LO VE IN DEFIANCE OF PAIN: UKRAINIAN STORIES

Love
in
Defiance
of
Pain

Ukrainian Stories

Edited by Ali Kinsella, Zenia Tompkins, and Ross Ufberg

Introduction by Adam Higginbotham

DEEP VELLUM PUBLISHING

DALLAS, TEXAS

Deep Vellum Publishing
3000 Commerce St., Dallas, Texas 75226
deepvellum.org · @deepvellum

Deep Vellum is a 501c3 nonprofit literary arts organization
founded in 2013 with the mission to bring
the world into conversation through literature.

Copyright © 2022, the authors and translators
Introduction copyright © 2022, Adam Higginbotham

This book was published in partnership with PEN America and the Tompkins Agency
for Ukrainian Literature in Translation.

LIBRARY OF CONGRESS CONTROL NUMBER: 2022935437

ISBN 978-1-64605-257-8 (TPB) | 978-1-64605-258-5 (Ebook)

Cover design by Jennifer Blair

Cover art: Sergey Kamennoy, 2021, two pages from photo book Ukrainian
Suprematism (RODOVID, 2021)

Interior layout and typesetting by KGT

PRINTED IN THE UNITED STATES OF AMERICA

CONTENTS

INTRODUCTION

IT WAS LATE AND GROWING COLDER; darkness gathered in the stairwell, and nothing broke the silence except the grinding of shattered glass beneath our feet. On the fourth floor of the apartment building on Budivelnykiv Street, Valeri stood amid the ruins of what had once been his living room: the gutted carcass of the TV set; the green botanical wallpaper curling on the floor; the striped shadow left by the radiator, long since taken by the looters who stripped the city for scrap metal, oblivious to the contamination. Valeri had been given just forty minutes to salvage what he could before his final evacuation; he filled five plastic bags with his wife's English textbooks, a few science fiction novels, and a handful of flatware.

"It's hard," he said. "I spent the best years of my youth here. But you can get used to anything."

It was February 2006, and I was on my first visit to Ukraine, reporting a magazine story to mark the twentieth anniversary of the Chornobyl disaster. Galvanized by reading *A Night to Remember*, in which author Walter Lord had compared the sinking of the Titanic to "the last night of a small town," I had set out to interview eyewitnesses to the catastrophe that had not only destroyed Reactor Number 4 of the Chornobyl nuclear power plant and poisoned hundreds of square miles of countryside—but had also necessitated the abrupt evacuation of almost the entire population of Prypiat, the *atomgrad* purpose-built to house the workers of the plant and their families. Gathering an armada of buses, trains, and boats from across the Ukrainian Soviet Socialist Republic, the authorities emptied the city of more than twenty-seven thousand people in a single afternoon, beginning an exodus that weeks later would culminate in the evacuation of hundreds of thousands of children and expectant mothers from Kyiv.

These scenes, so vividly described to me by dozens of men and women—former schoolchildren, bus drivers, teachers, nuclear engineers, and government officials—whose lives were changed forever by the disaster, came back to me as I watched the shattering coverage of the first weeks of this year's Russian invasion: the wrecked and abandoned homes, the streams of buses carrying evacuees away from Mykolaiv and Sumy, and the desperate crowds filling the railway stations in Kyiv and Lviv. The book that I eventually wrote about the Chornobyl disaster was inspired by the accounts I had been told by the people I had met on that first trip to Ukraine—by their individual spirit, courage, humor, and resilience in the face of a collective story that had seen their land swept repeatedly by war, famine, and genocide before finally falling beneath the mantle of a radioactive catastrophe, only to at last emerge intact from the ashes.

I could hardly believe that a country that had already suffered so much was yet again subject to such grotesque barbarism, still less that the homes of some of the same men and women who had been evacuated from Prypiat were now on the front line of the Russian assault. In the first days of the war, missiles fell on the Kyiv suburb of Troieshchyna, where the majority of the plant workers and their families had been relocated in 1986; Maria Protsenko, the indomitable chief architect of the *atomgrad*, who had overseen the city's construction before being forced to help permanently fence it off from the outside world, had been resettled in Irpin—a once sleepy community to the west of the capital turned into another devastated ghost town, this time by Russian airstrikes and artillery.

But it's that spirit—the same spirit that has helped rally much of the world behind Ukraine in the face of the invasion—that animates many of the stories in this book. Artem Chapeye's "The Ukraine," from which the collection takes its title, is a beautiful and heartbreaking story woven from resonant scenes familiar to anyone who has traveled the country on a packed microbus or tried in vain to snatch a few hours' rest on the unforgiving, plank-like beds of its sleeper trains. This is the Ukraine I recognize, where I was welcomed warmly into the homes of total strangers who were generous and hospitable even when, often, they had little—offering homegrown tomatoes from the garden, or *samohon* and lard straight from the freezer—and where each trip had the potential for the hilarious or, at least, the unexpected: whether fearing I would freeze to death in a bus stranded on the shoulder of a remote road in Polissia, fruitlessly chasing an escaped cat—a reluctant gift from an interview subject—through the dark in a snowbound village, or enjoying a champagne cruise on the Dnipro with a former Soviet Air Force helicopter pilot.

Love in Defiance of Pain is also a kaleidoscope of contemporary Ukrainian voices: the poet and writer Kateryna Kalytko's "Vera and Flora" takes the form of a dark fairy tale, telling the story of a magical island at the edge of a land ravaged by plague and war; Yuri Andrukhovych's "Samiilo, or the Beautiful Brigand" is a historical adventure, a political allegory set in the baroque Ukraine of the seventeenth century; in "Brooklyn, Forty-Second Street," Vasyl Makhno describes the trials of Genyk and Zenyk, two Ukrainian friends cast ashore amid the polyglot diasporas of modern New York; and "The Bell" by Stanislav Aseyev is an extract from his harrowing memoir

The Torture Camp on Paradise Street. Aseyev, a reporter who remained behind in his native Donbas when Russia-backed separatists seized the region in 2014, was later detained, tortured, and imprisoned for more than two years before finally being released by his captors in 2019. With his stark reminder of what is at stake in the current conflict, Aseyev joins a tradition of Ukrainian poets and writers who have cataloged centuries of their country's struggle against oppression. I look forward to a future in which their successors will be starved of new material—or hope, at the very least, that this current catastrophe is the last to overshadow Ukraine and that its people can finally enjoy the peace and independence they have sought for so long.

Adam Higginbotham
March 2022

Love in Defiance of Pain

ARTEM CHAPEYE

THE UKRAINE

translated from the Ukrainian by Zenia Tompkins

S HE AND I CONVERGED ON A sullen love for our country. A hate-
love, some might say. A love with a dash of masochism, I used to say.
A love in defiance of pain, she used to say. And that was how she and I
loved each other, too—through pain and a bit frantically.

Almost every weekend, she and I would get on a train or a bus and
head off somewhere. And, in Ukraine, you can get far in the course of
a weekend. And make it home, too. Only once were we late for work
on a Monday—when we were hitchhiking back from Milove, in the
Luhansk region, in January. It's the easternmost point of the country. We made it there on buses and headed back on foot along a snow-
covered road, hand in hand. We had just fallen in love then. Guys in
Soviet-style Zhiguli four-doors were giving us rides, no problem, but
each time they'd give us a lift for only a few kilometers, then drop us at
the side of the road and turn off toward their villages. We shivered in the
blue twilight, but we were happy.

We felt a melancholy love for precisely everything in Ukraine that
annoyed many of our acquaintances. The random thrashiest of thrash
metal on intercity buses. The obligatory multihour sessions of awful
comedy shows like *Evening Quarter*. The flat-screen TVs at the fan-
cier bus stations, like Dnipro, where the thrash on the speakers is even

3

harsher—like that little rap that goes "The best feeling's when you're the coolest of 'em all"—and performed by Ukrainians who write their names in the Roman alphabet because they think it will be more familiar and appealing in the West. The sour smell of the alcohol that's poured in semidarkness on the lower bunks of the economy-class sleeper car while we're trying to fall asleep on the top ones. The instant coffee in plastic cups and the plasticky sausages in hot-dog buns. The cheap train station food, like cabbage-filled patties or meat pies wrapped in paper; even back then I wondered why it was that she didn't at all care about her health.

Or the more tender things: the slightly squat, chubby mother and daughter speaking Surzhyk, that slangy combo of Russian and Ukrainian, so alike in appearance—dark, cropped hair, their faces wide, a deep beet-colored flush on their cheeks—who wouldn't have been all that pretty if it weren't for the huge, kind, gray-green eyes that made them beautiful! They were the proprietors of a cheap café at the bus station in a nameless town, with tables covered in oilcloth carelessly slashed by the knives of previous guests, which the daughter rubbed with a gray rag before bringing out plates of food that her mother had prepared for us. We had a meal there—for less than a dollar, if you add it up—of mashed potatoes with a sun of butter melted in the center of the plate, pork chops fried to a crisp, and homemade sour-cherry juice in tumblers. Or the people with gray faces, smileless and weary after a long shift, on the buses of Donetsk. The wet autumn leaves stuck to the footpaths of the Storozhynets Arboretum in Chernivtsi, where we had gone just to take a stroll—likely the only people ever to make a daylong excursion to have a look at a city where, when push comes to shove, there's nothing much worth looking at.

She was quoting Serhiy Zhadan, her favorite poet: *"Ya liubliu tsiu krainu navit bez kokainu"*—"I love this country even without cocaine." I prosaically chimed in, "And without antidepressants either." It was then that she stopped taking antidepressants: she said they made her gain weight—the only vanity I noticed in her in all those years. And now she always resurfaces in my mind along with a line from *my* favorite poet, Tom Waits: *She was a middle-class girl* . . . She had spent a few years living in the US: her father had gone to earn some fast cash, then brought her over, too. While there, she finished college, got married, and quickly divorced. It was a past I was jealous of, and that was why we rarely talked about it. One time, she told me that her friends in the US, and even her ex-husband, used to call her home country "the Ukraine." With the definite article. Even though they knew that in English it was correct to just say "Ukraine," their tongues kept reflexively pronouncing "the" first. Why, she would ask her ex-husband. One time, after some thought, he said, "I think it's the *U* sound." The US, the UK, the Ukraine. She and I laughed about this, but from then on we began to notice and point out to each other situations and instances when it was actually correct to say "*the* Ukraine"—because there's Ukraine as such, but there is, in fact, also a *the* Ukraine—a "*voilà*-Ukraine." A Ukrainian Dasein.

For example, it's the middle-aged men in peaked caps, with long mustaches and leather jackets over their warm sweaters. It's the middle-aged women in chunky knit hats. The college girls who, on their way back to the dorm after a weekend at home, step over puddles of oozy mud in their fancy white boots, clutching the handles of checkered plastic tote bags with fingers red from the cold, trying to not chip their long, painted nails. It's the old lady in the ankle-length brown overcoat and cheap white sneakers who's carting apples on a hand truck. The coiffed, aging blonde behind the wheel in a traffic jam in Donetsk who's calmly smoking out the car window, watching life pass by.

Once in a blue moon, during the worst frosts or protracted rains, she would plant me in the red Škoda Fabia her father had given her—because, of the two of us, only she had a license—and then we would look out at the country, separated from our fellow Ukrainians by glass and music: usually Tom Waits, who, for some reason, perfectly suited the Ukraine. But, in the end, the trip would sour her mood because, separated in that way by music and glass, we could only watch and not experience, not identify. The following weekend, we would once again buy tickets for a train or a bus and be among the people.

The Ukraine, for us, was a gigantic and empty new bus station, dusted with snow, at the edge of, I think, Cherkasy. I didn't understand why it was so gigantic or so empty. She and I stood in the bitter cold in the middle of a snow-covered concrete field beneath an open canopy, alone. Opposite us was a single microbus, a white Mercedes Sprinter—ours. I opened the door, but the driver barked, "Shut the door! Don't let the cold in! This isn't the stop."

So we stood and blew on each other's fingers until, fifteen minutes later, he pulled up fifteen meters. Her face flushed in the frozen air. In the van, too, our breath turned to vapor. We paid the driver, who grumbled, "This is the stop." She giggled softly and whispered in my ear, "This here is the Ukraine."

She was generally quick to laugh, though sometimes with a dark sense of humor. For instance, one time in Khotyn we were taking a selfie at her prompting in front of a store called Funeral Supplies and Accessories. She let out a ringing laugh and said that this, too, was the Ukraine.

When the bus stopped on the highway north of Rivne and in climbed an old woman whose sheepskin coat smelled of hay and cows, the people turned up their noses, not appreciating that this old woman was, in fact, the Ukraine. The official folk kitsch—that stereotypical woman with ribbons flowing from her hair, holding bread and salt on a traditionally embroidered towel—is a fake, but that dilapidated mosaic at the entrance to the village, depicting a Ukrainian woman with ribbons in her hair—only she's missing an eye—now that's the Ukraine. The Ukraine is also the romance of decline. The unfinished concrete building on the outskirts of Kamianets-Podilskyi. The bottomless, purple-green lake in a submerged quarry in Kryvyi Rih, which you're looking at from a tall pile of bedrock, fearfully watching as a single minute swimmer slowly does the breaststroke, holding himself up above the lake's impossible depth on the treacherous film of the water's surface. It's the slow destruction of the Dominican Cathedral in Lviv, grayed by rains, and the faded-white plaster Soviet Pioneers with lowered bugles in Kremenets, in a gorge between the creases of mountains, unanticipated among all the fields overgrown with withered grass. The abandoned Pioneer camp outside Mariupol, where we sat on rusted swings, thermoses in our hands, with a view of the Sea of Azov, which swished with ice, pushing its surf, layer by layer, onto the shore. And even in Kyiv— the gray, multilevel concrete interchange at the Vydubychi transport hub, framed by the smokestacks of the TETs energy plant, which belch a thick, dense smoke into the deep-blue sky.

We were wanderers: we glided on the surface and often saw the Ukraine through misted windows. In the final years, she'd have her treatments in the summer, and we couldn't travel then. That's why the trips I typically remember were in late autumn or very early spring, when the country is in a palette of gray, rust, faded yellow, and pale green. It is unimaginably beautiful. Side roads along alleys of poplar or birch trees, barely winding through hills, lead you to places where you haven't been and aren't visiting, and you feel the urge to stop, to climb out of the bus and go—actually go—to those places where you haven't been and aren't visiting.

One time I dozed off, my head resting on my hat against the steamy pane, and, when I awoke, through the window I saw, right next to the road, large and seemingly metallic waves frozen in time.

"Is this a reservoir?" I asked her. "Where are we?"

She laughed softly and stroked my temple.

"Rub your eyes."

Those waves frozen in time turned out to be large mounds of plowed black soil.

Once, at night, behind a belt of forest bare in November, a tractor was running with four blinding headlights, two on the bumper and two above the cabin, and this detail struck me as particularly romantic for some reason, yet somewhat mysterious. Another time the minibus driver stopped at a café in the middle of the woods—near Chudniv, I think. The café was encircled by a wall of logs, sharpened on top like pencils, with the frightening, elongated, crested faces of Cossacks wearing large earrings carved on them. It was trash and kitsch, but it was the Ukraine. The night was frosty, and star-pierced deep space loomed black above the forest road.

I think that fatigue, too, affected our perception on these trips. We were under-rested, and everything struck us as a little unreal and simultaneously uber-real. Blurred objects and people emerged through the fog, becoming distinct as they approached. In silence, with a shared pain and delight, the two of us could spend whole minutes watching a droplet trickle down the other side of the pane. Even then, she was succumbing to mood swings, which were rubbing off on me, too. One time, I recall, the other people in the bus were mouthing, "Starkon, Starkon. We're heading to Starkon." There was something cosmic, futuristic, and damply mysterious in this word. When, an hour later, it turned out to be Starokostiantyniv, for some reason she grew disenchanted, pouted, and withdrew into herself. For the next hour, everything seemed horrible.

In Starkon, two young men sat down behind us, reeking of alcohol. All the passengers were gray in the partial darkness of the cabin and swayed like sacks on the rugged road; no one was smiling. Then, suddenly, one of the drunks behind us began to tell the other one about his little son.

"I look over, and he's got a snotty nose and he's crying. I tell him, 'Open up your mouth, I'll take a look.' He shows me his mouth, and he's got a little side tooth that, you know, had pushed through in two places. I felt so sorry for him. 'Poor little kid!' I say. And I start kissing him, and I grab him in my arms . . ."

The bus was suddenly bathed in love and beauty. All the people who had been sitting silently, swaying with the bus's motion, lost in their own thoughts and their own problems, ceased to be gray mannequins: inside each of them, behind the mask of weariness, was an entire universe, a gigantic cosmos brimming with internal stars, and she leaned over and whispered in my ear, "People are beautiful, even if they don't realize it."

Sometimes she and I would set out on our weekend journeys on foot. In the early years, when it was still possible. Outside Yuzhnoukrainsk, on a Polovtsian grave field in the steppe, we ate a stolen watermelon. Outside Konotop, we got lost in the meanders of the Seim River; emerging from waist-high mud, we walked onto a farmstead, and a young woman, whose husband had gone off fishing in his boat, fed us boiled perch and polenta flecked with scales. And, when we paid her, the woman tried to refuse, but her hands began to tremble because it was an enormous sum of money for her. While it was still possible, we climbed a mountain overlooking Yalta, and from a kilometer up we saw clearly that the earth was round: the deep-blue sea segregated itself from the pale sphere of sky in a distinct arc.

I had anticipated that, during our early trips, she and I would be constantly making love, particularly in the fields or in secluded and beautiful spots like that mountain over Yalta. Yet she almost always said, "Ew, we're dirty." Once or twice, during a mood swing of hers, she initiated lovemaking on her own—like in the Transit Hotel on the highway in the bogs of Polissia, where we startled the long-haul truckers—but I quickly understood that, for her, our trips weren't at all about that. She was catching time, which was trickling through her fingers. Particularly in the final years, when she needed more and more treatments, and we traveled less and less.

I was jealous of her past in the US, of her learning, which came from I don't know where. Or, rather, of her chaotic erudition. For example, she had this category: "random fact." We could be traveling in a black vehicle through a snow-dusted field in the boondocks, which, between the two of us, we referred to as "Kamianka-Znamianka," and we'd be marveling at the greenish hue of the asphalt when, out of nowhere, in response to some mental association, she'd burst out, "Random fact: when Voltaire died, his relatives sat him up in a carriage as if he were alive. And just like that, seemingly alive, the corpse was driven to a remote eastern region. You know why? To beat the mail. So that the Church wouldn't have time to give the bishop there an order prohibiting Voltaire's burial in consecrated ground."

I was jealous of her past in the US, the past from which these paroxysms flared, while she, it seems, envied me those years that she had missed in Ukraine. I would tell her stories. I told her about how in the nineties, as a schoolboy, I was forever digging in our gardens with my parents because, at the time, we had amassed as many government-issued plots as we could till from elderly relatives and relatives who had gone abroad for work—so that there could somehow be enough food for all the children through the winter. I told her how the electricity would get shut off in winter, and my entire family—clad in thick sweaters, because even the gas heat wasn't all that warm—would gather in the kitchen, first around candles and eventually around the car battery that Dad had bought, whose light bulb emitted a pale glow; and how, on those kitchen evenings, Mom would bake flat biscuits with a dollop of jam in the gas oven or fry crepes on the stovetop, which we ate with preserves; and how at the time, of course, I didn't understand that these would be the happiest memories of my childhood.

I told her how my brother and I traveled to my grandfather's funeral from Kyiv. I was living at the polytechnic institute then, not far from the train station, while my brother lived in a hostel in the Vydubychi neighborhood. We bought tickets for the no-frills train that was leaving for Radyvyliv in the middle of the night, when the metro wasn't running, so my brother came to my place, so as to be walking distance from the station. We sat and sat, talked, smoked, but, when we headed out, it turned out that we were running late, and so we sprinted the last kilometer, as fast as we could, panting and sweating, and jumped onto the moving train, teetering on our bellies on the already raised steps. The conductor saw all this and scolded us. "Dumbasses, you could have had your legs chopped off!" I wanted to laugh in relief but thought that laughing wasn't appropriate. We ended up late for the funeral all the same, and, when we arrived in the village of Boratyn, our dad and the neighbors had just returned from the cemetery and were sitting at a table beneath the old pear tree in the yard set with cheap booze, cheap smoked sausage, and homemade pickles. They tried to force me and my brother to have a drink. A minute later, the neighbors were recounting how good each of them had been to the deceased old man and what he had promised to bequeath to whom. Our dad, his son, sat at the table in silence and later, as he led me and my brother to the grave, he complained, "The body isn't even cold yet, and they're already divvying up the inheritance. I don't need anything, but at least don't start in front of me."

After I told her this, I recall, she and I took to saying that thoughts of the Ukraine always, sooner or later, led to memories of funerals. Why?

"Maybe love is more acute when it's mixed with the feeling of inevitable loss," she surmised.

I think I finally understand what she meant.

One time, in her final year, I told her about how my best friend's mother was dying of cancer in the hospital. And about how he had to take a syringe to the head nurse and give her a twenty-hryvnia bribe each time he wanted her to fill it with morphine for his mom.

She laughed. "That is most certainly a contender for *the* the Ukraine."

And then she began to cry.

For the two of us, the booming talk of "official" patriots about their "love for Ukraine" that you hear everywhere—that talk was pompous and stilted, hackneyed, and, above all, it was what the Russians call *poshlo*: passé, tacky. Or, if you prefer English, it was lewd. Paraphrasing an American saying, she used to argue that patriotism was like a penis: irrespective of its size, it's not a great idea to go waving it around in public. Choral singing and walking in formation. *Sharovary*—the bright-colored ballooning pants of the Cossacks—and everyone on the same day sporting traditional embroidery, on shirts and even plastered on cars. Waving flags on sticks or, better yet, flying the biggest flags possible! Ukrainian tridents on chests. It was all a pretentious demonstration, a showy show. It was an aesthetic on the same level as putting up a billboard beside the road with a picture of your beloved holding a photoshopped bouquet and the caption, "Natalka! I love you! Your Tolia!" Only in this case it was done collectively: "Natalka, lookie here at how you arouse our patriotism!" It was group exhibitionism.

Sincere feelings don't need megaphones. Love is quiet, barely audible. It's in the comma and in the reiteration, "I love her so, I so love my poor Ukraine." Today I almost let out a sob when I came upon this line. Taras Hryhorovych Shevchenko. In defiance of pain, a bit frantically. Tenderly. Acutely. With a fear of loss. In love, the imperative is acceptance.

During one of our final trips, in the heart of winter, the rural bus we were on broke down, mid-ascent, outside Dunaivtsi. Little by little, the cabin of the bus began to freeze. Outside, a cold, damp wind blew, piercing through our flesh all the way to the marrow. The driver was poking around in the engine. The bus was old: that was why it had broken down. Someone began to grumble, "And here we have the perpetual 'Are we part of Europe or are we not?'" I, too, was growing irritated. But she was warming her hands in her armpits and smiling. She said, "I've never heard that someone up and froze to death in Ukraine from a bus breaking down. Okay, it isn't pleasant. But it happens."

I was learning acceptance from her. When her mother called and invited me to the funeral, it was bitterly sad, but I wasn't surprised. She hadn't said anything to me directly, but now, looking back, I saw that all along she had been living a life short on time. Just as she had gleaned satisfaction from depression and from a sullen love in defiance of pain, I was confident that she had even gained a certain pleasure from her suicide. I only hoped that the physical pain of it had been less than the pain she had had to live with.

> *But now she's dead,*
> *She's so dead,*
> *Forever dead and lovely now . . .*

I didn't notice when I stepped on the edge of the freshly shoveled, soft mound of earth. Her mother looked at me judgmentally. Lips compressed into a thread, painted with dark red lipstick. A thin, properly contoured, made-up face. Her mother had a wonderful figure for her age; she would have had a similar one had she lived as long. Her mother wore a light-colored business suit, a white overcoat, and black high-heeled shoes: that was why she stayed on the concrete path and didn't approach the mound. She had a scarf on her head because, after all, it was a cemetery. Her mother probably thought I wasn't displaying enough grief. All those years her mother had thought that I was a bad influence on her daughter. That it was me dragging her "who knows where or what for." That it was me refusing to formally start a family or at least live together full-time. I'm curious, did her mother understand the pain her daughter lived with? Someday I'll tell her about it. Or maybe not. Her mother was very Orthodox and concealed the truth so that her daughter's body—her body—could be buried in accordance with the rules. In consecrated ground.

I was learning acceptance from her. Clay from her grave stuck to my shoes, and I recalled how she and I had walked around the cemetery in Krasnoilsk the previous spring. Fake flowers adorned almost all the crosses. We read the inscriptions, written in a mix of Romanian, Russian, and Ukrainian, and yellowish clay stuck to our feet in just the same way then.

Her mother and I heard muffled cursing behind us. Apparently, the two cemetery workers who had filled the grave were squabbling over the tip that her mother had given to one of them. If I recall, they were a little drunk. Her mother glanced at the workers, her painted lips clenched, then turned away and snugly tightened her scarf, which she would take off upon leaving the cemetery.

"What horrible people," her mother murmured.

The gravediggers asked my forgiveness with a gesture. They quieted down and walked past me and her mother, their shovels over their shoulders. When they thought I could no longer see them, one punched the other's shoulder, then gesticulated: *idiot*. Yes, they had had a bit to drink. They smelled. They were filthy. Gray, in tattered jackets. They probably consume that TV trash, I thought. They weren't European, they weren't civilized. What else was there to say? Inside everyone there's a universe, a gigantic cosmos brimming with stars. And so be it that an uninviting exterior, humdrum labor, thoughtless amusements, and squabbles over money often keep it from being seen. Sometimes people forget that it exists inside them. Sometimes we do, too.

I turned to her mother: "You know what she used to say? People are beautiful, even if they don't realize it."

KATERYNA KALYTKO

VERA AND FLORA

translated from the Ukrainian by Ali Kinsella

I T WASN'T AN ISLAND, BUT A land bagel tossed into the water. In the middle was a lake that itself was home to a small island. There was water all around, big water. Beyond the big water was a far-off shore with trees. A river flowed from the north into the double ring formed by the land and water, so that the landscape looked like a key when viewed from above. Downstream from us the river narrowed but flowed on. The sea lay ahead of it. This is how Ivan once described it to me. He flew into our lands on a medical helicopter, so I had no reason not to believe him. I never saw Heavy Sands from the air. Heavy Sands was the name of my home. It was always simple and natural to pronounce this name, but writing it, which I now do well, is very strange.

≈

The order was as follows: buildings were on the earthen ring and the market was on the isle in the middle. A few streets had bridges that extended to the isle. It always reminded me of a flower. Every year, winter squeezed this flower in its icy fist. It was good that the utility poles the electrical lines were strung up on along the shore were strong enough to withstand this compression. On short winter days, the seagulls that

17

hung out on the wires squawked endlessly. When the ice retreated from the strait, men went out in boats to make sure the floe hadn't broken the piles, and they strung new ropes. Then they agreed on a schedule for the ferry. Two of them set up on each side, dug their feet in, and pulled the rope hand over hand. It was strange to watch the ferry piled high with people jerk across the channel, kind of like an enormous water strider. The ferry carried women with fruits and vegetables away from us and brought us sea people with fish and salted meat in barrels. Then they switched places. Our market was always noisy. We loved crowds, even crowds of foreigners as long as they weren't Gypsies or Indians and didn't have any holes in their bodies or drawings on their skin.

≈

Ivan arrived in Heavy Sands just as the thrushes started to sing. He walked out onto the wet planks of the dock and looked all about in wonder. No one paid any attention to him—his kind often showed up. He had a crate of books and a large, gray sack with straps slung over his shoulder. He could easily have been a trader. He was clean, pale, and quiet. He stood staring for a long time, and then began to ask people where he could settle in. Uncle Nemai stopped and pointed to my house. He said to go see Orphan. She'd find him housing and explain how to live here. She always does. Only her.

≈

That day I had been collecting coltsfoot and shepherd's purse along the shore and digging up sweet flag and garden angelica roots. I saw the stranger from a distance and went to meet him. They call me Orphan, but it's complete nonsense, and not the only bit they're guilty of. I was my parents' child; I spoke to them every day. I was flesh of the flesh of Heavy Sands and the place was mine. My name is Vera. But in the fifty years since the new people arrived, they have never once asked me about that. Still, I taught them how to live in Heavy Sands. I explained that it settles a little more in the water every year; taught them how to build houses on piles; told them how to fertilize and wrap the trees for winter, when to sow for the best vegetables, which birds bring spring and put an end to summer, what kind of ferry to build and how to move it. They listened to everything I said and never asked me anything. They grew here along the water like sweet flag. The new people are always worse than the old ones.

≈

The old people were here a hundred years ago. When my father thought up Heavy Sands, the settlement wasn't a land bagel bulging from the water, but a mountain amid a river bed. Right after my mom and dad were married, they rode for a very long time in a rickety cart until they could no longer hear the last echoes of the wedding songs. Then they got in a yellow-sided boat and floated downstream. Their two black beauties—a mare named Ṣàngó and a stallion called Bandit—who had earlier been harnessed to the cart, swam after the boat. They were alone in the clear blue water, and the boat was all they wore. Mom sang and Dad stroked her unruly black hair, tousled by the wind. Every night he told the same story: that he would give her an island in the water to reign over. Their island was growing for them, just then, while they floated, and would appear before their horses got tired of swimming. The horses withstood seven full days and one more night. On the morning of the eighth day, Heavy Sands came into view right in front of them. It was Mom who named it. When Dad lifted her from the boat and the horses clambered ashore, Mom lightly touched her bare feet to the earth and said, "The horses' tracks are barely visible. The sand here is heavy." I was already a seed in my mother's belly when she and Dad first set foot on this shore.

When I was born, the mountain only grew toward the sky. My hair also grew fast, just as black as Mom and Dad's. And our herd of horses grew, black like hot wind. I grazed our ninety-nine horses. I would graze the herd, brush and braid my hair, and sing, because Mom had told me as long as we sang our mountain would grow and Heavy Sands would hold us. The fish swam up to the shores and jumped into Dad's nets without a fight. The falcons from the riverbank flew in and landed on his shoulders, and when he asked, they brought us quail they'd caught. Every time a full moon rose over the mountain, Mom and Dad got in the boat and floated away. They always returned with the waxing crescent, bringing with them trees: shoots, some seeds, pits. Mom remembered each one's origins and could name precisely which corner of the Land of the Lost she brought these new friends from without error. She planted the first tree at the very top of the mountain. It was a cherry plum. It always bloomed first, consumed in a white spring fire as soon as the weather turned warm. And it was the first to roll its red-yellow fruits down the mountain when the nights grew longer. Month after month, year after year, new trees sprouted on the slope, reaching from top to bottom. Peaches and plums, cherries and quinces, pears and apples, walnuts and mulberries, chokeberries and hazelnuts and almonds. Finally Mom and Dad brought red grapevines that only had female flowers, and green grapes that had only male ones. They planted them right on the shore among the rocks that poked out of the water. Mom sang, our island grew, and even the banks of the river parted in a semi-circle to make room. Then spring came. By the time the herd's one-hundredth horse was born, I could plait my black braid, and the fruit trees bloomed all at once. Then people emerged from the forest on the distant shore. There were a few dozen of them; some fell over with exhaustion. Dad and Mom rowed over to them in the boat, and I stood with the horses on the slope and read the whole conversation on their lips. The people said they had come from a war that was being waged far away. They were from a city that had been burned to the ground and they had nothing. They walked for eighteen days and thought they were going to die, when in the middle of the woods a fragrant white wind full of flower petals blew out to meet them. They went in the direction of the wind and came upon our island. They were peaceful people, mostly women and children, and only a few men. They had a cow to give milk to the sick. They wanted to stay. Dad transported them to the island in his boat until late at night. They lay down to sleep on the shore, one next to the other.

"Who are you?" the new people asked Dad the next morning. "I am Rasul and this is my wife, Maria, and my child, Vera. We're the people of Heavy Sands," Dad said. "How are we to live now? Which god shall we believe in?" the new people asked. "Live as you can. Believe in the god you brought with you," Dad said.

Mom strictly forbade the cutting down of fruit trees, but she showed them where they could get wood on the opposite shore and stones in the water. She showed them our small house among the trees. Their men first built a few boats, and later cut down oaks and pines to build houses that looked like ours. They carved furniture and dishes. They tilled small plots in front of their houses and planted the seeds they'd brought with them. That was how our first vegetables grew.

They were all related. The noise they brought with them scared my horses, and my horses scared them in turn when the black whirlwind rushed down the mountain and trampled their gardens. But they didn't dare talk to me. They stuck together and looked askance. Then the cow they'd dragged along died, so they buried it in the field. My horses went to graze in the field and within a week they were all sick. First the young, then the old ones, the sturdiest, stopped eating. Painful nodes swelled in their necks. Then wounds opened on their withers and backs and on the joints of some of their legs. They lost weight and limped; their gums bled. I stroked their bowed heads and they were all hot; their eyes watered. The colt that was born last died first. Then I took to my bed.

My arms were first covered in red splotches that turned to blisters. In a few days they appeared on my neck, too. They would have hurt if I hadn't had a fever. Lying on my pillow, my head felt like it belonged to someone else; it was like a die filled with liquid metal. My hair became hopelessly tangled. Mom wiped my body with a broth of calendula and put poultices of mint leaves wrapped in wet canvas on my forehead. The canvas dried in minutes. Mom would step outside the door to consult with Dad in anxious whispers, repeating words that sounded like an incantation: papules, vesicles, pustules. I would fall asleep and wake up, drift off again, hearing the constant beating of hooves. My horses! The glass pane blown by Dad had bubbles in it. When the sun shone in through the window, the bubbles cast shadows on the earthen floor that looked like a snowfall. This snow dissolved in the river, turning into water-bound air bubbles, and then spring came, May and the spawning; hundreds of spawn floated in front of my eyes and burst and the fry played on the sunny bottom of the transparent bay. Then the spectacle was gone. I recovered, only I no longer heard the knocking of hooves.

Mom explained that we no longer had a large herd. While I was in bed with my fever, the sick horses hobbled up to the doorway with their last bit of strength, and stood for a while as if they were saying goodbye. They then turned and went into the river, one by one. That was how they disappeared. Only nine of the sturdiest remained—five stallions and four mares: Fog, Agate, Blizzard, King, White Mane, Pinto, Thyme, Song, and Yarta. I stayed with them. My hopelessly tangled hair had to be cut off. Reddish scars remained on my arms and neck, eventually turning dark. The farmers became even more afraid of me.

New people came in the fall. There weren't many of them, only a dozen and a half. A few of them had terrible injuries: a young boy was missing an arm and the belly of another was split open. Two others carried him in a blood-soaked blanket. The rest were simply exhausted. They were the remains of a garrison of some defeated fortress a five-day walk away. Dad said that they couldn't enter Heavy Sands armed, so they tossed their weapons into the river. Then he again carried them across in his boat to our shore. They were all worried whether the one who was holding his guts in his hands would live, but Mom said that people don't just die like that on our shore. And, indeed, she sewed him up so well that he survived the winter with just a single bottle of poppy tincture, and in the spring even tried to work the fields.

In spring, the newcomers started divvying up the land with the old newcomers. Heavy Sands wasn't growing as fast as it used to, and there wasn't enough land. It became harder and harder for Mom to convince people not to cut down trees. Once, coming down the mountain with the horses, I saw a soldier and a farmer quarreling. The soldier wanted a plot of land with a garden to feed himself and his one-armed son. The farmer said that it was his parcel and he wouldn't share it with anyone. He struck the soldier in the neck with his spade. Blood spurted in both their faces. The soldier crawled along the ground, but Mom had spoken the truth: people don't just die like that on our shore. The wounded man made it to his hut and went inside for some time. He came out leaning on his one-armed son and carrying a pistol. He didn't even hide it. They went to the field where the farmer had continued to work and there the soldier shot him in the breast.

Mom and Dad went to the field where both wounded men lay spilling their blood. All around, the crowd of settlers frowned. It always rained when Dad got angry. I have never since seen a deluge as fell that day on the field.

"I ordered you to drown your weapons!" said Dad, steely calm. The settlers maintained a gloomy quiet. "Are there more?" he asked.

The people shook their heads no.

"We're not going to help these two," he said then. "Punish them yourselves. On this land, no one raises a hand against another."

"It's because of the trees! We haven't enough land!" someone from the crowd shouted, then stopped short.

The deluge grew so strong people could hardly remain standing. They fell to their knees and covered their heads with their hands.

"Punish the guilty yourselves if you want to have any land at all," Dad said and walked away.

I saw the people tie up the wounded, not heeding their unearthly screams. Saw how they bound great riparian stones to their legs. How they tossed both in the river. The next day, everyone in Heavy Sands except for our family woke up with the same blisters I'd had on my arms and neck all over their bodies.

The disease was rapid and ruthless. It spared neither the young nor the old, neither women nor children. On the third day the people's blisters turned into bloody wounds; on the fourth, black scabs. Fever so enfeebled them that they lacked the strength to even dress their wounds.

A thick, incessant moan hung over Heavy Sands. Mom conscientiously visited each house in turn, but her cures—ever infallible—this time did nothing. On the seventh day a few of the sick still lay breathing in their homes, but they knew they'd never get up again.

That night Mom quietly said to Dad, "We must do something. The disease didn't take our child and now this is her land. We can't put the dead into it. Heavy Sands must remain pure."

The next morning Dad ordered those who could still walk to carry the sick, place them in the boats, and then get in themselves. He said he'd take them to the shore, to the place where they could find a cure since we didn't have one. The people didn't argue. With their final strength they went to the boats, dragging the infirm. Either they believed him unequivocally, or they had accepted their inescapable fate. I watched the boats drift away from Heavy Sands and couldn't shake the feeling that the distant shore had grown even more distant. It was as though Heavy Sands was retreating, shrinking away.

The boats never reached the opposite shore. They sank in the middle of the strait. In the dark of night Dad had carved carefully disguised holes in their bottoms with a knife. He swam back, but the sick couldn't swim. The river swallowed them all, every last one. When Dad got out of his wet clothes at home, I noticed a swath of scarlet blisters trailing down his neck, across his shoulders, and onto his breast. "Remember, Vera: he who betrays must share the fate of the one he has betrayed," was all he said.

Mom refused to sleep apart from Dad. She said they had a single destiny. That she would experience what he experienced. Although the disease had emaciated their bodies, it didn't affect them as it did the settlers resting at the bottom of the river. They remained strong enough and their minds stayed clear. Now it was I who brewed the healing tincture of calendula, but they ministered to themselves. One moonlit night, I heard their voices and got out of bed.

I thought they were calling me because they needed something. They were sitting in the middle of the room, faces turned to the moonbeams at the window, and didn't notice me. They were talking not to each other, but to someone else, though there was no one else in the room. They spoke quietly and decisively, pausing as though they were listening for an answer. I thought their fevers had finally taken their minds. For the first time in my life I cried, long and despairingly. Everything in our life up to now had made sense—for the first time it didn't.

As soon as the sun came up, Mom and Dad dug two pits in the yard. They were finished by evening. I didn't help, but they wouldn't have let me anyway. Come dusk they bathed in clean water and dressed in elegant clothes. They called to me. I already knew why.

"You've grown into a beautiful, strong girl, Vera," Dad said.

"You will live long, very long, I know," said Mom.

"We're not leaving you, you can feel that yourself," said Dad.

"Everything must cross new frontiers. This isn't the first time," said Mom.

"There is no land but love," said Dad. Mom added, "You have a lot of land. It is all yours. Be strong, Vera. New people will certainly come."

They both kissed me and lay down to sleep in the earth. In the morning I looked and saw they were stiff and radiant, like two precious minerals. I purposely did not cover them with earth. I let them shine.

That night the earth shook thrice and then let out a long moan. Our house trembled and from under the girder fell three falcon feathers: one large, one larger, and one smaller. When I went into the yard in the morning, everything was much changed. Earth had fallen into the pits on its own, burying Mom and Dad. The mountaintop slumped as if its base had simply melted away, entombing a number of the fruit trees. Now it barely stuck out of the water. "Out of the water" since the earth now extended in a perfect circle from our house and again ended with it. The rest had been taken by the water. Between me and the mountain there was now a dark strip of river but the river was also at my back; it continued climbing higher, swallowing up my parents' vineyards. I walked along the strip of land left to me. A few houses and old trees survived. When I got back, two shoots had already broken through the freshly plowed earth in the yard: a walnut and an apple tree.

From that morning on, I never sang again and Heavy Sands only slipped further into the river it had once grown from. But this happened very, very slowly. I observed it for fifty years until the arrival of new people. The nine horses remained with me. They no longer bred, but neither did they grow old or die. My hair never grew back. During the long winters when the horses and I were cold on the pasturage, I burned the bodies of the trees felled by the movement of the ground and the local yellow loam in the stove. I pounded the cinders from the stove into fine dust. I made drawings with a needle on my arms and neck along the black scars and then rubbed in the ashes of a noble ocher color. On my right arm from my elbow to my fingertips, I fit a map of the entire Land of the Lost with its most secret corners. I had never seen such a detailed map; I only had stories and Dad's schematic drawings in the sand. But strangely the whole of the Land lived inside of me as if it were drawn on the undersides of my eyelids. I similarly worked out a network of all the rivers of the Land of the Lost on my left arm. On my neck I marked the characters of the ten winds that most often blew over Heavy Sands in straight, winding, and jagged lines. When new people arrived here after fifty years I went out to meet them. After all, I knew they were coming. They took fright. Romani woman, they said, Indian, they said, all painted, they said. Then they asked, "How old are you, girl?" They didn't believe me when I said I was seventy. Nobody needs the truth. They declared me not all there. They named me Orphan. But how was I an Orphan? I have a name.

Then they searched out my house and came on their own. No one else could explain how to live in Heavy Sands. I told them that the settlement sinks into the water a little bit each night, but that if they were running from something, they wouldn't find a better place. So they stayed. I showed them which of the old buildings were still inhabitable, taught them how best to build new ones. How to gather the harvest from the old trees and thin out the young ones. Where in the backwaters of our river the fish still nibbled. How to tame falcons and teach them to hunt for you. But they were afraid of the falcons. They had brought their own domestic fowl and devoured their meat and eggs. The morning noise of chickens straining on their nests was unbearable. But I put up with it all. They came to me for advice fifty years in a row. I told them how to build the ferry, and when the time came to connect Heavy Sands to the electricity from the mainland, I supervised the work. Every time I turned around I heard that I was a Romani or an Indian or a witch all painted with pictures.

"You see, Vera," Dad said once when I returned to our yard and sat between the walnut and the apple tree. "You yourself know that the new people are always worse than the old."

≈

Ivan was the first newcomer who asked my real name. The first who wanted to listen to my story. And he didn't laugh. He believed me and he knew that I wouldn't eat domestic fowl or their eggs. Or honey from the hives that the new people dragged here. And I wouldn't drink milk from under their ruddy cows. He said that he understood everything perfectly—I wouldn't absorb cosmogonic substances. I didn't understand his words and explained that it's no different from gnawing on the stalk of a worldly flower and drinking up its juice. No different from cracking the Heavenly Egg, sucking up everything alive inside it plus the sun for good measure. You can only eat what has separated from the beginnings of life, from the divisions that accompany the beginnings. Ivan smiled

28

and said that he had approximately the same thing in mind. He fished in the river himself or bought fresh and salted fish from the sea people for me. He made sure they didn't have roe or milt. He brought game from the market. He couldn't call the falcons himself and I already knew this wasn't something you could teach. We gathered apples together—the first harvest he was in Heavy Sands for.

When Ivan first came to live with me he was strange. I often heard him nervously pacing his room at night, stomping loudly. He once forgot to close his door tightly and I saw for the first time how he unbuckled the straps and rested his artificial leg on the bed. Then he took a bottle of some clear liquid from his trunk, drew this liquid into another bottle, one with a needle, and then plunged this needle into his arm. And then he sat motionless for some time with his head thrown back, his lips utterly white.

Ivan explained that the war took his leg. Officially, it was unjust, because he was a doctor in a field hospital, not a soldier, but the war didn't ask. The war had lasted a few years all around the world and was so large that he couldn't believe I didn't know about it. Enormous and toothy, the war swallowed his leg and didn't even notice. It was nothing unusual—I had seen such wounds before. He also explained that the bottle with the needle was called a syringe and sticking it into his arm was an injection. The clear liquid in the syringe was called morphine and it helped equally with pain and memory. He had wanted to escape to a place where no one would stop him from poisoning his memory to the point of death. So here he was.

I didn't ask him for any morphine. It wouldn't have helped with my memory anyway. But I thought: Ivan knows and has lived through so much that I can tell my one secret only to him. Namely, how Dad drowned the sick settlers and then he and Mom lay in the earth to sleep and I often went around to the surviving houses. I touched their things, lay in their beds. Thus I grew accustomed to the wasteland and the new flow of time. In one hut, thrown together helter-skelter by soldiers, I found a book. An enormous, heavy book bound in calf's skin with laces. It was damaged in a few places, as though someone had tried to stab it with a knife. For some reason I knew this was a book even though I'd never seen one in my life. Mom and Dad preserved their knowledge another way. I immediately recognized Ivan's books as books. It was like I had always known they existed, just like the grass or birds or river. The book left behind was heavy, so I understood it was important—otherwise they wouldn't have hauled it to who-knows-where from their vanquished fortress, especially while they were carrying the wounded. I didn't take the book home, but I flipped through all the pages, more than once. I remembered every symbol drawn in it, but I couldn't make sense out of anything because I couldn't read. It's a shame to be unable to comprehend what you believe to be important. So then Ivan got out his books and started showing me letters. Every day he showed me letters and taught me their names. When I memorized them all, he asked me to put them together. Next he began underlining words printed in the books and speaking them out loud to me. Then I tried drawing a few of them myself. I dreamed of words; letters sparked and formed chimerical figures like bubbles in the green glass of the window pane. Finally I could read, slowly, touching each letter with my hand and helping myself by whispering. All at once the pattern on the paper came to life and spoke to me. I didn't need to return to the abandoned house to the old book covered in shabby leather. I remembered it cover to cover. All the familiar words flashed in it, piled on top of each other like stones in a wall. Names, people, places. Heavy Sands had the most complete chronicle of the Land of the Lost. And all of it had taken up residence in my head.

When the trees bloomed, I decided to tell Ivan something genuine and intimate. One night I took him to the threshold and asked,
Can you hear how the orchard makes love? He answered, "I can hear it.
I've always heard the air quietly humming with pleasure like this." This
ardent, shameful flower, it rings and copulates both with witnesses and
without, for it cares not, it is denuded, open, full of desire. Everything
would have been different if Ivan had heard nothing.

The day we first touched bellies fell on the summer solstice. A current lives on the skin of the belly, the same current that was in the electrical wires above the strait. Stars fall from the sky when lovers touch
bellies, and the wave from their current runs across even the dark skin
of the sky. All mutual penetrations and intertwinings are worth nothing
if you have not lain upon each other, touching bellies, and did not freeze
that way. Ivan and I did so many times that summer.

But he always loved like autumn. He was strangely submissive. His
wrists and lips had skin as tender as a crime. He lay down before me
like tired, laden grass in a foggy meadow. He was formed of resin and
honey, and when I leaned over him I could see the tiny kisses of the
sun, the transparent gingery flecks on his nose, the rounded moles on
his body. He responded to every touch, moaned faintly, writhed and
squirmed, but stubbornly never said a word, holding on to the head-
board with white fingers and hiding his eyes behind their lids when his
gaze flashed too sharply. When he entered me, he grew like a tree, but
with his every movement it was like he was apologizing and I laughed.
Does an oak really apologize to the sky into which it grows? I boldly
unwound him, as I wanted, I grew like a heavy yellow moon, got large
and powerful like swelling water; but he got small, easier, melted in my
embraces. Only his enormous, wide-open, green eyes remained. Every
morning he again appeared in my sheets as if from nowhere. Every evening we started from the beginning. But we never, ever spent the night

together. When we were both worn out, I stood and returned to my bed. Ivan was at first surprised, but he got used to it.

A few important events happened while Ivan was in Heavy Sands. A few children were born in quick succession and he delivered them all. People trusted him and also always wanted to touch him with their hands. Later, the first of the new people died, and Ivan witnessed the death. The funeral was in winter. The shovels squeaked, overturning the frozen earth, and the bottom of the hole was damp. We returned from the funeral and couldn't make love. Someone else's death hung under the ceiling; it smelled like the sweaty armpits of the gravediggers; and a dead man lay in the earth beneath us. Nothing would ever be as it had been.

≈

The next summer the duel between water and earth that was taking place here came to an end. Heavy Sands no longer grew. It didn't get bigger like before, but it also stopped sinking into the water. I marked a few old trees along the river with paint and checked the water level every day. Since Ivan and I had slept together, the water hadn't once climbed higher than the white stripe. Not once all summer.

Flora came to Heavy Sands in the middle of August. That day we were penning in the river waters as usual. The children released grass wreaths into the water, candles fluttering on a few of them. Flora stood, her head tilted slightly to one side, and observed how the current carried the wreaths off into the distance to the sea somewhere. A dry wind blew over the dock and the water also seemed dry, flat, and harder than the earth. Anticipation of winter, which began right after penning the waters, always worried but didn't scare me; no, nothing ever scared me. It's just that we again had to get used to the long, deep nights, to daily feeding the worm of anxiety that wouldn't vanish until the next spring. But that day, in Flora's presence, the worry was different, bulging. In some strange way, after her appearance my time palpably sped up. And I also somehow knew that there'd be no winter.

Flora also came to me for advice—and stayed on to live. She came with an interesting goal: to study plants. I liked this. Actually, she said, the local flora. She chuckled and said it's a bit funny: Flora studying flora. Then she thought that she needed to explain this to me and she clarified—the local plants. She'd heard that we had a lot of interesting ones. But I had long known the word *flora*. I learned it from Ivan when we were talking about the trees, flowers, and grasses of Heavy Sands. He was initially extremely displeased by Flora's appearance. He twisted up his face as if he were in pain; he wouldn't stay at home, spending entire days tramping along the river, his artificial leg giving him bloody blisters, but he explained nothing. But one night, the morphine, rather than taking away his memory, loosened his tongue and he told me Flora was from the land that waged war against his. I objected: Flora couldn't fight. Flora's suitcase was full of heavy books. Some had maps with the geographical distribution of plants; others with their portraits and descriptions of their properties. By the time you read all that, is there even time for war? Ivan smiled bitterly and stroked my cheek.

No one knew the local flora better than I. Over our years of sharing the island, the trees had formed genuses, passing along their properties to the new generations. A few of them I had grafted, but the majority I left free to grow as they pleased. Large herds grazed on the grasses, each summer changing their habits and temper, running farther away from people. Sometimes I needed the deftness of a hunter to retrieve them for the winter. But this wasn't at all the information that Flora and her discipline—botany—required. More often, I couldn't shake the feeling that she was just jealous of the plants' relationship with me. Especially after that evening when we strolled about the orchard and our hands suddenly grabbed the same heavy apple.

Then I started avoiding Flora. And she, surprisingly, turned into my shadow. She was probably concerned she'd offended me. I suppressed a smile when she tried to talk to me in my language, the language of a savage. That's what she considered me. She wore a beautiful green stone around her neck laced with bright veins like the entangled roots of grass or thin seaweed. Once she touched her pendant and said, "You know, Vera, this is a turning stone."

"A turning stone?" I didn't understand.

She shrugged and set about explaining very patiently, as if to a child. It's a reversible stone. If you press it between your thighs, you'll turn into an earthworm and you'll understand all the secrets of the earth. If you put it under your tongue, you'll turn into a bird. What kind? It depends on what kind of songs you can sing. If you put the stone on your belly, you'll turn into a fish and dive to unknown depths. If you put the turning stone on your back, right here between your shoulder blades, you'll become a lizard that's not afraid of fire or water since it keeps all its fear in its tail, which it can easily get rid of. Flora most of all wanted to become a lizard because then she'd be able to slither into the smallest gap under the warm porch, close her eyes, and dream about whatever she wanted until winter came. And if you bury the turning stone in the earth, it will speak from there, always saying whom it belongs to and whose earth it is lying in.

"Children's stories," I said. "There's no such thing as a turning stone. To transform others, the magical object needs to be able to transform itself. Only things that move can transform. But the stone can't move without outside help. It's just a stone. Green jade.[1]"

---

1. Jade (from the Spanish *piedra de ijada*, "stone of the flank") — a general name for the minerals jadeite and nephrite. The Spanish conquistadors

I regretted what I said. When Flora was talking, her eyes were like two birds bathing in waters unknown to me and her tongue was happy, for it was tasting a foreign language, recasting it into words I'd know. But afterward, she turned away and bit her lip, and it seemed she was about to cry. What had I taken away from her? Had I stomped on the only fairy tale that didn't fit into the strict canons of her science? Had I insulted the legend behind a gift from a treasured friend? Or was it just hard for her to look foolish in front of a scarred simpleton from this moldy backwoods?

I comforted her like a child, embraced her and stroked her head. I was surprised that her large breasts were so hard. She hugged me and my shirt slid off my shoulder. Her lips touched my skin. Again. Flora got down on her knees and slowly undid my belt. My skirt fell with a rustle, and only then did I notice how many shriveled leaves already lay on the ground. Flora kissed me below my belly. She threw her head back, looked me in the eyes, and kissed me. A large hard stone had grown from the end of her tongue. But not a turning one—a stone of fear of oneself—which is why our union was silent and smelled of salt and doom.

When Flora and I first lay together, I realized how Heavy Sands had grown out of the water. I fully comprehended the mechanics. The force with which desire had penetrated the dark bottom of the water awoke sleeping currents, moved the pliable folds of earth, and that very moment, an earthly flower that only needed to be held in one's hands and formed began to grow up to the light. And it grew as long as my mom and dad were rays that penetrated down to the ancient bottom, damp and warm. In the world of people, this feeling is similar to working with clay. You knead your hands in nearly human flesh, poke your

---

discovered these stones when they were conquering America and believed in their ability to heal, renal disorders in particular, hence its name.

fingers, give it form, ennobling or distorting, turn the potter's wheel with your foot, the world turns, and something grows, grows, enveloping your hands, not letting you stop, wanting to absorb you completely . . .

Flora and I wouldn't have been able to stop either, had it not so suddenly turned to autumn. We always made love outside as if there were something preventing us from going indoors. It's unlikely we were really afraid that Ivan would see us. He also needed his alone time with his morphine. But we always stayed in the orchard as long as the sun was shining. Flora was more and more resolute. The western rays seemed to set fire to her light hair. Sometimes the now cool wind snaked between our bodies, trundling the dry leaves across the withered grass. Flora would catch languid brown grasshoppers in the grass and plant them on my bare belly. At first they'd freeze, then they would crawl, prickling me with their feet. I'd flinch and she'd just laugh. At the end of summer every novelty seems like the key that will open the last remaining door. And you will either run away, or you will see a world not worth running away from. When Flora showed up, for the first time I thought that I could go to a big city with her.

There is that especially preternatural moment before dawn when the sun is already peeking out over the horizon, but isn't yet visible. Space is then flooded with a bluish light almost like ink spilled in water—the ink I had used to draw letters under Ivan's vigilant eye. In these pre-dawn moments, things lose their borders. Nothing is quite like it usually is; everything presents its double nature, bares its demonic heart. That time is always restless.

One such tender dawn I realized that I was afraid of sleeping alone. That three figures stood in the doors of the house—fog, rain, and the great river water—and for the first time in as many years I was frightened by their presence. In order not to scream, I needed to go to Ivan, who was sleeping on the other side of the wall, and crawl into the warm nest of his sheets. Bury my face in his hair, knowing that it also smells like rain.

Walking—from door to door, two worn thresholds—for some reason I remembered an old song that Dad used to sing to Mom:

O bird with the white stone, taste my heart.
Take a piece to the sky, let the sun feast on it.
Grant us a long night, let heavy rains
Or a great river shroud my maiden's windows.

On the other side of the wall in the bed where I was supposed to peacefully spend this endless night, Flora was sleeping with Ivan. She had spread herself so freely that she'd kicked the covers to the floor and Ivan, cold, was bunched up on the edge of the bed. There was no space for me between them. I lifted the blanket and covered them up. Then I left so quietly on tiptoe that even the floor froze in fright and didn't creak.

So one love died with the final warmth like a butterfly. And another grew moldy after last year's hibernation. Or I was just a bee carrying pollen from a male to a female flower. I fertilized someone else's love. I still had to check some things. I went into the orchard and walked to the banks. I wasn't wrong: the water was covering the white stripe on the trunk of the old cherry tree. I went back. I sat then on the twisted roots and wept for the second and last time in my life. For again what was happening made no sense. The next morning people woke up in every house in Heavy Sands with red blisters on their arms. In every house but ours.

≈

The medical helicopter landed on the island in the middle of Heavy Sands. For many years I had watched these machines fly over the forest and mountains of the far shore, but I'd never seen one so close. Ivan said his friend whom he had summoned by mail had come. That the friend had brought medicine. That now everything would be fine. But the man in the blue jumpsuit backed off when he saw Ivan and me running across the bridge. He looked at Ivan and then at me and retreated, step by step. He only stopped when he sensed the water behind him.

"What're you doing?" Ivan attempted to laugh and extended his hand. "We're vaccinated. In the military, remember?"

The pilot shook his head and stared at me.

"Ah, she's got immunity! She's already survived a mild case. We're healthy, come on. Don't be afraid!" Ivan shouted at him and reached out his hands to meet his friend.

But the man in the blue jumpsuit would never believe us, I realized right away. He leapt up to the helicopter and tossed two cloth sacks out of the cabin onto the ground. He shouted that he wasn't coming back, this was all he could do to help. Then he climbed in the cockpit and yelled, "Get back!"

Ivan screamed as loudly as he could with a sort of desperate bitterness, "You have to at least tell people!"

There was no point. I knew right away. People don't tell others about these things. I helped Ivan run back across the bridge. He staggered and lurched; I caught him so he wouldn't fall into the water. A vortex of air whipped around us, space shuddered from the roar, and in a few minutes it was over. This was the last time Ivan and I touched each other. The sacks turned out to contain syringes and vials. I still couldn't read very well and the letters on them were sort of slow and

detached on their way to my head: i m m u n o g l o b u l i n, p e n i c i l
l i n . . . For the next few days I drew up the liquid into the syringes and
injected people in the arm like Ivan taught me. But this medicine did
nothing, just like my mom's grasses a long time ago. The anguish of the
ill in Heavy Sands moved into its fifth week.

~

When the moonlight fell on the floor, a woman in black with a small
veneer suitcase entered the room. A true lady. A high-necked dress with
long sleeves, a hat, a small, natty veil. She sat quietly on a chair near
the window, her suitcase alongside her worn-out shoes. The shoes contrasted strangely with her outfit. I got up and sat on the bed. She lifted
her veil and took off her gloves. She had noble skin, very white and thin.
Only on each cheek and on each wrist she had three deep, scarlet scars
laid out in a row.

"I'm leaving," she said in a wan voice.

I nodded.

"You will live for a long time. Your parents have requested it."

I nodded again.

"Do not long for people," the woman in black went on. "You see
how small they are. They fit into one suitcase. Don't linger here."

"What about the earth?" I asked then. "I feel bad for the earth."

"The earth is made from love," the woman said and she scratched
the scarlet scars on her left hand with her right. "Take yours and go."

I nodded again. She got up from the chair.

"I'm going now while it's dark. The air at dawn is very taut—you
can't slip through it."

"What's your name?" I shouted after her.

She turned around and smiled, "Variola Vera."

"Mine's just Vera."

"I know," she kept smiling, gently, almost maternally. "There's a language in which *vera* means 'summer.'"

"Are there lands where summer is eternal?"

"There are. Not that far from here. You'll find them."

The door creaked and the woman disappeared. The moonlight moved from the floor to the wall.

"Who are you talking to?" Flora said sleepily from behind the wall.

"I was dreaming," I answered.

And I quietly jumped out of bed. I had to hurry.

≈

Everything started with water. It would end with water, too. I released my horses from the corral and they followed quietly after me, flattening the grass covered in its first frost. I went from house to house—almost all their doors were ajar. I entered everywhere bravely since I knew Variola was still present, even if she'd said goodbye to me forever. There had been no living souls in many of the homes for a long time. Some they had managed to bury; others were less lucky. Here and there people still breathed and moaned, but there wasn't a miracle in the world that could have saved them. I stooped over the beds of the doomed and took a last look at them. Some of them seemed transparent: I could even see their infected, putrescent throats and guts. A few had blood running down their throats and noses—even their tears were bloody. Some had skin black as night. The ones who saw me through the fog of their fevers pressed their children to themselves, with more and more force, taking the right to life from them. They put them in bed between two dying parents, sang them a last lullaby. They preferred to carry their children with them into death rather than give them to the dreadful Orphan. Only Uncle Nemai and Aunt Myrta had sent those of their daughters—there had been nine—whom the infection hadn't taken away into the cellar and locked them down there. The Second, Fifth, Eighth, and Ninth—the smallest, whose umbilical cord Ivan had cut. The girls were tired of crying, but when I heard their whimpers, I brushed aside the moss their mother had covered their hiding place with and lifted the dark lid. When the girls came out, they needed no explanations. They stood and blinked in the first rays of morning light, they snorted. Eighth held Ninth in her arms. That was it. There was no one else to take. We didn't even take food for the road, so the disease couldn't tag along. We quietly headed for the ferry crossing. I left the children to wait with the horses. I myself returned briefly to my almost former house. Almost.

The serpent of the last dawn had already shed its dark pink skin in the room. Flora and Ivan were intertwined in a deep sleep—it was like she was trying to grow into him with all her limbs, adorning her body with his truncated one. Let them sleep. They have some hard days ahead. They'll have to decide what to do with all these people after Variola leaves. That is, if the river doesn't take care of everything itself. But I didn't doubt that even the water would leave them alive. Ever since the dead had begun to be buried there, Heavy Sands was no longer my land. It now belonged only to Ivan and Flora. It was too much space for me alone and too little for the three of us. It would be easier for Ivan than the rest; he kept only one foot on the ground. Flora was another matter. Flora was everywhere. Besides that, they still had a choice. Earth or water, death or life. This is much more than many people in the world have.

I got a knife and went outside. The shoots around the roots of the walnut and apple trees swayed with their youth. I nodded in response, squatted, and dug up a few with some quick motions. The roots I wrapped in a wet rag. The clump of earth on these young roots would be enough until I got settled. I put the shoots in my basket. Now everything was finally ready.

≈

The children climbed aboard the ferry first. Behind them, treading carefully, the horses boarded and stood around the girls in a protective circle. I got on last. I set the basket of seedlings near my feet and grabbed hold of the rope. How could I have miscalculated? I didn't understand anything and now the ferry wouldn't move. The girls went white. They didn't say anything, but they were afraid of the same thing I was. How could one woman move a ferry that four men barely pulled? The horses stood as still as if they were carved from wood. I took one last look at Heavy Sands, at my house where Flora and Ivan were sleeping, and then grabbed hold of the rope with my other hand, too, a bit in front of my body, and gave a jerk. The ferry creaked and moved.

We were in the middle of the strait when a cold wind suddenly whipped up. It came from nowhere, from the clear blue sky, but it was so strong that the river seemed to boil from its breath. The horses neighed and reared; the girls fought with the luxurious locks of their hair that whipped into their faces. I hurried, leaving bloody stains on the rope. But I passed hand over hand and the ferry moved. The far shore grew irreversibly nearer and this miracle of mine was enough. The wind couldn't stop me. At this moment a sharp, synchronized cry sounded out from behind. And a splash. The horses fell silent. I looked back.

Eighth stood in the middle of the group. She held her arms like a baby—Ninth—was still lying in them, but her arms were empty. Eighth's eyes were full of horror; she couldn't even cry. The other girls were lamenting and speaking over each other, repeating that just a minute ago Ninth was lying calmly in her arms, not crying, not even squirming, and then she suddenly wriggled like a fish, jumping from her sister's arms and splashed into the cold river.

"It wasn't me," Eighth said stiffly and kept repeating the whole way, "It wasn't me, not me. I didn't throw her in the water."

Meanwhile, the wind had quieted.

"Of course it wasn't you," I said. "The wind came for her."

A few more jerks and we reached the shore. We stepped out onto the white grass and never again returned to Heavy Sands.

≈

I passed the places I had once tattooed on my arms, not yet knowing how they looked. The Solstice Mountains and Serpent's Neck, Stone Eye and the Fortress of the Recluse, the City of Seven Brothers, the Forest of the Hanged, the Cursed Hamlet, the Valley of Hungry Dogs. We walked for a long time along the Three Rivers—south of Heavy Sands our dark river indeed divided into three like it was spreading its roots. It was between these roots that I went out to the sea.

We left Heavy Sands behind in the fall and Eighth and I reached the coast before the start of winter. Rather, there was no winter here at all, just as Variola had promised. I stood at the edge of the water panting as though I had run the whole way there, not ridden on a horse. I felt like I was being born. With my forehead and shoulders I parted the folds of the old world's skin and came out of the darkness. Another minute and I'd shout. Eighth and Agate stood nearby, both quiet. I hugged the walnut and apple shoots and they said they felt good there.

Along the way we'd stopped in the City of Seven Brothers where Second and Fifth stayed behind. Having heard their sad story, the mistress of the inn cried all evening and said that her whole life she'd dreamed of having daughters. She had only boys, beautiful and wise, but still just boys. She said the girls should stay if they'd like and they'd never want for anything. The girls agreed. They liked this gentle woman and, even more, her sons with their wily dark eyes and large hands. I was happy for them. Second and Fifth entreated Eighth to stay with them, but she'd latched onto me and only shook her head no.

My mom was a sister to seven brothers, the architects of this city. They came out to see me off and each of them brought a seed—their favorite flowers and trees. And I gave them four black stallions and three black mares. To Second and Fifth I gave a song. I kept only Agate. And Eighth. We got on Agate and rode together. People and horses bowed down and watched after us for a long time. It was three days to the sea.

Many years have passed since then, but the sea is just like at our first meeting. Now I have a great old orchard here and a house built between the walnut and apple trees. My parents also like that there's no winter. Every morning and every evening ships sail through the bay and I'm a bit sorry that they're all made of iron now. They used to bear the souls and fates of trees. But times change—what's to be done? There was another war, an enormous one, just like Ivan used to talk about. Even the sea burned and the dead and wounded were everywhere. We harnessed Agate and carried the wounded when all the cars were over-full. I worked in the hospital and sometimes thought I might run into Ivan there. I didn't, of course, but the wounds I sewed up healed the best. After the war an enormous cemetery sprang up beyond the city. But I'm just an outgrowth on this land, not its master, so it's not hard for me to be in proximity to the dead. It has been very, very quiet here, for many years in a row.

Eighth lived with me her entire life into deep old age. She lived and died happy. Only sometimes, especially on windy nights, a sense-less fear overtook her. At those times she would cover her face with her hands just like that morning on the ferry and say: when she was little she was always afraid that I'd grab her and throw her into the water. For Ninth. And every time I repeated that she wasn't guilty of anything, that Ninth made her own choice. And that every body of water needs its own mermaid. And that thanks to her protectress, Ninth, the local markets still sometimes have apples from Heavy Sands. But they're strange, not the ones I remember, so I don't ever buy them. Eighth didn't like them. Now her daughter and granddaughter don't like them.

I've had women, but never one that could uproot me like Flora. And there were men, lots—it's a port city, after all, people find each other quite interesting. A few even heard about me and turned into this port on purpose. They brought gifts of exotic plants from far-off lands, stroked my map-covered arms, kissed the tattoos on my neck. In parting I told each one what awaited him, what happiness, what death. But few of them could handle this knowledge, so they didn't come back to me a second time. Some couldn't; some were simply afraid.

One dark-eyed boy stayed. When he came the first time, he brought a passion flower cutting from his first overseas voyage. I liked the name of the present. The plant took root and then I also liked the flower, looking at once like a man and a woman. I explained to the boy that he would survive a big shipwreck and lose his memory. From his whole memory only one thing would remain, and it would bring him here, where he belonged. He sailed off and returned a year later. He said it had all come true: the ship sank and he forgot absolutely everything, remembering only me. By some miracle he made it onto the shore, waited a week for a chance boat to pick him up, and then asked the travelers in various ports if anyone had heard of Vera who had lived for one hundred years in a large orchard overlooking the warm sea and who had the entire earth drawn on her arms. Some had heard. So he returned. He said that now his name was Adam. At first I objected that this name was from a different story. But he was very insistent and I agreed. He's sleeping upstairs while I draw these letters in my leather book. In winter—although there is no winter here—we're having twins.

OLENA STIAZHKINA

from IN GOD'S LANGUAGE

translated from the Russian by Uilleam Blacker

T HEY DID SEE EACH OTHER LATER, after his wife, Varda, had
left—and not just in their dreams. Not often, but they saw each
other. They would say hello, they would chat. "Here are mine," she'd
say and show him photographs. First in her wallet, later on her phone.
Revazov didn't show her any photos. Ten minutes. Five. Three. Too little time for anyone other than Inna to be "his" in that moment.

They didn't let themselves get carried away or fool around. Old
friends—family, you might even say. It felt comfortable. No reason for
yelling, sobbing, kisses. What would be the use? But each time, after
their meeting, Revazov regretted that he was leaving her without the
yelling, without the embraces that would be impossible to break.

Once a year he'd send her his best wishes on some holiday or
other—on whichever one was coming up next when he felt the longing
rising up in his chest. It was always a different holiday. She understood.
And about once a year, when the longing welled up in her, she wrote to
him. In the beginning it was telegrams, later emails and text messages.
"How are you?" Of course, they never answered one another. There was
just the one time. At an investment forum, where Revazov had brought
along two partners and Inna had come with her translators. The moder-
ators were disciplined, but there was chaos behind the scenes; the local

47

bigwigs who were meant to open the thing were late and messed up the whole schedule, and got the speakers drunk at the beginning and not at the end. The entire forum turned into a party in the hotel lobby, and it was impossible to get anyone to go into the conference rooms. Revazov's partners had dissolved themselves in vodka, and Inna's translators were practicing their Chinese, since the only ones who weren't drunk were the guests from China.

"Let's get out of here," Revazov suggested. She nodded.

It was autumn then, too. It was cold, but underfoot there were still leaves, and not yet puddles. She was wearing high, and most probably uncomfortable, heels. She speared piles of leaves with the narrow toes of her shoes; the leaves flew awkwardly into the air, and she managed to kick them as they descended, as though they were small, deflated soccer balls. His daughter, Miriam, walked through leaves in exactly the same way. First in her baby shoes, then in her sneakers, and now, more and more often, in shoes with narrow toes.

By the house where Inna lived (both then and now) they stopped and turned to face one another.

"Shall I read your palm?" Inna asked. He shook his head.

"No. I know everything about myself already," he smiled. She took his hand and pulled it to her. This had all happened to them before. And so Revazov wasn't surprised when Inna kissed him on the wrist.

This year he couldn't find a pretext to write to Inna. There was nothing to celebrate. But when Varda's absence stopped being so painful, he wrote, "Where are you?"

The commonplace of the whole summer. An essential phrase. It was the beginning of every conversation. Or every "contact," as they had begun to say. Beyond the front line, in the rest of Ukraine, there was a different life. And there was a front line of a different kind. His clients would report the shifting geography of the country. Friends, too. But Varda and the kids were in Mordor. And that was hard to take. And it was clear that everything was lost, precisely because they were in Mordor, clear that the shadow would lie across that land for far longer than Revazov's miserable new life.

Not everybody was leaving. Not everybody. Those who remained would say, "I'm in the city." The city no longer had a name

Inna wrote back, "Nowhere."

Revazov called her landline. Over the last twenty years, only the first numbers, the city code, had changed. There had been two digits, now there were three . . . The number of landline users had clearly gone up.

"What's happened?"

"They've taken my husband. They want money. I think they've killed him already. I can just feel it somehow."

Her voice was dull, her intonation resigned. Everyone had already learned to live in that resignation. And it was more or less clear that if not now, then tomorrow It, or They, would come. For us. For them. And you knew you should run away, but it was too late, there was nowhere to go, no strength left. No faith that, beyond the checkpoints, there was actually a horizon. And not just more Tiulpan rocket launchers spewing their bloody mess all around.

"I'm on my way," said Revazov. "I have connections." He gave a bitter laugh at these words and left. The taxis, unlike the trolleybuses, which were reliant on electricity, were running efficiently.

Revazov recalled, against his will, his son's former history teacher, who was now working for *them*; the unwelcome, shapeless, toothless, giggling apparition, wearing its pince-nez, looking just like Beria. The image of his face kept crawling its slimy way into Revazov's head, and just as the mythical seafarer couldn't escape Aeolus, Zephyr, and his other companions, Revazov couldn't get rid of this picture.

Revazov arrived at the local administration building, now occupied by *them*, and spent a long time searching for the "historian," wondering how this drunk had managed to carve out his new career selling human beings for peanuts. In the office marked "SMERSH" they said that the historian was now a colonel in the Interior Ministry, but in the Interior Ministry they were pleased to inform Revazov that the historian had become a general, only now attached to the public prosecutor's office. Revazov didn't know if he could handle a meeting with a marshal, but the prosecutor's office relieved this worry, informing him, "Your friend has been transferred to agricultural work." Revazov wanted to ask, "Where to? Central Asia?" From what he could remember of Soviet life, any kind of agriculture was a demotion. And the warmer the locations to which the party dross was punted off, the more humiliating the demotion. Having to earn your crust by hard work was a bitter pill to swallow for those who'd made their names breaking fingers and knocking out teeth.

He eventually found the historian in the Ministry of Transport. The office had no windows, and several other ministers of some description sat in the adjoining reception area. It stank of toilets and cabbage pies.

Everyone here looked despondent and out of sorts. You could feel that their revolution was over, that it had taken to drink from grief. Now it was wandering around somewhere nearby, its face blue and swollen, and the historian and his colleagues had to concentrate hard to respond to its dirty hints.

"They've ruined the transport system . . . It's a wreck . . . Can't even find a decent railway car or a cattle truck to send all that filth off to Siberia," the historian grumbled. And muttered something about himself, about his bitter fate and the vicious battle against the private minibus drivers, about the time before the Gregorian calendar was introduced, about the outdated methods of collecting taxes from the fat-cat taxi drivers.

He muttered, yelled, and fell silent by turns, as though pausing sometimes to listen to someone answering him. Above his desk hung a portrait of Givi, the onetime parking attendant at Donetsk's covered market who was today marshal of the United Armed Forces of the South of Russia.

"I have to find someone," said Revazov.

"The prices have gone up. I have to go through middlemen now, and that costs more," the historian said gloomily.

"First find out if he's alive. I won't pay for a dead man."

"You will, no avoiding it . . . Fucking intelligentsia—don't want to have to bury your friend in a ditch, eh? Well, just you wait!" The historian threatened Revazov with his index finger. Revazov thought the teacher looked like a cartoon dinosaur: big body, small head, and tiny little hands with little sausage fingers. Although dinosaurs didn't have sausages. Or fingers. And as Revazov looked at him it struck him that he'd be able to kill not only strangers, but also this guy—real, familiar, harmless, his son's old teacher.

His heart started racing again. And Revazov only now understood for the first time that the historian looked like Beria. But could Beria really be similar to a dinosaur?

≈

He really was dead. Inna's husband, Vlad, it seems, was his name. Revazov found him at what used to be a training complex belonging to a soccer club. The complex had been built out in the suburbs, and sparkled, as people used to say, like something foreign, something imported, with its blinding green fields like the green contact lenses in the eyes of Hollywood stars, with its gravel paths and subtropical bushes that flowered and gave off intoxicating, suffocating scents, and in winter wrapped themselves in white garments, turning into unmelting snowmen, with the neon-lined contours of its buildings. All of this garishness brought to mind the American oilcloth they used to cover Dostoevsky's murdered heroine Nastasya Filippovna. It was too luxurious, too foreign, too inappropriate, and somehow resembled a synthetic shroud covering the corpse of the grim suburb.

The complex had been taken in May. They started calling it "the barracks." They made a mess of it, trampled all over it, stole everything there was to steal, broke everything. Basically, they helped it blend in to the surrounding architectural landscape. In June, it started coming under fire. It was bombed with precision, professionally. And *they* couldn't quite believe at first that they could also be on the receiving end of something like this. They thought that their ticket to the war, issued to them somewhere far away from here, guaranteed them immunity, a sure-fire investment, a sort of insurance policy. For them, the enemy was a fictitious object. And therefore it was possible to kill him, who was fictitious, but not them, who were supposedly real.

The first stage of this surprise passed quickly, And when the complex became dangerous, they started calling it "the concentration camp." With no shame. To end up in the concentration camp meant you were so close to death that you were good neither for digging trenches nor for bargaining with your relatives. They didn't even guard the prisoners here very closely, because they didn't have the strength to escape . . .

The historian said that Vlad was at the training complex.

He needed someone to go with him. Not Inna. Someone who could drive a car or dress wounds. Who could, if necessary, call . . . someone, some relative, and say: you can stop looking for him now, or look in such and such place.

That was one of the simple desires people now had—to be identified. Nobody was too picky about being put into a mass grave, although ending up lying underneath a pile of *them* was something that neither *they* nor Revazov found appealing. To be identified is to put an end to another's suffering. To not force them to wait for you.

Revazov went alone. Because anybody who went with him would end up a target, a traitor, an innocent victim, or maybe even a guilty victim—an aggressive victim who got into a fight deliberately and got mowed down by a machine gun. Shot in the back, as usual.

His Grandad Lazar used to say that Jesus was a human being adopted by God. Not born, but borne by the passionless body of Mary. And that he had always had his eyes open wide. That Peter hadn't denied Jesus three times. It was He who had denied, together with Peter. That together with Judas He betrayed. That together with them He was ashamed, and died. And rose again.

"And if you," said Grandad Lazar, "give another more than he can bear, then you are a coward, and also a traitor . . . And you're the one who should die for this."

He could have called Igor, the neighbor with whom he'd killed the Russian mercenaries. That would be some party—you, me, and my ex's husband . . .

Inna's husband had been dead for several days. He lay among the other bodies in a room at the complex that they'd fitted out with refrigerators. By the door, there were three lawnmowers, two metal buckets full of bullet holes, the frame of a GAZelle truck, and some packs of yellowed leaflets that for some reason had never been distributed, but would come in handy soon as fuel for potbelly stoves, trash can fires. There was a shortage of paper now in the city, but not here. Paper is a great reason for hope.

"Take whichever one's yours," said the caretaker grimly.

"Can I call a hearse?" asked Revazov.

"A hearse?! I'll give you a hearse!" he spat, and snorted. Then he remembered he had a gun and shot lazily into the ground, almost without anger. He proudly adjusted his woolen *papakha* hat.

"Did you walk here or what?"

"Took the bus, then walked."

"Haha . . . riding the bus with a stiff . . . Hehe . . . Now that's funny."

"Where are you from, man?"

"We're from Nalchik."

The name of the foreign town rang out joyfully. Revazov gave a short, quiet sigh. He looked at the face under the *papakha* and caught himself trying to commit it to memory, so as to be able to recognize it later. It turned out that it was perfectly easy to call a hearse. The funeral business was booming. Wooden crosses, paper flowers, headstone carving. You could earn a bit of money if people actually paid for all this, Revazov thought. But judging by the texts on the headstones, they weren't paying much. They just copied, mixing stuff plagiarized from other graves with the drunken pathos of cinematic nonsense about "officer's honor."

During the siege of Leningrad they'd moved bodies on sleighs. In winter. But in spring, when the snow had melted yet there was still no food? How did they move them then? Did they sling them over their backs? Drag them by the legs? They just abandoned them, because the winter had drained them of the ability to grieve, to feel . . .

"Ivan," said Revazov to the body, "I'm Ivan. And I never touched her after your wedding. Just want you to know that."

He pulled the body onto his shoulder. He carried it to the bus stop. There was a smell. And the softness of a lifeless person. And yes, he began to feel sick. But it would have been even worse, impossible, to drag him by the legs.

The undertakers sent a car to the bus stop. They didn't ask any questions. Nothing surprised them anymore. They gave him a price that was bearable. He had saved some money on the historian by telling him that he'd pay for Vlad on receipt, at the training complex. And the whole time—on the bus on the way there, while he'd been talking to them, while he'd been identifying the body (by the jacket, by the most recent photograph, by the trousers with the white paint stain on the pocket), and while he'd been carrying him—the whole time he'd been thinking how he'd love to be a fly on the wall when the guy in the pince-nez demanded the money from the guy from Nalchik.

These thoughts made him smile.

But the other thoughts, about calling Inna and telling her to come and get the body from the morgue, about the emergency meeting point they'd agreed on, which was now already obsolete . . . He called her, and when he started talking he couldn't stop.

Two strangers can become communicating vessels filled with grief. It works well: a stranger's grief does not take up too much volume. It evaporates easily, like dew in the sun. But when people know each other, their grief multiplies, and both vessels become full, and the container is put under great pressure. The grief has nowhere to go, can't escape. The vessel breaks. For Revazov, if anyone had come to him with Varda, dead, over his shoulders, that person would have immediately become like Charon to him.

And Charon doesn't get telegrams or text messages asking "How are you?"

We don't care how Charon is.

These other thoughts made Revazov cry.

KATERYNA BABKINA

RICHARD THE CHICKENHEART

translated from the Ukrainian by Hanna Leliv

IT WAS CLEAR RIGHT FROM THE start that no one was going any-where. The clouds above the city had delivered rain, while we sat in the kitchen, laughing and making plans—where to have dinner and what to do afterward. Serhiy and I brought Richard along; Nadia and Radu joined us on the way. Three days in a southern city by the sea were even more precious, stolen from the country's latest political events which all of us—as journalists or photographers—had been following incessantly for a long while, with not so much as a break for some sleep. Summer was underway, and we sensed that it wanted some water, but really it was blood that summer wanted.

I met Richard two years ago in Hanoi. Every day at five, loudspeak-ers in the streets would blare upbeat songs—the Vietnamese going home from a hard day's work had to listen to children's voices praising the party. The Vietnamese returning from an easy day's work and roll-ing past in their big cars couldn't hear it. The loudspeakers had hardly fallen silent when the birds' voices drowned them out: every coffee shop, every hotel, every hair salon, and, certainly, every grocery store in Hanoi had birds in cages. Cages clung to the ceilings or the awnings over shop windows; cramped and narrow, they were lost in the tangled vines and electric cords. The birds were nowhere to be found; only twice a day—before sunset and sunrise—did they reign over the entire city for a few minutes.

One of our colleagues connected us. We agreed to meet near St. Joseph's Cathedral and then roamed around this Vietnamese Notre Dame, so out of place amid all the noodles, palm trees, and conical hats, gradually getting to know each other. There were old frescoes preserved in the churchyard, the three kings carrying their gifts across the desert. One of them pointed upward in wonder, "Look, Balthazar, look, Melchior," he seemed to say. "A fern has sprouted where the star of Bethlehem should be, what should we do now?" And so, for many, many years, the three of them wandered around the desert, having lost sight of their landmarks—ferns grew on every single wall in Hanoi. An old woman, a street vendor with a bicycle loaded with fruit, stopped for a rest nearby; she seemed to be sleeping standing up, her hat swaying and its round shadow also swaying to and fro on the stone slabs at her feet.

Richard was big and loud, American through and through; he was in a not-my-president T-shirt, but, judging from its look and the political views of its owner, he'd had it ever since the previous president was in office. Richard was obsessed with the dead.

He had spent two months traveling along the Truong Son trail and visiting Vietnam War sites. Richard took photos of the living as if they were dead; he had a knack for finding the right positions and angles—in his photos, surfers resting on their boards looked like the dead bodies of soldiers left after a brutal battle, and tourists' children squinting lazily, leaning against the walls of torture chambers, while their parents listened to the tour guides, resembled little massacred Vietnamese bush fighters. Even a group of elderly Dutch people checking out of a hotel and walking to their bus looked like downcast refugees, and the one clumsily holding a large backpack looked as if he was holding a dead child.

Richard's photos, all very strange and all about the living dead, were sold as stock photos to well-known magazines. Even *Time* and *Esquire* bought them. Richard came from Seattle, and it was his first time abroad. At any rate, he was very young and treated the concept of death and chronicling dead bodies in the living world as the glorification of fluidity and change, as a rebuke against wasting time, as social resistance and rebellion against everything that oppresses the vitality of the human body, and as many other things. We walked around all night long, and Richard kept babbling about death and groping for the camera on his neck, even though no one around us was dying, and he didn't have to take any pictures. Instead, there were too many people scurrying by, loud and alive, and unfamiliar with the concept of personal space; the twilight was packed with people. They tried to sell us food from every window and stand; they gutted chickens everywhere you could imagine, and slippery chicken hearts kept popping, snapping under our feet. Spitting blood. I asked Richard if he had ever seen a dead person.

"My grandma, before she was cremated. I was nine then," he answered gravely. Richard emailed me after people paid their last respects to the fallen in February. He offered his condolences; a mourning song, "Plyve Kacha," moved him, and he looked up its translation on the internet. "The Duck Swims." He asked me what was going on, said he felt bad and was there for us, but I knew what was really on his mind. He had sent a few scant words of support when it all started, and I appreciated that. He couldn't miss out on so many dead people all in one place. I talked to Serhiy about it, and we invited him over.

When Richard arrived there were no dead people left, only those taken hostage, arrested, or missing. There was already fighting in the east, mild fighting, not even any refugees yet. This all looked unbearable to Richard, but what were we supposed to do with him? He was plain bored, upset, like a little kid, that he missed the Maidan, charred and blackened from the burning tires, Molotov cocktails, and bullets. There were only drunkards and crackpots left in the tents downtown. For some reason, the foreign reporters, photographers, and camera operators he may have known had all dispersed right around that time. Richard was a new level for us in terms of nurturing tolerance toward "the others" who swarmed all over this world. He treated our deeply personal grief with purely consumerist curiosity, which we had to accept since, technically, he hadn't done anything wrong. He strolled around the city for a few days, while we worked like dogs to process the developments in Eastern Ukraine, yet he took only one picture. A little boy—about four years old—had fallen down, tripped where the cobblestones had been removed by the protestors on the Maidan, where traffic was still blocked. In Richard's photo, the boy looked dead, hopelessly dead, the background showing heaps of memorial wreaths and blown-out street lamps where people had been shot.

He must have been a genius, this Richard, a genius at documenting death where it seemed no longer present, a genius at pinning down death's ubiquitous presence even where it wasn't visible yet. At the very end of April, we escaped to Odesa, to the sea, and Richard came along.

We were sitting in the kitchen, laughing, almost till dawn—didn't even bother to go out for dinner. Radu had some wine. We didn't have anything to do the next day—no writing, no filming—and some rowdy soccer fans were planning a rally for later. Serhiy and Radu wanted to film it, and over the weekend we could go to the beach again and then head home.

We didn't feel like getting up. Serhiy and I had been lying there, watching how much sunlight pushed through the young leaves on the trees outside. Radu and Nadia had gone into the kitchen of the large apartment we were renting and started laughing softly about something. Richard joined them shortly thereafter. Radu didn't like Richard, but, then, he didn't seem to like anyone at all; he was too smart to overlook others' shortcomings, and too honest to forgive or ignore them. Or maybe he was just an irritable Romanian with whom, as with many others at that time, we'd crossed paths by chance only to part ways forever, also by chance.

We had breakfast in town and then went to the beach. We walked through an old botanical garden turned health resort for employees of the Ministry of Internal Affairs and their families. I went there on vacation as a kid, with my parents, but only in the spring—the summer months belonged to the officers of a higher rank than my stepfather. There was no one around, only the ripe spring, abundant light, young greenery, and endless statues of discus throwers and girls holding oars.

"Lie on the ground," Richard said to Nadia abruptly.

Nadia burst out laughing; she was always laughing no matter what was going on, and sometimes she really saved the day. You know, it's like when you want to drop dead, and someone next to you is enjoying a sincere, lighthearted laugh, and then you want to drop dead just a little less.

"What do you want?" Radu asked.

"Lie on the ground," Richard repeated and smiled, and Nadia, laughing, tossed her backpack aside and sprawled out on the warm cobblestones. She kept laughing, making faces, and talking—about how warm the ground was and how blue the sky was. She couldn't keep still or keep her mouth shut, not even for a second. Richard took only one photo and showed it to me. Back then, he shot in black-and-white; a dead woman lying on the cobblestones among neglected alabaster statues and old trees, one leg turned up, as if she'd been running and some bullets had caught up to her and pierced her back, her bags lying beside her. Serhiy also looked at it and said nothing. Shocking. Nadia was rising to her feet and brushing off her pants, laughing again, when Radu snatched the camera out of Richard's hands.

"She's dead, what did you do?" he shouted.

"She *looks* dead. Cool, isn't it?" Richard said, but Radu went nuts for some reason.

"Let me see, please, let me see," Nadia peered over Radu's shoulder. He was pressing some buttons on Richard's camera. Richard tried grabbing his camera back, but Radu suddenly shoved him, really hard. Radu was short, tenacious, and mad.

"Don't shoot people like they're dead. Don't shoot my girlfriend like that. Got it?" he said, looking at Richard. He couldn't figure out how to delete the photo.

"Let me see," Nadia repeated.

Richard tried to snatch his camera back again, but Radu shoved him away even harder.

"Chill," Serhiy said anxiously.

"I'm gonna smash it," Radu said, holding the camera up in one hand. "I'm gonna smash it."

"Give him his camera back," Serhiy said, standing between the two of them.

"Okay," Richard said, reaching for his camera. "I'll delete it."

Radu hesitated and then eventually handed him the camera. Serhiy was still standing between them.

"Deleting it, okay?" Richard said slowly, looking at Radu.

Silently, we went down to the beach, only Nadia let out the occasional giggle. The sea was so quiet and smooth as if it had been laying low—I'd only seen a sea like this at daybreak. But then the wind picked up, the water began to ripple, and a storm broke out; we wanted to hail a taxi but the seafront road was for pedestrians only, so we dashed through the rain to a restaurant. I was pissed that it wound up being much farther than Serhiy had thought when he suggested waiting out the storm there. Radu grew anxious because I wouldn't shut up about the rain. Serhiy was irritated by Nadia's incessant laughter. We finally made it to our apartment an hour and a half later, soaked and angry. We didn't even talk to each other once we got back. It was a relief when someone called Serhiy and asked if he could film the next day. Everyone agreed to settle up for the apartment, get in the car, and be back home in four hours. It was only after we stuffed our backpacks in the trunk that Richard suddenly announced, "I'm staying."

"Are you sure?" I asked.

"I'll be okay," he said. "Just a couple of days."

We hugged limply; Serhiy plopped down into the driver's seat.

When he called me on Saturday, bright and early, I already knew about the clashes in Odesa and the fire at the Trade Unions Building after the soccer fans' march, and that more than forty people had died. I also knew for sure that Richard had been there. This was all we knew— only dead people and accusations, endless accusations, fantastic grounds for inciting hatred. By that time, we were no longer surprised.

"I'm catching a flight to Seattle tonight," he said. "I land in Kyiv at seven thirty. I need my suitcase."

I texted him, asked him to come out of the terminal, as I would have to take him to international departures anyway, and he did. I stopped, and he hopped in the back, for some reason. He had no camera.

I saw in the rearview mirror that he was looking straight ahead, almost without blinking, that he hadn't shaved and his lips were bloodless, like those of an old man. I didn't ask him any questions. I thought about how those things we had to and did get used to, those things that turned into everyday life, the daily grind, were like this only for us, but remained, in essence, horrible and irreparable.

I parked near the international terminal. Richard took his suitcase out of the trunk, and we went to the check-in desk. Or rather, he went, and I, for whatever reason, followed him. Inside, he stopped, turned toward me, and said:

"All those people died for real. I saw them, less than two feet away from me, like this," he marked off three feet with his hands "They died. Burned alive. Slaughtered."

I listened to him in silence.

"Why?" he asked.

I didn't say anything.

Leaving the terminal, it felt like I and the all people around me were the dead ones, and the ground under my feet was strewn with chicken hearts.

SERHIY ZHADAN

A SAILOR'S PASSPORT

translated from the Ukrainian by Uilleam Blacker

1

IN THE MIDDLE OF MARCH WINTER ended and the warm mists
began to gather on the coast. In the night the air was dark and transparent, like well-washed bottles of green glass, but nearer the morning
the mist rose from the sea, filling up the empty piers. For a few hours
part of Crimea disappeared into the thick, damp air. The mist was so
heavy that you could hear it dissipating into separate drops. The first
to awake in the city were the drunks and the vegetable sellers. They
got out of their beds, pulled on their sturdy, manly clothes—Turkish
jeans, crumpled jackets, and beat-up leather boots—looked for their
cigarettes, went into the kitchen, drank boiled water from their kettles,
opened their windows, and let the mist into their rooms, which were
still warm from sleep. The wet air quickly filled the rooms, settling on
the everyday lives of these forty-year-old men—on their leather jackets, spare car parts, and old bicycle wheels tied to the ceiling, which
revolved sadly like weathervanes in the drought. The streets were
empty, just the dogs warming themselves next to the wine cellars and
bookshops, guarding the dusty shelves filled with fortified wine and
the counters selling old poetry. Around six the traders wheeled their
carts out into the street and dragged them to the markets. Some of them

stopped by the roadside at junctions and began to lay out their goods. After them the workers appeared, cleaners and random prostitutes who wandered the city trying to find their homes, having forgotten their addresses, who were unable to recognize the streets, wandered into the wrong buildings, greeted the shadows of strangers, which disappeared away lightly into the darkness, their footsteps echoing on the wet cobblestones. The bars with slot machines threw out their last nighttime customers, who got up and without a care dragged themselves off to their burrows, forgetting all their nighttime losses and adventures. They got home, waking their children and wives, dragged themselves along communal corridors, went into their wardrobes, went to sleep in old bathtubs, made yellow by time and love, broke fake crystal dishes, cut their veins with blunt razors, drank tea, thick and sweet like the sea mist, read last year's women's magazines, turned on their radios and listened to the weather forecast, not believing all the warnings about possible flooding, earthquakes, and the speedy onset of summer. After this the children ran out into the streets and hurried off to school, leaving long, deep corridors behind them in the mist.

At eight the first shops opened. The sleepy cashiers unbolted the doors, unlocked the padlocks, and let in the stray dogs. They ran inside and lay down beneath the shelves full of cans of sweet corn and pickled onions, and lay there, warming the damp storerooms with their hot breath. The cashiers raised the blinds on the windows and the shops were lit up by the first rays of sunlight, and then became filled with that dreadful, joyful music they usually play on shortwave radio. Soon the fresh bread and milk arrived, the delivery men cheerfully chatted to one another, the dogs followed them with their eyes, mistrustfully observing them as they carried the still warm bread in from the street. Then elderly women began to come into the shops where they bought bread and cans of food, slipped out onto the street again unnoticed, and returned home. The mist lifted and the sun warmed the rooftops. The walls of the buildings and the vine leaves were damp and swollen, like freshly washed linen. Half-empty sanatoriums, cafeterias, empty parks, and old Pioneer camps lined the coast, a dead springtime territory, long-neglected buildings full of state-issue furniture and heavy refrigerators full of fat and malt that shudder heavily in the night, their other-worldly sounds waking the inhabitants of the buildings. Endless fences among trees, guards at gates, ivy on the brick walls, sunlit dust on dead monuments, half-erased inscriptions from the seventies—the March resorts, like nighttime train stations, lived on in their memories of better times, of noisy crowds, in March all this calls forth gentle nostalgia and mild distaste, abandoned towns, swollen by the rain and dried by the sun, whose inhabitants have left behind countless personal belongings for security guards and burglars to stumble upon. The windows of most of the buildings were ajar, and were one so inclined, one could glance in and see the furniture gathered from all across the city, the rugs on the walls, the old record players and transistor radios—most of these things were accidental, didn't match the rugs, which made the rooms look like left-luggage offices. Most of the rooms were rented out only in summer and stood empty through the whole winter. In spring-time the owners cleaned them, aired the quilts and pillows, driving out the dead winter spirit, the spirit of a flat in which no one has lived for months. They washed the floors, finding letters, phone cards, and used condoms under the beds, that's to say, the traces of other people's passion and other people's pain.

At ten the drugstores opened, crowds of drunks already gathered round them. They entered the empty, echoing premises and timidly scanned the striped and colorful leaflets, the bright pills, golden mixtures and syrups, fragrant powders and expensive creams; cautiously and respectfully they peered at the chrome medical instruments, the sterile instruments, with the help of which those who teeter on the brink of life are returned safely to it; they spelled out the names of treatments for insomnia and immortality, regarded with curiosity all those love powders that you were supposed to rub into your gums, they stepped up to the shelves with needles and scalpels, mistrustfully glanced at the mountains of Chinese condoms, jealously screwed up their eyes at that whole pharmaceutical bounty; they then ordered two bottles of medical-grade ethanol each, and with great relief breathed out all that uncanny pharmacology from their chests and went out into the fresh air.

Before lunch solitary guests of the sanatoriums wandered along the seafront, lost and lonely deserters who arrived every day, escaping from the endless March sleet engulfing the valleys and river plains of Eastern Europe that lay to the north of the Crimean Peninsula. This sniffling public wandered in twos and threes along the beaches, empty as wintertime stadiums, observing the freighters creeping their way toward Sevastopol. They wandered along the paths in the parks, sat on the warm rocks to read detective stories, invariably taking the side of the villains.

At lunchtime they all dispersed back to their nests, which still hadn't quite warmed up yet, their rooms with their television sets cold as dead hearts, they set out for the cafeterias, greeted their friends, and began their endless conversations about weather and health, or to be more precise—about the poor state of both. In the town workers from the warehouses and building sites also stopped for a break, got out their stocks of alcohol, their ammunition, laid it out on the wooden benches, turning their tattooed backs to the sun, and began to tell stories of business, women, and crime, stories from their own lives. By the wine kiosks the usual crowds had gathered and occupied the best seats at the tables and watched as the fresh sun slowly drifted westward. Everything should happen at the correct pace and in the correct sequence, most of all—the consumption of alcohol.

Nearer evening the bars filled up with teenagers. They arrived on mopeds and in old Soviet cars, drank wine, and listened to the jukeboxes. Then after six the workers from the building sites filled up the bars, and then the drunks came crawling in, that is, those who were still able to crawl; retired colonels from the sanatoriums arrived, lonely women and abandoned housewives, drunk Roma women and naive college girls, outside it got dark and in the bars the first golden lights were lit, dim in the cigarette smoke. The shops began to close, though you could still buy alcohol and bread well into the night. The sun lit up the surface of the water, red flashes bounced off the windows of the attics and the rooms to rent, the shadows got thicker, like ink, and the monument to Lenin, who looked like a young beatnik in his foppish green jacket and late-fifties narrow-cut trousers, yes, the Lenin monument also fell into shadow, and around it schoolchildren gathered and listened to music on their cell phones. After ten the narrow streets of the center were filled with the merry, drunken cries and nervous sighs of those on their way home, unable to continue the unceasing celebration, this day of the drowned, who swam up to the shore of their town and stood on the sandy seabed, stamping their water-filled boots in time to the music from the cell phones. Nearer midnight things began to heat up and the atmosphere was soaked in passion, wine, and danger. In one of the bars a fight broke out—the teenagers had had a disagreement with some Moldovans about the jukebox, they couldn't decide what they were all to listen to, they all wanted to listen to sad prison ballads, but each of them had his own favorite sad prison ballad, then someone put a song on out of turn, and the fight broke out. The Moldovans were older, and so at first they had the advantage, they threw the locals out onto the street, drove them away from the bar, only for the locals' older brothers to come to their aid, along with the drunks, the unemployed, and passersby. Broken glass flashed, the first window was broken, the teenagers got out their knives, and the festivities reached their height. The night air dried throats and sobered heads, upon which bottles of fortified wine broke. The Moldovans made for the side streets, carried away their wounded, and dissolved in the park alleyways. The police were called, arrived, and chased away those who were left. Having done so the policemen entered the bar and finished the drinks the Moldovans had left, and listened to the sad prison ballads. Listened, and didn't interrupt.

In the silence of the night the birds began to sing, bloodstains lay dark under the streetlights, and by the Lenin monument the teenagers sat wiping their bloodied noses with their sleeves. They cleaned their knives, played some new sad prison melodies on their phones, and looked out to sea, where there was silence, mist, and darkness, that is, where there was nothing.

2

At first they thought about robbing a tobacco kiosk. They spent a long time circling it, sniffing out the territory. But one of them, Bodia, was allergic to tobacco, he immediately felt ill, and they decided to leave the kiosk in peace. Vietal, Bodia's friend, refused to speak to him after this, although secretly he was glad that things had turned out that way, since neither of them smoked, and no one really knew why they wanted to rob the kiosk anyway. The two friends were finishing school, were incurable romantics and losers, no one would sell them alcohol and women didn't like them. In fact, neither did men. No one liked them. One day, in their district on the outskirts of Kharkiv, they found a drunk businessman sleeping peacefully on a bench outside the gaming arcade. The friends immediately decided to rob him, take his phone, for example. Turned out the businessman had three, and so they took all three. Next morning the phones started to ring. The friends got scared, went to the secondhand phone market and sold the first two for practically nothing, but kept the third, just in case. Bodia began to panic, saying they'd be looking for them now, and suggested running away somewhere, say, to Crimea, to the sea. With the money they'd got for the phones they bought two second-class tickets, and that very same evening left the city for the dark, sweet unknown. In the night they dreamed of warships. They didn't have enough money for bedding and slept on bare bunks.

After changing trains in Simferopol, they traveled to Alupka, got off the bus, and went to see the city. They hung around for a while taking photos by the green monument to Lenin, whom Vietal didn't recognize at first because of the tight trousers, trying to convince Bodia that it was some local celebrity. They bought some chips. Their money ran out. The friends went to the seafront, sat on the stones and watched the skies, white as train sheets, and listened to music on the stolen phone. It was March and life seemed endless and sweet, like a free caramel. They could find work as sailors on a freighter, sail under the exotic flag of some unrecognized African republic, and have real sailors' passports— the entry ticket to the darkest and sweetest of gates—they would sail into black, hot ports, fill themselves up with alcohol and sleep with laughing, obliging Chinese women, smuggle drugs in their stomachs and trade stolen clothes, wear fake gold and hang around with the biggest scoundrels and rogues in town, wherever such company could be found. They would sail across the waters of the Black Sea, salty as tears, sail down the Eritrean coast, only fish and dope to keep them going, travel from city to city, mingle with the noisy port crowds, drink with sea cadets and ship doctors, sing with murderers and perverts, hunt sharks, dragons, and cunning predatory octopuses. They'd be able to choose life's best and tastiest morsels, start everything anew and depend on no one, speed blind through ocean mirages, fight their way through crashing waves, suffer thirst and hunger, freeze in ice and burn on slow fires, so as to finally reach their destination, where glory, respect, and sweet, insane love await. The main thing now was not to choke on their chips.

Toward evening the friends returned to the Lenin monument to sell the last phone. A Black kid began to talk to them. He was a couple of years older than them, was out walking his boxer, and was called Gabriel; he told them he had no money, but that he had a free room they could rent for a few days. In exchange for the phone, obviously. The friends hesitated for a moment, but only for a moment. In the room there was nothing but a bed, onto which they collapsed fully dressed and slept almost until dinnertime the next day.

In the morning Bodia found an old chess set under the bed. Armed with the chessboard they went to the sanatorium belonging to the Ministry of Defense, found a pair of worn-out old colonels on a bench, and challenged them to a game. They won twenty dollars and a pack of cigarettes and went to buy chips. In the shop they approached an attractive woman dressed in black, who was standing by the counter eyeing the bottles of Madeira, and asked her to buy them beer, the woman carefully looked them up and down, bought some wine, and invited them to her place. She lived in that very same sanatorium belonging to the Ministry of Defense, was the widow of an officer, and wore a very low-cut dress, golden rings on her fingers, and a heavy necklace around her neck, her hair was carefully dyed, she seemed somewhat confused and gazed dreamily out to sea. The two friends sat next to her at the table and didn't know what to do with their hands, were nervous and sweaty. The widow suggested opening the wine, first Bodia had a go, but the wine slipped out of his hands, then Vietal took the bottle, but with a similar lack of success, and the widow just waved her hand and got out

72

an open bottle of vodka from the sideboard. The friends took one shot and immediately became drunk. The woman smoked a lot, asked them about school, and told them about her personal life.

She told them that her husband had been a combat officer, that she'd dreamed of marrying a combat officer ever since she was a child, you don't know what the navy is like, she said, the heat, the hidden fire, those officers' families, she crossed her legs and the friends caught a glimpse of her dark red underwear, those long waits, meetings and passion, curses and farewells, the woman leaned forward and what the friends saw almost took their breath away, then the long months alone, waiting for news, languishing in unsatisfied desire, do you know how that feels? The friends nodded. The woman told them about submarines, empty barracks, salty spray, and the shimmering sun; she said she came to Crimea every year in springtime, when no one was there, and remembered the good times.

The friends then started vying with one another to tell the black widow about life, so that she didn't think they had absolutely no clue, so that she knew that even at the age of sixteen they had already tasted the might of fate's blows, that they had ten robbed tobacco kiosks on their CV and hundreds of stolen mobile phones, that they knew the real price of love and loyalty, that the glittering, sweet criminal world had taught them to treat women harshly but fairly. At this point Bodia lost his coordination for a second and fell off his chair, and Vietal ran to the bathroom to puke. But the woman found more vodka and their leisurely, friendly conversation flowed on, and the friends tried in vain to open the wine, until eventually they broke the bottle, and they smoked women's cigarettes, and sang pirate songs together with the woman, like real sea dogs, lying on her warm bed, which smelled of perfume, powder, and loneliness. By midnight they'd managed to sober up a little and began to think about going home, telling her they had to leave. Okay then, the woman said, off you go, but if you like you can stay, she added, and went out onto the balcony, offering her surprisingly well-looked-after sixty-year-old body to the nighttime wind, with its warm, soft skin, with all its curves and bulges, its clothes and underwear. And the wind tangled itself in her thick wig, and the ships' horns sounded from the bay, and the watchmen returned the signal, guarding their gates and towers, and cosmonauts, flying across the southern sky, sent her greetings via satellites.

The friends at this point tried to decide which of them should stay. Bodia insisted that he should stay, since it was he who had picked her up, back in the shop. Vietal didn't agree and claimed that he should stay, since it was he who had just moments ago broken the bottle of wine. Bodia then tried to be cunning and announced that he was falling asleep and didn't have the strength to go anywhere, while Vietal resorted to blackmail and threatened to puke all over everything. In the end the friends started fighting, turning over chairs, and breaking the wide plates with the emblem of the Ministry of Defense on them, and the woman watched them out of the corner of her eye from the balcony, trying to remember the last time someone fought over her. The adversaries, however, soon exhausted themselves and slumped to the floor, breathing heavily and wiping away tears. Vietal was the first to give in, he felt sick again, leapt out into the black night, slipped through the lobby, and disappeared among the palms, cursing the entire female sex and the transience of male friendship. But Bodia remained, and what happened to him that night deserves a story all of its own.

Toward morning, miserable, vomit-covered Vietal came upon their new Black friend in the middle of the street. He was on an Italian moped and invited Vietal to go with him to Yalta to sell some weed he'd bought from some Moldovans, because, as he explained, he needed a partner for security. Vietal put on a helmet, sat on the moped and off they sped,

scaring the seagulls and bats, and as they neared Yalta they drove into
the warm, fresh, bitter embrace of the mist.

3

The Moldovans lived in a junkyard, among snow, mist, and bro-
ken-down Ikarus buses. The junkyard was high up in the hills, below
it lay the warm, defenseless town, beyond that the surface of the sea
glinted sharply, and above their Moldovan heads a mountain ridge
loomed. They had arrived at the beginning of June, a ten-man team,
and had been hired by an eccentric general who was building himself a dacha on the grounds of a hospital; he put them up in the junkyard, in the garages. They were supposed to finish by October, and in
the beginning everything went fairly well—the team worked hard, the
Moldovans kept quiet and bothered no one. But by August the problems had begun—the general was arrested by the security services and
the Moldovans were left orphaned. The general's daughter came and
told them to wait until things blew over. The Moldovans decided to
wait. But not to work. In the burning August mornings they'd crawl out
of their garages, lie down on piles of old tires, and warm their thin bodies. In the evenings, when the heat subsided, they'd send one of their
number down into the valley for alcohol and food. Then they'd stay up
long into the night, watching a portable TV under the starry sky and the
jagged mountain ridges. They couldn't swim, so didn't go down to the
sea. What's more, since the general still had all their documents, they
had to try not to make themselves too visible. At the end of August the
general's daughter appeared again, told them that the police had found
the general's second passport, and paid them part of what he owed
them. The Moldovans, who now had no passports whatsoever, couldn't
decide whether this was good news or bad, and so decided to keep
waiting. But not to go back to work. In September, harvest time came.

Back in August the Moldovans had already noticed some sun-drenched plantations, beyond the forest that surrounded the junkyard, which had most likely been vineyards under the Soviets. The plantations belonged to some agricultural company in Kyiv, which had bought them back in the nineties, and every year stubbornly planted the dry Crimean soil with potatoes, corn, and other healthy but hopeless crops. The firm had recently gone bankrupt and had simply forgotten about the vineyards. Wild hemp grew there now, thrusting itself upward toward the warm, anxious, subtropical sun. For two months the Moldovans had been fondly watching their bounty grow and waiting for September, which would bring with it the blessed harvest. And in September, the hemp, as they say, ripened. The Moldovans wandered long among the warm, fragrant plantations, rubbed the ripe leaves in their hands, and dreamily sniffed their fingers, which had turned black from engine oil and green from the hemp. Afterward they returned with full pockets, fell down on the old tires, and smoked until nightfall, looking out at the fading sea and counting the satellites. On those very same tires they fell asleep and slept until the following afternoon. Their clothes were soaked in the smell of sunny hemp, their pockets, socks, and nostrils were full of hemp seeds. In the morning heavy September bees appeared, landed on their dark brown, time-dried skin, and gathered pollen right off their bodies. Swift-footed spiders wove webs in their pockets, and ladybugs crawled into their boots looking for shade, quiet, and oblivion.

The Moldovans were in no hurry to gather the whole crop, justifiably considering it their own property, and not believing that it would enter anyone's head to drag a combine up here to gather cannabis for the cows. Until one day, while they were still coming to from the previous day's excesses, and getting ready to begin those of the next, they arrived at the plantation and saw a group of strangers joyfully shaking the ownerless bushes. These were Rastas from Krasnoiarsk who'd been roaming around trying to find a railway station for two weeks, without any money, documents, or chance of success, and had quite by accident ended up on these unoccupied lands. A brief confrontation ensued between the Moldovans and the Rastas, as a result of which the Rastas were forced to admit defeat and retreat into the mountains. At first they wanted to report the Moldovans to the authorities, to get rid of those impudent Bessarabians, but they then realized that, together with the Bessarabians, the authorities would most likely get rid of the whole crop. The Moldovans also didn't dare report the Rastas to the police, while the Rastas themselves, it seemed, had no intention of going back to Krasnoiarsk. The situation was a tense one. The Moldovans decided to keep the Krasnoiarsk lads out of the fields at all costs, and set up round-the-clock patrols. At night they rolled black car tires up from the junkyard, set them on fire, and in the light of the burning rubber guarded their bounty. Above them, in the black, rubbery night, the eyes of the Rastas gleamed hungrily; they dared not come near, and watched the ripened leaves greedily from a safe distance. On the third night of not enough sleep and too much smoking, the Moldovans decided to offer a compromise—they'd let the Rastas fill their rucksacks with hemp, on the condition that they then disappear, preferably straight back to Krasnoiarsk. The Rastas didn't have to be told twice, quickly stuffed their bags, and with great hopes for their Rasta future descended into the valley. Here they were picked up by the law. As were their rucksacks. After a short but intense interrogation the Rastas gave in and told the police the location of the plantation. Yet to their credit, said nothing of the Moldovans. The police went to the plantation with scythes, the sergeants took off their caps and started work. From the cover of the forest the miserable, downcast Moldovans observed each stroke of each scythe. A couple of weeks later the weather finally turned, and the rains began.

In October, the general died in custody. The doctors gave the cause of death as a heart defect, and then painstakingly covered up the three bullet holes in his skull. The Moldovans watched the general's funeral on TV and drank aftershave for his soul's eternal rest. At the end of October, the general's daughter arrived, said that her father's bank accounts were still frozen and that they'd have to wait until spring, but in spring they could start work again, since, as the old Moldovan saying goes, work is no wolf, and until the accounts are unfrozen no one's going to pay for it. The Moldovans decided that there was no real point in returning home and that it would be better to spend the winter there. Besides, it meant they didn't have to spend money on the journey home. So they stayed in the junkyard. With no work or normal contact with other human beings they'd turned completely wild. In town they were feared and given grain and pasta on credit. One of the Moldovans got married in the town to a Romani woman he'd met at a bus stop, and left with her for an unknown destination without even informing his companions. Another one fell in with the Tatars and even converted to Islam. He found work in an underground coffee factory and had no intention of returning to his compatriots. A third broke into a drugstore in town and filled his pockets with some imported cold medicine that when mixed with cola gave a hallucinogenic effect. The next day he ended up in the hospital with a serious stomach disorder, from the cola, obviously, and spent a week lying in the ward, from where he was then deported to the unwelcoming Moldovan autumn. The rest of the Moldovans kept their heads down for a while and lived in the junkyard, like the seven dwarves, not particularly bothering anyone, trading all the scrap metal they could find and selling the remains of the autumn cannabis crop. The winter was warm and rainy, and in the early morning, before sunrise, they'd emerge from their garages, make a bonfire, warm themselves around it, and look out at the sea, which lay below them, dark as heavy silver.

When they went to town they'd sit in the bar, drink fortified wine, and listen to the jukebox. Every so often they'd start a fight with the locals. They'd throw themselves into the fight, working as a team, and when the locals became too numerous, they'd make a quick escape up the narrow side streets that led up the hill, carrying their wounded comrades on their backs. They'd return to their junkyard, sit down around the TV, and watch whatever was on—talk shows, news, even the commercials. But when soccer started they turned the TV off completely, since they didn't know who they were supposed to support up here in these hills.

4

In Yalta they stopped at the Tatar districts. These comprised a few multistory buildings that Tatars had occupied. The authorities had been trying to evict them for years, but the Tatar commune was solid and fended off all attacks. Gabriel, the Black kid, led Vietal through the back alleys and courtyards; they went into some back door and found themselves in the gap between two buildings, soaked in darkness and smells. Gabriel confidently walked ahead, up the dark stairwell, went into the apartments, which weren't locked, and where dozens of adults and children slept on the floors; he slipped into the darkness of the apartments. From some side door where the storage rooms and toilets were, suspicious-looking types appeared and shook Gabriel's hand, they talked about something, and Gabriel hurried on, up to the higher floors. There was almost no furniture in the rooms, the floors were covered in rugs, duvets, and army greatcoats, the inhabitants were sleepy and guarded, the women slept in colorful T-shirts and bright stockings, the men wore kerchiefs and scarves around their necks. They all greeted Gabriel, they made thick herbal tea, got out some eastern sweets and raw meat, shoved crumpled banknotes, cigarettes, and telephone cards into Gabriel's hands in exchange for his goods, and went back to sleep, diving under the duvets and greatcoats, covering their heads with old blankets and flags, turned off their lamps, and the rooms once again fell into silence and sleep. Gabriel came out of the building and went into the next, greeting passing tenants on the stairs, ones who were already awake. He went into different rooms, stepped over sleeping men, slid into the beds of women, woke them with quiet words and touches, the women were glad to see him, the men didn't notice him. Then they got back on the moped and spent a long time weaving through the Yalta suburbs, until they finally stopped by a private home surrounded by a slate fence, and for some time were unable to enter. Eventually they were let in, went through the courtyard, in which two crazy-looking German shepherds were prowling around, and went into the building. There they found some kind of strange commune, about two dozen ghostly members of some sect, mostly women, who looked like prostitutes who'd been sacked for failing to fulfill their quotas, though what they actually did was unclear. The women slept together, also on the floor, ate in the same big room, were quiet, and spoke little. They paid little attention to Gabriel, despite his best efforts. Having taken what he'd brought, they immediately shoved both of them out of the door and began singing some strange song.

We have to go to one more place, said Gabriel, starting up the moped. And off they went to their last clients for the day. These were underground entrepreneurs who'd set up a home coffee manufacturing business. They bought large quantities of cheap raw materials, sugar, and powdered creamer, and had procured some brand labels from somewhere, so that on the outside the product looked good and sold well with wholesalers. The entrepreneurs ground the coffee in cement mixers; they had two brand new cement mixers, bought especially with a view to the expansion of the business. They poured the beans in there, the work went quickly and well, and the profits grew. Every day this strange alchemistic undertaking produced up to a ton of perfectly drinkable coffee. Vietal looked at the cement mixers with admiration and immediately began to help the owner's daughters, carrying sacks of sugar and shoveling the finished coffee mixture with a child's yellow spade. The entrepreneurs invited them to stay until their lunch break; these underground alchemists turned out to be vegetarians and ate only salads and drank slowly brewed *chyfir*—impossibly thick, strong tea. They didn't drink the coffee, perhaps because they knew how much work went into preparing it. In the evening a happy Gabriel gathered his strength and they drove back, avoiding all potential traps and pitfalls along the way.

On returning to Yalta they found the Moldovans in the bar and joined their table. The Moldovans had been paid, and in their delight were buying every kind of alcohol available. After a while they got in an argument with the locals and threw them out of the bar together with the chairs they'd been sitting on. During the fight one of the locals smashed a bottle of fortified wine over Vietal's head, Vietal stumbled back down the street and crawled into the bar, hid under a bench, and somehow managed to dress his wounds with his Iggy Pop T-shirt. Before long the police ran in and began searching for the culprits. They dragged wounded Vietal out from under the bench. Having received a dose of first aid across the kidneys, Vietal told them what had happened; the officers shoved him into their car and set off to the addresses given to look for the protagonists in this complex story.

5

In the morning everything was strange and bright, nighttime fear and exhaustion had subsided, and Bodia went out onto the pier and sat for a long time counting the ships sailing out of Sevastopol. Everything that had happened to him, everything he felt at that moment, which only he could see under those cold, sunny skies, seemed to him strange and unlikely, so easy to believe in, so hard to deny. Hard men can look forward to a long life, laughing women, and easy hangovers. Especially if you're not afraid to submerge yourself in this beautiful, illusory world, which has just been waiting for you, preparing its countless trials and rewards for you. And when you overcome the obstacles and pass the tests, it opens its gates for you and hands you a sailor's passport, with which you can get off at any stop, cross any border. The world sparkles from the sun and the sea, merrily explodes like a firework, lighting up the sky in red and golden flames, and in this world you are a real scoundrel, a cheerful son of a bitch with a sailor's passport in your pocket, and you still have your whole life in front of you to wander through noisy Crimean towns, to stay in motels and squats, to run illegal businesses, seduce sad older women who will teach you unspeakably sweet things, to cross the sea, to alight in strange, faraway ports, wear the best suits, dance with the best girls, not be afraid of old age, not miss your childhood, to have real, trustworthy friends to whom you could boast about all of the above. Bodia felt bad that things had turned out the way they had with Vietal, he had already forgiven him entirely his nighttime tears, his drunken sniffling, and all his childish helplessness—friends should stick together. Bodia now felt responsible for his friend, and even worried about him, and also felt a light sense of contempt for him, but mainly—he wanted to tell someone everything that had happened to him!

When evening came he could stand it no longer and headed home. As he approached the building he saw the police and immediately stepped into the shadows, but too late—one of the officers saw him and ran toward him, Bodia jumped over a fence, ran through some courtyards, fell out onto the next street and hurtled down some steps, ran a whole block, turned the corner, passed some kiosks, down more steps, jumped over another fence, and came to a stop in the sanatorium of the Ministry of Defense. He passed the administrative buildings, keeping to the cover of the palm trees, passed by the cafeteria, and went into the cinema. In the darkness sat a few older men watching some old Soviet movie. Bodia sat in the first row. A few minutes later two officers peered through the doors, and, bending low so as not to disturb the viewers, made their way to Bodia and tried to take him outside, but Bodia asked in a whisper if they might not just watch the end of the film, there was only about ten minutes left, the most interesting bit, the officers looked at the screen and agreed, but remember, they said, if you try to escape we'll break your legs, and they sat down to watch, worrying and fretting over the fate of the hero.

Soviet cinema always gave you hope, left you with the illusion that even in this imperfect world everything wasn't so bad, that it was worth fighting for your place in the sun, that you shouldn't give up, that everything would turn out just like you wanted it to, as long as you had love and patience. The brave men and beautiful women paid no attention to their difficult circumstances, striving forward as though those circumstances didn't exist at all, without a trace of fear or doubt, uncertainty or sadness.

Ah, how differently everything could have turned out, everything could have come together, they could be sitting somewhere on some little street under the black sky drinking strong Madeira, smoking cigarettes, blowing bitter tobacco smoke into the freezing evening air, building plans for the future, painting in their imaginations hair-raising adventures and the unbelievable fortunes that would come along with their experiences, and he would share everything with his friend, wine and pistachios, the last draw of his cigarette and his most intimate secrets, laying out everything that he had in his pockets and in his soul, tell him how to get rich and how to spend what you've earned as quickly as possible, how to get visas and get through customs, how she had come up to him and begun to undress him, how he had clumsily resisted but had quickly got the hang of it, how she took off her dress and her wig, and how tired and deep her eyes were, even without the contact lenses, what she had done to him, what she had told him, how she had done it, how she had come, finally, and how she had fallen asleep exhausted, and he hadn't known what to do next, had tried to fall asleep but had been woken up time and again by the drumming of his own heart.

Beyond the voices of the film characters he could hear the hush of the sea, as though the camera wasn't showing something important that was happening outside the frame, and you could only guess what dangers and trials awaited the heroes, it was as though were they to relax for only a second they would immediately be set upon by all the monsters and fiends that live constantly alongside us, the spirits and demons, the dragons and other beasts, the sharks and the octopuses—lively, cheerful, and carefree, the color of carrot salad.

OKSANA LUTSYSHYNA

TRAPEZE ARTISTS

translated from the Ukrainian by Daisy Gibbons

THE EVENTS AS THEY HAPPENED: TODAY, on Friday, the eighteenth of September, at nearly ten in the evening (I'm beginning with the exact time, like in a novel from the nineteenth century), Nina and I left the house to walk around the center of town. Every Friday night, the little town is bustling, the bars are full, and there is something rather nice about this—on some nights. Not today. A sense of doom was oozing from the town. If I had listened to Nina, we would have just gone for a walk down the street we lived on—but whatever. Someone up there is behind some strange deeds, to the point that they're getting consistent.

We walked past a bar, very popular with the locals, called The Trapeze. Isn't a trapeze—the kind a tumbler launches himself from—something theatrical, mystical, out of a novel by the Goncourt brothers? On the way, I joked that we might run into Tom. And what do you know, there he was, sitting at one of the bar tables in the street. He lit up when he saw us, jumped to his feet, offered to buy us some tea (he remembered that I don't drink), and was very well behaved, despite being a little tipsy. We accepted his offer. We went inside and sat down; the tea came. Tom came with it.

Tom's first gimmick of the night: he always pretends as though he has a bad memory, but then he forgets himself and reveals that his memory is not just good, but horrifyingly good, like my own. I'm the only one who ever remembers my friends' and random acquaintances' culinary preferences. I know with absolute certainty that most people do not remember. So many people try and treat me to a beer, even when I have told them a hundred times that I only drink tea. Tom remembered the first time. When the moment comes, he hits you with things like this on his first shot, like a hunter. Which he is: one of his first drinking stories was on exactly this topic, hunting. He told us a story of one time in his childhood, in his tenth year of his life, as he put it, when he accidentally shot a crow and his parents made him eat it (the first rule of hunting is you must eat anything you kill). While telling this story, he also did a very convincing impression of a loving mother's gentle voice. The same mother he dances ballroom with, as seen in several pictures on the internet: both dressed as in a James Bond movie, he in a tailcoat, she in a ball gown.

Tom's second gimmick: he talked only to Nina, only looking her in the eye. He pounded the table with his fist, telling funny stories (mostly about guns or hunting, or about a suitcase full of frozen quail he had brought with him from Colorado) while drinking his dark, malty beer. He complained that he'd taken up drinking again, because one day he suddenly felt like some wine. Prior to that he hadn't had a drink in fifteen years. He started again at the age of thirty-seven. He is thirty-nine now. Those were his numbers, not mine.

His third gimmick: he asked me about R. He asks, have you seen him? No, I say, I haven't seen him—why? Oh, never mind, he says, I haven't seen the guy either. Well, I say, you'll see him. Ha, he guffawed, why should I see him, our relationship is nonexistent, you could say. I say that he has these nonexistent relationships with many people and makes up all sorts of stories about them. Ah, says Tom, (he stares at me for a while out of the corner of his eye) you could be right there. I've started *leaning* (adding weight to his pronunciation of the word) toward the same conclusion. I got to know him . . . uh . . . last year at a party. I thought right away, hey, look at you, you're a smart guy—you know, girls, our department is full of bores, not like yours—there's no one who's seen the world, or who knows foreign languages or anything else for that matter. I saw him, and I thought, look at you, what a smart guy you are! Smart as hell! Don't you think so, too?

Yes, we say, of course. So, I say, what did you want to tell us? You started telling us about . . . What, he says, what did I start saying? I didn't carry on the story because I have absolutely no desire to talk about it, can't you see that? That's why my story was cut short.

After that we talked about guns. Nina told him about a time when she was a child when she almost ate a piece of dynamite (her father was in the army). Oh, says Tom, how awful, I'm so glad you spat out that dynamite, you have such a beautiful little head. I can't imagine trying to have a nice conversation with a beautiful woman if she were headless. You know, Nina, I don't even want to imagine you without a head. It's such a sad thought! All those arteries, blood spurting out, it's horrible! He was sitting strangely, like a bird on its perch, legs tucked up underneath him. I say to him, why are you sitting like that? Ah, he waved his hand carelessly (not quite a wave, more like swatting something away: maybe he was still thinking about Nina being without a head)—because I'm ten years old.

Then he started asking Nina about how she ended up in the States. He listened and listened, and then for some reason he turned to the subject of marriage. I can't remember the pretext. Well, he says, I drink because I don't have a wife, I don't have children, I never have, and that's fine. That was when Nina (with her strange insight, the unclouded vision which is a gift of the very young) says, so, you decided to get married and have children? Tom crumpled and sank, like a bird shot in flight. Well, he says, how do I explain it to you? I didn't decide, someone decided for me. Oh, says Nina, are you going to have a baby? (What was I doing at that point? I kept quiet—things had been decided for me as well, more or less). Tom has an answer for this question, he says, isn't this the commonest story in the world? Look, Nina, you be careful now, otherwise—whoops!—you'll get knocked up, and what are you gonna do then? Oh, she says, I would like to have a baby. And he laughs— well, you'd better use condoms when you . . . you know (he makes an obscene gesture, poking a finger through his thumb and forefinger of his opposite hand). And then, he says, you'll have to get an abortion. This annoyed me, and I said, I see, she got pregnant and had an abortion. Oh, says Tom, I would've liked that. Unfortunately, she wanted something else.

There was a pause. Remember, (he turns now to me) I told you on Tuesday that I'm in trouble (he's still acting drunk, but his memory's as sharp as a knife). Yes, I say, why wouldn't I? Well this is why I'm depressed, he says. I see, I say, but things will have to right themselves somehow. Then Nina goes, listen, get married, really, you might even like it, perhaps. Have the baby—if you destroy it now, you'll regret it later. He blew up. Me? Regret it? Oh, sure! I'm really going to regret ruining my life (he turns beet-red) and all because of some useless *thing*! He laughs, slapping the table. Some *thing* that doesn't even fucking exist!

I tug Nina's sleeve. Let's go home, I say in Russian. Tom angrily tugs my sleeve. Don't you dare tell her what to talk to me about! Then, abruptly, he turns away from Nina and leans in toward my ear, taking me by the forearm. Nina tactfully turns away. Look, whispers Tom, imagine if you and R . . . if you and R (emphasizing the name) had a child. And your *husband* (emphasizing the word) . . . your *husband* found out about this. Well, he'd say, where did this child come from? He'd sue you! You'd have a paternity case on your hands—how would you like that?

He lets go of my arm. His lips had been practically touching the skin of my cheek. I should have been able to smell him, feel him, but I couldn't. It was like he was sterile—not in the sense of fatherhood—but a man without an odor, without a body. I lean toward his ear and whisper (again, without sensing his touch or smell), so this is what happened to you?

No, he says, after a pause, nothing. Nothing like that has happened to me. I've already told you what happened to me.

He looks at me and says, listen, I know that I was being a pig. How exactly, I ask. Because . . . because I blurted that all out to you. That's something a pig would do. I can't tell whether he was ashamed of himself now or whether he was playing with me, or whether his shame was more existential than contextual. I don't say anything. Finally I ask, why did you say that, then? Why did I say that? (He falls silent for a while. Sharp furrows appear on the bridge of his nose, and for the first time this evening, his face is thoughtful.) Why did I say that? Oh . . . What can I say? I could tell you, but I don't want to open up to you like that. Try, I say, you won't lie to me anyway.

No, he says, as if hurling away a stone. I won't lie to you; I'm not that stupid, I already know there's no point in lying to you. I felt like I broke loose and was falling, and I wanted you to fall with me. For the company (he nudges me, chuckling). I let my mouth run away with me today; but that's beside the point, he says. Sorry. I see he's not sorry, but he's lying—even if he doesn't want to.

I'm not angry, I say. I see that, he says. I see that you're not angry. He said it in the tone of voice you would expect from someone broken, someone remarking on their death sentence. I'm not angry, I say, because observing people is much more interesting than getting angry at them. Yes, he says, mournfully, not looking me in the eye, I know, I think the same.

Well, (Nina and I get up) it's time for us to go now, it's late. He cracks a wild smile, as if to say, you've figured it out, you stupid girls. He apologizes once again. I bend toward his sterile ear. Don't worry, I whisper. I do this because he expects me to react differently, to show some different emotions. But I don't have any. I've lost too much. I have lost so much that I can't lose any more, and everything happening to me from now on is only gain.

He kisses us on the cheeks, hugs us goodbye, and opens the door for us. As my auntie would say, sorry to see you, he says. We laugh and then we leave.

A thing . . . An unborn thing. I tell Nina what has happened when we are outside. She goes into the nearest tobacco shop and buys a cigarette. She smokes. I don't.

Once home, Nina goes to bed. I lie on the floor and hug my knees, pulling them toward my chest. I still don't know how much I can hold. Then I lie flat again, face to ceiling. Cleanse my face, I beg, please cleanse my face! I remember once how Tom was bragging to me about his atheism. So, he said, you're from the land of atheism? I said that I didn't know, that it's hard to know for certain. I'm from the land of the gulag, that's for sure, I'm from a gulag where everyone drinks. Gulags, alcoholism, said Tom, that's quite the historical burden—and atheism to boot.

Ah, but you see, I say, there were some people like that, but there has never been an atheist in my family.

VASYL MAKHNO

BROOKLYN, FORTY-SECOND STREET

translated from the Ukrainian by Zenia Tompkins

1

ORTY-SECOND STREET IN BOROUGH PARK, BROOKLYN, is unenticing and monotone, as are the rest of the surrounding streets. In the winter, it's cleaner than in the summer. In the fall, it's warmer than in the spring. The industrial zones on the shores—Sunset Park and Green-Wood Cemetery—cling to the harbor like tipsy bridesmaids trying to avoid getting the slip. It's intersected—or, more precisely, interrupted—by the Mexican Fifth, the Chinese Eighth, and the Hasidic Thirteenth Avenues, and in one spot the metal structure of the subway that covers all of New Utrecht looms above it. But everything else is as it is elsewhere: laundromats, shops, bakeries, hair salons, schools, churches, synagogues, residential buildings, cars that seem to never budge from their spots, and residents who seem to never die.

Standing on a hill of Sunset Park, the panorama of the bay opens up, you can see the spire of a Catholic church and hear the hubbub of Fifth Avenue. Fifth Avenue is populated by Latinos: you can buy sombreros, cowboy boots, and peeled yellow mangoes in the shape of a blooming flower on little skewers. Mexicans play soccer on the hills of the park from early spring through late autumn. Their prodigious families watch them, all the while sipping cool drinks and munching the time away on boiled corn. Mexicans have a lot of time: maybe that's why they're forever eating and playing soccer. They play soccer even with their language, volleying words in one another's faces, their corn-flecked teeth in wide grins. The little restaurants on Fifth Avenue smell of chili sauce, heels glint with copper spurs, children cry, and women complain, winding their long black braids round their shoulders and wiping their kids' faces. On religious holidays, they organize processions—with sweet singing that tickles the ear, and with an icon of the Virgin Mary of Guadalupe at the helm. The procession stretches across several blocks, and before the image, carried by four men on wooden poles, the festively dressed faithful strew red flowers that they immediately trample. The procession's route is gradually carpeted with a masticated floral pulp, marking precisely its beginning and end—that is, life and death.

Further on, leaving behind the singing Mexicans and their Fifth Avenue—sweetly sour like a ripe mango—and heading uphill, you'll pass the wholly unnoteworthy Seventh Avenue and find yourself in China. If it's late January, the Chinese New Year will come out to greet you, but if you didn't make it in time, then banners with golden characters painted on red backgrounds will advertise newly roasted Peking ducks hanging on hooks in wide restaurant windows or cheap goods in the little shops squeezed up against one another. The Chinese—paper-thin, like tobacco leaves, and barely speaking any English—will press you to come into their stores. There's the same kind of hubbub here, the same sleepy children in the withered arms of their mothers. The Chinese don't play soccer; instead, they smoke a lot. Their cigarettes are harsh and smelly. They smoke and play cards, talking loudly, and there's a faint smell of furniture varnish and the fat of plumped-up ducks. The

Chinese produce shops sell all sorts of seasonings and greens, the aromas of their spices clogging the noses of passersby, almost knocking them off their feet. The smell of fish trails after you, whipping around like the long tail of a freshly caught carp—slippery, and with bloodied gills. Eighth Avenue never sleeps, the lights are always on, it's always busy, there's no end of lovemaking or childbearing, and the street is, and will always be, Chinese—even here, in Brooklyn.

When apples are dipped in honey on the eve of Rosh Hashanah and when the shofar is blown in all the synagogues, the Jews come to pray at the banks of the river—because on those days it is decided in the heavens who will live and who will die. That's why the greatest river of Hasidim in Brooklyn—which flows through the air and courses through their hearts and stomachs, and to which they come most often—is Thirteenth Avenue. Thirteenth Avenue is a place of life and chaos, stores filled with diamonds and gold, of kosher restaurants, tailors' shops, and clock towers. The paths to the synagogues are carpeted with fur hats and silk robes, and the word that they read in the Talmud they carry around carefully like a hen's egg—because it's warm and white and pure. Beards and payot sway back and forth above the pages of the Talmud, and golden words are gleaned, and every Sabbath the men don starched shirts as the women place new wigs on their shorn heads, and candles are lit in silver candelabra in Hasidic homes. Wine is poured, and children laugh, and Thirteenth Avenue rocks with song, from white challah to white challah, from one roasted chicken to the next gefilte fish. And the rabbis and the Talmudists bless this life, awaiting the Messiah, as they have for five thousand years.

2

The brick townhouse with the black wrought iron gate and heavy padlock stood in a compact row of similar structures closer to Ninth

Avenue. The next building, which brought to a close the section of Forty-Second Street between Eighth and Ninth Avenues, was abandoned: the windows and front door were nailed shut with plywood, and raccoons and Atlantic winds would sneak in through holes formed by the heat and rain. The owners would sometimes come by the building with an inspector to check on the plywood and to make sure nobody had crawled inside and made themselves a nest there. The neighborhood was peppered with addicts and homeless folks who sought out these kinds of buildings, taking up residence until the cops dragged the squatters off to the nearest shelter. On the corner of Forty-Second and Ninth, the boarded-up building with the unpleasant odor wafting from inside patiently awaited a new life with new residents.

Number 895, on the contrary, was fully occupied. And whenever one or two apartments came on the market, new tenants turned up right away.

On the facade above the black doors was the inscription "Leonard Court." Inside—off the long corridor covered in white mosaic tile, with two sets of sepia stripes framing the path—were two stairways. One, to the left and almost at the entrance, led to the north wing, while the other, in the back, led to the south wing. Together with the adjacent building, 895 created an internal courtyard, the door to which was kept firmly shut. This space could be seen as you climbed up to the higher apartments in both of the building's wings. From the north wing, it was easier to spot the empty square of the courtyard, which had no other purpose than as the place residents tossed out their used kitchenware, broken chairs and paper bags, and strung clotheslines tied to metal hooks nailed into the buildings' walls. When the things were dry, they'd pull them to their kitchen windows along the squeaky little pulleys.

The building welcomed everyone. There were two families on the first floor: the Puerto Ricans—Gabriela, the grandma, Amanda, the mom, and Nicole, the granddaughter—as well as two old Jews from Latvia—Basia Moiseevna and Hryhoriy Markovych—together with their white lapdog and a cart they used to bring groceries home from the supermarket. There was always upbeat music drifting out of the Puerto Ricans' apartment, and the forty-five-year-old grandma was forever hanging out the window that looked out on Forty-Second, a pillow propped under her elbows. The building across the street was inhabited by her fellow islanders: other women, elbows propped on pillows, were hanging out the windows, listening to music, breasts tumbling over the windowsills, bopping around. The Puerto Ricans shared news and recipes without having visited one another in years. The super of the Puerto Rican building that faced Number 895 would sit on the stairs and drink coffee, listening to the music and the women's chatter. Twice a week he took out the trash in big black plastic bags, and then he'd go back to sitting on the stairs and drinking coffee.

There were two families from Bangladesh on the second floor of the south wing. When you passed this floor on the way up or down, the distinct cooking smell that wafted out would turn your stomach. A floor up, above the Bangladeshis, two American families had moved in many years before, but precisely when, no one recalled. The first was an elderly couple, the Johnsons, and their daughter Nancy, a hopeless addict who was joined sometime later by Michael, a younger addict. Nancy and her parents shared the apartment with Michael and her four children: sixteen-year-old Margo, thirteen-year-old Sapphire, and two more, Mary and Jonathan, roughly six and three years old. Next door to the Johnsons—as confirmed by the metal nameplate on the door— lived Lucia, who was part Hispanic, with her husband Jack and their son, an addict of more recent vintage, who left his needles all over the third floor. Lucia would sweep them up and toss them out the window into the abyss of the internal courtyard. Nancy and Michael often smoked pot out the open window between floors, ashing on Lucia's son, who was lying passed out on the sidewalk, and warning their children not to take one step, not even one little step, outside the apartment door. Old man Johnson supported the entire family working as a driver for a medical facility. He would park his white Chevy, tumble out of the seat with bags jam-packed with groceries, stuff them all under his arm, open the door to the building, and vanish into the dark corridor. The grandchildren, like hungry wolf pups, were always waiting for their grandfather because their mom and stepdad were capable of spending the entire day standing next to the building in a somnambulant state.

On the fourth floor of the north wing, Nadia from the Ivano-Frankivsk region of Ukraine—pushing forty, squat, with strong arms from scrubbing half of Hasidic Borough Park—rented a one-bedroom apartment.

"That she-goat from Church Street said she's got some Polish woman in Greenpoint."

"So what?"

"Well, she said that for five grand the Polish woman will arrange a fake marriage."

"Five grand ... Whoa!"

"Look, the Chinese couple is watching a kung fu movie again."

"Bruce Lee?"

"I don't know the difference."

"It'd be nice if they watched some porn once in a while."

"What porn, you idiot? They've got kids."

This was the sort of conversation you might overhear in the apartment rented by two men—Genyk and Zenyk—on the top floor, the fourth. They'd moved in a couple months before, having given the super a few hundred bucks to hold the unit while they cleared out of the semibasement apartment they'd been living in. And then, over the course of a few hours, they carried over their things in bags and backpacks.

Looking over the empty new apartment, they discovered that the previous tenant had left them his mountain bike, a white dresser with drawers stuffed full of electronics, and a few cans of beer in the fridge. "The kid was in a rush," concluded Genyk, standing in the middle of the living room that smelled of the previous inhabitant and cockroaches. Later, Genyk's hypothesis was confirmed by the super, a sixty-two-year-old Leningrad native named Kolia, who had stopped by to see how the new tenants were settling in and to give them the keys. According to Kolia, the kid hadn't paid in half a year, though you couldn't kick him out in winter, so they'd waited till spring, but the kid was no dummy: he split. To remove any suspicion and as a guarantee that they weren't there temporarily, Zenyk, Genyk's roommate, offered the super a beer. Grabbing a Budweiser out of the fridge, the new tenant rattled off his favorite toast and was the first to pop the metal tab on his can. The super, praising this apartment in particular, pointed out the kitchen window to show them a perk: "Since you don't have a TV, you can watch with the Chinese."

"What about the sound?"

"Consider it a silent film. Edik, who lived here before you, always watched the freebie Chinese movies."

As he said goodbye from the doorway, Kolia pointed at the apartment next door and warned them that the neighbors' son was a druggie and slept in the stairwell. The parents didn't let him into the apartment, so you had to step over him. You shouldn't let it bother you.

Since Genyk and Zenyk's move, the sweltering Brooklyn summer had passed and autumn had arrived. Every morning they got up and went somewhere. Genyk would hurry to the produce shop on

Thirteenth Avenue: he worked for David, a Hasid. In theory, the work wasn't difficult: all day Genyk set out vegetables, picking out the rotten ones. When the Hasid left for lunch, he would add some good ones to the rotten, then take them home in the evening. Pedro, the cashier, and Leszek, a Pole, worked with Genyk. The Pole had no more authority than Genyk, but he had worked for the Hasid a long time. All day the Hasid sat on a tall wooden chair and observed the customers and his employees. Occasionally, after a phone call, he would give instructions on who to make a delivery to. Genyk would then take the hand truck, because Leszek couldn't be bothered, load it up with paper bags, and deliver the orders. He would get his tips and return to the shop. Every week after the end of the Sabbath, Pedro and Leszek opened the shop at 10:00 PM. They were the only ones there all night. The Hasid would come the next morning, count the night's earnings, inquire about the customers, and then go into the small storeroom to look over the security video. When Genyk arrived, David would already be sitting on his chair in a white shirt, the fringes of his tallit hanging from beneath it, reading prayer books. David didn't talk to Genyk at all because Genyk didn't understand English; he relayed all instructions for Genyk through Leszek.

Meanwhile Zenyk went off every morning to build New York. He bought a coffee en route, then headed straight for New Utrecht. Next to a playground, at approximately 7:00 AM, a minivan covered in advertisements would pick him up.

3

Genyk and Zenyk had walked the length of the subway station to the end of the platform and were waiting for the train. This was an ordinary Brooklyn station, Ninth Avenue, with paint peeling off its walls and rusted communication cables. The station was located at ground level and was separated off with a metal chain-link fence. It was windy. And as always in October, it was raining, the Brooklyn sky releasing rain like an infected bladder releases urine. Toward the end of the platform, a young rat stubbornly wrestled with a plastic baggie next to a metal trash can that hadn't been emptied overnight, but no one was paying any attention to the rodent. Here and there passengers waiting for the train watched as, across the way, a cement factory and a handful of trees with signs indicating the spot was a park got drenched.

"You always have to pick this fucking spot," Genyk said with dissatisfaction.

They were waiting for a Manhattan-bound train.

Half an hour had passed since Genyk and Zenyk walked out of their building, but the cop cars blocking Forty-Second Street had delayed them. Behind the cops, a few fire trucks and ambulances from Maimonides Medical Center had pulled up. A twenty-year-old drug addict had died in a neighboring building, found on the stairs between floors. Ignoring the rain, people had come out and were watching in silence as the firemen carried out the deceased on a stretcher, shrouded in a body bag, and loaded him into the ambulance. Before the crowd had even dispersed, a candle and a modest bouquet of flowers had appeared in the walkway to the building. Twenty-year-olds just like the one who died came flocking from the outskirts of Borough Park to light a candle and commemorate their buddy over hits on a joint, while perched on their parked cars.

A seagull squawked above the tracks, then flew off toward the ocean; beneath the wheels sparks flashed and the train coming around the bend let out a piercing screech.

"You think she'll help?"

"Maybe she will, maybe she won't. But I can give it a try."

Genyk and Zenyk entered the subway car, whose windows had

misted from human warmth. It seemed as though the rain was flooding the whole world. The seats were all taken, so Genyk leaned against the doors of the car in his torn jeans.

He turned his massive face, speckled with mustard-colored freckles, and rubbed his coppery stubble. Zenyk, straightening his shoulder blades as if he was short on air, nodded in agreement. That instant the train slithered into the tunnel, pulling into the Thirty-Sixth Street Station a while later.

The following conversation took place after the Sabbath when Leszek and Genyk were opening the shop. Pedro had fallen ill, so on Friday, the proprietor had told Genyk via Leszek to be at the store at 10:00 PM the next evening.

Leszek, who was sitting next to the cash register in David's chair, said he was heading to Canada in a week to go fishing. He wasn't much of a fisherman, but taking a break at the Canadian lakes would be nice. According to Leszek, he did this a few times a year. He had friends in Toronto who had everything you need for a good vacation—a car, tents, fishing rods, even hunting rifles. "You're welcome to join," Leszek offered.

Genyk didn't have papers. He told Leszek as much: he couldn't join because no one would let him across the border.

"It's fucked up . . . I came to New York from Toronto. You know it as well as anybody. Before 9/11, you could run a herd of buffalo across that border and nobody would've noticed," he added.

Leszek couldn't see Genyk because Genyk was bent over sorting through oranges and setting them out in wooden containers.

"Have you tried getting papers?" asked Leszek with a yawn.

It was after midnight already, and they had to talk to stay awake. Even though it was quiet here on Thirteenth Avenue, anything could happen. David left Leszek a hundred bucks for those kinds of emergencies.

"There's no way," Genyk's voice floated up from behind the crates. "There's no US entry stamp in my passport. Can't find a lawyer to take a case like that."

"Yeah, but you should see the fish up there," Leszek said, holding a two-liter bottle of Coke as an indicator of size.

Around 3:00 AM they decided to have a bite to eat but were interrupted. A fire truck with lights flashing stopped outside the store, and the firemen opened the hydrant. Genyk ran to bring in the produce that had already been set out, as the water flooded the street and pooled next to the storm drain, bringing the street trash along with it. One of the firemen peeked into the store and explained something to Leszek, who in turn told Genyk that the Borough Park Fire Department was doing a nighttime hydrant inspection.

"There's this Polish agency in Greenpoint," Leszek said, pulling his phone out of his pocket and jotting down an address on a piece of paper. He handed it to Genyk.

4

They made it to Greenpoint with some mishaps, after exiting at the Lorimer Street Station. They transferred at the Metropolitan Avenue Station, but Zenyk carelessly took the train going the wrong way. They'd lost almost an hour by the time they found the three-story building on Nassau Avenue and rang the apartment. Without anybody asking who they were or what they were doing there, the lock buzzed with a whir, like a bumblebee, and Genyk and Zenyk entered a narrow hallway. They took a set of steep stairs to the third floor, and a young girl met them on the landing, in front of a doorway. She asked if they were there to see Ms. Maria. The apartment—that is, the agency—consisted of two rooms: the kitchen, which is where Genyk and Zenyk were now standing, and the room from which Ms. Maria rolled out in a wheelchair. The girl wheeled the chair up to the kitchen table, and Zenyk walked over to the window, signaling that he was just there to accompany his friend.

"So what's your business, gentlemen?" inquired Ms. Maria, holding a cup of tea.

"Well, Leszek from Borough Park sent me . . ."

"Leszek, Leszek . . . which Leszek?"

"From Borough Park," repeated Genyk.

"It's not important."

"Leszek said that your agency can arrange a fake marriage . . ."

"Why don't you just hire an attorney?"

"Well, I entered the US illegally . . ."

"From where?"

"From Canada. That's why I don't have an entry stamp in my passport, and without that a lawyer won't take the case."

"And where do you work?"

"At David's, on Thirteenth Avenue. With Leszek."

Ms. Maria turned her wheelchair around and rolled off to her room, closing the door behind herself.

She returned in twenty minutes, rolled up to the table and began drinking her tea. It crossed Genyk's mind that maybe the old woman had been released from a loony bin. She had on a red skirt, a thick wool sweater, and white sneakers with turned-down backs—house slippers or something. "How does she get up here, to the third floor?" he thought. "You couldn't even get a stroller up here. Someone must carry her up. Couldn't be this girl that Zenyk's been whispering with, could it?"

"At the present moment, only Gośka's free."

"How old is she?"

"Sir, you are only getting married for the sake of obtaining papers. Or would you like to take her to bed straightaway, too?"

"Yes, yes, for the sake of papers."

"Well, then the situation is as follows: Gośka is forty-five years old and a US citizen. If we agree on a price, then you must attend certain functions with her and take pictures, at least for the first few months. Those pictures need to be sent to the US Citizenship and Immigration Services every two months in order to demonstrate that you really do live together. The two of you will work out the details. It's fifteen thousand for everything. The first part of the fee is due before obtaining your marriage certificate in the city registry office, and the second before receiving your green card. The whole thing can take two to three years."

Genyk looked at Ms. Maria more closely and noticed a green tea leaf had stuck to the corner of her wrinkled lips. "Fifteen grand . . . holy shit," was his most immediate thought.

"Let me know what you intend to do by tomorrow, 10:00 AM. You have my number?" The old Polish woman was ever polite and thoughtful.

"I do," replied Genyk and, nodding to Zenyk, he said goodbye to Ms. Maria.

Nancy and Michael were standing on the corner of Forty-Second and Ninth when Genyk and Zenyk returned from Greenpoint. Genyk was relieved to see them, he even felt his spirits lift a bit. The feeling of home or something. He and Zenyk had picked up a six-pack on the way and he handed two of them to Nancy. "Right on," she said, and as they walked away, he heard her say to Michael, "I always told you these Europeans are cool, you dumb fuck." Michael mumbled something in seeming agreement.

Zenyk made dinner while Genyk, standing next to the window, held two plates and two forks in his hands and spied on the Chinese family getting ready for bed. The family had finished eating: two old people, a young couple, and their children. The old woman was washing the dishes, and the young one was wiping the table. The old man and the young one were smoking out an open window. They had hung an ashtray on one side of the window and a makeshift bird feeder on the other.

"So, whaddaya say, bridegroom?" Zenyk blurted as he sat down at the table.

"I'm going to look for the money."

"That's good. What other choice do you have? Die illegal? Fuck."

"I've got two and a half grand. I'll borrow the rest."

5

The telephone call caught Gośka as she was in her car, turning onto Delancey Street toward the Williamsburg Bridge. She slowed down and felt around in the inside pocket of her coat for the phone. The drivers backed up behind her, all heading toward Brooklyn, leaned on their horns. "*Słucham*," Gośka said, and stepped on the gas.

Gośka had everything except for a past—from the time she got to France, where she'd gone to study. Her father and stepmother in the provincial Polish town thanked their lucky stars when Gośka left them in peace, and her six-year-old stepbrother forgot her as soon as the apartment door slammed shut behind her. She'd found a Frenchman while studying at university in Lublin, and he was the one who helped her move to Paris and spend a semester at Paris Nanterre, studying French and art on a scholarship from the French government. Then the funding ran out, and Gośka became a waitress at a bar on Rue Trousseau between the Ledru-Rollin and the Faidherbe-Chaligny metro stops, almost in the center of Paris.

Gośka arrived in the US with one suitcase of stuff she'd managed to buy on the wages Pascal paid her. Pascal, the bar owner, would often corner her late at night in the kitchen. When Gośka was ready to split for the US, she obtained a six-month visa thanks to the State Department's lax policies. Gośka went to the bar a few hours before her flight and told Pascal that she needed to go see her aunt. As it turned out, she did in fact have a French aunt—okay, not exactly an aunt, but a descendant of a relative on her father's side who'd come to France in the 1920s to work in the coal mines. Gośka asked to borrow some money and promised Pascal she'd pay him back in a week. As she boarded her plane at Charles de Gaulle, she spat on the Paris pavement one last time, smoked a cheap cigarette, and laughed. She thought about Pascal, that dickhead, and how he'd be waiting for his money, how he'd be looking for her, calling her friends, turning up at apartments. She'd be exhaling her cigarette smoke into the New York skies by then.

It was Maria calling—the old twat, as Gośka called her, running her agency for dubious affairs or, more precisely, seeking creative ways of making money off immigrants fresh off the boat, FOBs who felt terrified and helpless in America, at least at first. Gośka had gone through all this long ago after the death of her husband—an old American who'd left her some shares of Royal Dutch Shell and half ownership of a building in New Jersey, too. The rest of the inheritance went to his daughter and a few organizations the old idiot had belonged to. The building in New Jersey was so mismanaged it didn't bring Gośka any profits, especially since the other half was controlled by the old man's daughter, who thought Gośka was a vile little bitch who'd taken advantage of the financial position of her father. And the father (in the daughter's opinion), well, he was a complete fucking moron for letting himself get talked into marriage and for rewriting his will in his lawyer's office a month before he died. So Gośka lived in Manhattan, in a one-bedroom apartment on Broadway, which she'd bought by selling all her stock, since the building in northern Jersey wasn't for sale yet. She needed money like she needed air. Maria's phone call was timely.

"A Ukrainian, of all people?" Gośka was rattling off into the receiver. "Seriously, a fucking Ukrainian, Maria? Are you serious? He'll call tomorrow? And then what? How much do I cost? Hooow much? Maria, you think I'm an idiot? Shit. How old is he?? Are things really that bad in Ukraine right now? Don't tell me any more right now. Call me tomorrow. I swear . . ."

Margaret Westwood—formerly Małgorzata Szymkowska, or Gośka to family and friends—pulled off the highway and turned down the empty streets toward Greenpoint.

6

On Saturday, Genyk was driving his Crown Victoria past Sunset Park to Second Avenue. Hundreds of warehouses and auto body shops were huddled in the industrial zone overlooking the East River. He was meeting with the mechanic who worked on his old car. Hrysha had come here from Belarus as a humanitarian parolee, and Genyk had gotten to know him during his first days in New York, when they both worked loading seafood in a Chinese warehouse. They would haul the frozen fish out of huge refrigerators, load it onto refrigerated vans, and deliver it to fish markets in Brooklyn and Manhattan. Back then Hrysha would tell Genyk that he dreamed of having his own auto shop in America. Hrysha was married, legal, and quit the fish warehouse before long because he had supposedly found a new job. With an old pickup he'd bought, he went out on calls to fix the school buses the Orthodox Jews used to take their children to yeshiva. Genyk ran into Hrysha a year and a half ago in a supermarket parking lot in New Jersey and they struck up a conversation. Since they'd last seen each other, Hrysha had become co-owner of a repair shop, and Genyk had bought a tenth-hand Crown Victoria sedan. Hrysha gave the car a professional once-over and offered his services. "For you, a discount," he'd said.

They exchanged numbers. And Genyk had in fact stopped by Hrysha's shop a few times.

As he passed Fourth Avenue, Genyk ran a red light and looked in the mirror. Luckily, there were no cops. He was heading to Hrysha's in hopes of borrowing money for his sham marriage with Gośka. Hrysha's was the first name on the list Genyk had made. He needed seven and a half thousand bucks for Ms. Maria to introduce him to the girl. Next would be all the formalities at City Hall. And in two years max, he'd have his green card and be able to go fishing in Canada with Leszek or visit Ukraine, wouldn't need to be afraid of the police anymore, and could stop holding his breath and waiting to be deported. Genyk wanted Hrysha to say yes so badly, his thoughts resembled something close to prayer.

Hrysha's shop was small, just two vehicle lifts. Genyk walked inside. Hrysha was examining the underside of a Ford using a portable spotlight. They exchanged greetings. Nearby, Hrysha's partner had opened the hood of a dinged-up minivan and was tinkering with the motor. The workshop smelled of all kinds of oils; plastic garbage cans stood in the corners. Hrysha motioned for Genyk to wait a bit and climbed farther under the car, which was on a lift. Genyk was in no hurry, so he walked out of the shop, sat down on the front left fender of the Crown Victoria, and lit a cigarette.

Genyk spoke to Hrysha for twenty minutes. He pulled at the words till they surfaced and watched as seagulls circled around the industrial zone. Hrysha stared vacantly at the ground without losing the cheerful look on his face.

"If we sign a loan agreement at a lawyer's, you've got two grand in your pocket."

"Thank you, I'll need it in a week."

"Great, my lawyer is on his way back from the Caribbean. I'll give him a call."

Genyk breathed a sigh of relief and squeezed Hrysha's shoulder.

And he drove down Second Avenue, this time with a song on his lips.

Gośka was sitting in a hair salon in Greenpoint reading Polish magazines. She had plans to meet up at a restaurant with Władek, and she
was fine on time: the hairdresser was combing out Gośka's hair and
describing the latest Polish soap opera she'd seen on TV. It was only a
few blocks to the restaurant, but Gośka stopped to buy a pack of cigarettes in the nearest shop and, while she was at it, a few videos of Polish
movies.

She and Władek had dinner together two or three times a month.

After the old geezer died, Gośka had managed to finish two semes-
ters at The New School. She still had plenty of money back then and
lots of free time she didn't know how to fill. There had been a trip with
some American guy to the Virgin Islands, horseback riding lessons, she
played the stock market. Every morning she turned on her computer,
logged into her trading account, and read the *Wall Street Journal* that
landed at the front door of her building. And she would trade. She had
a financial consultant who cost her a few hundred bucks a month. She
slept with him once, but after that, it was only phone calls.

Gośka would wake up late and make herself a Viennese coffee with
a dash of salt and sugar. Then she would buzz the doorman and ask for
the newspaper. Even when she'd been with the old man, whom she had
met at a consulate party for a Polish filmmaker who had come to show
his documentary at the Tribeca Film Festival, Gośka had kept her figure.
After Paris and their successful union, she had taken to working out at a
gym three blocks from their building. A young African American trainer
there stretched Gośka's muscles, massaged her calves and buttocks, and
taught her how to do sit-ups correctly. The man started inviting her to his
place in Flatbush, and Gośka only got rid of him by canceling her gym

membership. She was worried that the old man would find out about her romance with the trainer. When the old man kicked the bucket, she took to the courts and lawyers and traded letters with his daughter and her children, who called her every name imaginable. But per the court's decision and in accordance with the will, she had close to three hundred thousand bucks to her name. She was making money in the market, too, and she had no desire to be thinking about tomorrow.

It all happened unexpectedly. One morning, while Gośka was brewing her black coffee, sprinkling the salt and sugar into the coffee maker, the market crashed so hard that once she turned on her computer, she understood: she had been left with a tenth of what she had owned only the day before. Gośka burst into tears. She still had a decent-sized widow's pension, which she could live off fairly comfortably, but she'd have to say goodbye to the horses and cruises. Out of despair, she called a girlfriend of hers in Poland and they talked for a few hours. The girlfriend informed Gośka that her father had died—her stepmother had failed to let her know—and caught her up on the few classmates who had stayed on to waste away in their little town.

"Oh, bloody hell, you've lucked out as it is, Gosia," her friend chirped from Poland.

"Well, yes, yes, but you can't even imagine what life is like here . . ."

"Nothing like mine—I have two kids, a small apartment with windows overlooking the train tracks, and my man's only a damn railroad worker. Our apartment has been vibrating from those goddamn trains our whole lives. Even when we're making love, it feels like a train is going to run us over, Gosia. That's our shitty luck."

That day, as she dined with Władek, Gośka was thinking about how to tell him about the upcoming fake marriage. Władek had been her lover for several years now. He owned a construction business. The company was called Wladyslaw's Construction. He worked with three other Poles, taking jobs from New Jersey to Connecticut for a variety of work: roofing, concrete repair, home additions, even remodeling jobs. Władek's wife lived somewhere in eastern Poland—precisely where, Gośka never inquired. Every year she came to New York for three months, and then Gośka would be free of Władek. His older daughter Monika lived with him here in the States, but, as Władek put it, she had her own life and didn't meddle in her father's affairs.

To Gośka, Władek was essentially nobody.

"Władek, listen," Gośka began cautiously. "I'm going to have to leave New York for a bit, maybe for a year or so . . ."

"You're going back to Poland?" asked Władek, pouring Italian dressing on his salad.

"No, it's not that," Gośka went on, "but we need to not meet up for some time."

"But why?" he asked with dissatisfaction.

"It's just, my love, there are matters I need to attend to urgently."

"Gosia, what's going on? Is something about our arrangement not working for you?"

"Władek, stop. You know that you're exactly the man I've always dreamed of, but there are matters that supersede our desires—so said the priest who married my parents."

They walked out of the restaurant, and Gośka waved at Władek in farewell as she opened the door of her car. She settled into her seat. "Jesus, what an idiot."

7

The next person Genyk wanted to see about a loan was Petro, an acquaintance from Deliatyn in western Ukraine. Petro rented an apartment on Forty-Second Street, too, but lower down, between Ninth and Tenth. Genyk didn't see Petro often but had once jotted down his cell phone number. It was Saturday and he suspected he'd reach Petro with no problem. Glancing out the window, he saw the sky shrouded in gray clouds and scrapped the idea of going to the laundromat on Eighth. He found Petro's number in a notepad and dialed him. Petro answered.

"Who's this?" Petro asked matter-of-factly.

"Petro, is that you?"

"It is, and who are you?"

"It's me, Genyk. Listen, can we meet up?"

"Not today," replied Petro.

"But . . . it's urgent."

"I can't. We're celebrating Deliatyn Day today."

"What day?" asked Genyk.

"Deliatyn. All of us from town are meeting up in a restaurant today."

"It'll only be five minutes."

"Fine, meet me there. But come early, so I'm not drunk yet."

They chatted a little longer, and the first drops of a dense rain struck the window. Within twenty minutes, the clouds had migrated to the East River and sunshine flooded Borough Park.

Genyk knew the street he was walking down: he walked that way to David's store. Teenagers were playing basketball in the middle of the street as usual and once in a while a car would drive by. He passed Tenth Avenue. He pulled out the piece of paper and confirmed, yet again, that he needed to go down Forty-Second Street all the way to Thirteenth. "Don't turn off anywhere, just head straight down Forty-Second," Petro had told him. As he walked, Genyk saw Jewish women, young and old, sitting outside on wooden chairs, in their holiday dresses. The young ones were pregnant, with big bellies, as if they had deliberately been set out to warm under the September sun, while the old ones, with prayer books in their hands, squinted from the sun and nearsightedness. On

Thirteenth Avenue, Genyk breathed in the sweet summer air with a hint of halva, as if it had drifted there from childhood.

Deliatyn Day was being celebrated by a jovial little crowd in a small restaurant on Thirteenth Avenue close to Thirty-Ninth Street. Petro was standing next to the entrance, smoking. Genyk thought he'd lucked out and would be able to talk with Petro after all. Everyone knew Petro's fundamental flaw: when he was drunk, he was liable to get angry and break things.

"Hello, Genyk," Petro said first.

They shook hands and then embraced. Genyk and Petro hadn't seen each other since winter, even though they lived on the exact same street. Deliatyn natives, warmed up by alcohol and dancing, were beginning to exit the restaurant. First came the men, some of whom Genyk recognized from the laundromat, the shops, or even church, and then the women exited, too. There were so many of them, it seemed all of Deliatyn had moved to Brooklyn.

"Petro, there's this thing. How should I put it?"

"You need money?"

"Two thousand . . ."

"I can't. I swear."

"Well, it's just two . . ."

"I can't. I send money to Deliatyn every month, and I've got a broad I live with here. I don't put anything away. I'm building a house in Deliatyn. And I have to live off something here, too."

"Of course . . ."

"Don't take it the wrong way. I just don't have a penny to spare . . ."

As he said goodbye to Petro, Genyk noticed Nadia from his building, who'd also stepped out for a smoke.

8

The day before Genyk and Gośka's wedding, Zenyk came from New Utrecht and said that C-Town, the supermarket where they used to buy groceries, had burned down. Genyk wanted to have a little party after the marriage registration, which was why Zenyk was running around from store to store, buying up everything for the wedding feast.

When Genyk brought Maria the first half of the payment for the fake marriage—seven and a half thousand dollars—he asked the old woman about Gośka, whom he still wanted to meet. Maria called her on the phone while Genyk was standing right there, but Gośka said that she didn't have time to meet up and they'd see each other near the front entrance to City Hall. Maria said that Marysia would serve as the witness.

Genyk woke up at 6:00 AM. He pulled his suit out of the closet. But, on second thought, he put on a sweater and jeans, and tossed the suit on the bed.

Through the window, Genyk could see that the Chinese family had woken up and was making breakfast. And that thick clouds had shrouded the sky. For the wedding celebration, Zenyk had bought a few bottles of whiskey and stocked the fridge with various snacks and two-liter bottles of Coke. He brought an oblong table in from the street, which he placed against the wall in the larger room.

"She's Polish, after all. Everything needs to be classy," Zenyk was saying.

"I don't know . . . Is this necessary?"

The marriage registration office was on Worth Street in Lower Manhattan, next to a tiny park.

Gośka pulled up in a taxi and Marysia came on a bike. Leaning against the gray concrete building, Genyk picked them out—these two Polish women, Gośka and Marysia. But he was in no rush to approach them.

Gośka was in a luxurious cream-colored overcoat with a dark blue Parisian scarf around her neck. Marysia wore jeans and a jacket. Fixing her disheveled hair, Gośka spotted her prey with a sniper's eye. "I'm Gośka. Do you speak Polish?"

"I understand it," Genyk acknowledged and went on surveying his sham wife.

"This is Marysia," Gośka said. "You likely saw her at Ms. Maria's?"

Marysia was indeed the same girl who had greeted them at the door to Maria's.

"Do you have your passport?"

"Yes, I brought it."

"Then let's go get everything registered. I don't have much time."

"I wanted to ask if you could . . . come to my place today. You know, to have a drink and a bite to eat. I invited the guys over."

"Why?" Gośka sounded surprised.

"Well, just to . . . this is kind of our wedding . . ." Genyk was grasping for words. "To take a picture, you know . . . for Immigration Services . . ."

"At what time?"

"By the time everything's ready . . . maybe around eight?"

"Fine. I'll see if I can make it."

They walked the thirty feet to the front door, and Gośka yanked the massive door open. This was where the sacrament of holy matrimony would be taking place. Each couple got fifteen to twenty minutes. In the large hall, a guard asked for their IDs and also that they sign the visitor log. After a quick look, the guard chivalrously returned Gośka's and Marysia's passports to their owners, but Genyk's he began to inspect more critically. Gośka was becoming anxious that things were dragging out.

"What's wrong, sir?" she asked.

"His passport is expired. He needs a valid ID to get married, and this one's not valid."

"Excuse me?"

"Miss, I told you his passport's no good."

"Sir," the guard said, addressing Genyk. "Do you have another form of ID?"

Gośka translated: "He says there's something wrong with your passport."

Genyk arrived back in Borough Park late in the evening, dragging like a beat-up dog. There was such melancholy in his eyes that Zenyk spilled a bottle of wine on the white batiste tablecloth when he caught sight of him. Zenyk was waiting there with two other guys, and Nadia, whom he'd invited for no reason at all.

"Where's Gośka?" Zenyk asked.

"She couldn't make it . . ."

"Oh, we waited and waited . . ."

In a gesture of pity, Nadia took Genyk back to her place that evening, and he passed the night in the chasms of Nadia's body. In the morning, pale, he left her apartment. He said he was going out for cigarettes. He left the building and vanished in the Brooklyn rain.

SOPHIA ANDRUKHOVYCH

AN OUT-OF-TUNE PIANO, AN ACCORDION

translated from the Ukrainian by Vitaly Chernetsky

WHEN AIR BECOMES DENSER TO THE touch, when celandine's wet yellowness appears above pockmarked musty needles on the forest floor, when trash between the naked, sucked-bare pine tree trunks forms a white shimmer like giant flowers of a cosmic-sized apricot tree, then you can rest assured—the wandering ghost camp is already here, close by, in our forests.

It's your choice whether to believe in it, you can make your cute skeptical grimace: puffed lower lip like a moist cherry, an obstinate horizontal fold between the eyebrows, wrinkles on your little nose with its semitransparent winglike nostrils; now you'll shake the morning dew off of them, spread them out sleepily—and take off into the air, into the light blue broth of the sky, swimming next to Boeings and globs of sour cream.

The night exhales the first mosquito swarms, opens its jaws full of warm muck. A coarse crone with a jellylike body, nearly blind and hopelessly slow-witted—just think what its drunken grin and cloudless joy are worth.

Flowers fall off pear trees with a dry rustle; self-satisfied caterpillars lazily munch on arugula leaves, and irises—these crystal ritual daggers—fold like origami, Japanese boats and lanterns, and shine from the inside with a meager cold light.

Then you won't be mistaken: the wandering ghost camp has arrived. An indistinct melody spreads above the trees, multiplied by echo—like a tune from a Victrola or an old cassette player that constantly chews up tape. Girlish laughter resounds together with teenage shouts and giggles, with piercing playful cries. An insincere feminine voice declaims something solemnly into a microphone; you can distinguish lines of poetry, rehashed jokes, and mechanical reading off a page, but you can't make out the words. Every evening up until late at night, when the cooperative dacha settlements die down, hold their breath, and their dwellers sidle up to one another in pitch-black darkness, their expansive bodies sunbaked to a meaty shade of pink, the sounds of eerie amateur performance seep through the double panes. From the forest thickets a menacing stench and an otherworldly smoke come swirling, flashing with fuzzy shimmering lights that circle around the tree branches.

You can never tell precisely where they are now—at Krasna Poliana, near Poroskoten, or in the Babka Valley—their manifestations are omnipresent yet so uncertain, their music resounds, it seems, from tree trunk hollows and badger burrows, they spy on us from behind currant bushes, they rustle in the grass around the cesspit, their elongated greenish faces reflect in the glass walls of hothouses like in stagnant water.

Everything quiets down only at dawn, when the contours of trees slowly become clearer, birds shake their wings and clear their throats, and the air gets saturated with nanodroplets of moisture, invisible beads of a necklace—they refresh and make things easier. The shroud of stupor and fear falls off, the gaze becomes clearer.

Viola sits on a cold, wet terrace, her head thrown back, her mouth wide open. Her red eyes stare unblinkingly at one spot. She is exhausted, drained, finished. Her large, soft body has spread in the armchair like melting butter. Her wet dress sticks to her, its contact with skin unpleasant. Renat comes closer, dragging his left leg, and covers her with a yak-hair blanket brought from the Himalayas.

Renat is eighty. His left leg does not obey him; he has a glass left eye. It shines mutely, its pupil directed at you no matter where you go, wherever you retreat—the way icons, especially old ones, worn, damaged by woodworm and dry rot, look at mortal sinners. Renat's right eye, squinted and sly, darts about and peeks under the lining: what's hiding there? Renat's teeth are crooked and dark (he refuses to get dentures as a matter of principle, saying that nowadays bodies already do not decompose); his wide grin is open and scary at the same time; his face is a puzzle made of hundreds of wrinkles; his hoarse, ingratiating voice that of an old beast, once strong, and now simply warming itself in a sunny spot.

Renat always knew how to enjoy life. The starter kit of his life included starched white shirts with wide cuffs and gold cuff links, fragrant cigars, recliners, fancy building materials acquired through connections, the smiles of flight attendants, banquets in hotel restaurants, and also apartments, dachas, antiques, laundered linens, offices with lacquered furniture, cars with the latest sound systems, yachts, Cuban women, snorkeling, gravlax, getting to see the doctor without waiting in line, special deals, precious jewels, massages, yachts again, they really eat this stinky cheese, it costs how much? I'll be damned!

Even now, weathered and worn by life, lacking one eye, crooked, wrinkled, and dented, Renat hasn't lost his luster. He's like an old Steinway with a cracked frame. A 1954 Rolls Royce Phantom with a broken headlight and clumsy body and doors that don't close tightly—still, its interior preserves the scent of Queen Elizabeth: lavender, clary sage, vetiver, lemon mint, and patchouli; the luxurious leather seats creak heavily like balding gentlemen coughing at the opera after an intermission.

His first wife was the same age as he. They lived quietly together for thirty years, producing a couple of kids along the way, up until Renat met Viola. She was forty then, and she still remained striking and attractive: curvaceous, blond, and languid; ripe, juicy, and soft like a plum (you bite through the deep purple, almost black, skin and the purplish inside reveals itself moistly). Renat, understanding everything well (I am sixty, she's forty, I have two kids and six grandkids, real estate and savings; she has alcoholism, infertility, a room at a boarding house, and a messy personal life)—in fact, precisely because he understood everything so well—opened his embrace to her with luminous calm. He so loved watching her expose her face to the wind when riding in his yacht, try to correctly eat an oyster on a half shell, pretend to be a society lady, chasing champagne with strawberries. Her buttery voice and mannered way of talking moved him the way a child's babble can move you. She laughed loudly like a boor, opening wide her mouth covered in bright lipstick and throwing her head backward—and he, choosing a strategic seat beside her, magnanimously squinted his one eye, smiled quietly to himself, and mumbled something, paying no attention to the confusion and disapproval around them.

He, the kindly sixty-year-old daddy, showed her the world. At the dacha that Renat succeeded in wresting from his first wife, they made an alpine garden to which they kept adding stones brought from various corners of the world. It was surrounded by plaster gnomes—once so bright and cheerful, with the bright red cheeks and noses of drunks (which is the reason they had conquered Viola's heart), but decades of rain, snow, and piercing wind had bleached them and worn them out; the paint was peeling , and a few of their noses were missing.

In the spring, Viola, dressed in tight pink britches and a revealing blouse, crawled on all fours across their sizable garden with a jar of paint and a brush, refreshing the collection of plaster beasts and fairy-tale characters. Their well-tended lawn spread like a silk rug. The decorative bushes stood all covered with flowers.

As soon as she married Renat, Viola tried to become a good house-keeper. She studied reference books for home gardeners, bought seedlings, and planted several varieties of tomatoes: Aurora, Hussar, Turandot, and Calif. She tended them thoroughly, selflessly: that year Viola felt especially sharply her hopeless, unrealized maternal instinct. The tomatoes reciprocated: their elastic stems bent under the weight of plump red fruit.

And then she cried, loudly, uncontrollably, choked on tears, howled and yelled over sixty buckets full of sweet vegetables.

"What shall I do with them, Renat dear?" she screamed in an unrecognizable voice. "Who can I give them to? We won't be able to eat so much. I won't go to the farmers' market! I won't give them to strangers! To no one! They'll rot!"

The next day, shortly past noon, Viola was barely able to open her swollen, hurting eyelids. She had a piercing headache, her throat was burning, her neck hurt from a bottle of Greek brandy.

When she was finally able to focus her gaze, she saw Renat in front of her. He was holding in his arms a kitten, black, with a triangular white patch on the chest. This was Methodius.

Oh, Renat, how much did this sly old fox of a man love them, his kids. His short fingers dug into the edge of the table, so that the tips hurt—this is how much he craved to stay just a little bit longer here, next to them. Squinting his eye, he caressed with his gaze this corpulent woman in a bright, skimpy, low-cut dress, her shapeless forearms covered in freckles, her puffy hands ending in sharp claws painted with sparkly enamel, her swollen face covered by the purplish-black mesh of blood vessels, her misshapen nose, tiny bleached eyes that twenty years ago were still so blue, so full of surprise—and now hidden behind butterfly-shaped glasses. Methodius, as always, spread himself over her knees, his pink neutered belly up in the air, and purred like a freshly started engine. This was like the purr of the granulators, agglomerators, and shredders made by Berlingtong, the Japanese company Renat was a sales rep for (just one capsulator sale—and a trip to Sri Lanka is guaranteed!). "He is so smart, so smart, you have no idea, gentlemen!" Viola clapped her hands like a giant newborn. "He goes number one in the bidet, and opens doors with his little hands, like this, grabbing the latch, just imagine!" Viola tried to show with gestures how Methodius opened doors. "Our little son, I cried so much when he came back home all injured."

Methodius, the impertinent tomcat, went everywhere his heart desired. Neither someone else's territory, nor unhappy owners, nor guard dogs could stop him. He entered other people's kitchens and sipped broth right from the stove; he munched on parsley and scallions in vegetable beds, leaving stinky piles behind.

That morning Renat found him by the fence. Methodius was lying on his belly spread-eagled, his hind paws unnaturally twisted. His left eye was closed and a dark streak came down from it. The cat was maimed, badly wounded. Renat let out a sob, got on his knees in front of the cat—the way he did when pulling the heads off dandelions—and carefully pressed his forehead against the tiny skull.

"You are a strong boy, you won't get away from us," whispered Renat.

Methodius thought the same. He recovered, regained his health— yet he did not get a glass eye of his own.

"Only a human could have done this," said Viola, gesticulating wildly. "Neither an animal nor a car could have damaged him so much. I don't know where such cruelty comes from, gentlemen. But this must be a local, one of ours . . ."

Viola waited for the oppressive silence to thicken, scratching Methodius behind the ear. And then she continued coquettishly, "The boy has been with us for eight years now. He's the second man in my life. He won't let anyone offend me, my knight in shining armor," with her bright-clawed hand she lifted the cat's head, puckered her lips, and kissed the cat on the nose with a loud smack. Her voice was sweet, candied, with flies swimming in it. "Just like Renatie, isn't that right, my kitten? Do you remember, honey, how I almost got kidnapped in Istanbul? Just in the middle of the day, at the market, in a crowd of people. Renatie was walking slightly ahead of me, I was a step behind him, having stopped to admire a lovely, unbelievable coral necklace—and suddenly some man, short, below average height, grabbed me by the arm and pulled. He seemed so small but held me so tightly I couldn't pull myself free. He pushed me down some stairs, to some basement, opened the door—and then Renatie turned around, saw me, and was next to me, my friends, was right next to me—and that man disappeared into thin air . . . Right, Renatie? I will never ever get away from you."

Renatie was losing strength. With each passing day he felt that he was melting more and more into thin air, becoming semitransparent, like smoke from burnt grass. Sitting in a cool room, he listened to Viola outdoors continuing to imitate society life, greeting people cheerfully, her voice all sugar and honey, as always, "I am just so happy to see you! Have you been well? Perhaps you could drop by our place for a glass of wine?"

Fortunately, no one dropped by. Viola bawled next to him, sobbing like a little girl, and he first tried to calm her down, stroking her head and promising never to die, and then, finally, barked at her and chased her away, for she did not calm down and only continued to wail in a thin voice of a little bird in a large, worn-out body.

Feeling offended, neglected, for half the night Viola darted back and forth through dark rooms, threw pillows and dishes, smoked on the sofa, drank from the bottle. And then, having grabbed an uneven quadrangle of broken mirror in her palm, she thickly put on lipstick, wiped the running mascara off her cheeks, and quickly, in a determined fashion, left the house, shuffled over the gravel path, and disappeared into the forest, among the creaking melancholy pine trees that gently swayed like pendulums.

Soon the dispersed little blue lights started gathering around her. Viola passed by a gazebo filled with immobile hushed shadows. The path, paved with stones, led somewhere through the prickly thickets of sweetbrier. From someplace nearby came the musty, smothering scent of blossoming bird cherry; Viola's head was spinning.

Nobody sat on the benches under the unlit streetlamps; plaster children with lidless, never-closing eyes rose on the pedestals. The clearing in front of the building was likewise empty—but from somewhere, God knows where, resounded the familiar indistinct melody: too-too-too-tah-too-too, an out-of-tune piano and an accordion.

Viola stopped in front of a broken fountain, its basin full of dry leaves, and picked at a piece of whitewash with her nail. The wide-open entry doors beckoned with their gaping orifice.

Empty hallways covered with smashed bricks breathed stuffy moisture. In the rooms, through the cracks in the floor and the walls, plants broke through, little twisted pines, ferns, lichens in puddles of stinky brownish water. Iron beds with nets, bent, sagging like a tired udder. Decomposed sheets, saturated with the stink of decay.

The melody sometimes quieted down, then again crackled at full volume, its tempo quickening. Somewhere a window frame creaked nervously—although at times it seemed to Viola this was a ball bouncing off the floor farther up. In one of the rooms, it seemed that somebody wheezed or coughed in the corner. Viola gazed in that direction till her eyes hurt, but the darkness only grew thicker and stuck back together, safely hiding everything behind itself.

Viola decided to follow the tune. She wandered for a long time, passed though the same gap in the wall several times, until she finally found herself in a large gym with a rotted parquet floor, holes gaping in it here and there.

The accordion stood on a sports bench by the wall bars. Viola looked at the immobile instrument and continued to hear a melody. At the piano, with her back to the guest, sat a little stooping woman with curly hair. Her dark, shapeless clothes blended into the surrounding darkness, and only two pale arms, like the empty sleeves of a white blouse, continued darting back and forth above the keyboard.

Viola closed her eyes and made the first step. Her body was light, weightless; she no longer felt her weight, forgot her clumsiness and exhaustion. It was as if there was no floor beneath her feet, it seemed to Viola she was swimming through the thick and tender air, which carefully enveloped her, caressing her skin. She began spinning on an axis, a pleasant hum started in her head—no effort, but she spun like a top, and this made her feel so cheerful, so joyful and light, that Viola couldn't hold herself and burst into clear, loud laughter, delighting in its echoing all around.

Nearby, someone readily joined in her cheer. However, the laughter of those others was muffled, like a rustling. As if from all directions at once, plastic bags crept toward the woman in a bright dress who, forgetting herself, spun under the ceiling, her legs not touching the floor.

Sensing a dull pain near her neck, Viola opened her eyes. This boy, tall, abnormally thin, with an elongated face, with heavy lids weighing over his eyes, looked somehow familiar to her. He embraced her and led her into a dance, peering intently into her face. His bloodless lips were curled in a whining grimace. The boy held Viola tightly with his strong, bony hands, so tightly that it was impossible to break out, there was no strength left even to breathe—much more tightly than the short Turk who once grabbed her elbow—and the spinning grew so fast that a vortex appeared around Viola, an icy whirlwind it was impossible to resist.

And when Viola's heart started beating so fast that in a moment it surely would fail—right at that moment resounded a mad, piercing, wild scream, and somebody small and fierce jumped at Viola's partner and, twitching wildly, clawed and bit at the alien void of the gaping hole, up until the melody cut off, yelping with a torn string, and the accordion twitched convulsively several times, drooping halfway.

Renat woke in the middle of the night in an empty bed and, groaning heavily, got up on his feet. Viola was nowhere to be found. He passed one room after the other. His heart was beating anxiously, air came through the alveoli like through a dirty filter; his leg hurt as if white-hot knives had sliced it. But his baby was nowhere to be found—neither in the garden, nor on the path behind the fence. And Renat, the old diseased predator, dragged his hurting body into the pitch-dark space of the forest.

He gazed, feeling the path in front of him with a stick, passing the palm of his hand over the pine tree trunks. He looked up—the black treetops formed extravagant baroque ornaments against the sky.

Viola sat on a pile of dry leaves, staring at the space in front of her. Next to her, Methodius lay, bloodied and exhausted, in an unnatural pose. From his throat came muffled wheezes.

"What's with you, children, what's with you again?" Renat dropped on his knees in front of them, sinking into the pine needles covering the forest floor. "Let's go home."

Viola, the large white butterfly of a woman, sips sherry on the terrace. An opened tome of Pérez-Reverte chills on the table nearby. Viola thinks: septic amber brings Sept-ember, and this, kids, is a no brainer. Viola, oh, butterfly-brained woman. God, when will You let her go! When will You come to this Earth—it seems You did rise from the dead, right? Viola looks for miracles at the bottom of a greenish bottle. Her exhausted hips tremble, like a sandwich assembled with toothpicks; it seems, it was too much of a gamble: Viola, the lady bramble, Viola, an ear of grain . . .

". . . And we'll never ever leave each other," said Renat, covering Viola with a blanket. The cat was lying nearby; its pink belly calmly rose and fell with breathing. "It'll be time soon, kids."

PANDA

translated from the Ukrainian by Iryna Shuvalova

O KAY," I SAID, "THEN IT'S PROBABLY gonna be a panda."
"'Probably' isn't good enough," said the guy. "We need a firm commitment."

"A panda."

"Now you're talking! And may I ask why you've chosen a panda?"

"Well," I shrugged, "I kinda like pandas."

"I see . . . Unfortunately, that's not enough. Convince me that you'd make a great panda, one perfectly equipped to cope with all the related responsibilities."

"I guess I'm interested in this, and whatever I'm interested in, I kinda do well."

"That's better," the guy said, nodding. "Now could you please list your three greatest strengths for me?"

"I don't really like talking myself up . . ."

"That's not what I'm asking you to do."

"Fine then . . . So, I'm kinda persistent. And I always consider things carefully before doing them. Well . . . And when I decide on something, I'm, like, gonna achieve it no matter what."

"You read any libertarian stuff?"

I shook my head.

For a moment the guy seemed deep in thought. He was around forty. His expensive suit was perfectly tailored, but his shaved head wasn't a good look for him. He appeared even more tense with the fake politeness and puffy eyes—signs of sleepless nights, drinking, and, most likely, kidney problems.

"Alright," he concluded. "Let's just say you passed the first interview. Now if you could fill out this questionnaire and wait to be called into the supervisor's office."

I started filling out the form in the waiting room. It was a list of stupid questions I did my best to answer honestly. I answered "yes" to the question "Have you ever lied?" and when I reached "What are your dreams," I wrote, "It's a secret."

After ten minutes or so they showed me into another room. I found myself alone with a businesswoman. Conservative suit. Nice boobs—a C-cup, I'd say. Hair slicked back in a ponytail. Thick-rimmed glasses. In fact, she would have looked much more appropriate in a German porno than as the boss of this place.

She scanned my application indifferently.

"Looks like you're a liar. Is that correct?"

"Yep," I said, and nodded.

"And when, may I ask, did you last lie?"

"Well, like, fifteen minutes ago."

"Excuse me?"

"I told your colleague that I'm perfectly suited for the panda position, but I'm actually a little afraid of heights."

The woman was silent for a while. Then she asked me why I'd applied.

So I told her—trying not to lie.

≈

Yesterday I was on a train, returning home from the capital. Riding third class, which meant no sliding doors dividing the train car. Four people in my compartment. Two more huddled on the bunks across the aisle from me. The group I was going to spend the next several hours of my life with hardly looked inspiring. There was something wrapped in a blanket lying down on the bottom bunk across from my top one, and a Catholic nun and a rough-looking fiftysomething man sitting on the other bottom berth. I plopped down beside them, not bothering with a hello.

Soon the shabby-looking man produced a chunk of smoked chicken from his sack and started chewing on it, informing the nun how good life used to be under the Soviets and how shitty things were for him now, poor thing. Judging from the nun's behavior, she could have easily been the man's wife: as soon as he got started on his chicken, she pulled out a couple of hard-boiled eggs and started hammering them on the table to break the shells. These sounds briefly awoke whatever was sleeping on the opposite bunk from its slumber. It tossed around for a while, causing its blanket to partially slide off. Turned out it was not an "it," but a "she," and a "she" with a reasonably nice ass peeking out of a miniskirt. I couldn't help admiring the view, even as the nun hurried to readjust the blanket.

I did not really feel like climbing onto the upper bunk to sleep, so I started contemplating how likely it was that the chicken being chewed on by the guy could actually have produced the eggs the nun was gorging herself on. However, on that particular occasion the laws of probability escaped me. Besides, the guy was already done with his meal and had started yammering away. He seemed positively hell-bent on talking about his childhood years. (He was obviously one of those perverts who, even well into adulthood, like to tell scary stories to women, hoping to bring them to tears.)

So the guy told the nun the following story. When he was in the eighth grade or so, their biology teacher was hard on him and his group of friends. He promised "those little pricks" the lowest grades possible that term, because they had taken bites out of the wax fruits and vegetables that the district authorities had sent to the school as learning aids. The little pricks realized they had to do something and decided they'd soften their teacher's heart with a gift. First, they caught a good-sized fish, waited for it to kick the bucket, and stuck it on top of an anthill. In a couple of days the only thing left was a perfectly white fish skeleton perched on the anthill. They placed it in a cardboard box, which they even fitted with a glass lid. This was to be a specimen for the teacher to use when explaining the bone structure of fish.

The nun crossed herself and I walked out to get myself a beer from the train attendant. My idea was to sip on my beer in the vestibule of the train car until the clowns in my compartment finally went to sleep, still in their wigs, rubber noses, and makeup. Then, I thought, I could climb onto my upper bunk, hang my head over the side a little, and keep an eye on that cute ass on the bottom bunk: if, of course, she let her blankets slide off again.

Armed with two bottles of beer, I was cautiously making my way through the train car, avoiding the feet in stinky socks sticking out from the bunks right at face level. Finally I reached the dreamed-of vestibule. Unfortunately it was already occupied by two thugs, their faces swollen black and blue. I found myself a spot in the corner across from them and downed my first bottle almost in one go. The thugs, meanwhile, regarded me in silence. Then one of them started saying something to me.

I couldn't make it out, though, because he was speaking a strange language. They must be Moldovans, I thought. Yeah, for sure, Moldovans. The question remained: what the hell did they want from me? Moreover, what did they want from me in my own country? Were they looking for work? But what kind of work can Moldovans do? Digging holes? I've got nothing to dig. Apartment renovations? Well, I don't even have an apartment. Maybe they wanted to be my bodyguards? I'd never hire such ugly thugs. Unless, of course, I armed them with shovels and convinced everyone they were migrant workers or something.

For a moment I even imagined myself sitting at the bar in some posh joint while these two hung out discreetly at a nearby table, earning their keep. Then this big shot in leather pants strolls by me. He accidentally catches me with his elbow, so that I spill my Becherovka on the rocks all over the bar. My Moldovans jump up and close in on the guy.

"Hey," says one of them. "Don't you know how to behave?"

"What was that?" says the guy, pretending nothing has happened.

"Tell the boss you're sorry," says the other Moldovan, gritting his teeth.

"Watch yourself, buddy," the big shot says, and half opens his jacket, showing them his piece.

"You better take it easy and apologize, or else we'll bury you."

"You'll what?"

"You heard me," says the second Moldovan, grinding his teeth and pointing meaningfully toward the two shovel handles sticking out from under the table.

The big shot buttons up his jacket immediately and turns toward me.

"Sorry, brother, I was out of line there, you know. What are you drinking?"

"Becherovka."

"Get my brother here a bottle of Becherovka, and put it on my tab," the big shot calls to the barman.

At this point one of the talkative Moldovans probably got tired of my standing there and staring at him in silence. He started talking louder.

"Man," he said—my internal translator was helping me out—"we'll put down tile in your kitchen, man, a tile floor you can only dream of. We can dig, too, man, we can dig real cheap."

"Dig in my kitchen?"

"Say what?" The Moldovan looked puzzled.

I used a lighter to open my second beer and sipped on it loudly.

"Either of you speak Ukrainian?"

"Course we do!" The Moldovan nodded happily, and I began to see that his speech really did sound Ukrainian.

"We're boxers from Ternopil," he explained.

"What the hell happened to your faces?"

"Shit," squeaked the other Moldovan, who until then had been silent. "Remember, Ivanko, I told you we shouldn't have gone out in the capital, man. I fuckin' told you!"

Then they started their confession to me. Their story was simple. These two guys were working their asses off, training in Ternopil, until they were invited to tournaments in Kyiv and Kharkiv. Unfortunately, in Kyiv they faced an unexpected blow—and a double one at that. First, they found out that their coach had signed them up not for a boxing tournament, but a kickboxing one. "Nuh-uh." One of the Moldovans was miffed and he was ready to go back to the train station, "Nuh-uh." The other Moldovan didn't approve of his friend's moping. "Quit bitching. Kickboxing is just like boxing. Only difference is, you can beat the shit outta them with your legs, too!" So the Moldovans gave it a shot.

Afterward, they sulked into a local joint to drink off their bitter defeat. Someone relieved them of their cell phones, which resulted in the Moldovans thrashing half of the bar crowd and even pummeling the barman. Sadly, their phones were gone forever, and they couldn't even contact their trainer to tell him what's gonna happen when they get back. Nor could they ask him what kind of tournament he'd signed them up for in Kharkiv.

Having finished their story, the Moldovans sighed simultaneously. I was also done with my beer.

"We should go find a chick. Or bump someone off," said one of them.

"Good thing I'm not a chick," ran through my head. "Although . . ." However, the Moldovans did not do anything to me. Instead, one of them punched the wall a few times, as hard as he could.

"Don't punch so hard, Ivanko," the other guy said ruefully. "Or you'll punch through the wall and land on somebody's ass."

The one who was punching froze for a moment, confused. Possibly, he realized that the bathroom was on the other side of the wall. Then suddenly his attention shifted to me—or rather to my empty beer bottle.

"Ever see someone break a bottle on their head?" he asked.

Unsure of which head he was planning to use, I protested energetically. The Moldovans calmed down a bit and for some reason grew eager to know if I had a "chick" at home. I said I did not. This must have caused the Moldovans to sympathize with me about the eternal sorrow and shitty nature of our existence, because they hooked their arms through both of mine and dragged me to their train car, confiding happily that they had some vodka there. I was trying to resist, though— quite predictably—in vain.

A few minutes later we were in their train car. However, there was an unpleasant surprise waiting for the Moldovans: they'd hidden their booze inside the luggage compartment, the top of which doubled as the mattress for the bottom bunk. And on top of that mattress, was a woman of voluminous proportions.

"Ma'am, we're going to need you to get up, please," one of the Moldovans said.

The old lady opened her eyes, saw the two thugs leaning over her and proclaimed loudly, "You get away from me, or I'll call the police!"

"Ma'am, please, we really need you to get up," the other Moldovan whined.

"I'm old and I'm not getting up!"

"To hell with her," the first Moldovan hissed into the other one's ear. "Let the old bitch lie there. I'll lift the mattress up a little and you pull out the bag."

Moldovan 2 does what Moldovan 1 says.

After the lady had closed her eyes again, one of them tiptoed to the bunk, placed his hands strategically on the bench top that served as her sleeping surface, and braced himself like a weightlifter about to perform.

"Lift!" signaled the other fellow.

A moment later, with a squeak and a squeeze, the old lady was sandwiched between the wall and the pleather mattress of the bunk. She looked like a burger squished in a bun. Meanwhile, the other Moldovan reached into the luggage compartment and pulled out a bag. They let the old lady back down.

"Help m—" she started saying, but the Moldovan who'd done the lifting looked at her in a way that made her shut up immediately.

"God daaaamn it!" The second Moldovan looked upset.

"God damn what?" the other one asked.

"I grabbed the wrong bag. The vodka's in the other one."

The old lady got squeezed and squeaked again, but this time she kept her mouth shut. The Moldovans did finally manage to get the right bag, where there really were two bottles of shitty vodka nestled beside the boxing gloves. Three's the magic number, they say, and the

Moldovans squeezed the old gal against the wall one last time to put the bag back inside the compartment. Then they dragged me back into the vestibule.

"Drink!"

"The whole thing!"

"In one go!"

Both of them gave me a look to make me understand that if I didn't drink, I was done for. I grabbed the bottle, opened it, took a deep breath, like I was really going to chug it, you know, and—I smashed it on the floor in front of the Moldovans. It's go time! I burst out of the vestibule, through the open air to the next car, slam the door open, and run—I run for my life, trying to avoid the smelly socks. I run, knowing I'm a few seconds ahead of them, since it probably took them a moment to recover from the shock of seeing some son of a bitch smash their bottle of booze right before their eyes. I race through a couple of cars and stumble into another vestibule, and then realize that there are no more cars. I've run out of room just like you run out of bullets. For a moment, I stand and stare at the rails disappearing into the darkness. Then I look back and see the angry Moldovans crashing through the car, headed my way. Even without their shovels, they look scary enough. "They'll bury me," I tell myself, and I pull the handle of the door opening onto nowhere. As I pull it, I realize it's not locked, for some reason. I yank it open all the way, look back one more time, and jump . . .

≈

I regained consciousness in the office of the guy with bags under his eyes.

He was really talking up the company, praising it up and down, but he finished on a solemn note. "In these times of global financial crisis we don't have a great number of positions open. Still, there are a few

SASHKO USHKALOV

we're trying to fill: we're looking for an ant, a swordfish, a cocker span-
iel, and a panda. These are what we can offer."

After the conversation I'd just overheard on the train, I wasn't too
keen on becoming an ant or a fish. And I can't stand cocker spaniels,
since they pee on every vertical surface they can find.

It stands to reason that by the time you read these lines, I'll be
chewing bamboo shoots somewhere high up in the Himalayas, really,
really high up . . .

TANJA MALJARTSCHUK

ME AND MY SACRED COW

*translated from the Ukrainian by Oksana Maksymchuk
and Max Rosochinsky*

1

I HATED MY COW AND SHE hated me.

Even though we were like two peas in a pod, both of us crazy.

We competed with one another in mental abnormality, and the cow always won because she was the better runner. She had four legs and I only have two.

Take this, for instance: we are walking across the village, it's high noon, the sun burns, the skin on my nose is peeling. The cow, black as tar, cautiously wobbles in front of me, prudently glancing back now and then, trying to assess my mood. I say to her, "Bitch, now that it's all over, will you explain to me why you ran off into the woods?"

Daisy glances at me with a large black eye and doesn't say anything.

"Have you thought about how I feel?" I am beginning to raise my voice. "You saw me reading a book. And the book was very interesting! Had you read but one book in your life, you'd know how it feels: when you're reading and some stupid cow you have to watch runs off into the woods!"

Daisy hopes that I'll blame the gadflies.

"What about those gadflies? They bite me, too. Do you see me running off into the woods?"

We are passing the Vulan household. Liuba Vulan is standing at the gate—a large deaf-mute girl who's always getting raped in the pasture by her younger brother. She roars with laughter, and it makes me shudder.

"You know how much I wanted to kick your ass?" I keep going. "A lot! But you run so fast I can't keep up! Wait till we get back to the barn—then I'll get you. I'll get you, believe me! With a broomstick! That'll teach you!"

We're passing Kamaikina's house. I'm hurrying the cow because I'm scared to run into her—the old senile woman who's been after me for the past two years. Daisy's mother once knocked down her hay pile while I was reading Hugo's *Les Misérables*.

We pass yet another house. Ours is coming up next. It's right next to the store. The store sells only apple-flavored sparkling water, Turkish chewing gum, and matches.

"I'll kick your ass alright! Like there's no tomorrow!" The cow glances at me anxiously with a large black eye and lowers her head as if she's going to graze.

"Don't even try to make me feel sorry for you! I've pitied you before, and you just keep doing your thing."

Grandma's gate is wide open. Secured with a brick. Daisy will dive in, drink from a bucket under the ash tree, even though I'll yell to Grandma to give her some pesticide instead of water, because she's already managed to fill her gut from the puddle near the compost heap. Daisy will stare at Grandma sorrowfully, as if I hadn't tended to her, but tortured her with a hot iron rod. And I'll yell at Grandma to give her a taste of the whip, or to hobble her legs, or to tie her by the neck, because she's mad.

Daisy slows down, hesitates. The gate is a few feet away. I can see the Vasyliovskas' yard from here. A tall, thin mother and her three girls with their mousy-red hair are sitting on the staircase of the brick house waiting for an old aunt to die.

"Come on now, don't worry. I won't beat you too hard."

Daisy makes a radical decision and, picking up her pace, instantaneously passes the gate and gallops away.

"You bitch!" I yell, running after her. "Come back! Where do you think you're going? You won't get away from me!"

The cow knows exactly where she's going. She's going to the store. Before I can manage to call her a bitch one more time, she enters its wide iron doorway and disappears into the stony coolness.

Once upon a time the store was the village elementary school. My grandma attended the first two grades there. Then she quit because she had to tend to a cow. What is happening is deeply symbolic. Daisy ran into the schoolroom to pray for the redemption of all of Grandma's previous cows, especially the one on account of which she remains illiterate.

Auntie Ant sits at the store counter. She is an aged shopkeeper who thinks it's a matter of honor to remain in the empty store to the very end. She eyes my cow with a melancholy expression and the cow pleadingly eyes Auntie Ant. If I hadn't come in right then, Auntie Ant would surely have said to the cow: "Hello! How can I help you?"

"Daisy! Come home! I promise I won't beat you," I say wearily.

"Hello, ma'am," I address Auntie Ant. "How about slaughtering this cow? You'll finally have something to sell."

Auntie Ant is delighted, but quickly comes to her senses:

"Wouldn't your grandma mind?"

"We won't tell her. I'll say that the cow's been taken to the insane asylum."

At last, we two crazies arrive home. Grandma anxiously peers out of the gate.

"What took you so long?" she asks, and lets Daisy drink the cool well water out of a bucket.

"Better you should give her some pesticide!" I cry out defensively.

Daisy rubs her neck against my grandmother's thin torso. Just like a dog.

"My sweet baby," Grandma pets her. "Tired? Would you like some water?"

"I am very tired," says Daisy. "And she's the worst of all," Daisy nods in my direction, "How she torments me! When will her parents finally come get her?

My parents will come in a few days. In a little while. I have to be thoroughly scrubbed before school. Especially my feet. And I have to be rid of head lice. They have to buy me notebooks and textbooks. So they could be here any minute now. Bitch.

2

Liuba Vulan has not always been a deaf-mute. She fell from a cherry tree as a child, when the owner of the tree caught her red-handed. She had such a scare she hasn't spoken since.

But some people say that she was born with no upper palate and has never spoken a word.

She wears long, ragged skirts and goes barefoot in all seasons. To save on shampoo, her mother always crops her hair close to her skull. Liuba is in a perpetual state of growing her hair back. During her period, she's splattered all over with blood. Her younger brother Vulan rapes her daily in the pasture, and she laughs eerily. Sometimes, when it's over, Liuba hugs him and kisses him on the forehead. Meanwhile, I keep an eye on Liuba's cows. If anything happens to them, Liuba's mother will order her son to lash Liuba with a whip, and he will gladly do so.

Liuba is her brother's first woman. Soon he will become her first and only gynecologist. To save money, he'll give her a home abortion.

She roars with eerie laughter, and sometimes I think this is her way of smiling.

3

The Vasyliovskas, the tall thin mother and the three redheaded girls, sit on the staircase of a gray brick house and wait for their ancient aunt to die.

When she dies, the house will become theirs. They have no other place to live. Meanwhile, the four of them live in an old summer kitchen next to the house. They, especially the redheaded girls, are anxious to move into the luxurious quarters, mossy and moldy, just like the old aunt herself. They will jump on the mildewed embroidered pillows, sleep on the chicken featherbeds.

The youngest girl's first words were:

"Auntie, when will you die?"

The aunt's reply was:

"I will die, child."

The girls take turns bringing food and drink to the old aunt's quarters. They quietly enter the room, stand next to the bed, and keep silent for a while, hoping that the aunt will not wake up.

Their aunt has lived through the whole century.

Every day, Mother Vasyliovska takes the train to Kolomyia. She works as a security guard at the historical museum. When the museum personnel don't show up for work, which happens almost every day, Vasyliovska locks herself up in the museum and doesn't let anyone in. The occasional visitors—lovers of antiques, or tipsy Polish tourists—bang on the door, plead with her to let them in (because it's not a holiday and the museum has to be open), and Vasyliovska peeks out from behind a curtain, like a frightened ghost, like a sixteenth-century museum piece, and bobs her head, as if to say, "History is not available today, she is depressed, and I am only a Vasyliovska, with three red-haired daughters and an immortal aunt."

The young Vasyliovskas have nothing to eat. They wear bright, colorful dresses that the villagers gave them. They wear bows in their hair, but no underwear. Their noses always run, and the girls lick off the snot. Their legs are covered with mud up to the knee.

The Vasyliovskas are so redhaired and their freckles are so bright that each of the girls reminds me of a dirty-faced sunflower.

4

When the cow got sick, Grandma started taking her out for an evening walk.

Daisy's milk turned red and she mooed mournfully.

I am sitting at the gate, waiting for my parents to arrive. Grandma is walking Daisy in circles around the yard.

"Don't just sit there, child. It's getting late," Grandma tells me. "I don't think they're coming tonight."

"They may come late at night. It's not so scary when you travel by car."

"Or they may be busy," Grandma keeps thinking out loud.

"Life's hard, so hard!" Daisy adds. "There's blood in my milk."

I'm waiting for my mom, and I'm scared. I imagine her pressing my head to her breast, then suddenly pulling back:

"Tania, your head is full of lice!"

I'll pretend that I'm shocked:

"What are you talking about? What lice?"

"The lice are prancing around in your hair like horses! How did you let it come to this?"

"Mom, I don't have lice!"

"And what's this?" She pulls a large chubby louse out of my hair. "Do you ever brush your hair? Do you even wash it? Where in the world did they all come from?"

"Mom, all the kids around here have lice! It's not my fault! They just leap from head to head!"

I am really nervous about my mom's arrival. Some time ago she reacted like this when she discovered I had worms. I hid behind the barn and picked the worms out of my turds to convince her that I didn't have them.

"Don't leave me at Grandma's for so long! Soon enough I won't just be expected to take the cow to the pasture, I'll have to milk it too."

Grandma pets Daisy on the forehead, and slowly walks her around the yard. Daisy obediently shuffles back and forth.

"Gran, why are you dragging the cow around?!" I yell from the gate.

"She wants to walk around a bit. You're enjoying this, right?"

"Right," says Daisy.

5

Kamaikina has a beautiful young daughter, Liuda. At one point, she initiated the transformation of the local children's library into a pool hall. The portly old librarian was forced to donate some of the books to a library in a nearby village and to distribute the rest among the village children. That's how I got *Adventures in Electronics* and *Little Baba Yaga*. So I felt really good about the pool hall.

Liuda was a brilliant pool player. She also played the guitar and sported a tattoo on her left arm. She had a boyfriend from Kolomyia who came to see her on a motorcycle. The wedding was planned for the fall. At the end of the summer, she went to Tlumach with friends and jumped from a third-floor window.

"Don't come near me. I'll jump," Liuda told her drunken boyfriend, climbing onto the windowsill in the dormitory where they were staying.

Her boyfriend didn't believe her and kept going.

Liuda broke her spine and became forever wheelchair-bound. The village council bought the wheelchair. Her boyfriend came a few more times, made sure that Liuda would never walk again, and the wedding was canceled with mutual consent. The last thing he said to her was this:

"I love you, and will always love you. If you ever get better, let me know. Even if I'm already married, I'll come back to you."

And right away he married another woman.

Liuda quit playing pool, but she learned to embroider and to do without walking. Her arms became her legs.

That's when my cow, Daisy's mother, knocked down Kamaikina's hay pile with her hoof. I lost sight of the cow because I was busy reading *Les Misérables*.

The old Kamaikina was immediately informed whose cow had ruined her hay pile. And right away she came by to pick a fight with me. I muttered something in my defense, but I had nothing to say to the last thing she kept repeating. She screamed, "Who will pile up the hay for me now? Who will pile it up?!"

6

And then there is Little Hoodie, a boy of about eight years, who is constantly sent to foster care by his mother, and who always escapes. The mother also escapes. A few times a year. To Odesa. With lovers. But she always comes back.

Little Hoodie suffers from epilepsy. When you say something to him, he answers: "Wha'?"

I go to the cemetery, which I call "the fruit and berry medley," and Little Hoodie follows me there. Everything I love most grows at the cemetery: wild strawberries the size of a fist, sweet cherries, sour cherries, apples, pears, and plums of two kinds, yellow and purple. You can pick anything you want, gather it into the bosom of your shirt, and then go for a pleasant stroll among the tombstones and study the inscriptions.

Little Hoodie breathes down my neck.

"Little Hoodie, I'm going to the cemetery. Are you coming along?"

"Wha'?" says Little Hoodie and takes a step away.

"You'd better watch the cows. They'll kill us if the cows get into their vegetable gardens."

"Wha'?" says Little Hoodie, and comes one step closer.

"Aren't you scared to go to the cemetery, Little Hoodie?"

Little Hoodie doesn't know what to say. He wavers between "Wha'?" and "I'm not scared." Finally he says, "I'm not scared. What's to be scared of? When I die, I'll lie there."

"Maybe you won't. By the time you die, there won't be any room left for your grave there."

"Why not?" Little Hoodie dives indignantly into the bushes.

When Little Hoodie's mother escaped to Odesa yet again with yet another lover, Little Hoodie went to the Beremiany lake, swam five feet from the shore, and drowned. His disease caught up with him in the water.

"Little Hoodie," the angels at heaven's gate asked him, "why did you go for a swim at the Beremiany lake? Didn't you know that your disease might catch up with you in the water?"

"Wha'?" Little Hoodie replied.

"Watch out, Little Hoodie. This isn't foster care. You won't run away from here."

Little Hoodie didn't know what to say. He wavered between "Wha'?" and "I will too if I want to!" Finally he said, "I will too if I want to!"

147

7

Some pears are best left unpicked. They grow right out of the graves. These pears are large and juicy, they resemble human skulls. But I am not superstitious and can easily eat a dozen.

Suddenly I see Liuba Vulan and her younger brother.

"Climb the pear tree," the brother orders Liuba. Liuba roars with laughter and tries to kiss her brother on the forehead.

"Climb the tree, I'm telling you!"

Liuba starts climbing. Right under the pear tree is the grave of Vasyliovsky, the father of the three redhaired elves. Vasyliovsky says to Liuba, "Liuba, don't climb the pear tree. You've climbed the cherry tree before and look what happened to you."

"Keep climbing! Move on!" Liuba's brother hurries her up.

Liuba has climbed onto the first thick branch and is roaring with laughter.

"Climb higher," her brother orders.

"Liuba, don't!" Vasyliovsky persists. "Your brother is evil. He wants you to die. Or at least for your baby to die."

Liuba climbs higher and reaches the next branch up. She hangs over all of us and smiles. Her skirt flares up and I see that she is not wearing any underwear.

"And now jump, Liuba!" her brother yells. "Jump down to the ground!"

"Liuba, don't jump!" I roar. "Don't jump, no matter what!"

Vasyliovsky sorrowfully shakes his pear-shaped skulls in the branches.

"Jump, Liuba, jump!"

"Don't jump, Liuba!"

"Jump, Liuba!" Liuba is getting ready to jump.

And that's when my cow makes an appearance. Daisy. Her milk

is red, and she moos mournfully. Soon she will die. But right now she knows whose side she is on.

Daisy bellows like a bull, shoots fire from her nostrils, stomps her hooves on the ground, and attacks Liuba's brother with her horns.

Liuba's brother doesn't even have time to get scared, hurled as he is into Little Hoodie's freshly dug grave.

Daisy waits at the grave for a few more minutes, watching Liuba's brother. Then she goes back to the pasture to graze the withered grass and moo mournfully.

"Liuba, why do you listen to that freak?" I say, helping Liuba down from the tree.

"Because I love him," Liuba replies.

"Listen, you fell from the cherry tree, right? Or were you born without an upper palate? Is that why you are a mute?"

"I don't have an upper palate." Smiling, Liuba opens her mouth to show me.

I give her my underwear.

8

My parents arrive on Sunday morning. They bring me chocolates and apricots. Mom presses me to her breast, then abruptly pulls back and starts yelling about the lice. Just as I imagined.

"Mom, the people here are so miserable that they don't worry about lice. Everyone has lice around here, even the chickens. How was I supposed to stay away from them?"

In the evening, my parents are getting ready to leave.

"I am going with you," I say.

"Stay another week. The cow died and Grandma is heartbroken. How can you leave her here all alone?"

Grandma sits beside the summer kitchen, stares at my dad's car, at the dog in the doghouse, at her lousy chickens, at the empty barn, and doesn't say anything.

"I can't stay here anymore!" I cry out on the verge of tears. "I just can't! Who knows who else will die this week!"

"Stay," Mom insists. "There're things to eat here. There are pears and apples. The grapes will ripen in a few days."

"Yes, child," Grandma says. "Stay. There's this and that to munch on."

"Wait for me," I start crying. "I'll go get my things! I'll be back in a minute! I'm going with you."

I run into the house and quickly gather my shorts and tank tops into a bundle. I grab my toothbrush, books, an outdated Soviet tape recorder, and some other stuff.

I hear my parent's car, an old Zaporozhets, starting.

"Wait for me!" I run after them, almost breaking my neck. I come out just in time to catch a glimpse of their car disappearing in the distance.

"Why did you leave me here?" Tears are rolling down my cheeks like large peas.

Suddenly my cow Daisy appears. She bends her front legs and I jump onto her back.

"Go Daisy! Run after that car!"

Daisy gallops like a good horse. I am bouncing on her back, the wind tousles my hair and dries out my eyes. I look like a louse on horseback.

"Daisy, we can't stay here! It's a graveyard, not a village! I can't help these people!"

The little Vasyliovskas run out of their yard doing a little happy dance.

"She died! Our aunt died!" they yell.

"How nice," I say to them and ride on.

"I'm ready for a snack," Daisy tells me, turning her head. "I won't catch up with the car unless I have a bite to eat."

I tear off a piece of my thigh and toss it into Daisy's mouth.

My parents notice us approaching their car. Mom says to Dad, "Go faster! They're catching up with us."

"I can't go faster," Dad answers irritably. "The gas tank is leaking."

"Daisy! Let's do it, sweetie! We can pass them!" I yell victoriously. "Turns out, it feels really great to not wear any underwear! Come on, Daisy! We're leaving them behind! We're running away!"

"Oh, Tania," Daisy giggles flirtatiously, "we're so crazy! So crazy!"

TARAS PROKHASKO

ESSAI DE DÉCONSTRUCTION
(An Attempt at Deconstruction)

translated from the Ukrainian by Ali Kinsella

I

THE ANALYSIS OF TIME-CONSCIOUSNESS IS an age-old crux of descriptive psychology and theory of knowledge. The first thinker to be deeply sensitive to the immense difficulties to be found here was Augustine, who labored almost to despair over this problem. Chapters 14–22 of Book XI of *The Confessions* must even today be thoroughly studied by everyone concerned with the problem of time.

Autumn is the refinement of concepts. In October I can have more interesting thoughts about time, about Augustine, about summer. The fact that back in spring I stopped publishing articles and giving public lectures, that I ceased work on my dissertation and broke off all communication with European correspondents, wasn't caused by any surveillance or prohibitions on the part of the regime (the regime, on the contrary, was interested in my productivity—I was the only one who could conduct research on the flora in this part of the mountains, which was closed off to the whole world. All the European botanical societies had to make do with my herbaria, and my silence led to misunderstandings, putting the brakes on a few continental projects), nor due to any form of disobedience or resistance. I hadn't at all lost interest in botany (I had just then started putting together a principally new field guide based on nonbinary logic) or in life. I simply couldn't cope with all the minutiae established by the regime regarding the layout, cataloging, and publication of texts. I was lost. I was completely at a loss. I preferred not to write. This didn't, however, apply to my summer diary. For me, everything that happens throughout the year happens during the summer. It is by the events of summer that I distinguish the years. Each summer I take some notes, often in the strangest ways. Maybe this is somehow connected to the herbarium—plants come about in summer, specimens are gathered and wait around all fall, until they are sorted and studied during the winter. The herbarium is a post-summer story. The collected plants are wrapped in adventures, people, places, conversations, and moods. Summer diaries are a separate culture: travels, expeditions, hunting seasons, hikes, new places and ways of living, photography, rivers and shifts in the aesthetics of being, and later vacations, revacations, boyish valor, wars of the imagination, juices, fruits, and mirages. Summer is truth because it is openness.

But autumn is the refinement of concepts. All summer I read only St. Augustine. I read only a little at a time, but every morning. If Anna was around, I read out loud. We would set out the three-tiered Viennese coffee pot, held together with wire, on the uneven chair near the bed in the evening, having already ground the coffee in the coffee grinder that had the drawer with the cracked bottom. We'd carefully pick up every last ground, since that summer there was nowhere enough coffee to go around and Ms. Viki gave everyone who lived in the boarding house an equal amount, which was supposed to last three months. The beans came in tins of different sizes with different pictures and words (and also different former smells). None of the containers was actually for coffee. I got a flat box that used to hold Grand Café cigarillos from

Holland (for some reason objects are remembered best). We all brewed our own coffee knowing that our boxes wouldn't be refilled. Anna would come from the citadel—she didn't live in the boarding house—and I had only enough coffee for us to drink in the morning. I would get up first and pour the boiling water into the ready and waiting coffee pot.

That was when we would lie together, waiting for the coffee to percolate and return to the bottom chamber of the pot. We drank the coffee at the table, which we'd pulled up to the unusually deep window-sill; there were always cigarettes and a volume of Augustine lying on the sill. We had enough for four small cups of coffee, four (two each) cigarettes, and one and a half pages of confessions (for me, each fragment of Augustine is now connected to the subtlest topography of our mornings: Anna's flannel nightgown, all of Anna's micromovements that combined to form the endless topology of her plastics. It's easier for me to hold on to this nostalgia—remembering everything, I will never forget what we said, what was spoken—it can be read word for word in St. Augustine). I still can't break myself of those coffee pots. Even after I got to Prague, every morning I ordered a full pot on the square near the old town hall (likewise a few years ago when Anna and I stopped living together, I would order a now unnecessary second coffee, always without sugar, at first unconsciously but later in hopes that she'd turn up, since it's hard to change one's routines). Ever since that summer I have been "concerned with the problem of time." I know that the past lives on in habits, and that today an hour from summer will last as long as there's coffee in the pot (if only I could smoke those cigarettes that Ms. Viki had). In early evening I go to the wine bar on Vodičkova Street and drain a jug of *burčák* in a couple hours. It's dark in the basement. There's only a table lamp glowing in a corner on the floor with its shade flipped upside down. I read my summer diary. I realize that despite the compactness and totality of that summer in the boarding house—it was the time of Irzhi—the diary is nothing but records of conversations with him. The lighting doesn't change; as I read, I speak the words aloud in my mind and the *burčák* further dissolves the clot of intonations on the paper, their durations becoming almost identical. I always carry in my pocket at least one of Irzhi's drawings and this typed fragment: "Edmund Husserl. The Phenomenology of Internal Time-Consciousness. Introduction. The analysis of time-consciousness is an age-old crux of descriptive psychology and theory of knowledge. The first thinker to be deeply sensitive to the immense difficulties to be found here was Augustine, who labored almost to despair over this problem. Chapters 14–22 of Book XI of *The Confessions* must even today be thoroughly studied by everyone concerned with the problem of time." Irzhi only managed to translate the first paragraph. It is thanks to the absence of Husserl that I came to know Augustine. Even now I'm not going to write anything until I've written a book about Irzhi. And this diary, dictated by Irzhi, will finally be it. Nor will I compile a field guide because I won't be able to find an illustrator like Anna, the wife of my Anna. Since Anna showed me her botanical sketches, I've refused everyone else. It's better for there to be no field guide. Instead there will be Irzhi. He will be more than a hero; he will be discourse, he will be style, writing. Irzhi as a way of writing. I couldn't wait for the Husserl, but Irzhi and I created our own phenomenology. We shifted our ontology from being to living and put prose above all, right alongside God's plan.

Irzhi was prose lived. Prose was his essence, and he regarded prose as a sign of life. Just what his prose was I saw at the beginning of summer when we went to the city for a night. We crossed through yards, passed by garages, trees, chin-up bars, and trash cans; mixed with sand, the pollen from the poplars still lay around the tumid roots of the biggest trees. All of this, he said, these yards, garages, trees, chin-up bars, trash cans, this pollen from the poplars on the roots of the biggest trees, the lighting, the state of the atmosphere, temperature, even the latitude, all of this is Handke's prose. I thought then that we really were living in someone else's prose, with someone else's prose, for and by someone else's prose. But only until we could come up with our own (let's set loose the totipotency, name the unnamed, choose the unchosen, make possible the impossible). You can study your whole life without coming to any conclusions. He really liked Anna. For her he spared not even his most precious things. Irzhi, his room, everything captured in the frame, reminded me of the Chesterfields ads. "Study without coming to any conclusions"—he said this to Anna when we were sitting in the overly large restaurant near the lake smoking Chesterfields and talking about their ads, their aesthetics of life. We thought up a general slogan for this series of photographs. He knew Anna better than I. He told me what I would learn from her, even though I had just introduced them in the middle of summer.

Every time the regime announced a state of emergency, they detained me, arrested me, and took me to a special camp outside the city. There was never a trial or sentencing. They fed us pretty well at the camp; there was a lake and a library, and they brought in beer. They just didn't ever let us go outside the boundaries. The people interned there weren't dangerous, just disagreeable to the regime. My grandpa was an officer in the army that existed before the current regime, and I myself took part in performances put on by a forbidden ecological organization. This was my sentence.

That year summer was so unusually hot that the warmth hung around until the end of October. The water in the rivers didn't even cool off overnight; every night the walls further heated the air in the city; one's vision went yellow-green from the intensity of the rays; and almost all the insects squeezed in a few extra, overlapping generations. Allergies to the genuine haze of unrepentant pollen were the order of the day because the plants hadn't even the minimum humidity necessary for pollination, and the unrealized grains of pollen tumbled and died off in whole clumps. I really didn't want to go to the camp. What saved me was that I stopped going in to the department—it had become uninteresting. Therefore they couldn't find me on the first day of the state of emergency. It was announced in the morning and by lunchtime I had already gotten pretty far on the train headed to the mountains. The train was strangely empty save for a few old country folk who were hastily returning over the pass with their fruit since all the markets had been closed. I bought a whole backpackful of apricots from them for next to nothing. The train was hot so I spent the whole day and all night sitting in the vestibule near the open door. Meditating, I watched the flight of passing landscapes, objects, buildings, and then, staring continually at the movement of everything beyond the train, I most likely hallucinated. I hadn't even been smoking. Then my friend the entomologist came into the vestibule from one of the other cars. He and I met after we had spent the night on different sides of the same rock a few meters from one another, completely unaware. In the morning we saw each other and realized that we had the same method for overcoming depression—without preparing, leaving everything unfinished, bringing nothing along, to come out to these rocks, make our way to the top, and spend the night there, no matter the time of year, sitting, standing, sometimes lying down, but always holding on and always sleeping. Later I offered him my laboratory to hide from a mobilization campaign.

The entomologist told me about Ms. Viki's boarding house. I knew the station well from back when I studied the flora of the railroad tracks, the various immigrations, emigrations, migrations. I used to ride from station to station on the ladders of the freight cars. There was a citadel on the hill there: a real curiosity of a fortification from the beginning of the century. It was even armed with cannons and a funicular rose up the hill from the station. Not once was the citadel needed; somehow all fronts of war passed it by. In the end, the garrison was moved out and a few of the bastions were converted into a luxury hotel. I really liked it there. I had a room in a machine-gun bunker a little ways outside the citadel, like a separate building. One time Anna waited there for me for several days when I had set out into the mountains on foot away from the tracks on the trail of some expansive population, leaving Anna, who had gone with me for the entire hunting season, behind. Another time we were there in winter right after Christmas. It was terribly cold and we went sledding. The sled spent the night inside; the walls took forever to thaw out. Anna ate snow and we warmed ourselves upstairs, heating our clothes near the stove before we got dressed. Everyone talked only about the frost; Anna didn't allow herself to smoke. For some reason the mirror was hung high, so Anna, who was developing a series of scenes for a new photo album, was forced to stand on a chair. I watched her strange poses, the thick wool socks on her feet, stoking the stove with seasoned beech wood until the tiles glowed. We had a lot of grapefruit with us and we made ashtrays for our bed out of their peeled skins. Our lips were windburned and raw, our hands frozen, and we had to tilt the glass of alcohol past our lips since the ethanol burned them. I rubbed lotion into Anna's hands. Although we had made a blanket tent on the bed to heat up a little bit of air for ourselves, the scent of the hand cream always overpowered my and Anna's smells. At some point we bought some frozen plums. Frozen, they tasted almost exactly the same as fresh. When they thawed, though, they were completely different. We also thought we were being reborn each time we warmed up after that penetrating cold, which made every cell in our entire bodies painfully palpable. The road on the side of the mountains opposite the station, which was lined with pitch-black (especially against the backdrop of snow), twisted plum trees, led from the citadel to a narrow, room-like hideaway, closed in on all sides by rocks. Yet it was big enough for a lake, a rather large one. There were several picturesque huts standing on the shore. One housed a pub, and across from every hut was a long wooden pier with boats tied to it. A little farther along the shore, far apart from one another, two-story villas appeared from among a thicket of mountain pine; these were the remnants of the prewar sanatorium. It would appear that Ms. Viki's boarding house was the last of its kind.

I still didn't know where I was going to live, but the entomologist said that everyone at Ms. Viki's was a runaway like me and recommended the place. My grandpa's last name is still well known and popular today. Ms. Viki took me in despite the fact that the boarding house was overcrowded. I got a room in the attic, which mostly served to dry all sorts of grasses. That same day I found the Grand Café box near my mug in the common dining room. Besides mine, there were five other mugs. Ms. Viki herself always ate separately.

It was a little tight with groceries. Ms. Viki had thought up all sorts of dishes to make for us with whatever she could get. For breakfast she would make us each a large mug of hot cocoa (strangely some luxury items actually made it to the village store in great numbers). She'd serve it with heaps of perfect French toast. For lunch she only ever cooked soup: a soup civilization, the sacrament of soup, very complicated soups. A few hours later we'd sit down to herbal tea with cake, baked from "austerity" recipes—from practically nothing at all. To compensate, our rather late dinner comprised innumerable vegetable dishes— haricot beans, squash, onions, tomatoes, pulses, potatoes, mushrooms, peas, cabbage—boiled, stewed, stuffed, fried, sautéed, deep-fried, baked. There were sauces for everything and a great big dish of boiled rice. Dinner ended with proper tea and a degustation of fresh preserves. Besides that, we took a spoonful of honey on an empty stomach each morning. Honey was a cult object for Ms. Viki. We could pick currants, gooseberries, apples, and cherries ourselves in the garden.

There was a large round table and a sideboard with dishes in the dining room. All the dishes were Secession. It was good that, in addition to everything else, the table service included ashtrays, also of Secession porcelain. We could smoke during tea. Stairs from various floors and alcoves with separate rooms all converged in the dining room. The whole of the topography of the villa resembled the Prague Castle the way it looks from Smíchov, when the most diverse of fragments are combined in one structure. The villa had an irregular shape due to its hodgepodge of annexes and offshoots. On every side it ended in verandas, galleries, porches, balconies, or stairs. The stairs leading to some of the rooms went straight through windows. The whole building was terribly overgrown with grape, moss, ivy, and vines I couldn't identify, all cultivated by the lady of the house. Because of this it sometimes looked bigger and sometimes smaller than it actually was.

II

June 10. Irzhi. For me, he was the most important person in the boarding house. Everything manifests in parallel—through his judgments and conclusions. A translator hiding from mobilization. A translator of Roth, Heidegger, Rilke, Trakl. He almost never left his room. He would walk around the lake. The aesthetics of being. Everyday hermeneutics.

June 14. Irzhi on Ms. Viki. Her garden thinks; it can move from place to place. The Alps imitate the Himalayas. Wild strawberries until the snow comes, but only a few berries a day. Stale, old fur coats can serve as furniture. Moths fly out of the credenza because Heidegger lives there.

June 15. At Irzhi's. Rasta and Stronzitska came over from their rooms. Rasta is a Rastafarian guru. He's being threatened with arrest again. He tends to the marijuana in Ms. Viki's greenhouse. Ms. Viki accidentally ended up with some high-grade marijuana through a correspondence seed exchange, probably from someone in Holland. We smoked with him and Stronzitska. Rastaman vibration. Irzhi caught a wave. Stronzitska is an essayist from Vienna (she could have been a spy in the service of the Hapsburg house, Irzhi says). She smokes incessantly. And only Drum shag, but one paper isn't enough for her cigarettes so she sticks two or three together in advance. Stronzitska has Raynaud's syndrome. She brought her own blanket. Now she has all the blankets in the whole house because her hands and feet are always freezing. She was interested in me as a famous botanist, as a former friend of a world-famous model—Anna. She recorded an interview with me for her radio program. I wasn't afraid to tell her about everything I'd seen in forbidden zones—provocative radio is her format. Things often happen only after Stronzitska tells about them. I refused to talk about Anna. She is afraid of moths. An invitation to a conference of opposition journalists from our country, Stronzitska is organizing the conference, it will take place in the boarding house where we live.

June 16. We went even farther into the mountains with Rasta and hired ourselves out to pick apples for a couple days. Discussions on drug-induced and sober ways of achieving visions. Attempts to analyze and systematize the visual laws (high optics) of vision. Rasta is the former European champion of cannabis reframing—two competitors go somewhere together, smoking weed the whole time, conjuring up each other's fears, phobias, provoking obsessive ideas, manias, ulterior motives, and unjustified conclusions. Whoever leads their competitor to a level of reframing from which they can never return wins.

June 20. Life in the boarding house is straight out of the nineteenth century—that's what it feels like. Our daily existence with our shared breakfasts and evening teas, the culture of preserves, the old paintings, everyone talking all at once, everyone having private conversations. Guests coming for a day or two. The absence of a storyline—there is no plot. Everything sort of stretches out in time, which ceases to be events any bigger than drinking tea or an abundance of moths at night. There is no determinism, but the logic—just one of the many possible—of the register, of the description, of the inventory of "traits." Reading Antonych with Irzhi: every day the verse with that day's date.

June 22. Took the night train to the city with Irzhi. We wanted to sleep, we smoked in the vestibule. It was on trains like this that *Being and Time* was thought up. We had to use a razor to defend ourselves from the patrol. We wounded them and jumped off the train to immediately hop on another, headed back to the mountains.

June 25. With Irzhi. We decided to listen to Ms. Stronzitska's tape—a recording of conversations with everyone who lives at Ms. Viki's. On the tape recorder our voices sound almost the same. We listen to the conversation with Ms. Hiba (it was for her sake that Ms. Stronzitska came to the boarding house for the summer): a film and theater director of situations—modeling scenarios, creating events directly in someone else's life, at times in reverse, at times not, at times commissioned, at times unexpected, her involvement in a host of strangers' lives, but the absence of her own is very dangerous for the regime. A consummate psychologist. Irzhi says she's bored at the boarding house without drama and intrigue, she rides her bike to the citadel to play bridge with the bishops, she's looking for a plot among us that could unfold, climax, and resolve with a performance.

June 27. The invariability of phenology. Stagnant days, like the summer of '92, '94. A nighttime trek with Irzhi to the blackberry patch. A few odd lighters in our pockets. My plant philosophy is the denial of self-expression, tropisms, and contemplation. To stay, to endure. Tracelessness, coexistence, the constant feeling of existing, non-rhetoric, extra-erotica, the unattainability of the idea, and much more.

June 30. With Irzhi at the citadel. Anna is there. She is at once both happy and sad. My inability to choose. Her inability to endure. Anna lives with another Anna, a graphic artist and photographer. And Anna is her model and lover. Irzhi's lecture by the lake: conclusions for the sake of harmony with the world, the hermeneutics of holes and niches; wanderings through niches and aesthetics; free flight from being into being; entanglement as the guarantor of nonpredestination, freedom as unnecessity, freedom freely freeing itself.

July 1. Anna at the boarding house. We become lovers again with ease and nostalgia, realizing that our bodies belong to each other. Shades of various unshared experience. Anna suggests positioning her body to pose together for the other Anna. We think up compositions. We drink mineral water at night at Irzhi's.

July 2. Anna and I drink with the colonel at the pub. He has admired Anna and only now acknowledges me. In the colonel's room. Maps published under the regime—he adjusts them. He's a geographer, a former minister of lands for the government, unseated by the regime, he ran illegal border crossings. A photograph with my grandfather, whom he once saved from enemy fire. After some rum he hangs by his fingers from the edge of the balcony. Deplorable memories of the First World War: during the war he helped chart mountain routes, decipher enemy symbols, and make additional false marks (there were six coding systems).

July 3. The marijuana plant Rasta gave me is in the white porcelain vase.

July 7. Anna and I swim in the lake in the morning, daytime, evening, and night. We row the boat and the citadel floats across the lake, we swim behind the boat. We do sit-ups and strengthen our backs— the longest muscles of our backs are wet. Later I wash her hair, but I can barely hold it all in my hands. We each smoke one of Rasta's cigarettes and experiment with that kind of eroticism. We fall asleep in unexpected places a few times.

July 9. We spend the night at Irzhi's. The floor is made up with blankets, life on the floor, bitter Japanese tea. We burn walnut shells specially collected for this in winter. Irzhi says, the more you really love people, the happier you can be.

July 10. With Irzhi. My bygone history with Anna. Growing closer over a very long time, very gradually, very completely. We became true lovers only when there was nowhere left to expand. Subtleness is holiness. She was my existence and essence, my singular motif of the riskiest, boldest, frankest, sincerest, and most grateful advances. Dances of the imagination. Standing at the edges, it is forbidden to cross. The intensification of existence is a philosophical technique. Someone who has never said anything empty or extraneous, and gradually I said everything I wanted to. The conversation could be written as a continuous text without separations between the speakers. A day can only be held if it's not torn into night. Cyclamens. Rum, persimmons, large cafés. The long fear of touching each other and not getting used to it. A very thin arm whose hairs are standing on end from cold. Winter turns into spring, the sun aquariumizes the room, there's wet snow in the garden, the evening unwinterly illuminated by indirect lights. Yet at some point it had to turn bad. One time I returned from an expedition and immediately went to my study. She embraced me and the photographer took a picture. We contrasted too much, yet complemented each other remarkably. The photo appeared on a few covers, by then Anna was already quite popular. A few things are important to me: we achieved the impossible, we learned very much from each other, we evoked unusual joy in everyone. And now we are we again, even if just for one summer.

July 13. Into the mountains with the other Anna for a few days. We look at plants. I show her the fine aesthetics of botany. We think up a series of designs based on this. She photographs me. Sketches for my field guide. The designs let loose more and more creatures from other forms of reality. The unexpectedly quick appearance of a shared past. Destruction as a real state of the world, as a sign of vivacity. The phenomenology of a rock covered in a few layers of lichen is the phenomenology of lichen, not of the rock. The bunches of lichen are the phenomena. Superficial, planar, topological, rhizoidal phenomenology.

July 18. At Irzhi's looking at photographs that Anna took, that Anna and I staged and posed for. The color of umber. Asymmetries and symmetries. The faces of medieval monks. Around the lake. Life on a single rock. The sky along your arm. Trees variously infected with mistletoe, existence among mistletoe. The silhouettes of the uninvited on invited surfaces. Irzhi says, you come up with photographs based on how you lived. But in the end the photos are totally different. And then you use your own photos as scripts. You are finding your own prose, freeing yourself from citation.

July 20. I'm afraid that Anna will get pregnant from Anna when she turns away from me. Anna, my lover, and Anna, Anna's lover. In this way, Anna and I are getting dangerously close. We caress each other through Anna. The traces of our touches coincide. Anna is happy and laughs both with Anna and with me.

July 22. With Irzhi. Coming up with stories. Attempts at destruction and reconstruction. Derrida. It's impossible to evaluate stories without taking up residence in them. Attempts at deconstruction. Irzhi says, I'd write a story about our summer in the boarding house. I say, to really let your imagination loose. The joy of thinking up a world. I wouldn't know any motifs, I wouldn't know any reasons, I wouldn't know why. I'd see it for what it is. I'd see what shows itself. There would be no evolution, only an agglomeration of phenomena, properties, occurrences, facts. Inconsistent logic. I'd even be able to think up more than I knew. I wouldn't want to achieve anything other than to imagine what could be possible. Irzhi says, writing like stones thrown into water, circles of varying intensity rippling out from each one, entering one another. Don't worry that your story won't have much in common with your own experience; don't try to drag that into the story. I say, prose on the level of auxiliary verbs, prepositional phrases. Irzhi says, a complex structure—this story is like the first chapter in a great post-summer novel of intrigue, a refined and worthy debut, yet only the first chapter exists. I say, but none of this should make the story heavy. Write lightly, with joy so that it likewise is read with joy.

July 25. A whole other world. Anna and I take the radio operator's place and stay for a few days in the armored personnel carrier that guards the citadel during the state of emergency. Life in the contained space, life within iron, life at the radio station. We heard that they were in fact leading the military into our mountain province and introducing martial law. They were threatening everyone with arrest.

July 28. Ms. Viki planned a holiday for all of us on the first of August. I invited Anna and Anna. With Irzhi. We'll see what happens in the middle of the story. How it ends. If something happens during a night of revelry. Anna's hoping for an orgy that would let her pay attention not only to me. The colonel's dreaming about getting drunk and dancing with Anna. He doesn't even know if he'll be able to drive us across the border if they bring the military in and we find the courage to steal the APC near the citadel for our escape. Ms. Hiba probably knows everything: how the situation will eventually play out, who will have which roles. It's looking likely that Anna and I could become the object of the game. Rasta is going to try this year's marijuana, he's going to try to smoke up as many people as possible. Ms. Stronzitska, Anna, Irzhi, Anna, and I might agree to smoke. It's curious what inhibitions of Anna's the grass might evaporate. Rasta is also going to attempt a group reframing session. What's more, participants in Ms. Stronzitska's secret conference are going to start arriving on the night trains. The military might come too.

July 29. It turns out that Irzhi is competing in this year's October finale for the European reframing championship. And Rasta's training him. "Irzhi isn't a real Rastaman," Rasta says, "but Irzhi's potential is greater than anyone in the entire history of the championship." Irzhi has reframed moths—there were more than usual this summer. They would fly in through the window toward the lamp, until it became difficult to walk across the room without running into at least a few moths. They even landed on our hands. In the gleam of the table lamp their eyes were bright and translucent red. Irzhi would raise the moth on his hand until it was even with his gaze and stare into its eyes. Their eyes, it turned out, were large and compound. The moths couldn't hold Irzhi's stare and looked away. "Another requirement for writing"—one's gaze can never be narrower than one's peripheral vision (but this doesn't take literature into account at all).

III

Dying is the collateral of any experience. It is impossible for there to be too much experience, extraneous experience, erroneous experience. And there can be no direction other than toward experience, toward dying. The maximum coincides with death. Maximal experience is needed in order to die in your own way. So that in your death you can become an entire death forest, a whole heath of additional experience for someone else. Later the text becomes life that after it appears can only die, getting squeezed out by experience.

You never know which period you live in, whose, what field you're entering. This becomes clear when the period ends, when the force of the next death ushers us into new territories of the experience of dying.

OKSANA ZABUZHKO

GIRLS

translated from the Ukrainian by Askold Melnyczuk

D ARKA SAW HER IN THE TROLLEY, the sweaty, June-soaked trolley, brimming with people and their smells: sweet, almost corpse-like, female, heavy, equestrian, yet oddly palatable, and even stimulating, sexual, distinctly male. Suddenly all the smells switched off, leaving only a girlish profile on the sunny side of the car, angular as a Braque: abrupt, soaring cheekbones, a fine pug nose, full lips, and a sharp, childlike fist of a chin—a capricious, fragile geometry which occasionally seeps from an artist's pen, piercing the heart, as when in childhood you pick up a new Christmas ornament (I remember it: a blinding white ballerina, tutu frozen in an upward sweep, an inconceivable liquid legato of arms and legs, so delicate and small-fingered that touching them with your brutish five-year-old's stumps seemed blasphemous), such faces catapult into the world in order to reawaken us to life's fragility. She had the disproportionately long (instead of Braque, Modigliani) neck of a wary fawn (Fee, Fi, Fo, Fawn chanted the other girls, but Darka couldn't bring herself to say it: the fawn was simply Effie and none other, because these slopes and angles, lines pushed to the breaking point, suggested something else entirely). It was the same kind of neck that had emerged from the open collar (stiff, angular, extending over the shoulders in that style from the seventies) of the school uniform, flashing cleavage. Ah, Effie the fawn! In the chemistry classroom her spot was near the window where the light fell on her face and neck that same way, trailing down the trench between her breasts. It deepened as she bent over, giving the sun her downy left cheek. Only, Darka realized now that this couldn't be her childhood friend, that the real Effie would be well over thirty, and yet amazingly enough, it was her, newly returned in her incomparable, not-quite-twenty-year-old prime: every woman's beauty has (like every figure, its ideal size, where one pound more or less makes all the difference) its own moment of perfection, one in which everything opens to the fullest, and which can change in a minute like the bloom on a desert flower or may, in happier circumstances, depending on care and watering, last for years (so, optimistically, thinks Darka, whose expenses for moisturizing, for creams and lotions, have recently begun exceeding her outlay for clothing), and Effie at the start had been junior-sized. Yet who knows what life turned her into eventually? Effie: ephebe, the word exactly.

Effie or non-Effie on the sunny side of the trolley senses she's being watched and turns her head (the butterfly brush of lashes), glance sharp as an elbow: Look, look, said Effie, sweeping up her sleeve, see how sharp, want to feel it? And here too—thrusting forward her neck and, already disheveled and spooked, pushing out her collarbones: held breath, the gaze dead, strange, a little frightened, whether through its own daring trustfulness or because of your unpredictability: she loves me, she loves me not (or, as she played it: love, kiss, spit)—of course it's not her, and neither is this one as young as she looked in profile—Darka turns her eyes away and looks politely out the window where at this moment out of the dappled green of Mariinsky Park rises the monument to Vatutin—dull, bald, and smug, a sculptural epitaph to Khrushchev's era—my peer, Darka sneers (the monument went up the year she was born), and at that moment she decides about the school reunion (a stiff envelope with a gold seal, an invitation, removed yesterday from the mailbox, and uncertainly set aside—there will be time to think about it), dammit, she'll go to the reunion though the prospect wearies her: what could be interesting about this pathetic act of self-assertion before the face of one's own adolescence, what's intriguing about the gray and the bald blissfully morphing to boyos again, and artificial, elaborately decked-out women who sneak glances at your wrinkles, hoping they have fewer themselves? But she'll go—whatever happened to Fawn-Effie-Faron? Suddenly, she needed to know.

≈

Once Darka read an article by an American gender-studies guru which claimed axiomatically that boys tended to be competitive, girls cooperative. Only a boy could have blathered such nonsense so glibly.

The struggle for power, not for its dividends in the form of grades (suggestive of subsequent financial achievement), nor for success with the opposite sex (which had not defined itself as being opposed to anything yet), and not even for the applause meter running high at the Christmas Pageant (which principally feeds the vanity of one's parents, and only later flexes the muscles of your own), but for power in its nearly unalloyed pristine form, like the sweet narcotic of pure, dry white spirit, and all the more intoxicating: the exclusive right to lead the class either from the schoolroom to the playing field, or after class to what they called a "recital of cats"—below a window where you torment the tubster from the front row, the one who chews her sandwich wrapped in wax paper from home during the break and then leaves hideous grease stains on textbooks—to lead the class no matter where, no matter whether for good or ill, because the difference between good and evil doesn't exist, just as it never exists in the presence of absolute power—this struggle, aside from its earliest form in tribal war, you see precisely among girls from ages eight to twelve. Later, thank God, they develop other, more civilian concerns.

By fourth grade, when Effie appeared in their class, Darka already had the rap sheet of either a budding criminal or a political leader (the boundary between them is of course narrow, and depends not on nature but nurture): at least two girls from her class had to change schools, one in the middle of the year, black-haired Rivka Braverman with bluish-white starched bows in her glistening braids, whose father's chauffeur drove her to school in the company's glistening black Volga, and after school drove her to music lessons.

Rivka had a plump, confident ass and a disdainful mouth melding into folds of flesh. She smelled of homemade vanilla cookies, vacations at a spa in the Caucasus, third-generation antiques confiscated during the Revolution, and a five-room apartment of the sort reserved for only the most privileged of Soviet families, in a building erected by prisoners of war for the new Soviet elite. Such a start in life does little to encourage an instinct for self-preservation, so that Darka, whom Rivka carelessly attempted to treat with all her studied arrogance toward others, none of whom had ever darkened the threshold of such a five-room apartment in a building erected by prisoners of war, forced on Rivka her first lesson in survival training in a society sufficiently transformed that neither her grandfather the prosecuting attorney, nor her father the director of X, was able to secure for her what was most valuable: a more bankable nationality to declare in that fifth blank on her passport. After Darka sicced on her a group of classmates, including red-haired Misha Khazin and Marina Weissberg, who chased her from school to the entrance of that apartment building built by prisoners of war, in one breath chanting "Kike, kike, running down the pike"—and Rivka really did run like the Wandering Jew of all Treblinkas, her plump bouncing ass suddenly,

pathetically deflated, and the next day in class the whole group murmured to themselves so that the teacher facing the blackboard heard
only a monotonous hum as though the room had been filled with bum-
ble bees—"Zhid, zhid, zhid," the word sounded especially greasy, thick,
repulsive. "Let the damn bee out," the teacher snapped, at which point
the bee fell silent, and then Rivka suddenly leaped up and shouted
"Again! There they go again!" and ran out weeping. After this, no matter
how Braverman the Elder threatened the school, no matter how many
parents were called in for meetings, it was no longer possible for Rivka,
proudly upholding the propellered bows of her braids, to stay in class.

Darka herself was shocked and frightened by Rivka's unexpected
collapse. Her hysterical crying had aborted their game of king of the hill
and for a few days Darka herself lay in bed with an inexplicable fever.
Her principal sorrow lay in the fact that Rivka, arrogant and hateful,
with her muscling into the class presidency, with her hideous pout-
ing mouth (a clear legacy from her grandfather, an agent of the Cheka,
the brutal secret police, a fact Darka could not have known at the time,
though she registered it instinctively) with which she talked her way
into the coveted position of sanitary inspector, where she would examine her classmates' hands and send the ink-spattered back to the wash-
room for a scrubbing, with her methodical nerdiness and unblemished
faith in her own perfection, who had once dared to point out reluc-
tantly that Darka too was an A student (it's you who's an A student too,
Darka blurted back), with her glistening satin sleeve protectors, and
that second pair of shoes in a special pink bag, real pumps, delicate and
also pink, like a little princess's, with heels—You don't have any like this
and you never will. My daddy bought them for me in Copenhagen—
that Rivka suddenly appeared to be a child, just like Darka, and because
of her, because of Darka, that child was screaming with grief. Her
mother and father also grew worried as Darka began groaning in her

sleep. She'd gladly have made peace with Rivka, would have apologized, made it up, cheered her up, had she only known how. Her experience of peacemaking involved only her mother and father, who, no matter what happened, always found themselves in the pastoral position: Go and sin no more, they'd say after a time, and it was possible to skip out with a leap, lighthearted, with quickly drying, as in a sun-shower, tears. Here, however, something had broken irreparably, in Rivka, in the world, in her very own self, and through the break, as in a fence, there crawled a thick, hot, brown darkness, and when Darka's fever finally fell and she returned to school she found that Rivka was no longer in her class.

The remote consequences of these events revealed the mixed feelings of guilt and shame which from then on dogged her in her every encounter with Jews and which only faded on closer acquaintance. The direct, immediate consequence was that Darka shrank, grew subdued, and dove deep into books (that began the period of intoxication by reading) right up to the end of the school year.

Then, the following year, a new girl appeared.

Darka remembered her first meeting with everyone who'd played any real part in her life, even though it may have been hidden—the bottom of memory's drawer, a snapshot of another-other-stranger, who God knows why your eye alighted on, cutting him out of the chaotic backdrop that became the rest of the world, like a promise, that when laid out in a row, with the rest of the sequence, reveal various unexpected poses, from the lightning glance of direct eye contact, creating a voltaic exchange across the short distance between two points (blue eyes, gray eyes, green eyes, each with the same enchanting glassy gaze of antique crystal, men's eyes, but who knows how hers looked to them?), to those taken as though with a hidden camera, when the object has not yet noticed you and not begun to suspect that he or she will soon be someone in your life, profiles, three-quarter shots, even shots from the back of the head: napes can be outrageously singular. Yet, no matter how she rummaged through her memory, she could never find that first shot of Effie.

Effie hadn't come from the outside; she'd unfolded from within Darka like one of her own organs. Like the dormant gene of an inherited disease.

What Darka remembered were Effie's pantyhose—most of the girls in the class still wore white and brown cotton ones, wrinkled, droopy-kneed, and for some reason eternally sagging too short, oh this damned command economy (or had socialism set as one of its goals the breeding of short-legged and suspiciously tubby little girls?), with the crotch always sagging out from under one's skirt so that everyone, above all the wearer, expected that any moment they would fall off, and so our childhood passed, in the Land of the Falling Tights. Toddlers were constantly hiking up their skirts and purposefully yanking up their stockings. Once tubby Alla from the front row did it in fourth grade when she was called up to the blackboard, the most natural gesture, the same as rolling up your sleeves or smoothing your hair, but in fourth grade they mocked her mercilessly, the boys practically fell out of their chairs, pointed their fingers, and the treacherous girls too yukked it up, and maybe because of that Darka remembered Fawn's legs, those of a long, vulnerable, lanky newborn fawn, but covered smoothly with a fine transparent wrap. In the sun-drenched classroom they looked golden. It was as though Fawn had no childhood, nothing to outgrow, all the barely visible, minute women's ways of sculpting, transforming themselves into women, which take one's entire adolescence to master (some even dedicate part of their youth to it), all that plucking of eyebrows, trying on various haircuts (the shag, the flip, Sassoon bangs—a chirping already incomprehensible to boys), nail polish with glitter and flowers until settling in tenth grade on, thank God, one's natural color.

She seemed to have been endowed with everything at birth, a fully drawn, breakable gold-legged figure: Braque? Modigliani? No, Picasso, *Girl on a Ball*.

Effie, Effie, my love.

And she remembers something more about the legs—that unbearable internal burn which you eventually learn to recognize as jealousy when the English teacher (and really as though copied from life, from the grotesquely bland, flat-chested, formless, ageless English women of de Maupassant, whom Darka was already devouring surreptitiously) makes Effie stand in the corner: teachers, that is, female teachers (there was only one man, who taught phys ed), somehow teachers did not love her, but why? And Effie stands there in her uniform, in front of the whole class, lightly rocking on her golden fawn's legs and Marinka Weissberg whispers to Darka: Doesn't Fawn have nice legs, Darka pulls back, this isn't a subject for discussion, but Marinka keeps on, Long, too. Mine are twelve centimeters shorter. We measured. You know how you measure, here, from the hip, the blow seems so strong that Darka inadvertently opens her mouth to catch a breath and then under her breast the burn spreads with a slow fire, just yesterday she and Effie sat late on the lake in the park, first feeding the Effie-necked swans, and when the swans went to sleep the girls watched the sun set on the burning, splintered, intense dark purple streak of water, wide-eyed as though frightened. Both gazed with Effie's wide-open eyes: so much beauty, she said, her thin—so thin they looked shadowed with blue—eyelids butterflied: So much beauty in the world, how to grasp it all? You know, Dar, sometimes I can't sleep all night, I keep thinking, my head goes round and round, how to hold it, this world's so huge? And you know, the lids dropped, along with Darka's heart, full lips puckered as though for a kiss sprinkled with dewdrops, the result of an extraordinary internal effort, You know, Dar, I think either something very beautiful or very terrible will happen to me, her knuckles squeezing the bench turning white. Something, some way in which I'll finally be able to capture everything, hold everything, contain everything, you understand? Darka trembled within, not from the cold, because her cheeks and mouth were hot, but from the feeling that in her cupped palms fluttered a butterfly, because from childhood, because everyone knows that if you blow all the pollen off the butterfly's wings, it will certainly die. Never again in her life would she so desperately want to protect someone, before no one else did she feel such numbing awe as then, with Effie, all later connections were mere shards of this sensation, like those splinters of purple fire on the water (a bit like loving a man, bodies dissolving, and after a few minutes you hungrily move toward him again because you don't know what else might be done with this flesh, impenetrable as a wall, aside from taking it one more time, because there's no way to come together so as to never part again—but that's coarser, more primitive. For that matter, as you develop your self-conscious flesh, everything becomes simpler and more linear, or maybe, Darka assumes now, being a sister, an older sister, is the same as being born with the instincts of a mother, and it was her sisterlessness which had been an absence swelling inside her for years and at the right moment shifted onto Effie, Effie who in fact needed something different)—deafened and blinded, Darka bent low over her notebook, trying not to look at Fawn standing in the corner, though she smiled wanly in her direction as if she knew what she and Marinka Weissberg were whispering: that Effie yesterday entrusted to her the most precious part of her inner self meant to Darka a kind of vow to eternal and absolute fidelity, so, aside from the shock that the beloved turns out not to be transparent, that she leads a separate life and can have secrets from you (measuring legs with silly Marinka, giggling, hiking hems to press their hips against each other—she never did such things with me, not even a hint of it). In addition to that shock, there was the grief of insulted love which demands everything at once, unsatisfied with bits and pieces, and therefore is destined to doubt that which it has actually received: is it possible she lied to me yesterday? How is it possible to be so, so hypocritical—Darka remembered she'd used just that word; during recess, she passed by Effie in proud silence; it took her stupefied senses an entire class to recover from the shock, while at the next recess Effie herself approached her: What's up? You mad at me?

I have to talk to you, said Darka in a tight voice she didn't recognize herself, a lump in her throat. After school they again sat in the park at the lake, wrapped like fairy-tale heroes in a cloud, an air of Shakespearian thunderstorm, a tempest—the sweet sorrow of parting—Effie, flashing eyes full of wobbly tears, passionately assured Darka that the thing with Marinka had happened long ago, implying that it was before her friendship with Darka, that it was all silly and meaningless and didn't matter, and Darka brightened, the sky cleared, as though pulled out from under an avalanche, yet for a while she still pretended to be offended, partly from an innate sense of form and partly out of an unconscious bartering with Effie for new concessions, new guarantees of undivided and exclusive affection, a scenario which Darka later on inevitably repeated with men except that with them it was much easier, while Effie was about as supple as Picasso's acrobat, dodging to avoid Darka's onslaught, from despairing repentance to a sudden collapse into a complete and trancelike absence and a self-absorption, to half-hysterical recitals of poems meant to explain everything (that year they buried each other in poetry), until, exhausted by the endless back-and-forth, Darka heard her own voice cry: Forgive me! then sinking to her nylon-warmed golden knees, embracing them and at the same time greedily snorting in, through tears, their surprising smell of bread, the odors of home reached after long travels: in the bedroom under your parents' door the light pours, let me fluff up your pillow, the ticklish scent like a kitten's on her hair on your cheek, two girls cuddling under the covers, hugging each other, whispering, sudden outbursts of laughter, stop, you're deafening me—like you, but different, that's what a sister is, that's what I'm embracing, tightly, so tightly that it can't be tighter, never to let it go— two wildly intertwined girls on a bench in the park of an evening, her swollen breasts under her school uniform thrust into yours, her lashes tickling your neck, like in that myth where the cloud of the gods rendered the lovers invisible to mere mortals—nobody walked down the path, nobody rustled the fallen leaves, there was nobody to be surprised when Effie began kissing the trail of tears under Darka's eyes and then pressed her lips to hers and gasped, Effie's heart beat inside Darka's chest and both froze, not sure what to do next, and then Darka felt between her lips something quick, wet, salty, and very large, it floated in her mouth like a naked, hot fish blacking out the rest of the world and she did not immediately understand that it was Effie's tongue but once she did she was seized by another, incomprehensible sort of sobbing, inhaling her tears and Effie's tongue, squeezing the skinny body even tighter: shoulder blades sharp as wings, the keyboard of the vertebrae under the coarse uniform, suddenly brought to memory her first realization of what it meant that something was alive. She was three years old, standing speechless above a basket full of tiny fluffy white rabbits, unable to step aside or turn away, until one of the adults said from above, "Would you like one?"

She struggled to come to terms with the idea that such an astonishing creature breathed and moved, and then with the equally astonishing news of what one could do with such a miracle: one could possess it (at that most honest of ages, possession meant just one thing: it meant that, out of an excess of feeling, one could put the thing in one's mouth and swallow it, as one did the petals of the prettiest flowers from the courtyard garden which you plucked and chewed, your saliva turning bitter and green when you spat, and over years that original meaning of the word doesn't change, only gets clouded over). It takes a lifetime to understand that long ago the grown-ups fooled you, that in fact nothing living, neither a flower, nor a rabbit, nor a person, nor a country, can be had: they can only be destroyed, which is the one way to confirm they have been possessed.

≈

And here too, said Effie, but it was another time, at home, before a large tarnished mirror in a dark brown frame—she first unbuttoned her dress, exposing two bra straps on a cubist shoulder of protruding horizontal bones; she'd long ago begun wearing a bra, Darka saw, when they changed before gym class, Effie's expensive snow-white underwear unavailable in any store though there amid the smell of mats stacked up in the corner which were old and rough to the touch reeking of old sweat, there, in the middle of it, it was just underwear, but here, when Effie, not turning her hypnotized, dark eyes—pupils dilated—away, slipped off her bra, a tender, pearl-pink nipple popped out of its cup like an outthrust tongue and at the same time Effie's fingers stumbled over buttons as though asking permission, began cautiously unbuttoning Darka's shirt and she saw, alongside Effie's, her own nipple only darker, redder, like a cherry pit, here blood rushed to Darka's head and everything grew blurred, Effie leaned lightly over her breast and Darka felt her wet gathering mouth, and goose bumps, and her own rapid breathing, and everything began flowing, was it her, Darka, who was slipping into the unknown, something heady and hot, something forbidden and tempting, compared with which all of Darka's steady will to power, being first in her class, academic triumphs, captain of the volleyball team, all this was small and insignificant as she went down and emerged new, dark, dangerous, and big as the world—oh, Effie, two girls with their shirts undone in the depths of the mirror where Effie touched her kissed breast with her own and said: Here too, pointing to the other one, and that was how it began.

And so it whirled, sweeping all away. All their school recesses spent together on the windowsill, wandering through the park after class, drunken talking talking, insatiable as two mutes who'd suddenly discovered the gift of tongues or infants who'd just learned to talk, but they really were just learning to speak, learning to translate each other into words and speech different from what the adults had expected, about the meaning of life, the future of mankind, will there be war, about their own childhoods, it was frightening to see how many reflections surfaced at that age—I remember when I was little—and then you don't remember a thing until you're old, when, they say, the sluices finally open again, you can't even remember what those things were—you spent hours gushing at each other so that the day felt too short, except a few splinters, of poems for instance, "So Long Had Life Together Been" by Joseph Brodsky (Effie), "Lady with Eyes Larger than Asters" by Kalynets (Darka), but that was passed on from the grown-ups, it was the frigging legacy of the sixties generation that was passed on from family to family in a thin stream from a closed tap, while all of one's own content that filled the cup to over-flowing had drained away somewhere, leaving only silt after the passing of a stream—the memory of a bench, of a windowsill in a school corridor, a memory of Effie's concentrated face—did she know how to listen with shiny eyes and half-open mouth, and all that in the shadowy, autumnal light of sad, nostalgic longing for the long-gone unreachable heights—that whole visible daily aspect of their friendship (sixth grade: just as, among kids, that boiling process of clinging and dissolving molecules begins, friendships forming and dissolving several times a year, so that none of the teachers ever paid these two much attention)—it

OKSANA ZABUZHKO

all continued, this material world, yet invisibly tightening and shrinking the dress (now pinching her armpits) under the abrupt combustible wind of that suffocating, heady element of their friendship which unfolded without witnesses and gathered strength, to be more precise a lot more energy, at least with Darka, went into supporting it because all their trembling falling into each other, all their hot kisses and more frequent, growing caresses exploded not on their own, not from a purely physical compulsion, as later occurred with boys, but each time moving to some kind of emotional resolution, a little drama, the improvisation of which they were wonderfully adept at: in the feat of peacemaking after a new argument that took them to the edge of breakup (regular as storms in July), in an ecstasy of simultaneously recognizing the music of the Doors, to which Effie responded by collapsing onto the carpet and pounding her forehead into it, shouting, I can't stand it, I can't stand it.

And Darka, seizing that dear warm downy head (smelling like the fur of a kitten), her whole body trembling at the unfathomable mystery of feeling things, at how far more subtle and spiritually richer Effie was than her (that was what Darka wrote in an essay titled "My Friend": *My friend has a richly subtle and spiritually rich nature*; she was stuck for a long time on the repetition: one of the two had to be crossed out, yet neither was willing to leave), really, it's quite puzzling, Darka now wonders, how on earth did they manage to study that year, where had they found the time for it, or, to be more precise, where had Effie found the time, since she never managed things as well as Darka, yet succeeded in passing all her classes, even earning As, and not only in music and gym (an honor student, which automatically meant a good girl, or, as the vice principal said during the PTA meeting about her, a girl from an honorable family, because that was what she was, with divorced parents who spoiled her competitively: stereo, French linens at twelve)— where did she find it, the time and strength?

182

And they read, insatiably, with all their might, living through the work as though it were their own inner life—their own times fit them like a glove: these were the years of the book boom: the hunt for hard-to-find books from Moscow (special access), bound in smelly fresh leatherette the color of dark amber or bottle green or marine blue, all spines gilded like the epaulets on an officer's uniform (yet looking for all that like the expensive cognac boxes next to which these books were meant to cohabit on Yugoslavian shelves symbolizing lives of cultured leisure and the ever-expanding well-being of the Soviet people), and Darka, whose family connections gave her access to risky mimeographed samizdat materials, borrowed from Effie high-ranking uniform volumes of Akhmatova and Mandelstam, as well as *The Master and Margarita*, which Effie read first, before loaning it, rehearsing for her most of the first chapter up to and including the part where the head's cut off by the tram, but Darka never managed to memorize the final chapter: as she was finishing the book she was called out and interrogated by the police, and in one moment her childhood came to an end.

Much later, as a grown-up, Darka finally risked asking her mother just what horrible thing had been discovered at that point (oh if only it hadn't been) and which had stormed through the entire school for over a month? To an adult, the story seemed utterly banal: a girl from a well-to-do family, not yet thirteen, secretly, without anybody knowing (not even me!), hangs around with sexually mature seventeen-year-old boys, goes with them Sundays to the deserted Trukhaniv Island, and later the mother of one of these boys (you can imagine this mother, someone should have drowned the bitch!), raises a fuss across the whole school (idiot!) because her dear little boy had the bridle on his penis torn, or rather, bitten through (so what's the big deal? It would heal before the wedding!). Darka's mother was only able to tell her about the torn bridle because the story had been an unforgettable lesson in anatomy.

Okay, I agree, said Darka insincerely, hoping to coax more information from her, the story's not pleasant, certainly not for the girl's parents, but when you think about it, there are many worse ways to lose your virginity, which don't always lead to broken lives, and a girl with such a turbulent debut might, in twenty years, why not, surface as an affable matron with a decent university job, while the poor mangled boy may, to the delight of his mother, yet become a PhD, an oceanographer, a selenographer, or a stylographer, why not?

(What Darka herself remembered was her first glimpse, through a crack in the principal's office door, of Effie's mother—young and dazzlingly beautiful, sheathed in leather, draped in pendulous Roma jewelry, in sheaves of turtledove-gray veils of smoke which swirled like burning incense round an unknown goddess—apart from the brief shock at the fact that someone had the nerve to smoke in the principal's office, she remembered it as the first time she became aware of a different species of human which somewhere, no, here, beyond the glass wall, though you can't get there, thrives—a richer than rich, glamorous movie idol with an unfathomably intense life, who has been given the world for her pleasure forever.) Darka's mother, however, also remembered the arrival of a detective, something Darka barely noticed (maybe because the children were questioned in their parents' presence and parents were, to kids at that age, more significant than any strangers, so Darka retained the vague impression that it was her own parents interrogating her). A detective? That means it wasn't simply a matter of children's games under clear skies. What else was up? Chewing gum, American jeans (the height of luxury) given or traded by these kids near the, oh God, Intourist Hotel (where all foreigners stayed), that terrible word—the most terrifying word there was—for-saling, because trading with foreigners was, after all, a crime.

What had all this been about? Were they plotting entrapment at a later date, or hoping to keep the kids from racing into the future with extravagant appetites, teaching them instead to sin in secret?

Did you see, Skalkovska has (Effie immediately became, and remained, Skalkovska) that badge with the American flag? Did she tell you where she got it?

Chills, my God, what a nightmare (plus the reek of political informers—was it the mother of the victimized, unbridled, half-circumcised boy who'd used this as a way to break up the circle once and for all?). What could Effie, her Effie, have to do with this? And above all how could she have maintained her life on such parallel tracks, as invisible as pantyhose without a wrinkle, without ever giving herself away to Darka?

(There was, however, one moment during which Darka, with the sudden jealous clarity of all lovers, did get after all one barely visible splinter: Ihor M., from tenth grade, passing them in the corridor, the red-scarved peons whom the upperclassman shoved aside blindly like ants, suddenly stops: Fawn, he says, with an unusually intimate, creepy, utterly adult tone and a strange smile on his lips, and Effie steps toward him like a ballerina, leg suspended in the air, heel to toe—and while they exchange a few hushed words, Darka sees nothing but the bent leg, toes lightly pressed to the ground, and, her heart breaking out of the pain of uncertainty, suspiciously asks Effie after she returns, Where do you know him from?

(We're neighbors, says Effie, puckering her full lips into a chicken's ass—it was the kind of grimace she put on when called on in class, driving the female faculty wild. This was the single glimpse, brief as a scratch, of a distant and incomprehensible, beautiful and frightening— and could it be otherwise—secret: because she was all mystery, that's what she was, and neither I nor those hideous boys whose brains leaked out in their sperm, not that there was much there to begin with, could have dreamed of holding her for more than a moment, a moment brief as the flutter of a butterfly's wings.)

At the time, of course, Darka knew nothing about any bridle, and for that matter neither did anybody else, except for the parents, of course, among whom the news might even have caused a surge of sexual activity: the atmosphere was electrified. All Darka knew was that Effie had been dishonored, irretrievably thrust into some dark nightmare, into a muddy bog suddenly opening where the ground was supposed to be hard and well lit, and Darka's parents loudly complained about the little prostitute and even went in a delegation from the PTA to the school director insisting that Effie be immediately removed from school and that the rest of the children, implicitly tender and pure, be forever segregated from her immoral influence. (What Bolsheviks they in fact were, what monsters, Darka discovers, with cold surprise, twenty-five years after. The entire generation, the Orthodox, the Orwellian newspeakers, and the dissidents, the thinkers, the free thinkers, and the thoughtless, my God!) And she also knew that Effie had betrayed her, this time not childishly, but in fact.

Forever.

Shameful, and frighteningly obscene, and at the same time so unsettlingly grown-up, the head spins: with boys, with the thing that dangles between their legs which just two years ago they'd spied on in gym class, elbowing each other: you can see everything on B! And exactly what was it they saw? With big boys who know everything and therefore do with her who-knows-what and she lets them, the strangers and grown-ups, and they look at her as did Ihor M. It's curious that no images from their own Sapphic games flashed before her, only this: how could she, with strangers? How could she let strangers take off her panties? Never mind what followed, which blurred in her imagination.

But the worst thought was: Effie, what about me? What about me? A mixture of feeling ignored, disrespected, for her gender, her age, and of course for her sex: no matter what, Effie was chosen, this was obvious, chosen by those boys for a different sort of life, while me, I'd metamorphosed in a stroke into one of those comic, clumsy, hunched honors students accompanied everywhere by parents, even to the movies, as though by bodyguards: she didn't let me in, didn't let me touch something essential in her, which means that everything about our friendship was a lie because under the best-lit, most ecstatic explosions of our union, which seemed so transparent, there always hid this gigantic dark cave full of sealed shameful treasures, oh what an idiot I was! And nightly tears into the pillow, deeply buried so her parents wouldn't hear. And therefore, when at the class meeting—as the chairman of the Pioneer unit (Tovarish Chairman—the drumbeat as before an execution, the red flag carried in, red plush with yellow fringes) and as a former friend of Skalkovska's, sure because there was no getting around the need for distance, as she was told by everyone, the vice principal, the class tutor, and all the king's men, otherwise Effie's fall might drag her down so low she could hardly imagine—when she had to announce the Case of Comrade Skalkovska and be the first to speak (and again at first the strange resonance of a voice squeezed by your own throat so you can't swallow, it echoes inside your head, you're constantly aware of the feel of your own head), she turned Effie in in a way no one would ever have imagined, she least of all.

This must have looked like the unbridled attack of a mean little dog, nipping at her ankles, drawing blood, and again, to the meat: Remember! Remember what you said about all the classmates, that they're all narrow-minded nonentities! (Naturally these good-for-nothings closed ranks and Effie wound up completely isolated.) You put yourself above the class! Above the collective! You decided you were better than the others, that you were allowed more than the others were, and look where this has led you—your friends (no: first you gather up the unit, then you speak in its name) are now ashamed of you! And so on, A+ and !!! but alas there's no such grade.

And it was not an excess of administrative zeal (as it might have appeared to a dull outsider), and even less was it a desire to save her own skin (as it might have been appropriate to say had they not been children) but rather an ardent, overwhelming drive to possess Effie, even if for the last time, to have her back, begging forgiveness, repenting her betrayal. (And because Darka didn't have that power over her, she pursued instead the one path offered her by the adult world: Tovarish Chairman of the Unit Council—and the drums beat, oh how they beat, a chill went through her, this shaman's drum and timpani, that's right, all turning points in life should be staged as solemnly as tribal initiations, and what is one's first act of collaboration if not a kind of initiation?) Consequently, Darka's words should have been read like a secret message, revealed in ultraviolet light: Remember! Remember how you said I was your only soul mate, the only one you could talk to. Remember what I said about the Doors as though the doors were really opening, and you immediately understood, those cast-iron doors! Heavy as those at St. Volodymyr's. And I really saw them as that, and I screamed with joy that you, you too—we stood before the doors together, we breathed as one, Effie, why did you slam them in my face?

But Effie-Skalkovska stayed silent. And didn't intend to remember a thing, nor to repent, nor to beg forgiveness.

She didn't even look at Darka—she looked out the window, at the playing field lined with poplars, occasionally biting her lower lip, she cried—and it was clear it was something very personal, something a galaxy away from Darka, her fiery speeches, and this endless meeting.

The doors, which Darka hadn't been asked to enter and tried to break down, remained shut.

Maybe, Darka speculated now, she'd been pregnant? That, thank God, I'll never know. Because you won't find everything out at a reunion over a glass of wine with a semi-stranger whom you can't exactly ask: Listen, remember, then, at the end of sixth grade or at the start of seventh, did you have an abortion?

Now out of this dull, bare plateau which is called experience, Darka could assume something else: namely that Effie with her innate vulnerability was like a package, its contents bubble-wrapped, stamped "Fragile" on all sides in runny ink, and sent on its way, yet without an address, this perfidious, secret, gracious, spoiled, truly vicious and irresistibly attractive, inwardly aflame Effie-Fawn, simply had to find, at an early age, her own way of protecting herself, especially from the suffocating Darka, defending herself with what was most obviously hers, her body. Putting it between herself and the world like a cardboard shield: take it, take it, feel it, you want it?

(I certainly didn't leave her any other options—why should others have?)

For one, two, or three years after that—in seventh, eighth, yes, and ninth grade too, they passed each other like planets on separate orbits, greeting each other with a nod, though for a long time Darka avoided Effie's eyes and was careful not to get stuck alone with her: the awareness of her betrayal, which couldn't be undone, poisoned her, lying somewhere on the bottom like an immovable rock raising up muddy miasmas so that in the upper grades Darka even had fits of nausea, something approaching morning sickness, problems with her gallbladder, and she had to take a spoonful of sunflower oil in the morning and a heating pad for her side—and then she noticed, with embarrassed relief, that when they were in groups Effie began to answer her remarks, calmly, almost warmly. She stopped pretending that Darka didn't exist, so Darka decided finally to risk speaking with her one-on-one, politely and purposefully—what's the big deal, really, let's get over it—asking Skalkvoska when she'd be on class duty, and Skalkovska politely answering it would be Thursday, and so it went, sideways, as between strangers, and by that time they really were strangers to each other, having outgrown their childhood episodes along with the pantyhose and splayed children's shoes, snub-nosed, which get tossed into closets or storage spaces, where they gradually air out the pigeon-toed warmth that once filled them, and all the falls, scratches, and bruises they witnessed, the jump rope, hopscotch, the sand carried into the house (while mother scolded), and, sticky as lacquer (to be pulled off with fingers), traces of jam, and after some years, when you find them again, amid the dust and the cobwebs, you drag them into the light to see they have become old rags.

No, they weren't girls anymore, they were ladies and young women, sighing, well.

Lies, because in fact nothing passes—no matter how deeply you bury it, what happened keeps growing darkly under the skin of years like an indelible bruise, hematoma.

Somehow, the turmoil passed. Maybe some influential parent from the Bad Company managed to turn down the heat or maybe the school wanted to protect its own reputation—the school had a fine one!—and who needs it, the endless meetings, commissions, inspections, good Lord, enough, and so it all dried up. Dried up. For a while Skalkovska suffered her isolation but it too slowly dissolved. Only the teachers, or more precisely the female ones, continued to rage (rumor had it only the gym teacher—a man—tried to defend her at the meeting but it sounded silly, what kind of defense could he mount?), treating her badly, really badly, which she definitely did not deserve, standing straight, expressionless, an honor student to the end, and she was once even sent to the regional academic tournaments, from her English class probably. And yet a teasing, seductive spirit seeped out of her like that slightly nauseatingly sweet, yet barely noticeable (except up close, along with the body's warm smell) and thus all the more lascivious (so they thought) scent of what must have been her mother's perfumes, it tickled their noses, entered their bloodstream, darkened their faces: Skalkovska, leave the room! (Shaking her head like a pony with its new mane, biting her lower lip, whether getting ready to cry or to laugh, concentrating as though she were leaving forever, she would pack her books and notebooks in her bag: a long narrow back with a keyboard of buttons running down it, a short skirt, walking down the aisle between the desks to the door, never turning around: Darka could never keep from staring at her back, as though she were expecting something, but her back was buttoned tight as the door that had just closed quietly behind her, which teachers were eager to take as a provocation, repeating her punishment, again and again: Leave the room, Skalkovska, that'll teach her.)

And in ninth grade, before the end of her last term, she finally did leave for good. And after her, the gym teacher, an Olympic medalist in swimming, a forty-year-old with thick gray hair (why do sportsmen so rarely go bald?), with acidy sweat and hair sticking out of his nostrils, was also let go. It turned out that he and Effie had been carrying on an affair all spring. Someone had seen them.

Heaped in a corner of the girls' gym room, the old mats, rough to the touch as though steeped a long time in brine, and a dry, sunk-in smell, familiar as the odor of old stables, the smell of children's sweat, or not only children's, but also that other, violent and acidy?

All the time, somebody is living your life for you, one of its possible, never-to-be-realized versions. All those feelings that really do bind us to others, from love to envy, grow out of this half-secret longing for other lives intuited, recognized, our lives which we will nevertheless never have. And somebody defends us, something shields us, lives them out for us.

And we sleep without nightmares.

Of course, said Darka's mother, it's all the fault of the parents: one look at Effie's mother tells the whole story. She said this while cutting her nails with a sharp, whipping sound: she was using a tailor's scissors, because they didn't have a manicurist's pair. Her triumphant voice a monument to motherhood, utterly beyond reproach. And something apart from this, which even then forced Darka to get her fur back up, though keeping it to herself: faceless and impersonal, with all the pressure of the ten atmospheres at the bottom of the ocean, the truly terrible eternal righteousness of the community, against all breakers of the rules.

Darka's mother also had her most intense life experience at thirteen. She'd stood at the top of a hill with her sled, red and gasping, awaiting her turn to go down—and suddenly she saw how the snow-covered slope was flowing underfoot in the lilac-colored shadows of the trees: in the sun the snow glimmered with billions of sparks and each one was a planet. The planets burned, shimmered, and as the poet whom she had not yet studied at school said, spun into alignment.

The girl stared while the light grew brighter until she could almost hear the ice tinkling. She didn't know that that sound had once been called the music of the spheres. That this was the voice of the infinite. She knew only that she had to look away otherwise something terrible and irrevocable might happen, otherwise it's all over, I'll go mad! a bolt of black lightning flashed a boundary marker: get back, get back!

And she turned away.

Everything that followed in her life was fine with her: marriage, poverty, children, sickness, work she didn't like, as well as the little joys, like a new apartment or a leather coat. It's true, the leather was only pig-skin, but had been well tanned.

It could have been worse. Much worse.

After all, thinks Darka, going through the outfits hung in her closet: the club jacket will reveal the burn on my forearm, the yellow dress begs a tan and I'm pale as cheese, and so on (it's fine to laugh at yourself, but a reunion is yet another test, this time of your life-in-progress, which hasn't exactly fallen into place perfectly but for that reason you hold your head high, dress to the nines, flawless makeup, silliness, but there it is, and what for, what's the point)—after all, you can't have infinity, can you? Yet that apparently was what Effie wanted—but this second idea, following the first, plays over the surface of her thoughts, never sinking in: Darka sees herself in the mirror holding a hanger from which flows a long silk dress. She wears an unexpectedly stupid, entirely child-like expression: an obvious discovery, you can't have infinity. And all our striving to gather up more: money, men, impressions, diplomas, dresses, cars is nothing but our pitifully meager effort to reach infinity by adding one thing to another and then another. There has to be a better way, but what is it?

At the entrance to the restaurant they were figuring out who wouldn't come, for whom not to wait: Misha Khazin emigrated to America, long ago, back in the early eighties, Kraichyn's in Paris at a conference, Artemchuk is somewhere abroad as well with a sick child—thyroid problems (Chornobyl)—and Soltys, well they'll commemorate him separately, and it would be good to someday take a trip to the cemetery, absolutely (at this moment everyone is confident that someday they'll certainly go)—at Berkivtsi, that unfenced area where row on row of short pillars topped with red stars stand at attention, announcing that they all did their noble international duty in Afghanistan, though they say it's permitted now to put up crosses. That overwhelming feeling at the very first moment—of a group of strangers, unusually silent (everyone overwhelmed by the same feeling perhaps), graying, balding (men) and decked-out (women)—and then at the next moment, as though the film projector has rewound, there begin to emerge from them the figures of children from twenty years ago until the two frames, the past and the present, finally click together and then from their lips come the sincerest of cries: You haven't changed! You too! You haven't changed a bit! (Who but our classmates will give us back those selves that no longer exist—not for anyone, hell, not for anyone? Of course if you don't count your parents, but then, they're parents.) So who else are we waiting for?

Holding before her bent fingers: Khazin, Kraichyn, Artemchuk (the Soltys forefinger remains half bent and uncertain: where should it go?). Hey, look, Sashko Beheria's here too, though he didn't graduate with us—he went to the technical school after eighth grade—at last Darka gets up the nerve, as though she'd just remembered:

And Skalkovska?

You know, what's her name. That's how it comes out. And yet she thinks that for a second everyone falls silent. Meanness is meanness, my dear Darka, and there's no time limit on it.

But no, that's not why. And almost immediately after, Darka realizes that none of them really remember the incident from all those years ago. Nobody remembers Darka's speech at the meeting, and even if they do recall something, nobody gives it the weight it's gathered for her over the years (one may say over her whole life, because she never did anything like it again, maybe cruelty too requires a single vaccination, though vaccinations sometimes also prove deadly). Dear Effie, my beloved golden-legged girl, my lost sister, with an addict's blazing pupils in which tears burn like candles at the impossibility of taking the whole world into herself, or all the men in it, what are they saying about you?

Because they are talking, with increasing liveliness, the ice of estrangement melted by the insatiable human craving for sensational stories: You're kidding! No! Really? Starting with a plane crash that leaves two hundred dead preferably with a list of passengers along with their ages (taking special note of the couple with an infant who were going to show him off to his grandparents) to all the mighty who have fallen and now allow us to pity them: presidents caught with their pants down before the entire planet, bankrupt oil magnates, pop stars busted for drugs, and the one who yesterday was crowned the king of the Jews and who today appeared weaker than the weakest of us, thereby revealing how he'd cheated us and so we with all due rage shout: Crucify him, asking for revenge for yesterday's humiliation.

They're talking, or rather it's a little plump brunette with a dark mossy mustache talking, who turns out to be Marina Weissberg, while around her the others have gathered with their What? Really? And then?

Last summer, by accident, on the street, I didn't recognize her. She says, Effie, that you now weigh about a hundred and ninety pounds, huge, a barrel, because they gave you insulin when you needed lithium—but lithium also adds weight, one of the boys, now a chemical engineer, says authoritatively, while another, a doctor, though not a psychiatrist, in the same professional tone, interrupts him (oh, men, how hard you work to earn your self-respect from us!), taking an interest in the diagnosis: If it's lithium, then it's manic-depression, and that's that, you can't cure it, you spend your life on medication, Oh my, coo the girls, a gust of self-satisfaction (or does Darka imagine it) wafts through them, the whisper of wind in the treetops, then gone—but does Marinka know the diagnosis? Did she tell her why? She told her she'd had a miscarriage after which her husband left her, they'd just come back from vacation, from where, from Switzerland (another round of leaf rustling, this time sharper-edged, and Darka sees a few suppressed sarcastic smiles), where she swam under a sign saying Polluted Water where she caught something, some infection probably from that.

The pseudo psychiatrist, alias Vovka Lasota (former nickname: Bucks, who knows why, but nicknames no longer apply), now claims the stage (one of two: either a really good doctor, or this is his only way of asserting himself because there are no salaries being paid and his wife at home nags endlessly) and again, from on high, he declares (for which Darka quietly begins to loathe him) that mental illness doesn't necessarily depend on specific causes, they, that is, not the rest of us, the ones separated from us with a high wrought iron fence, are always seeking a cause, often making it up, and they're good at it (but you, Darka sends him angry pulses, of all people should know that that fence is no boundary, that tomorrow you too might appear on the other side in a washed-out dark blue robe like a sailor and even more washed-out pants with food in aluminum bowls and a dazed, drug-induced gaze, don't you know?). And if it's really serious manic depression, the guy blathers on (and in his voice evidence of a certain skepticism about the diagnosis, as though to say, I'm not sure, of course, I haven't seen it myself), if that's the case, then it's not psychosomatic, it's organic, like schizophrenia or petit mal epilepsy (in a minute he'll rehearse everything he's learned at the institute, a real boy, what, he isn't married, where's his wedding ring, how is it possible such a catch is still available?). In such cases, the etiology isn't clear, the disease surfaces only later, usually after thirty (once more the female rustling, bees, on and on). You go on and on and never even taste it, Darka says aloud, trying to derail the conversation, and the conversation turns, your school-girl authority hasn't faded, immediately defrosts your present appearance into your former self, but the tracks turn unexpectedly: You know, says one of the girls, it's a nightmare, of course, it's awful, but she, Skalkovska was always, well, weird, wasn't she? Everybody nods in agreement, gathering together defensively, hastily erecting between themselves and Skalkovksa that wrought iron fence with the sharpened pickets at the top, hammering them in one by one, as though it might really protect them from something: someone with servile readiness remembers the time she danced a rumba on the chemistry table, *Girl on a Ball*, of course, she took ballet lessons, and at that moment everyone was going crazy until the vice principal walked in, but there was something in that dancing, the far-sighted sage had already noted it.

Then you should have said something then, why did you keep it to yourself all this time, Darka grins through her teeth, You might have saved her life.

They fall silent and embarrassed. They are in general not bad people. We are all of us not bad people. And yet why is it that, no matter what we turn to, it all goes so bad? Marinka comes to the rescue: it turns out it's not the end of the story because she then invited Skalkovska over, it was nearby, they'd just moved uptown, finally leaving her parents, and it worked out very fine, they now have a two-bedroom apartment on Mykilsko-Botanical Street with windows on the garden, the subject is a live one and everyone has something to say, especially the girls who immediately take a warrior's interest in the details of the trade-up: what kind of apartments did they leave, from what neighborhoods, how much more was it, Marinka is puffed out with the pride of responsibility, she promises a few interested parties her top-notch real estate agent's phone number, Tell him Marina and Vadik sent you.

So that's it, Vadik's the husband, and this fine upstanding Jewish husband, can you imagine, Effie tried to seduce when Marina, a good-hearted soul, went out to get a snack, leaving them alone. He told me later, I literally didn't know where to hide.

Literally. Nymphomania, Vovka Lasota confirms the new diagnosis—and why nymphomania, Darka wants to object, why not the hysteria of an abandoned woman, and, quite possibly, an easy one to get, with that instantly recognizable defenseless fragility of hers, which not even two hundred pounds can hide, and which for many, and above all for men, is balm for all their wounds at once, so that our upstanding husband may not be the innocent sheep that he claimed to be. Marinka convinced herself, though—and what other choice did she have. And what's left for Darka but to force out what she intends to be a caustic remark but which instead comes out mumbled and pathetic: Isn't it nice for medics, they have a diagnosis for everything, and here, have some pills.

In response Vovka Lasota winces and asks her not to refer to him as a medic since he is neither a male nurse nor an orderly but a doctor, and the head of his department, and as a matter of fact he specialized in gynecology and so if she wants he can leave her his number. Thanks, laughs Darka, and it comes out in a bass, otherwise her voice would have betrayed her, So far, God has been good.

Meanwhile the crowd has begun moving to the tables which glimmer from afar with coquettish kitschy bouquets of white napkins blooming from the glasses, why the hell did I come here, and what am I to do here, God, what emptiness—get drunk, maybe?

Vovka Lasota sees Darka home. In the taxi she notices that his Chekhovian beard smells of cologne, Givenchy she thinks. He kisses her under her dress strap, mutters something about his divorce, Darka says please shut up and wants to add or I'll scream, it's the last thing she needs at this moment, male confessions, but she decides to leave such a complex sentence for better days, focusing herself instead on getting the key in the lock, which she manages on the third try. The worst thing is that she remembers everything, even more clearly than before: instead of drowning in the drink, it all rose to the surface and swirled through her mind, horrible. Lasota meanwhile has turned into a hot bumblebee and buzzes in her ear how from eighth grade on he was afraid to approach her, attacks her from all sides with his heavy breathing and the pressure of a strange body under the bulging, already superfluous dress, and okay, actually not okay, and it won't save you from anything, and she can't even focus, but she'll try, she'll try, why not—the dress strap pops and the thing drops to the floor, and when he enters her with a groan, and the familiar inner warmth awakens the stilled bodily memory which grows instantly louder than everything else, she surrenders herself gladly, out of genuine gratitude to Lasota for this brief respite which he naturally takes as a sign of his own male irresistibility and so encouraged, he does it well, yes, quite well, and hey look, it's getting really good oh, oh God, oh, and then she lies like a stone with her face buried in his shoulder and he asks her, leaning over in a voice deep with emotion until she feels ashamed for her absolute lack of responsiveness:

You knew that I loved you?

It looks like he also needed revenge. Isn't it convenient. Men, oh yeah. How all of them are one-dimensional, linear, like a simple arithmetic (x:y=z; z+a=b). Slipping into sleep, as consciousness loosens its bulldog grip, she remembers how Lasota, who himself was not the worst of students, once asked timidly for her help in math—the only time she might have discerned his wish to be alone with her, and with this pleasant thought, or rather, using it to squash, like a beetle under a saucer, a different thought, the dark and formless one, for which she has no more strength, Darka finally falls asleep.

She awakens as though pushed and pops out of bed, where, shamelessly, as though he belonged there, lies a loud, breathing, snorting man, along with all the bed smells of a stranger. What was it, a fit of nausea? Sour mouth, room dark, in the window a lone streetlamp burns, what time is it? She's prodded by some internal, physiological fear but her foot gets caught in a cold pool of silk, her crumpled dress on the ground, her best one, she picks it up, straightens it, tosses it in the direction of a chair (it rustles, landing), God it's cold, she's trembling, her teeth chatter, goose bumps on her forearms, feeling like scattered grains, yes, she fell asleep naked but that's not why she's cold, could it be the alcohol, it's bad—she wraps herself in her husband's robe (when will that idiot finally get his things?), she stumbles, blind and shaking, toward the kitchen where the digital clock says 3:30, holy shit, and she drops herself down the edge of the seat carefully as though she were made of glass, trying to breathe evenly one two three inhale one two three exhale, a meditation session, almost fucking yoga, ah, okay, now she can put on the kettle, a few familiar stabilizing gestures, and the blue flame flickers peacefully below, very touching. No, it wasn't her teeth that were chattering, that was something rising from within, with the rhythm of castanets, this line of poetry, which repeats itself mechanically as though the needle were stuck: So long had life together been—Brodsky, stupid verse, stupid as green firewood and crackling just the same, and yet it stuck—and suddenly, hands leaning on the oven, Darka starts to cry, the sob coming not from her throat but from her belly, like a groan, and she again has to hold her breath one two three so that she does not shatter: why, why, what is all this for, this fucking life, my God? And it's no longer clear whose life she's talking about, if only she could somehow learn to stand this terrible unfairness, somehow digest this burden of injustice, this eternal human scream to heaven: My God, for what? And this grief, live and burning, for all those things we did not become and never will become.

Blotting her eyes with her fingers, she reaches for the cigarettes on the table, strikes a match, and standing there in the kitchen with a cigarette in hand she seems to herself larger than the darkness. Okay, let's sum up, and what have we got? Some reputation in her field, some financial independence, provided such a thing is at all possible under our circumstances, and two published books, one of them based on her thesis, and one textbook for the university, and two divorces, and honorary membership in three Western academies, which is worth exactly shit but will do for an obituary. E la nave va. The show must go on.

Why the hell, of the two of us, did I have to be the survivor?

And here this disgust with herself, this nausea, the toxicity of the self—the eighth grade, the gallbladder, a spoonful of sunflower oil, yes, then, just like now, in a lightning flash changes direction, and Darka is at last rattled to the core, she is turned inside out like a sock, her stomach in her throat, she barely makes it to the bathroom and there, leaning against the cold tiles above the toilet, with more and more tremors, doubling from a silent cry, half falling in a cold sweat, no longer a human figure, mere intestines pumping backward, she throws up last night's dinner, and herself at the dinner, and the night with Vovka Lasota, dose after dose, brown sharp-sour-stink-kasha, all of life's undigested garbage spilling over the top, how does it all fit inside us, the decomposing corpse of her last marriage, all the scandals and humiliating accounts, all the pent-up hatred for the world and herself, hot burning spray of bits through her mouth and nose, she tries to take a breath between fits of heaving, her knees shake as she bends, that's right, that's right, that's how it should be done, to the bottom, to the scraped-out dregs, to childhood, to those first jealousies and first foul things, to become sterile, pure, and immovable, like the white tiles which hurt the eyes in the light, because nothing either very beautiful or very terrible, nothing like this ever happens to us, you poor child, and you would still have to work really hard to get either one of the two—and here again Effie made it, it came out as she predicted—while normal life just rushes through us with this jiggly, thick brown stream, just look how it glistens in the toilet, even the walls are brown, and the flushed water roars like Niagara, and the otherworldly cold because your whole life has been cast out of you, and you are standing in the bathroom like a Jew in a gas chamber, leaning against the tiles, struck by tears and your own shit, with bluing fingertips, empty, empty as after an abortion, and those you loved have been flushed out of you down, down the sewer pipes.

≈

Later she takes a long time washing, brushing her teeth (three times in a row because the odor seems permanent), and when she steps out of the bath it's starting to turn gray outside. Vovka Lasota lies in her bed with his head wrapped in the sheets like the corpse of a Bedouin ready for burial, and just like the dead Bedouin, he has nowhere to go (sure, divorce isn't easy on anyone, especially on men who soon seem like abandoned dogs who'll lick anyone, seeking a master). With Darka's appearance the corpse shows some signs of life: he pulls his head out of the sheets and smiles, somewhat like a victorious man after a successful night, and somewhat like that boy who approached Darka during recess and, looking past her, ears red, asked her to help him after school with this math homework.

Which, in fact, she never did.

And only now does Darka understand that she can't tell him to get out. At least, not right away. She can't turn on anyone the terrible megaton gush of the uncovered, naked, nothing could be more naked, and merciless because indifferent to the human, essence of life, the stream which, breaking through, flushes out adolescence, childhood, whatever scrap of warmth we've managed to collect around us over the course of our lives, leaving a person face-to-face with things as they are. And no human can be left there like that, alone with things as they are. Nobody deserves that.

For this insight she is grateful to Effie. For at least this.

"Get up," Darka says to Vovka Lasota, in the most casual voice on earth. "Let's get some breakfast."

OLEG SENTSOV

GRANDMA

translated from the Russian by Uilleam Blacker

I HAD A GRANDMOTHER AND I didn't like her. It happens.

≈

It also might happen that you're born a woman, you live in a small village, you work your whole life, of your four children only one survives, your husband eventually leaves you for another woman, and you're left alone. Okay, not entirely alone—with a child. The child then grows up, goes off to study, then to the army, then gets married, and goes to live far away and forever. And then you're left entirely alone. I can't imagine how all this would feel, and I don't want to.

≈

Your son visits very rarely, brings a grandson or granddaughter. But their visits are short and reluctant. Then you hit seventy, your son comes to visit for the last time, you sell the old wooden house and move in with him, into a stone house far away. Apart from your son, your grandson, your granddaughter, and your son's wife live there.

They're not pleased to have you. They're not mean to you, they put up with you, it's called "caring for an elderly parent."

The room is separate and new, but the things in it are all old, from the wooden house. The room quickly absorbs the smell of old age. They bring you your pension on time, nobody wants to take it away from you, they never even ask, and you can spend it however you like. How you like is usually on grocery shopping, sometimes you give some to your son's wife—there's never enough money in any family and this family is no exception. The rest goes into your savings account, like it should. You do it, the family you live with does it. That's the best way, it's safer.

Every other day they bring you newspapers, you can read them. Sometimes they invite you to come and watch television in the living room. They make food for you regularly. On Saturday, they go to the bathhouse and "do you need anything washed?" In the evening you can pray, kneeling in your old nightgown. At night, you urinate into a one-liter jar—it's too cold and dark to go to the outside toilet. You can also write letters to grandmas just like you who live far away and sometimes get replies. As the years pass, the letters are sent and received less and less frequently.

All of these activities take up most of your time. The rest of the time you can sit in your room and look out the window. You can see everything: who comes, who goes, who came through the gate from that direction, who left in that direction, who walked along the street, who drove. True, you can't see the street so well, you have a better view of the gate, but the window is big, with curtains. You can hide behind them sometimes, so nobody can see that you're watching everybody.

≈

Twelve years passed like that. Twelve years . . . For twelve years my grandmother and I lived in the same house. What did I know about her? Nothing. What did she know about me? Even less. Did we speak to each other? Yes. About what? Nothing. She'd pester me with her old-folks' conversations, but I wasn't interested in them and I'd try to avoid them, or I'd just leave the room. She wasn't very smart, a bit unpleasant, quite fat and old, and I didn't love her. Did she love me? I don't know. I didn't think about it then, I was young, skinny, sometimes smart, and reasonably polite, so I wasn't mean to her and I put up with her. And secretly made fun of her. Everybody in our family made fun of her, and we often got annoyed with her, for a good reason or otherwise. She didn't exactly suffer with us, but she wasn't happy either.

≈

Her granddaughter got married and moved out and soon had a baby, her great-grandchild. Her granddaughter and her husband lived nearby and came round often with the baby in the stroller. The child was still very small and so was always sleeping, but grandma still carried her stool out of her room and put it down next to the stroller. This was called "caring for the grandchildren." Then the child got bigger, and her son's wife began to look after him—they joked about her new status and now started calling her grandma. And the old grandma was no longer entrusted with her great-grandchild. They didn't entrust her with much in that house, in case she did something wrong and upset her son's wife. Nevertheless, grandma always managed to do something or other, and do it wrong, of course, and of course it upset her son's wife.

Every evening they'd have a conversation about washing up that was so well worn it had practically become a ritual:

"Liusia, leave those, I'll wash up."

"I'll do it, there's nothing to wash."

And so it was every evening, every day, and in everything—quiet, wordless resentment and putting-up-with instead of respect and tolerance. But grandma didn't get offended. She grew up and lived her whole life in a village, read with difficulty, was simple, not too smart, a bit fat and old, and on top of that she was going deaf. Grandma was in good health, she was almost never ill, though she complained about her health a lot, especially about her heart, but nobody really worried about that too much.

And then one quiet summer's day her son died, and she sat on the bench in the garden of the stone house and cried, her eyes were red, and she kept clapping her hands on her lap. People came in the evening, lots of them, and comforted her. They comforted the whole family, including grandma, and she liked it that they were paying attention to her.

≈

But life went on anyway. It didn't finish. Life never finishes, even if someone leaves it. Grandma started to forget things more—names and dates, the kettle on the stove, the tap or the gas. She didn't get ill more often, but she felt worse, she aged even more and started causing even more problems. Her grandson had long ago moved to the city, her great-grandson had grown up and was going to school, he was the least interested of all of them in grandma's business. She lived alone, or rather, with her son's wife, and she was already well past eighty. Her son's wife was also aging and getting ill, and she was finding it harder and less convenient to look after this superfluous and unloved person. A few more years passed like this, and the last one was full of phrases like: "She's no one to me now . . . I can't look after her anymore . . . She'll be better off there . . . My friend works there, it's a good place . . ."

There was no meeting and no vote, just silent consent. One day they gathered grandma and her things together and loaded them into a car. They said they were taking her to the hospital, which pleased grandma—she was already pretty far gone by then—and they took her to the old people's home. They sent her pension there, gave them her documents, and that was it, grandma was gone.

I lived in the city where the old people's home was. I had already started a family, had kids. I rarely thought about my grandma, never asked about her, and never wanted to see her. It was shameful and unpleasant. I didn't love her, she was old, a bit unpleasant, fat, and not too smart. I tried not to think about her and almost forgot about her. My mom visited her infrequently at first, and then stopped completely. She was no longer young herself now, she was old; and she was no longer healthy, but sick.

We didn't speak any more about grandma in our family. A few years passed and one day someone said she had died. Who said it and to whom weren't exactly clear, but nobody really wanted to figure out what had happened, and somehow we just carried on living. And then a few more years passed and one day out of the blue we got a call from the old people's home saying that grandma had died a long time ago and asking if the relatives were going to bury her. The relatives answered that yes, they would, although they thought they'd been told that . . . Well, it doesn't matter, we'll get to that bit soon. The grandchildren went to get their grandmother from the old people's home. As soon as she saw the nurses drinking tea and eating chocolates in the staff room, the grand-daughter put on a mournful face and gave them our name and the reason we were there. The grandson went to the morgue to identify the body. They rolled her out on a trolley. She was lying on her side, very old, curled up and dried out. The grandson didn't recognize his grandmother, he recognized only the clothes. But he didn't say anything and helped the nurse move the very light body into the coffin. They nailed the lid on immediately. A hearse in the shape of a yellow bus with a black stripe down the side took grandma back to the village, to the earth, to her son. The grandson held on to the coffin so it didn't rattle around too much on the bus. The driver was in a rush, they dug the grave quickly, there was no one around, it was a gloomy November day.

~

I have another grandmother. She lives far, far away and is very, very old. I see her very rarely, but I at least I see her, and I love her. She is old and capricious, but she's cheerful and kind. She's very small and thin. She is really old now, and really ill, she's not all there and causes a lot of problems. She lives with her daughter, that is, my aunt. My aunt is also old now, not young anymore, and sick, not healthy. They constantly argue. This is called "caring for grandma." Grandma's daughter's daughter also lives with them, in other words, her granddaughter. This is called "looking after the grandchild." This is how they live together: the old, the very old, and the young.

My grandfather I saw only once. And the other grandfather I also saw only once, but that was in a photograph, but maybe it wasn't him, I'm not sure. Also, it's easy to love the person who is far away, but hard to love the person who is nearby. It's also easy to write about all this, but hard to do anything about it. Especially now.

NATALKA SNIADANKO

WHEN TO START, WHAT NOT TO PAY ATTENTION TO, OR HOW TO FALL IN LOVE WITH GEORGE MICHAEL

translated from the Ukrainian by Jennifer Croft

TOLIA WAS THE TALLEST, FATTEST, CURLIEST-headed kid in the whole class. That his school uniform rode up his rotund little stomach and that he couldn't quite button up his jacket and that his mom made him put on knee socks instead of normal socks in the summer and warm woolen long johns that his grandma made him in the winter were sources of perpetual shame for Tolia. I sympathized with him, because my mom, too, made me wear a lengthy pair of granny panties made of thick wool called—for reasons unbeknownst to me—"reformers," which would sometimes stick out from beneath short skirts, or anyway so it seemed to me at the time. Just that awareness—that you had something that hideous on—would be enough to ruin anybody's life. I don't know what Tolia did with his long johns, but starting around sixth grade I would take my underwear off at the base of the stairwell of our apartment building, stuff them into the mailbox, and then extract them again coming home from school. At least until my mom came home from work early one day and found my "reformers" next to her *Science and Life Magazine.*

Tolia was easy to embarrass in general and would blush every time our math teacher would call him up to the board. During recess, while all the other boys were scampering outside to play ball or hopscotch or leapfrog, Tolia would find a little nook where no one would see him and remove from some secret jacket pocket the slender forest-green booklet he would read all recess, in secret, it not being the type of thing to especially impress his classmates. Tolia would usually go to the top floor of the school because it was always deserted and quiet in the corner by the physics lab: the physics teacher felt recesses were not for pupils to run wild and make a racket but rather for teachers to rest and ready themselves for the next class.

And so it was that she would make absolutely sure that nobody jumped rope or played truth or dare, let alone leapfrog, anywhere near her office. Anyone that sullied the sanctity of that spot was risking considerable unpleasantness; this having already been confirmed by several students, everybody avoided her office and its environs like the plague.

But back in first grade neither Tolia nor I could have known about any of that: we hadn't taken physics yet; we didn't even have classes in multiple classrooms like the older kids. We had all of them in the same "Starter Classroom" in the opposite wing. Out of our whole grade it was only Tolia and I that conducted expeditions to the wing with the physics lab, both of us with a slender forest-green booklet that actually turned out to be the same book in the end, namely *Cosette*—a selection from the novel by Victor Hugo—which I was ultimately able to recognize from a distance thanks to the standard Soviet cover that still graced the bulk of the books in our parents' libraries back then, when you could still get paid for recycling them afterward.

I don't know why Tolia and I both happened upon that particular book for our secret recess reading. It now occurs to me that there was little childhood romanticism in it and more just that that book of Hugo's was the littlest and lightest and—of course!—the easiest to smuggle around under a school uniform. Then, though, that coincidence struck me as enigmatic, mysterious—a secret message.

Tolia had been the first one in our grade that had learned how to read, and he always got As in writing. He wasn't a geek, per se, and his preference for the humanities was strong, but the other kids made fun of him nonetheless, as mercilessly as if he were already on the math team. They never even took him with them when they went to watch the older kids play soccer.

At the end of first grade, Tolia's mom had a talk with the principal, and Tolia skipped second grade so as to not stand out too much now that his peers were shorter and petiter than him. He made up the materials over summer vacation. His parents worked with my parents, and sometimes they would all come over; once we even went on a trip together.

As was in fashion back then, we drove down to Odesa and stayed in a cheap place near the city. The whole way Tolia tried to get me to play chess with him, or checkers, or to talk to him about books. We had such bad carsickness, though, that our parents had to pull over every half hour so our moms could take us by turn out along the side of the road, where with the good influence of the fresh air we would deposit the contents of our stomachs. We would then get back in the car clutching plastic bags in case next time we couldn't stop soon enough. It must have been that that kept us from coming up with mutually stimulating topics for discussion; our friendship failed to flourish over the course of the trip. Tolia did try talking me into badminton, but because I could still remember the details of the voyage and the fact that Tolia just about barfed all over my skirt and would have had I not leaped out of the car with a brimming bag in my hands, I refused.

Besides which I disliked intensely the green polka-dot underwear Tolia's mom put on him in lieu of swimming trunks, besides which there was the matter of Tolia's rotund stomach lolling over the waist of his green polka-dot underwear. Add to which barely had we crossed the threshold of the dining hall when Tolia would be held up as an example for me to follow.

"Look," my mother began and finished every meal, "Tolia finished ages ago, and you're still sitting there pondering your plate."

Equaling Tolia, who with an expression of bliss would in ninety-degree heat devour several servings of pasta salad with warm dried-pear compote and then, while taking a walk on the beach, jam into his mouth the four pieces of bread with butter they gave out at breakfast to accompany the tea, was absolutely impossible.

Basically, Tolia did not arouse in me even the slightest sympathy nor friendly interest, even though there was no one else our age in the whole hotel.

Even by the time I was bored out of my mind I didn't give in, and instead of going to Tolia I began to read the *Science and Life Magazine* my parents packed at the last minute—my mom having brought nothing else to read, so as to prevent me from "wrecking my eyes." The optometrist had recently recommended a break from reading so that I wouldn't have to wear glasses.

It was with unusual frequency, then, that I read the article dedicated to the latest discovery in the field of chemical crystallography, perhaps because the issue began with it. When for the umpteenth time my parents tried to force-feed me a piece of meat, and I discovered I couldn't take it anymore, I wound up reciting the following:

"A central place in the study of mineral evolution in heterogeneous mountain geological formations ought to be occupied by geocrystallography, as a new branch of traditional crystallography; a sizeable role ought also to be given geocrystallography in the exploration of defined-property fluid synthesis from a crystal-energy perspective, as well as research in isomorphism and polymorphism utilizing x-ray diffraction, electron diffraction, and neutron diffraction, as much for chemical properties as for the entire aggregate of physical properties. And you all are busy with your same stupid nonsense."

I then exhaled victoriously, drank the rest of my compote, and left my stunned parents to keep watching Tolia finish his meat and kasha.

Tolia was within earshot of the grand finale of my monologue: he had actually just finished his lunch and was walking by our table with his mom when I delivered it. After that my parents hid *Science and Life Magazine* somewhere, and Tolia never asked me to play badminton with him again.

Much later it occurred to me to regret my youthful arrogance, when in the eighth grade I realized that, for the first time in my life, I had fallen in love.

Michael Jackson, Poetry, and Gracious May

Actually May that year was particularly ungracious to the female half of our grade. A particular type of epidemic had struck, and there were three subtypes of sick: the first kind was head-over-heels in love with Michael Jackson, the second with George Michael, and the last—and least numerous—with the then-popular band Gracious May. It was unclear which among us were the worst off.

Symptoms of the illness, independently of whom it had befallen, were always identical. Every single one of them—even the biggest dorks we had—suddenly raised the hems of their school uniforms, stopped wearing the required ribbons in their hair (sky-blue on weekdays, snow-white on Sundays), pilfered their mothers' heels, and ignoring the various inconveniences of them not fitting at all attempted to wear them after school and then at school.

The next stage of the illness was characterized by the painting of fingernails in the unlikeliest of shades as well the application of artificial eyelashes, the meticulous plucking of eyebrows, and the application of considerable amounts of other cosmetics, to the point that periodically some girl would even wear bright red lipstick. That was what it was like at school.

After school the makeup got considerably more intense. Everybody looked like somebody out of a James Fenimore Cooper novel. Skirts were peculiarly abbreviated, and sometimes you couldn't see them at all from underneath a jacket, even if you were looking hard. Add to that the perfumes our moms had, only in greater quantities, and our very first cigarettes at our buildings' entrances.

The most advanced phase was walls covered in the posters that came with *Peer*, a kind of *Seventeen* magazine that we all read religiously, private collections of photographs from other sources, and still more radical changes in outward appearance. This last symptom depended upon the type of illness.

The friends I had that were amassing Michael Jackson memorabilia ordinarily dyed their hair black and used mass quantities of henna. The George Michael girls focused less on hairstyle and more on owning as many black turtlenecks, jeans, and jackets as they possibly could. They would just wear their hair gently combed; they would also wear several earrings in each ear.

Those devoted to the oeuvre of Gracious May didn't pay even the slightest attention to outward appearances, taking a page from their idols' book, not to mention the fact that their parents were generally less well-off than those of the girls that were in love with "Western pop stars." Physical symptoms, then, were less evident; the less observant might take them for totally normal teenagers.

Nor was I immune, although the epidemic cropped up in me only after everyone else was already violently ill. Plus it did not happen how I wanted it to. I had already begun to worry about whether or not I waſ going to actually undergo the process of sexual maturation properly— if I underwent it at all.

This is why every morning I would run into the bathroom when I woke up and examine the posters of Michael Jackson and George Michael I had carefully cut out of *Peer*, as well as the little black-and-white picture of Gracious May. Here, inspecting each of the men in turn, I would try to detect my heart skipping beats at the sight of any of them.

Ashamed of my belated development, I would try to artificially stimulate the process of falling in love and think intensively about each of the potential candidates for object of my affection. At first I consoled myself by thinking you probably had to get used to the way your crush looks before you designate him as such. Then I tried going into the bathroom twice, once before and once after breakfast, figuring probably love arises slower on an empty stomach than it does when you're full. After a week I took up regular visits, on the half hour, which only ended up making my mom inquire as to the state of my stomach; she force-fed me two pills of something. And my heart kept beating the best at breakfast and not while I was gazing at any of the objects of my girlfriends' ardent desires.

The situation became critical when one day in the cafeteria I happened to glance at Tolia. My heart began to pound with the intensity of someone who has just run multiple meters to catch a tram. I refused to believe this was actually happening to me. I took a close look at my old classmate, who had just wolfed down a third helping of wieners and mashed potatoes. But the more ardently he shoveled in the sauerkraut, which was dangling down his chin, the closer I wanted to watch him.

As we'd grown up, Tolia had indeed grown, but he hadn't really changed. He was still the tallest kid in the class, his school uniform was still riding up his rotund little belly, he would still run to the cafeteria every chance he got, and he still never played soccer. He still took a book (Sir Walter Scott's *Quentin Durward*) with him everywhere he went, including to the cafeteria; he now made no attempt to conceal this from anyone. He spent every free second reading, even the time he was waiting for the hall monitors to deliver his tray of plates heaped with steaming wieners and potatoes. He didn't even notice that the kids sitting with him were using that same waiting period to bang their elbows on the table in an attempt to eject the last kid sitting on the bench from said bench, nor did he notice their mad cackling whenever they succeeded in doing so. No one dared pick on Tolia, no doubt due to his powerful build: if he were to exert himself even a little, he would be able to knock them all off the bench with the whack of a single elbow.

I was reading *Quentin* myself at this stage, albeit at home and in secret, firstly because the doctor had forbidden me reading yet again, and secondly because the book was too heavy to drag to school along with all my textbooks. And this coincidence, which then seemed to me to be mysteriously significant, made my heart pound even harder.

I was in over my head. My situation had no actual exit. Up until then I had been ashamed of my overdue adolescence, and when my friends had asked solicitously, "So? Which one do you like?" (the results of my attempts to fall in love with one of the pop stars being tracked tensely by the whole female half of Grade 8A), I would avert my eyes and wind up having to admit that I didn't like any of them. I was risking the last shreds of my authority at that school and might have been considered underdeveloped. Things, however, had gone from bad to worse. Settling upon Tolia as my love object was like signing my own death warrant. None of my friends would be in a position to understand it. Such a blatant lack of aesthetic values—of good taste—such absolute incomprehension of the essence of masculine beauty, such an absence of enthusiasm for muscles, for the very symbol of masculinity, sheathed in tight spandex swimsuits, of their trembling, breaking voices, suggestive of a subtle eroticism I just didn't get. I couldn't even appreciate a great haircut or a wide array of earrings. And so it was that I had sealed my fate as a deserter. All the girls were doing the same thing, and yet I had been unable to pull it off, even out of feminine solidarity.

The object of my affections looked more like he had spent the last few decades working himself to death as a CEO: it was clear that not one of his muscles had ever even heard of exercise equipment, let alone free weights.

This was the absolute worst-case scenario. It had become apparent that this wasn't just overdue adolescence. This was something pathological. Although it was tricky, I could in fact imagine myself confessing to my best friend the fact of my indifference to Michael Jackson, but to tell her (even having sworn her to secrecy) that I was in love with Tolia would be unthinkable.

First of all, the whole school would find out about it immediately, because what friend would be able to keep something so sensational to herself? Secondly and worst of all, Tolia might find out. Which I would never survive.

The only reasonable way out was suicide. Before I decided to do so, however, I thought I might just pour my suffering out onto paper. My first work was titled "For You."

My heart in gloom
Rain down the window in my room
I'm not going to tell you
I am crying for you
The moon is shining bright
But all the same it's night
You are a glorious sight
I am so sad

Despite my doubts about whether the word "glorious" really suited Tolia, I really liked how the poem turned out, and I decided I'd wait on the suicide so as not to deprive mankind of my immortal works. The next poem was penned that very night and bore the title "Of You."

I'll be thinking of you
I'll always be true
As a woman damned
For this my yearning
You don't even know
You suffer nothing
But I suffer everything
I'm not the same

Without a doubt, this marked poetic progress. "I'll always be true / As a woman damned," that was really something. Only such a rich poetic image could do justice to the conflicting emotions that came with first love. Short, powerful, cruel. Reminiscent of Ukrainian writer Vasyl Stefanyk. I was unlucky in love, but maybe, just maybe, I would go down in history as a poet, and by breakfast the next morning I had already written "From You."

But for you I'm blind
The world is so unkind
And live I cannot
Without you now
What the future holds
No one can know
Yet this heart cannot
Be taken away from you

There was a hint of folk-song lyricism in this, and even if it wasn't overly original, then at least it was abundantly sincere, and if you looked hard enough, you might just see a certain flair for style. I was extremely pleased with myself. I copied all three poems out into a special note-book, which I titled *You.*

Over the course of the next few days I filled up an entire pad of graph paper with my poetry, and then another one, until I realized I needed to put together a larger notebook more befitting of my feelings. My work from that period was characterized by a certain stylistic unity, as evidenced by the titles themselves: after the *You* cycle I'd written a collection of five sonnets called *Me,* and then an epic poem called "You and Me," until ultimately and upon my third sleepless night I had come up with such a sum of poems as to require compilation in volume form in said proper notebook. I titled it *About Us,* at which point I felt I had exhausted the prepositional as well as pronominal possibilities of the Ukrainian language. Their extensive use in that first volume ought to interest, if not literary critics, then at least linguists. If they study "The Role of Exclamatory Particles in the Late Works of Nineteenth-Century Ukrainian Philologist Panteleimon 'Panko' Kulish," why would some-one not write their dissertation "On the Interaction of Prepositions and Personal Pronouns in the Early Work of Olesia Pidobidko?"

*Literature in Notebooks and Literature in Life: Mysteries
  of the Male Soul*

The days passed, my feelings increased, and humble nighttime scrib-
blings no longer satisfied me. I'd composed multiple notebooks of con-
fessional verse, and yet what had any of this changed? I longed to share
my feelings with someone, most of all with Tolia so as to get some idea
of whether or not I could count on his returning them. The only advantage I had over my girlfriends was that no matter how much less they
were currently suffering, they would never have any hope of reciprocity.

On the other hand, Tolia's behavior had not changed at all despite
having recently become the center of the universe. Either he was con-
cealing his feelings as diligently as I was, or he felt nothing.

I tried to tell myself that fate could not possibly be so cruel as for
the latter to be the case, but still I wondered, and with each passing day
my desire to find out for sure increased.

I ruminated long and hard as to how to do so, until finally I discovered a way.

Over the course of the subsequent sleepless night I translated
Tatyana's letter to Yevgeny Onegin—the classic declaration of feminine ardor—from Pushkin's Russian into my own Ukrainian and determined to slip this very missive into Tolia's jacket.

The letter begins, "I love you, Sir—what more do you need?" and
ends with "I'm stopping, it hurts to read it." Afterward I put in a little
P.S. that told Tolia to put his response in the pocket of his jacket, which
he would hang in the coatroom on the third bar on the second hanger
from the right and not request a rendezvous nor ask anything else of
me. I signed the letter "Mrs. X" and addressed it to "Mr. Y."

Several feverish days passed with my checking the coatroom
repeatedly and always expecting but never actually finding Tolia's jacket
in the agreed-upon spot. A week passed, and then a second, and Tolia

was still taking his jacket off same as before. His pockets were empty. I had been concerned that Tolia had mixed up the instructions and put his response in his pocket but hung the jacket up in its old place, so naturally I had had to check.

So passed two feverish weeks, with me frantically searching my would-be mailbox and the hall monitors giving me funny looks all the while, no doubt elaborating their own theories as to my motivation for digging around in other people's pockets.

After two weeks I couldn't take it anymore. In my next Tolia letter, I abstained from poetic expressions of my feelings and reported everything in my own words, trying to be as clear and straightforward as possible. I was aiming for maximum sincerity so as to make the best possible impression upon Tolia and convince him that I was deserving of his love. The result was as follows:

"Do not think ill of me, but I believe that under circumstances conducive to the development of an appropriate situational context the emotional slant of our extraordinary conversation might well produce a positive vibe. Given my desire to preserve anonymity I suggest starting with a virtual-verbal relationship with the intention of transitioning later into direct contact."

Once more I asked Tolia, or rather Mr. Y, to hang his jacket with his response inside it on the second hanger from the right on the third bar in the coatroom and to not ask anything else of me.

At that point he gave up, and for the next three months he couldn't even bring himself to wear a coat to school, despite the fact that it was winter.

This might have meant either that Tolia had misunderstood my letters and thought someone was playing some kind of trick on him, or that Tolia had understood perfectly and decided to play some kind of trick on me, thereby confirming my worst suspicions.

NATALKA SNIADANKO

If the former, Tolia was a coward. If the latter, I had suffered a major defeat. The next night I wrote the last poem cycle on the subject of my love for Tolia, titled *You Don't Deserve Me*, ceremonially burned a piece of paper with Tolia's name on it, and swore to never again fall in love unless it was reciprocated, and for the rest of my days I would avenge upon the male race my first failed love. The poem commemorating this ritual I entitled "Oath." It contained exceptionally strong, as I saw it, lines:

> *Taking a solemn oath to forget them all*
> *I seal my lips, until into the grave I fall*

SERHIY ZHADAN

THE OWNER OF THE BEST GAY BAR

translated from the Ukrainian by Mark Andryczyk

NYONE WHO HAS EVER EXPERIENCED TRUE despair will surely understand me. One morning, you wake up and realize that everything is wrong, terribly wrong. Not too long ago—yesterday, for instance—you were still able to induce change, to improve things, to make your mark, but now—you stand by the wayside and no longer have an effect on events, which unfurl like bedsheets around you. This very sense of helplessness, estrangement, and disassociation is what a person feels, I guess, before death, if I correctly understand the concept of death—you seemed to have done everything right, you kept everything under control, why are they now trying to disconnect you from the twisting red wires of the system, to delete you, like a file, and cleanse you away, like a skin infection; why does life, in which you had just been playing an active role, ebb, like the sea, heading east, quickly becoming distant and leaving the sunshine of slow death in its tracks? The unfairness of death is felt most harshly during life; no one tries to convince you of the purpose of your relocation to the territory of the deceased, they simply won't have enough arguments to accomplish this. But everything is wrong, you yourself suddenly start believing in it, you fathom it and become silent and you let certain charlatans, alche-mists, and pathologist-anatomists rip out your heart and display it at fairs and museums of curiosities, you let them smuggle it out for the purpose of conducting suspicious experiments and performing gloomy rituals, you let them talk about you as if you were dead and let them fon-dle your heart—which has become black from love lost, recreational drugs, and a bad diet—with their smoke-scented fingers.

Behind all of this stood the tears, the nerves, and the love of your contemporaries. Tears, nerves, and love, in particular, because all the misfortune and the problems of your contemporaries began concur-rently with puberty and ended with default, and if anything is ever able to silence these smoldering Slavic tongues and these strong smoky lungs will once again be capable of containing air—it'll be love and economics, business and passion, in their most improbable manifes-tations—I have in mind both passion and, of course, business, every-thing else remains beyond the flow, beyond the dark turbulent current into which you all jump, having just reached adulthood. Everything else remains scum, circles on the water, superfluous additions to a biogra-phy, dissolving in oxygen, which, although it may also seem to be nec-essary for life, in reality—is not. Why? Because, in reality, no one really dies from a lack of oxygen, they die from a lack of love or a lack of cash. When, at some point, you wake up and realize that everything is terribly wrong, that she's gone, that yesterday you still had a chance to stop her from leaving, that you could have fixed everything, but that today—it's too late, and now you're left on your own and she won't be around for the next fifty or sixty years, depending on your desire and ability to live without her. And from this realization you suddenly become enrobed with vast and endless futility, and beads of sweat prance upon your hap-less skin, like clowns at a circus, and your memory refuses to cooper-ate with you; but then people don't die from this either, it's actually the opposite—all faucets are flipped on and all manhole covers explode, you say that everything is okay, I'm fine, I'll get through this, everything's good and you painfully battle on, ending up in those vacuums, which were created in the space where she had been, into all these wind tunnels and corridors, which she had filled with her voice and in which the monsters and reptiles of her absence begin to nest, everything's okay, you say, I'll get through this, I'm fine, no one has died from this yet, one more night, just a couple more hours in territories sown with black pepper, shattered glass, on hot sand mixed with bullet casings and bits of tobacco, in clothes, which you both wore, beneath the sky, which is now just yours, using her toothbrush, taking her towels with you to bed, listening to her radio, singing along during especially significant parts—the ones she never sang, singing those parts for her, especially when important things are mentioned in a song, like life or one's relationship with one's parents, or religion, for that matter. What can be sadder than this singing alone, which, occasionally, is interrupted by the latest news—and then a situation arises in which each upcoming news update could really be your last.

The only thing that could be sadder than this is the situation with money. Everything that has to do with finances, with the business which you conduct, with your personal financial stability, leads you into an increasingly darker and more hopeless corner from which there is only one way out—into a black, little-known space, in which the region of death is found. At which point you wake up and realize that, in order to prolong life, you need outside support and, hopefully, this support comes directly from the Lord God or from anyone within his closest circle. Well, forget about support. Put this word out of your mind. Everything in this world revolves around you, so you've got to pull it off yourself, be wary of business and love, sex and economics—yes, yes, economics—that prostate of the middle class, that tachycardia for the

boy scouts of the stock markets; a couple of unsuccessful policy decisions and you are a soon-to-be drowned person, in the sense that they'll
definitely drown you, probably in cement, and fatal cement waves, the
color of coffee with milk, will overcome you, distancing you from life,
and even from death, because, in this situation, you don't deserve a normal, peaceful death, whether you pull it off or not, it doesn't matter,
financial debt hangs above you, like a full moon, and all you can do is
howl at it, attracting the attention of the tax inspectors. So many young
souls have been swallowed up by the inability to come up with a good
business plan, so many hearts were torn by privatization politics; wrinkles on their wizened faces and a yellow, metallic reflection in their eyes
are all that remain after the long battle for survival—this is our country, this is our economics, this is your and my path to immortality, the
presence of which you sense, waking up at some point and unexpectedly realizing that, in life, there is nothing but your soul, your love, and
your, goddammit, debt, which you will never be able to pay off, at least
not in this life.

And that's precisely what we're going to talk about.

The story about the nightclub was told to me directly by one of its
founders. I had heard about it for quite some time but I hadn't crossed
paths with him, which isn't so strange, considering the specifics of the
establishment. Rumors of the city's first official gay bar had been circu-
lating for several years, various names and addresses were mentioned,
and, because no one really knew where it was actually located, every
place was considered to be suspicious. The place where the nightclub
was most often discussed was at the stadium—the city's right-wing
youth staunchly condemned the appearance of establishments with
such a profile, they promised to burn down this nightclub together

with all the gays that gather there for their so-called soirées. Once, during the 2003–04 season, they even burned down the Buratino café, which is located right next to the stadium, but the police, rightfully, did not trace a connection between this incident and the existence of a gay nightclub, because, just think about it—what kind of gay night-club could be established in a Buratino café, the name of which, itself, is xenophobic. On the other hand, the nightclub was often mentioned in mass media outlets, in various chronicles of cultural events, or in features about the city's vibrant nightclub scene. Usually, stories on the city's nightclub scene recalled letters from the front lines—tele-vision reports on this theme featured various toasts being announced which were then followed by machine-gun shots, and sometimes, if the cameraman didn't neglect his, let's say, professional duties, in other words, if he didn't get shit-faced off of the complimentary cognac, the machine-gun shots would ring in unison with wedding toasts and part-ing gestures, and the pulsating bullets would poke holes in the warm Kharkiv sky, like a salute to faithfulness, love, and other things rarely seen on television. In this context, news about the gay nightclub was intriguing because of the lack of any clear picture or any mention con-cerning the direct ties between the government and criminals, it was just that there was a party, it took place in a gay nightclub, the pub-lic behaved in a civil manner, there were no casualties. In any case, rumors about the nightclub kept spreading but, in reality, the wave of interest fell, which wasn't hard to predict from the start—our city has much more exciting establishments, like the Tractor Plant, for exam-ple. And, generally speaking, who's really interested in the affairs of sexual minorities in a country that has such substantial foreign debt. And even the fact that the nightclub, according to rumors, was part of the governor's racket didn't create any special resonance—this is what they expected from the governor. Everyone, in essence, runs his own business, what's most important is a clear conscience and the timely submission of tax forms.

San Sanych and I met during the elections. He looked like he was pushing forty although he was younger than that. It's just that one's biography is stronger than one's genes, and Sanych was a prime example of that. He would walk around in a black, squeaky leather jacket carrying a piece—a typical, mid-level mafioso, if you know what I mean. Although, for a mafioso, he was rather melancholic, he seldom spoke on the phone, occasionally calling his mother, and, as far as I can remember, nobody ever called him. He introduced himself as San Sanych when we first met and gave me his business card, on which "San Sanych, Lawyer" was written in gold letters on vellum paper, along with several phone numbers with London area codes; Sanych said that they were office phone numbers, I asked whose, but he didn't answer me. We became friends at once; Sanych pulled the piece out of his pocket, said that he is a supporter of free elections, and mentioned that he could get a hundred of these pieces, if necessary. He added that he has an acquaintance working for the Dynamo sports club, who takes starter pistols and transforms them into normal guns in his home workshop. "Look," he said, "if you file down this thingy"—he was pointing to a place where, obviously, the thingy was once located, having earlier been filed down —"you can load it with normal cartridges, and what's most important is that you won't have any problems with the police, it's just a starter pistol, right? If you want, I can get you a set, it'll run you forty bucks, plus ten more to file down that thingy. If necessary, I can sort you out with a Dynamo worker's card, to make it fully legit." Sanych loved weapons and he loved talking about them even more. In time, I became one of his closest friends.

One time, he told me about the nightclub; he just happened to mention that before becoming a lawyer and a supporter of free elections he had been in the nightclub business and, as it turns out, he was directly involved with the first official gay nightclub—that very mysterious establishment that the city's progressive youth unsuccessfully spent so much time trying to burn down. That's when I asked him to tell me more about it and he agreed, saying, okay, no problem, it's all in the distant past, why not tell the story.

And his story went something like this.

It turns out that he was a member of the Boxers for Fairness and Social Adaptation Association. He told me a bit about it; they grew out of the Dynamo sports club as a fraternal organization of former professional athletes. What Boxers for Fairness and Social Adaptation actually did, nobody really knows, but the fatality rate among members of this organization was quite high, every month one of them would be shot and then pompous memorial services would take place, which police officials and members of the regional government would attend. Occasionally, every couple of months, Boxers for Fairness and Social Adaptation would organize friendly matches with the Polish national team, at least that's what they called it; several buses would pull up to their office, they'd fill them up with boxers and a large array of domestically produced electronics, and the caravan would set off for Poland. The regional directors and the trainers would travel separately. Having arrived in Warsaw, the boxers would go to the stadium and unload the whole freight, after which they would celebrate yet another victory for the national Paralympic movement. What was interesting was that Sanych was not a boxer. Sanych was a wrestler. Not as in a Wrestler for Fairness and Social Adaptation, but as in a freestyle wrestler. His grandfather introduced him to it; at one time, his grandfather was quite serious about wrestling and even took part in a competition featuring all the peoples of the USSR at which he had his hand broken, which he was quite proud of—not of the broken hand, that is, but of his participation in the competition. And thus, his grandfather brought him to Dynamo. Sanych started out doing quite well. He took part in city matches, he showed much promise, but after a few years he also had his hand broken. At this point he had already finished his studies and had begun setting up his business, but was having difficulty, especially with the broken hand. And that is when he came to Boxers for Fairness and Social Adaptation. Boxers for Fairness and Social Adaptation looked at his hand, asked him whether he supported fairness and whether he supported social adaptation, and, having received an affirmative answer, accepted him. Sanych immediately joined a brigade that dealt with the markets in the Tractor Plant district. It turned out that making a career in this business was not so hard—no sooner had your superior been killed than you immediately filled his position. Within a year, Sanych was put in charge of a small unit, again he showed much promise, but he didn't really like the business: Sanych did possess a higher education and dying before he turned thirty from a dealer's grenade didn't tickle his fancy. Even more importantly, business took up all of his free time and he had no personal life, if you don't count the prostitutes which he would personally pick up at the markets. But Sanych didn't count the prostitutes, they probably didn't consider it part of one's personal life either, it's more like one's societal-economic life, which may be the best way to put it. And thus, Sanych began to seriously contemplate his future. The incident with the bulletproof vest was the turning point. One time, in the midst of a prolonged alcoholic stupor (obviously it must have been some kind of holiday period, the Birth of Christ, I believe), Sanych's underlings decided to give their young boss a bulletproof vest. They had gotten the bulletproof vest from the workers of the Kyiv regional militia in exchange for a latest-model copy machine. They partied for a while to celebrate the gift and then decided to try it out. Sanych put on the bulletproof vest, his boys got a Kalashnikov. The bulletproof vest turned out to be a pretty reliable thing—Sanych survived, having only gotten three semiserious bullet wounds. But he decided that this would be the end—a career as a freestyle wrestler hadn't worked out, a career as a combatant for fairness and social adaptation also wasn't progressing in the best manner, it was time for a change.

After licking his wounds, Sanych went to Boxers for Fairness and Social Adaptation and asked to leave the business. Boxers for Fairness and Social Adaptation correctly observed that it's not so easy to leave the business in this line of work, not alive, at least, but they eventually took Sanych's battle wounds into consideration and agreed. In parting, they expressed their hope that Sanych wouldn't sever his ties with the association and that, in life, he would continue to serve the ideals of the fight for fairness and social adaptation and, in the end, they wished him a speedy recovery and set off to load the bus with stacks of domestically produced electronics. In such a manner, Sanych ended up on the street—with no business or personal life, but with a wrestling background and a higher education; the latter, though, was of little interest to anyone. And in his time of crisis he meets up with Hoha—Heorhii Lomaia. They had been classmates, after which San Sanych went into wrestling and Hoha went into medicine. They hadn't seen one another for the last few years—Sanych, as has been noted earlier, was actively involved with the movement for the social adaptation of boxers, while Hoha, being a young specialist, went to the Caucasus region and took part in the Russian-Chechen war. But it was unclear with which side he was actively involved because, in the capacity of a middleman, he would purchase drugs from the Russian Health Ministry and would then sell them to the administrations of the Georgian rehab centers treating the Chechens. His downfall, however, came with the anesthetics, when, having purchased too many of them, he provoked the Health Ministry officials to review the packing list and to pose a completely reasonable question: why does the regional children's medical center, to which the funds were allocated, need so many narcotics? Because of this, Hoha was forced to return home, getting into several shootouts with pissed-off Caucasian dealers along the way. Having returned, he immediately picked up several shipments of gypsum boards. Business was going well but Hoha became obsessed with a new idea, which occupied an increasingly larger part of his imagination and ambitions—he decided to go into the nightclub business. And it was precisely at this anxious time that our protagonists met up.

"Listen," said Hoha to his childhood chum, "I'm new to this business and I need your help. I want to open a nightclub." "You know," his old friend replied, "I really don't know much about any of this, but, if you want, I can ask around." "You misunderstood," Hoha said to him, "I don't need you to ask around, I already know everything, I need a compadre, you dig? I want you in this business together with me, it's better for me that way, you see—I've known you since childhood, I know your parents, I know where to find you if I need to, should you decide to bail on me. And, most importantly, you've worked with everybody here. You're a true compadre." "What," asked Sanych, "you really think you'll make some money off of this?" "You understand," answered Hoha Lomaia, "I can make money off anything. You think I'm doing this for the money? Hell, I've got five freight cars full of gypsum boards at Balashovka, I could sell them right now and it's 'Cyprus here I come.' But you have to understand why I'm so enthralled with this idea—I don't want to go to Cyprus. And do you know why I don't want to go to Cyprus? I'm almost thirty, just like you, by the way. I've done business in four different countries, I'm being pursued by the law agencies of several autonomous republics, I should have been lying dead from disease in the tundra long ago, I've been under artillery fire three times, I had President Basaiev as my client. I was almost shot to death by a Krasnoiarsk special forces unit, once, a lightning bolt hit a car I was driving, and later I had to replace the battery. I'm paying alimony to a widow in Northern Ingushetia—she's the only one of 'em getting any money from me—half of my teeth are implants, once I almost agreed to sell off one of my kidneys, because I needed to buy up a shipment of machine lathes. But I've returned home, I'm in a good mood, and I sleep soundly, half of my friends have been killed, but half are still alive, like you, you're alive, but the odds were against you. So you see, somehow it turned out that I stayed alive, and once I was still alive, I thought to myself—hey, okay, Hoha, okay, now everything is alright, now everything will be good, if the Krasnoiarsk special forces weren't able to wipe you out and the lightning bolt didn't kill you, well then what do you need Cyprus for? And then I suddenly realized what I had wanted my whole life. And you know what that is?" "What?" San Sanych asked him. "My whole life I wanted to have my own nightclub where I could sit every night and no one could throw me out, even if I started puking all over the menu. And what did I do? You know what I did?" Hoha chuckled. "I just went out and bought that dreamed-about fucking nightclub, you understand?" "When did you buy it?" Sanych asked. "A week ago." "What kind of nightclub?" "Well, it's not really a nightclub, it's a sandwich shop." "What?" Sanych asked, confused. "Yeah, the Sub, you know it? There's a shitload of work to do but it's a great location, in the Ivanov neighborhood, I'll unload the gypsum boards, renovate it, and all my problems will be behind me. All I need is a compadre, you dig? What do you think?" he asked Sanych. "I like the name." "What name?" "The nightclub's name: the Sub."

And so they agreed to meet the following day in the nightclub. Hoha promised to introduce his compadre to the proposed art director.

San Sanych arrived on time; his school chum was already there, waiting outside by the entrance to the Sub. The Sub was in bad shape, it must have been thirty years since any renovations had been done here, and, taking into account that it had been built about thirty years ago, it can be said that the place had never been renovated. Hoha unlocked the door and let San Sanych in before him. San Sanych entered a half-lit space furnished with tables and plastic chairs and he sadly thought to himself—well I guess I should've stayed with Boxers for Fairness. But it was too late to do anything—Hoha followed him in and closed the door behind him. "The art director will be here shortly," he said and sat down at one of the tables. "We'll wait for him."

The art director's name was Slavik. Slavik, as it turns out, was an old druggie, he looked to be about forty years old, but it could have been the drugs. He was a half hour late, saying that there was a lot of traffic, and then later saying that he had taken the subway—in other words, he was full of shit. He was wearing an old jean jacket and big, nerdy sunglasses, which he categorically refused to take off, even in the dark basement. "Where'd you find this guy?" Sanych asked quietly, while Slavik was walking around and checking out the space. "My mom recommended him," Hoha replied, also quietly. "He was an art instructor at the Pioneer Youth Cultural Center, but was later thrown out for, I think, amoral conduct." "Well, obviously not for his religious convictions," said Sanych. "Well then," Hoha replied, "alright." "So," he shouted to Slavik, "what do you think?" "I like it, in theory," Slavik replied anxiously, coming up to them and sitting on a plastic stool. Just try not to like something, you asshole, Sanych thought to himself, and even turned his phone off so that no one would bother them, and, because no one ever called him anyway. "Well then," Hoha was visibly excited about the situation, "what do you say, any ideas?" "Okay, here's the deal," Slavik dramatically exhaled and pulled out a cheap cigarette, "here's the deal." He remained silent for a bit. "Heorhii Davydovych," he finally addressed Hoha, "I am going to be frank with you." What a moron, thought Sanych. Hoha was joyfully relishing in the depths of the sandwich shop. "I'll be frank," repeated Slavik. "I've been in show business for twenty years, I've also worked with the Ukrainian Concert Organization, musicians know who I am, I have contacts with Grebenshchikov's people, I organized a U2 concert in Kharkiv . . ." "U2 played Kharkiv?" San Sanych interrupted him. "No, they shot down that idea," Slavik replied, "and here's what I want to say to you, Heorhii Davydovych," intentionally ignoring Sanych, "the fact that you bought this nightclub is a *fabulous* idea." "You really think so?" Hoha asked, in doubt. "Yes, it really is a *fabulous* idea. I'm being frank with you, I know everything about show business, I organized the first rock jam in this city." At this point he, apparently, recalled something, lost his train of thought, and became silent. "And?" Hoha asked, unable to contain himself. "Yes, yes," Slavik shook his head, "yep." Man, this guy must be totally wasted, Sanych thought emphatically. "What do you mean, yes?" Hoha didn't understand. "Yep," Slavik again shook his head, "yep . . ." San Sanych, out of options, went for his phone; in principle, at his previous job, he would just whack someone like this, but this was a different situation, a different business, let them settle this on their own. "This, Heorhii Davydovych, is what I have to say to you," Slavik suddenly began to say, and, to everyone's surprise, came up with this gem—

"The nightclub business," he began from afar, "is a real shitty affair, first of all because the market has already been established, you understand what I'm getting at?" Everyone looked like they had understood. "It's all because of mid-level business, goddammit, this mid-level business developed first. So, you bought a space," he addressed, more than likely, Hoha, "you want to set up a quality nightclub, with a quality clientele, with a cultural program, blah, blah, blah." "Come on, Slavik, cut the bull-shit," Hoha interrupted him. "Fine," Slavik agreed, "but what is it that is most important? What's the most important thing in show business?" Hoha gradually stopped chuckling. "What's most important is—the format! Yep, yep," Slavik merrily nodded, even clapping his hands once, "yes, that's it . . ." "Well what's the deal with the format?" Hoha asked after a long pause. "The format is a real fucking problem," Slavik replied. "In this business, all the spots have been taken, all the spots," he chuck-led. "The market has already been formed, you understand? You wanna do fast food—go for it, but there are already a hundred fast-food joints in the city, you want to have a fancy restaurant—go ahead, I'll organize a cultural program, you want a dance club—let's do a dance club, you want a pub—let's do a pub. But you won't make dick off of it, Heorhii Davydovych—you'll have to excuse me for being so direct— you won't make dick." "And why is that?" an offended Hoha asked. "Because the market has already been established and they'll crush you. You've got nobody backing you up, right? They'll just burn you down together with your nightclub." "And what's your proposition," said Hoha, visibly upset, "do you have any ideas?" "Yep," Slavik smugly said, "yep, there is one *fabulous* idea, a truly *fabulous* idea." "Well, what's the idea?" asked Hoha, wary of where this was leading. "We need to fill a vacant niche, if I'm expressing myself clearly. And in this business there is only one niche—a gay nightclub needs to be opened." "What kind of nightclub?" Hoha couldn't believe his ears. "Gay," Slavik replied, "in other words, a nightclub for gays. That niche needs to be filled." "What, are you com-pletely fucked in the head?" Hoha asked after another pause. "Are you serious?" "Well, why not?" Slavik asked defensively. "Wait, you seri-ously," Hoha was getting fired up, "want me, Heorhii Lomaia, to open a gay bar in my space?" "That's it, you're fired," he said and hopped off the table. "Hold on, wait, Heorhii Davydovych," now Slavik was getting nervy, "nobody's going to write 'Nightclub for Fags' in big bright letters on it, right?" "Well then what will you write?" Hoha asked him, putting on his overcoat. "We'll write 'Nightclub of Exotic Leisure,'" announced Slavik, "and we'll just give it an appropriate name. For example—the Peacock." "Moose-Cock" said Hoha, imitating his voice. "Who's going to come to your Peacock?" "But that's just it, lots of people," Slavik assured him. "It's like I said, there is a niche to be filled, in a city of two million people and not one gay bar! We're sitting on a pot of gold. You won't even have to work to draw a crowd, they'll come on their own, just open the door for them." After these words, Hoha grimaced and once again sat on the table but didn't take off his overcoat. Slavik saw this as a good sign, got another cigarette, and continued: "I myself was stunned when I came up with this idea. This is capital, lying right on the street, just pick it up and it's yours. I still can't believe that no one has thought to do this yet, another month or two and they'll steal this idea, you can bet on that. Mark my word!" Slavik was becoming increasingly edgy, perhaps truly fearing that they'd steal it. "In essence, we'll have no competition! Tell him," he finally turned his attention to San Sanych, looking for support. "Okay," Hoha said at last, "on the surface, it's not a bad idea." "Are you being serious?" Sanych asked him. "Well why not, it's doable." "Of course it's doable!" Slavik cried fervently. "Hold on," Sanych interrupted him and once again addressed Hoha. "Listen, you and I are friends and all that, but I'm against this. I worked almost two years for Boxers for Fairness, they'll destroy me, are you kidding me? We agreed to set up a normal business, not some peacock." "Would you forget about the peacock," said Hoha, "nobody is planning on calling it the Peacock. We'll come up with a good name. Or we'll leave the old one." "What old one?" Sanych didn't understand. "The Sub! Of course," said Hoha, now once again becoming jovial. "It sounds great: 'The Sub: A Nightclub of Exotic Leisure.' What do you say, Slavunia?" Slavunia

SERHIY ZHADAN

nodded and then nodded again. It was difficult to expect any more from
him. "Don't sweat it," Hoha said to his compadre, "the gays will be dealt
with by that guy over there," he pointed at Slavik, "our job is to finish
the renovations by summer, and then we'll see." "And you know what,"
he was thinking out loud, "why not a gay bar? At least there won't be
any whores there."

And everybody went to work. Hoha unloaded the gypsum boards,
Sanych introduced him to some necessary people, and they began renovating. Slavik, for his part, came up with the idea to register the gay bar
as a youth nightclub, in order to avoid coughing up money as a com-
mercial enterprise. As it turned out, everybody did indeed know Slavik,
evidenced by their determined efforts to avoid him. In the morning,
Slavik went to the Cultural Events Committee, visited their cafeteria,
drank tea there, talked about the weather with the ladies working at the
cafeteria, and then went to the Office of Cultural Affairs. They wouldn't
let him in, he became offended, rushed off to the nightclub, argued
with the workers renovating it, hollered that he had been in show business for over twenty years, and threatened them that he would invite
Grebenshchikov to the opening. And, by the way, about the opening—
spring had passed, the renovations were completed, the nightclub
could now be opened. Hoha once again gathered everyone, this time
in his own freshly renovated office. "Well," he asked, "anybody have any
ideas for the opening?" "Okay, here's the deal, Heorhii Davydovych,"
Slavik began in a very official tone, "there are several ideas. Firstly, fire-
works . . ." "Give me the second idea," Hoha interrupted him. "Okay,"
said Slavik, not being distracted, "I propose we serve Japanese food."
"And where will you get it?" Sanych asked. "I have some acquaintances," Slavik replied, not without dignity. "They're Japanese?" "No,
they're Vietnamese. But they pretend they're Japanese—they have two
freight wagons at the Pivdennyi train station, in one of them they sew

238

fur coats and in the other one they run a kitchen." "What else you got?" Hoha again interrupted him. "A circus striptease show," Slavik haughtily offered. "What kind?" Hoha asked. "Circus," Slavik repeated. "I've got some contacts, four chicks in bikinis, they work twenty-four-hour shifts, every third day, they can't work any more often—they moonlight at the Pioneer Youth Cultural Center." "Alright," Hoha cut him off, "not gonna happen, I said—no whores in my nightclub. It'll be bad enough with the gays," he added worryingly and once again addressed Slavik. "Is that all you got?" Slavik got a cigarette, lit it leisurely, blew out some smoke, and began: "Well then, fine, fine," he made a distinct pause, "okay, Heorhii Davydovych, I understand what you're getting at, okay, I mean, I'll talk to Grebenshchikov if you want me to, but I don't think he'll do it for free, even for me . . ." "Enough," Hoha waved his hand, "Sanych, be a pal, get me a few musicians, any musicians, okay? And you," now addressing Slavik, "think about who we will be inviting." "What do mean, who?" Slavik asked, animatedly, "the fire department, the tax collectors, anybody from the cultural affairs office. We'll make a list, in other words." "Good," Hoha agreed, "but you make sure that, besides all those fags that you mentioned, there will also be some cool gays there."

The nightclub opened at the beginning of June. San Sanych got a vocal-instrumental ensemble that regularly played in the restaurant of Hotel Kharkiv; their program was well rehearsed, they didn't ask for a lot of money, and they didn't drink on the job. Slavik put together a list of invited guests, a hundred or so people, Hoha spent a lot of time studying the proposed list, crossed out the names of the ladies working at the Cultural Events Committee cafeteria and of four workers from the Pioneer Youth Cultural Center, the rest of the list was agreed upon; Slavik tried to argue the case for including the cafeteria ladies but gave up after a long debate. Hoha invited his business partners, middlemen to whom he'd sold gypsum boards, some childhood friends, and the Lykhui brothers. San Sanych invited his mother; he wanted to invite an acquaintance of his, a former prostitute, but then thought of his mother and gave up that idea. The opening ended up being quite pompous. Slavik got drunk within half an hour, San Sanych asked the security guards to keep an eye on him, Hoha told everyone to relax—it was an opening, nonetheless. San Sanych's mom did not stick around for long, complaining that the music was too loud; Sanych hailed her a cab and returned to the festivities. The middlemen took off their neckties and raised toasts to the owners, Slavik sang loudly and kissed the representatives from the tax administration; in essence, out of everyone there, he was the only one who was acting gay, at least the way that he understood it, and he did this entirely on purpose, in order to engage the guests. The guests, finally, became engaged, and in the end, the Lykhui brothers got into a fight with the middlemen in the men's bathroom, basically a good old fisticuffs—in essence, that's what they're paid to do; from the bathroom one could hear an offended Hrysha Lykhui shouting, "you're the one that's a faggot!" His brother, Sava Lykhui, supported him. The fight was quickly contained, Sanych separated everyone, and the drunk middlemen set off to continue their drinking at a strip club, because the Sub wasn't offering a striptease show. The drunk representatives of the tax administration also set off for the strip bar, not taking Slavik with them, in order not to spoil their reputation. All the guests were almost gone, except for a girl who was sitting on a stool by the bar and two middle-aged men whispering in the corner, who kind of looked like the representatives of the tax administration, in other words, it was hard to find something that was memorable about their appearance. "Who's that?" Sanych asked Slavik, who was beginning to sober up and was now recalling who he had kissed. "Well, them," he said, focusing his look at them. "I don't want to offend anyone here but, I think, they are authentic gays." "Do you know them?" Sanych asked, just in case. "Yes, I do," Slavik nodded his head, "it's Doctor and Busia." "What kind of doctor?" Slavik replied, "I don't know—a doctor, come on, I'll introduce you. Greetings, Busia." He was addressing the guy who looked younger and looked more like a representative of the tax administration. "Howdy, Doctor," he shook the hand of the guy who looked more together, in other words, he looked less like a representative of the tax administration. "I would like to introduce you, this is Sanny." "San Sanych," a fearful San Sanych corrected him. "He's our manager," interrupted Slavik. "Nice to meet you," Doctor and Busia said and invited them to sit down. Sanych and Slavik sat down. Everyone became silent. Sanych became nervous, Slavik reached for his cigarettes. "So, Slavik," said Doctor, trying to relieve the tension, "so you're here now?" "Yep," said Slavik, lighting his cigarette and putting out the match in their salad, "my friends asked me for my help and I thought to myself, why not, I've got some time to spare. Of course, things aren't running all that smoothly just yet," Slavik continued, taking Doctor's fork and pricking the salad with it, "let's look at tonight's opening, for example: in essence, we could have taken the high road and had a cultural program, I had already cut a deal with Grebenshchikov . . . But, it's okay," he placed his hand on Sanych's shoulder, "it's okay, I'll advise them, a little bit here, a little bit there, everything will be fine, yeah . . ." Sanych carefully moved Slavik's hand off of his shoulder, stood up, nodded toward Doctor and Busia, implying—have a nice time, we'll talk again later—and went up to the bar. "What's your name?" he asked the girl, who had just ordered another vodka. She had a pierced lip and whenever she drank, the metal balls would clink against the glass. "I'm Vika," she said, "what's your name?" "San Sanych," San Sanych replied. "Gay?" she asked, seriously. "Owner," Sanych defended himself. "I see" said Vika, "can you give me a lift home? I got pretty trashed here." Sanych once again hailed a taxi, and bidding farewell to Hoha, escorted the girl outside. The taxi driver turned out to be some kind of hunchback, Sanych had seen him around before, and now it turns out that they're riding together; the hunchback joyfully looked at them and asked them—"Did you order a pickup at the fag bar?" "Yeah, yeah," San Sanych replied uneasily. "Where to?" he asked Vika. Vika started getting head-spins in the taxi. "You aren't going to puke, are you?" the hunchback asked. "Everything's fine," Sanych said, "we're not going to puke." "As you wish," the hunchback said, somewhat disappointed. "So, where are we going?" Sanych put his arm around Vika, pulled her toward him, reached into the inside pocket of her biker's jacket, and pulled out her passport. He looked at the address listed in it. "Let's try this," he said to the hunchback, and they set off. It turns out that Vika lived very close by; it would have probably been easier to carry her home, but who knew? Sanych pulled her out of the car, asked the hunchback to wait for him, and carried her into the entrance of her building. He stood her up on her feet by the door. "You gonna be okay?" He asked. "I'm fine," she said, "fine, give me back my passport." Sanych remembered that he still had the passport, pulled it out, and looked at the photo. "You look better without all the piercings," he said. Vika grabbed the passport and put it in her pocket. "If you want," Sanych said, "I can stay with you tonight." "Dude," she replied, smiling smugly, "I'm a lesbian, don't you get it? And you're not gay, you're just the owner. You dig?" Vika kissed him and disappeared behind the door. Sanych tasted coldness and felt the piercing on his lips. It felt like his lips had touched a silver spoon.

The tribulations of everyday business started to kick in. The tribulations lay in the fact that the nightclub was wholly unprofitable. The target audience doggedly ignored the Sub. Hoha was infuriated, Slavik tried to stay out of his line of sight, and, when he wasn't successful in doing this, he would loudly holler about the niche, about the Ukrainian

Concert Organization, and about the Vietnamese diaspora, he even proposed to turn the Sub into a sushi bar that would focus exclusively on the Vietnamese diaspora, after which he received a smack in the face from Hoha, and, consequently, stopped showing up at the office for some time. Hoha would sit in his office nervously trying to solve crossword puzzles published in *Accountants' Review* magazine. San Sanych tracked down Vika and invited her to a dinner date. She told him that she was on her period and asked to be left alone, but then added that someday she'd stop by the Sub. The summer was hot. Juice trickled down from the air conditioners.

Slavik showed up. Diligently trying to hide his black eye, which was still visible behind his sunglasses, he entered Hoha's office. Hoha asked Sanych to come in. Slavik was seated, sadly shaking his head and not saying anything. "How long are you going to keep sitting there without saying anything?" Hoha asked, smiling joyfully. "Heorhii Davydovych," Slavik began, carefully selecting his words, "I understand, okay—we were all very upset, I was wrong, you flipped out." "Me?" Hoha asked, continuing to smile. "You know, we are all professionals," said Slavik and then adjusted his glasses. "I understand—business is business, and we have to save it. I'm used to everything being up front, yeah ... And if you have a beef with me—I'd like to hear it, I won't be offended." "But," Slavik continued, "I understand completely, maybe we don't fully agree on some matters, perhaps our ways of seeing things are not always the same, okay, that's just the way it turned out, I understand—you're new to this business, that's why, no, everything is okay, I'm part of the team, everything is fine." "Slavik," Hoha said to him, "it's absolutely fantastic that you are part of the team, but the problem is that our team is being kicked out of the big leagues." "Yes," said Slavik, "yes. I understand— you have every right to say this, I would have said the same thing if I was in your shoes, I understand, everything is okay . . ." "Slavik," the boss addressed him again, "I'm begging you, give me something to work with, I'm in the red, that's not how businesses are run, you understand?" Slavik continued to shake his head, talked about how great this team to which he had returned was, mentioning his belief that, if they had been in his shoes, they would have done the same; he bummed some cab money from Hoha and said that he'd return tomorrow with some good news. He called the following morning using somebody else's cell phone and enthusiastically shouted that, at this very moment, as it turned out, he was at the Cultural Events Committee office, and that at this time, decisions were being made on a regional level, regarding the idea of awarding them the right to host this year's Embroidered Rushnyky! "What?" Hoha asked him. "Rushnyky," Slavik patiently repeated, you could hear the phone's legal owner grabbing at the phone and trying to get it back, but Slavik just wouldn't give it up. "Embroidered Rushnyky! Hey, would you just back off for a second!" he yelled on that side of the conversation and, once again commandeering the phone, continued: "It's a talent competition for children and youth, backed directly by the governor; it gets funded by the budget, if we pull this off—they'll give us the status of an artistic center, and then the tax police won't fuck with us." "But are you sure that this a good fit for us?" Hoha asked him, just in case. "Well of course it is," Slavik yelled, "this is exactly what we need—painting on asphalt, a children's fashion show, older schoolgirls in bathing suits, fuck, we'll come up with a program, we'll run the dough through the accounting office, we'll give the firemen a cut so that they'll include us in the budget next year, and that's it—we'll be talent-showing for the whole year on the public's money, ze show mast go on, Heorhii Davydovych, I've been in this business for twenty years, goddammit!" This was, probably, shouted into empty space, because they had indeed managed to take the phone away from him. Hoha sighed heavily and returned to his crossword puzzle.

In the afternoon, four guys in track suits came in, but they didn't look like athletes, unless they all played for a goon squad. The security guard asked them what they wanted but they knocked him down and went to look for the director. Hoha was sitting with Sanych and finishing up a crossword puzzle. Sanych saw the four of them and quietly turned off his cell phone. "Who are you?" Hoha asked, already knowing the answer. "We're the Copy Kings," the first one, the one in the blue track suit, replied. "Who?" Sanych asked. "What are you deaf?" The second one said, also wearing a blue track suit. "'The Copy Kings.' That building across the street from this joint, it's ours. The parking lot around the corner—ours." "And an office at the Pivdennyi train station as well," the first one, wearing blue, again entered the conversation. "In essence, we are the leaders in this market, you got it?" Now this was said by the second guy wearing blue. The third, wearing green, turned awkwardly, and a sawed-off shotgun fell out from under his track jacket, the green guy quickly bent down, picked it up, and put it back, apprehensively looking around. "We have a network of wholesale dealers," the first one said, "we receive direct deliveries from Sweden." "What," said Hoha, trying to prolong the conversation, "you want to sell us a copy machine?" The foursome disconsolately became silent, sternly moving their glances from Hoha onto Sanych. "What we want," the first one finally began to say, wiping his sweaty palms on the blue fabric of his track pants, "is for everything to be sorted out the right way. You guys are new here, you were not here before. This territory is ours. You gotta pay up." "We do pay up," Hoha tried to joke, "to the tax police." The third one once again turned around awkwardly and his shotgun once again clanged onto the floor. The fourth one flicked him in the face, bent down, picked up the weapon, and put it in the pocket of his crimson track pants. "Yo, *brother,* you didn't get it," the second one again started speaking, putting all his disgust into the word *brother.* "We're the Copy Kings, we control the whole region." "What do you mean?" San Sanych asked. "Hey, don't interrupt, alright?" the first one said sharply and turned to the second one, "go ahead, Lionia, continue." "Yeah," said Lionia in reply, "we've got connections in the administration. This is our territory. So, you gotta pay up." "Well we're not complete strangers here either," Hoha tried to say something, "You could say that we are known around these parts." "Yeah, well who knows you, *brother*?" the second one exclaimed, making a fist, but the fourth one took him by the elbow, as if to say— easy there, Lionia, easy, they don't know what they're doing. "So, who knows you?" "What do you mean, who?" Hoha tried to buy some time. "I deal in gypsum boards, I know people in the Balashovka district, plus I've got connections in the tax administration. The Lykhui brothers, for example..." "Who?" the second one asked, and Hoha immediately realized that it was better for him not have mentioned the Lykhui brothers. "The Lykhuis?! Those morons?!! Yeah, they got a set of printers from us, from Copy King, and resold them to some dorks from the Tractor Plant district! They claimed that they were copy machines for the next generation! And the latter guys, for their part, resold them to the military academy, together with our warranty! We barely got out of that one!!! The Lykhuis!!! The Lykhuis!!!" The second one was tugging at his blue track jacket and was hollering, for the whole nightclub to hear, that accursed last name. "Well that's not it," added Sanych, just to add something, "we're also on the Cultural Events Committee..." "What?!" The second one didn't let him finish. "On what cultural events committee?!! You want to tell me that you're also under the protection of the Cultural Events Committee?!!! Are you standing by your words?!!!!" The fourth one resolutely reached into his pocket for his weapon. Shit, thought Hoha, it would have been better if those Krasnoiarsk special forces had killed me, it wouldn't have been as revolting. All four of them began approaching threateningly, blocking off half of the room with their bodies. And it looked like neither Hoha Lomaia, nor, even less so, San Sanych, could expect anything other than serious bodily injury from this situation.

And, at this point, the door to the office opened and Slavik walked in, merrily smiling and waving a stack of xeroxes like a fan. The foursome, with raised fists, stopped in their tracks. Hoha slowly sat down onto a stool, Sanych shrank himself and touched the phone in his pocket. Everyone turned to Slavik. "Hi, hello," Slavik called out, failing to notice the surrounding tension, "hello to all!" He walked up to Hoha and shook his lifeless hand. "Partners?" said Slavik, playfully referring to the foursome and, smiling, shook the hand of the one on the end, the one in the blue track suit. "Voila!" he shouted emphatically, tossing the stack of xeroxes in front of Hoha. "What's this?" Hoha asked, barely able to speak. "We got it!" Slavik emphatically called out. "Embroidered Rushnyky!" "Embroidered Rushnyky?" Hoha asked distrustfully. "Embroidered Rushnyky?" Sanych asked, walking up to check out the copies. "Embroidered Rushnyky, Embroidered Rushnyky," the foursome whispered in fear, backing out of the office. "Embroidered Rushnyky!" triumphantly repeated Slavik and, leaning down to Hoha, confidently said, "So here's the deal, Heorhii Davydovych, I sorted everything out with the fire department, we'll run the money through their account, I figured it out, we take the cash and write it off as an overhead expense," he anxiously giggled, sharply cut off his laughter, and, turning to the foursome, commandingly asked them, "Can I help you with something, gentlemen?" Hoha also inquisitively looked at the foursome, but lacked the guts to ask them that very question. "Brother," the second one finally said, zipping up his blue jacket, "you're gonna tell me that you're really under the protection of the governor?" "Yep," Slavik impatiently answered him and whispered to Hoha, "we'll list the deficit as an expense for the children's choir, I settled it with the administrators, they'll register it in the quarterly report as a one-time payment to the orphans." The foursome nervously lingered by the door, not knowing what to do. The fourth guy tried to give the shotgun back to the third guy but that guy glumly spurned him. "What, leaving so soon?" Slavik turned to the foursome. "By the way, Heorhii Davydovych, are we inviting these gentlemen to Embroidered Rushnyky?" "Embroidered Rushnyky, Embroidered Rushnyky," the foursome groaned and slid out of the office. When the door behind them closed, Hoha sighed heavily. "Give me a smoke," he addressed Slavik. Slavik pulled out his cheap smokes and stretched one out to Hoha. Hoha grabbed the cigarette with trembling lips, Slavik instantly gave him a light. The boss took a drag and immediately coughed. "What just happened?" Slavik didn't understand. "Slavik," Hoha addressed him, "you're a guy who has seen his share of things, right? You've been in show business for twenty years. You know what's his name . . ." "Grebenshchikov," Slavik helped him. "You organized U2's Kharkiv concert, you've worked with the Pioneer youth. Now tell me—does God exist?" "Yes, he does," said Slavik. "Of course he does. But it doesn't really matter."

Vika stopped by the Sub. "Howdy, gayboys!" she said to the compadres, who were sitting by themselves at a table. Hoha grunted. "Okay," he said to his partner, "I'm heading home." "Alright, I'll close up," Sanych promised. "Ah, sure you will," Hoha laughed and, timidly letting Vika pass him, went outside. "Haven't seen you in a while?" Sanych asked. "What do you care." Vika answered. "What happened to that piercing you had?" Sanych inquired. "I sold it," Vika answered. They then set off to drink some vodka, Vika cried and complained about her life, saying that she broke up with her girlfriend, who had left the country for good. "So why are you still here?" Sanych asked. "Well, what about you?" Vika countered. "Well, I've got a business," he said, "plus, I don't know any foreign languages." "Neither does she," Vika said, "she's an actress, her body is her language, you understand?" "Not really," Sanych honestly replied. "Listen," Vika asked him, "you're almost thirty. Why haven't you gotten married yet?" "I don't know," Sanych said, "I've been busy with business. I've got three wounds. Plus, a broken hand." "Just find yourself a gay guy," Vika suggested. "You think it will help?" Sanych doubted. "Probably not," Vika said. "Hey, let's go to your place," he proposed. "What, you wanna fuck?" "Well, maybe not fuck," Sanych said, "we can just . . ." "We can just—not," Vika authoritatively declared. And then added, "Yeah, it's too bad you're not gay."

Then they just lay on the floor of her room for a while. The air was dark and warm. Vika counted his gunshot wounds. "One," she counted, "two, three. That's it?" She asked somewhat disappointed. "That's it," Sanych said apologetically. "It's kind of like having a piercing," she said, "except that they don't heal." "Everything heals," he answered. "Yeah, yeah," Vika didn't agree, "my girlfriend would also say that. And then she takes off for Turkey." "That also counts as an experience," Sanych said philosophically. "Uh-huh," Vika replied with anger, "you know, experiences like that are like those things on your body—you can always track how many times somebody has tried to kill you."

Things weren't going well for the nightclub. And even the successful presentation of Embroidered Rushnyky—during which Slavik almost got beaten up by the older Pioneer youth, because he had entered the dressing room where the older girls were changing without knocking— didn't save the situation. Hoha would spend his evenings in the office, computing their debt on a calculator. Sanych fell into a depression, Vika wasn't calling him, she wouldn't pick up the phone, he was running out of money. Sanych smoked by the nightclub entrance and looked on jealously as the Copy Kings began constructing a penthouse on top of their building. Business was obviously not happening, it was time to return to Boxers for Fairness.

One morning, Slavik showed up and said that he had some good news. "We're going to present a show," he said. "You didn't want a strip show," he addressed Hoha, "so be it. Let it be. I respect your choice, Heorhii Davydovych, I do. But I've got something that will amaze you." Hoha became tense. "I," Slavik said lazily, "have made arrangements with Raisa Solomonovna. At first, she categorically refused because, as you know, she has a very busy schedule, but I got through to her using my connections. She'll be here soon, it would be nice if everything was very civilized here, well, you know what I mean," and Slavik threw a concerned glance at Sanych. "And who is it again you've made arrangements with?" Hoha asked him. Sanych laughed. "With Raisa Solomonovna," Slavik repeated somewhat vociferously. "And who is she?" Hoha asked carefully. "Who is she?" Slavik smiled arrogantly. "Who is Raisa Solomonovna? Heorhii Davydovych, are you kidding me?" "Alright, alright, take it easy, answer the question," Hoha interrupted him. "Well," Slavik said, "I don't even know what to say. How could you have gotten into the nightclub business without having heard of Raisa Solomonovna? Hmmm . . . Alright. You gotta be kidding me . . . Raisa Solomonovna—she's with the Roma municipal ensemble, an award-winning Belarusian actress. You must have heard of her," Slavik confidently yelled out and then reached for his cigarettes. "So she's coming here to pick up something she left behind?" Hoha asked with dissatisfaction. "Well that's what I'm trying to explain to you," said Slavik, taking a drag, "we're going to present a show. On Tuesdays. She can't do it any other day, she's got a very busy schedule. I've made all the arrangements. Everybody has heard of her, we'll fill a niche." "Are you sure?" Hoha asked without enthusiasm. "Of course," said Slavik, sprinkling ash onto a crossword puzzle that had just been solved. "So what does she do, this actress of yours?" Hoha asked, just in case. "She has her own repertoire," Slavik informed him seriously. "An hour and a half long. To prerecorded music. Roma romance songs, and movie hits about gangster life." "And in what language does she sing?" Sanych inquired. "In Belarusian?" "Why Belarusian?" Slavik was offended. "Well, I really don't know. In Romani, I guess, it is a Roma ensemble." "Is she going to perform alone," Hoha asked, "or with bears?"

Raisa Solomonovna arrived around 1:00 PM, out of breath because of the heat. She looked to be forty-five years old, but she wore a lot of makeup, so it was tough to tell. She was a skinny dirty-blonde in leather go-go boots and wearing some kind of see-through slip, explaining that she had come straight from a concert she had at an orphanage, adding that she brought along a poster, to illustrate. Printed on the poster, in large red letters, was: "The Kharkiv Philharmonic Invites You. The Award-Wining Belarusian Actress Raisa Solomonovna in 'Twilight Shout-Outs.'" At the bottom were the blank lines reserved for "Time" and "Price of Admission." "Alright then," Raisa Solomonovna said excitedly, "show me the nightclub!" Everyone went into the main hall. "So what do we have here," the actress asked, "a fast-food joint or a pub?" "What we have here is a gay bar," Hoha replied, uncertainly. "Fuck yeah," Raisa Solomonovna said and climbed onto the stage. Slavik, being a show-business pro, turned on the prerecorded music.

Raisa Solomonovna began with songs about gangster life. She sang loudly, addressing the imaginary audience and waving her arms emphatically. Surprisingly, Hoha liked it; he smiled and started singing along, obviously familiar with these tunes. Slavik stood edgily behind the mixing board and monitored his boss through the corners of his eyes. Sanych watched all of this perplexedly. After the fifth song, Hoha clapped his hands, said that it was time to take a break, walked up to the stage, and, offering the singer his hand, led her to his office. Sanych hesitantly followed them. "Good stuff," Hoha said to Raisa Solomonovna, "real good stuff. Raisa, what's your . . ." "Solomonovna," she helped him. "Yes," Hoha complied. "Let's have a drink." "What, we won't be singing anymore?" the singer asked. "Not today," said Hoha. "Let's agree that today we will drink to our having met." "Okay then," Raisa Solomonovna agreed, "but, if I may, I'd like to change my clothes, it's so hot in here." "Whatever you want," Hoha said merrily and, dialing up the bar, ordered two bottles of cold vodka. Raisa Solomonovna took off her go-go boots and pulled a pair of slippers from her bag that looked like puffy cats. Hoha looked at the cats and opened the first bottle. Sanych understood where things were heading and sadly turned off his phone. Slavik was not invited to come to the office. He came anyway.

First, they drank to celebrate their acquaintance. Then they started singing. Hoha suggested that she get back up on stage, Raisa Solomonovna agreed, and slid back up onto the show-business stage, as she was dressed, in house slippers. Hoha followed her onto the stage, wearing her leather go-go boots. Wearing go-go boots and in his silk, fake-Armani shirt he looked like a nineteenth-century Russian intellectual. Slavik turned on the prerecorded music. Raisa Solomonovna returned to the mafia-themed material, Hoha sang along. The go-go boots glistened in the stage lights.

Upon entering the bathroom, Sanych found Slavik in there. The latter wasn't feeling very well, he was splashing water onto his face from the faucet and breathing heavily in the hot air. "You feel like shit? Sanych asked him. "I'm fine," Slavik groaned, "fine." "Slavik," San Sanych said, "I've been meaning to ask this for a while, maybe this isn't the best place for such a conversation, but, you know, I'm not sure if we'll get another chance—what, in general, is your opinion on gays?" Slavik stuck his head under the cold stream, breathed out, and sat up against the wall. He remained silent for a bit. "I will tell you this, San Sanych," Slavik began speaking, trustingly, spitting out the water. "I am not thrilled with gays. But," he lifted his pointer finger, "there are reasons for that."

"What reasons?" Sanych asked; he didn't feel like returning to the main hall, that's why he decided to linger here. "The reasons are of a *personal* nature," Slavik informed. "I've got allergies. People like me are constantly popping pills. I, for example," Slavik said and pulled out a cigarette, "am a pill popper. For ten years now. My doctor used to write me prescriptions. They, however, stopped having any effect, you understand? But my sister works for a pharmaceutical company, they opened a factory just outside of Kyiv. The Germans gave them a half a million worth of equipment and they constructed an entire lab as part of a revitalization program. They promptly divvied it all up and threw an extravagant grand opening for the factory. Joschka Fischer, the president of Germany, came for the opening," Slavik nervously exhaled some smoke. "The ex-president," he added. "So, they began working, they created a sample batch, and then the attorney general's office says: fuck this—it does not meet the necessary standards, it has too much morphine in it." "Too much of what?" Sanych didn't understand. "Morphine," Slavik repeated. "The whole problem was that the equipment was theirs, while the raw materials were ours. And because their machinery is geared for nonwaste production, in other words, it produces no waste, they ended up producing massive quantities of incorrect-strength drugs. The whole program, obviously, was shut down. The factory went bankrupt. The unions raised a ruckus, our environmentalists backed them. They wrote a letter to Joschka Fischer. But he did not write back. So, to make a long story short, they laid off everyone, my sister included. And, in order to ease the tensions with the unions, the workers were paid with the product which they had produced. These days, they stand by the side of one of the main roads leading out of Kyiv and sell these tablets to tourists, along with squeezie toys. And my sister brought me a couple of boxes. So, I have allergies, just so you know." "What does this have to do with gays?" Sanych asked after a long pause. "Well, hell if I know," Slavik disclosed. "Here, take this," he said and offered Sanych two tablets. "It's good stuff. It'll knock your socks off." Sanych took the pills and swallowed them, one at a time. It can't get any worse, he thought to himself. It didn't get any worse.

Raisa Solomonovna got completely drunk. She ripped the microphone out of Hoha's hands and began singing movie soundtrack hits. She put her red wig on distressed Slavik's head. Hoha tried to take the microphone away from her but she grabbed him by the hair and began screaming. Slavik tried to pull her away from his boss but was unsuccessful—Raisa Solomonovna was holding on tightly to Hoha with one hand, while trying to poke his eyes out with the other. At first, Hoha tried to push her away but then, later, also got riled up and started blindly waving his fists. With his first punch he knocked Slavik to the ground. Slavik grabbed his bruised jaw and once again tried to pull Raisa Solomonovna away. Raisa, having met resistance, became incensed and attacked Hoha with renewed strength. After a few attempts she connected with his left cheek, leaving bloody scratches and breaking off her press-on nails. Hoha bellowed, stepped back, and kicked Raisa Solomonovna right in the stomach with the toe of his shoe. Raisa flew back and, together with Slavik, who had been holding on to her, stumbled into the main hall. Hoha, cursing, wiped away the blood. "Sanych," he yelled to him, "do me a favor, lug that witch outta here. And turn her music off," he yelled. Sanych walked up to the singer, grabbed her, and pulled her to the exit. Following in the tracks of all the crying was Slavik, still wearing the wig. Hoha looked at all of this from the stage and cursed. "A witch," he yelled, standing in the middle of the stage, "the devil's witch!" Sanych hailed a cab, slid Slavik some cash, and returned to the nightclub. Hoha was sitting at the edge of the stage, wiping away blood with his silk sleeve and drinking vodka straight out of the bottle. "A witch!" he cried, and buried his nose in Sanych's chest. "What did she do that for? Damn witch!" "It's okay, buddy," Sanych replied to him. "Let me take you home." They went outside. The hunchback was standing by his car, looked at Hoha in go-go boots, shifted a ponderous glance at Sanych, and silently got behind the wheel. Nobody spoke on the way home, except for Hoha's occasional sniffling. "You know, I have a gay neighbor," the hunchback tried to get a conversation going. "Big deal," Sanych said sullenly. "My apartment building is full of homos."

In the morning, Hoha woke up at home, in bed, fully clothed and wearing go-go boots. Ponderously looking at the go-go boots, he tried to remember everything that had happened. He couldn't. Shit, Hoha thought, what the hell am I doing? Soon I'll be thirty, I'm a good, established businessman, chicks throw themselves at me. Well okay, chicks may not throw themselves at me, but nonetheless—what is it that I need this nightclub for, that I need these gays for, that's worth ruining my life over. He grabbed his phone, dialed up his middleman buddy, and hastily bought a batch of gypsum boards.

Sanych arrived at the Sub sometime in the afternoon. A frightened security guard stood at the entrance. "San Sanych," he said, "Heorhii Davydovych is in, uh . . ." "We'll sort it all out," Sanych succinctly replied and entered the nightclub. The main hall was littered with a bunch of boxes. They were all over the place. The tables were folded up in the corner. The bar was closed. Sanych went to see Hoha. Hoha was sitting with his legs propped up on top of the table, and cheerfully conversing with someone on the phone. The go-go boots were on the table in front of him. "What's all that?" Sanych asked him, pointing at the main hall. "What?" Hoha asked him, calmly. "Oh, the stuff in the main hall, they're gypsum boards. I got a good deal." "Well, what about the Sub?" Sanych asked him. "Not happening," Hoha replied. "It's useless, this Sub. I'm in the red, Sanych, fuck the Sub. Soon I'll unload these gypsum boards and I'm off to Cyprus." "Well, what about the exotic leisure?" Sanych asked him. "Yeah, what about the exotic leisure?" Hoha nervously smiled. "We just don't have the mentality for this, you understand?" "Well then, what kind of mentality do we have?" "Hell if I know what kind," Hoha answered him. "Our mentality is that we gotta have vodka and a babe for exotic leisure, right? And, with these gays, you can forget about vodka. Let alone the babes," he added sadly.

A piercing scream could be heard coming from the main hall. The doors flew open and Slavik raced into the office. "What?" he yelled. "What's all that?" He was dejectedly pointing toward the main hall. "Heorhii Davydovych, Sanych—what is all that?" "They're gypsum boards," Sanych told him. "Gypsum boards?" "Gypsum boards," Sanych confirmed. "What do you need gypsum boards for?" Slavik didn't understand. "Gypsum boards, Slavik," Hoha explained to him, "are for building architectural structures." "Heorhii Davydovych is shutting down the business," Sanych explained to Slavik, "from now on he's going to be dealing gypsum boards in Cyprus." "In Cyprus?" an affronted Hoha disagreed, but Slavik was no longer listening to him. "What?" he asked. "He's shutting down the business? Just like that? What about me? What about our plans?" "What plans?" Hoha nervously interrupted. "Oh okay, I get it," Slavik breathed in, "I saw this coming from the start. For you guys it's *like this*—today we open it, tomorrow, we close it. It's *like that* for you guys. I understand you, if I was in your shoes I would act just *like that* too. Sure. When you need something, when you need to put on Embroidered Rushnyky, then it's—Slavik, take care of it. Or when you need someone to invite Raisa Solomonovna, then it's Slavik, no problem." "Your Raisa Solomonovna is a witch!" Hoha responded, yelling. "The devil's witch!" "Oh yeah?" Slavik, for his part, yelled, "Raisa Solomonovna is an actress! She has her own show! And you kicked her in the stomach." "What do you mean I kicked her in the stomach?" Hoha was confused.

"Yes! You kicked her! In the stomach! And she has her own show!" Slavik couldn't contain himself, dropped onto the chair, and, grabbing his head in his hands, bellowed. A rotting silence took hold. "Sanych," Hoha finally began speaking, "Sanych, what? Is it true? Did I really kick her in the stomach?" "Well, you were just defending yourself," said Sanych, looking away. "I can't believe it," Hoha whispered and also grabbed his head with his hands. San Sanych went outside. Across the street stood two Copy Kings in green track suits who blended nicely with the July greenery.

Maybe Hoha was just reacting to this whole story about the stomach, about Raisa Solomonovna, that is. Something clicked inside of him after all of this, maybe it was because he felt ashamed in front of this group, but, the next morning, he unloaded the gypsum boards to the director of the amusement park and asked Sanych and Slavik to come over for a talk. Sanych was beset with depression but he collected himself and came over. The last to show up was Slavik, who was quite together and had a stern look about him. Hoha tried to avoid making eye contact with him. The go-go boots were still on the table, it seems that Hoha just didn't know what to do with them. Everyone sat down. No one said anything. "May I?" Sternly, and in somewhat of a schoolboy manner, Slavik raised his hand. "Please, go ahead," Hoha allowed, trying to move things along. "Let me go first, Heorhii Davydovych," Slavik began. "I created this mess and it's up to me to save this project." San Sanych looked at him with despair. "I understand," said Slavik. "We all made a lot of mistakes. You guys are new to this business, maybe I didn't stay on top of it as I should have. So then. No need to point the finger of blame," said Slavik and then looked directly at Sanych. "But not all is lost. I always have an ace up my sleeve." "Well now," he said, "they should be here any minute." "Who?" Hoha asked in horror. "The Bychkos!"

And Slavik told them about the Bychkos. He found them through the strippers from the Pioneer Youth Cultural Center. The Bychko duet— father and son—were circus clowns but, a few months ago, because of the financial difficulties that the city circus was having, they were laid off and began focusing on their solo career, according to Slavik. According to him, they had an *awesome* show program, an hour and a half long, with music, acrobatic numbers, and card tricks. Slavik laid everything on the shoulders of the Bychkos, they wouldn't disappoint them.

And so the clowns arrived. "Bychko, Ivan Petrovych," the older Bychko introduced himself and shook Hoha's and Sanych's hands. "Bychko, Petia," the younger one, lacking the guts to shake their hands, greeted them. Hoha invited everyone to sit down. "Well, then," Bychko Sr. began talking, pulling off his glasses and wiping them with a hand-kerchief. "I was told about your dilemma. I think that Petia and I can help you out." "What's your show like?" Hoha inquired. "Our show is all about dysentery," Ivan Petrovych said. "Dynasty," Petia corrected him. "Yes," Ivan Petrovych agreed. "We have a circus dynasty, from the year one thousand nine hundred seventy-four. It was then that my older sis-ter applied to circus school." "Was she accepted?" Hoha asked. "No," Ivan Petrovych replied, "—so then, for us, the circus—it's a family thing. I, just so you know, young man, back in the year one thousand nine hundred seventy-three, received second prize at the all-republican competition of young stage performers in Kremenchuk. With my num-ber 'Africa—A Continent of Liberty' I caused quite a furor during the interregional shindig in Artek, in one thousand nine hundred seventy-eight. No," Ivan Petrovych abruptly contradicted himself, "it was in seventy-nine. Yep—it was in one thousand nine hundred seventy-nine, in Artek!" "So you're," Hoha tried to join the conversation, "so you're proposing to present the 'Africa—A Continent of Liberty' show for us too." "No," Ivan Petrovych calmly countered, "no, young man. We always try to stay in touch with the new trends. Petia and I have a show, we perform for an hour and a half, any overtime will cost you extra, debit or credit, everything is legitimate, everything is legal. You may wire the payment, but then you have to pay an extra 10 percent service fee." "Well, okay," said Hoha, "that's clear. But do you know about the specifics of our establishment?" "Well what specifics?" Ivan Petrovych asked, throwing a displeased look at Slavik. "We operate a gay nightclub," Hoha told him. "That is, a nightclub for gays, you understand?" "So let's see, what do we charge for gays," Ivan Petrovych pulled a tattered notebook out of his sport coat. "Eighty dollars an hour. Extra for overtime. Plus 10 percent service charge," he added, as a decree. "But have you ever performed for such an audience before?" Hoha continued to doubt. "Ahem, ahem," Ivan Petrovych coughed heavily. "Recently we did an office party for a consulting firm. Well, that audience, I must say, was quite special. And, just imagine if you will, the executive director walks up to Petia and me and says . . ." "Alright, alright," Hoha interrupted him, "I know that consulting firm." "So then," Slavik voiced. "Are we booking the Bychkos?" "We'll book them, we'll book them," Hoha replied, "but how do you see all of this coming together?" "Okay, here's how it'll be," Slavik grabbed the initiative. "Heorhii Davydovych, I thought of everything. How's your calendar look?" "Well, what do you got?" Hoha asked him. "Kupala Night! We'll do a gay Kupala Night!" Slavik said, and cheerfully laughed. The Bychkos also laughed—Ivan Petrovych's laugh was rough and congested while Petia's was ringing and clueless. Hoha also laughed, his laugh was particularly nervous and uncertain. Later, as they were leaving, Ivan Petrovych turned away from the door. "Are those yours?" he asked Hoha, pointing to the go-go boots. "Yep," Hoha said. "My friends sent them to me. From Cyprus. But they're the wrong size." Bychko Sr. walked up to them and felt one of the go-go boots. "Quality material," he said, well versed in such things.

They prepared for the gay Kupala Night particularly earnestly. Hoha no longer trusted Slavik and personally took care of the task of attracting an audience. Once again, among those invited were business partners, middlemen, childhood friends, and the Lykhui brothers, of whom, however, only Hrysha showed up because Sava had gotten beaten up during a fight in the Tractor Plant district and he was lying at Regional Hospital Number 4 with broken ribs. Slavik was given permission to invite the workers from the Pioneer Youth Cultural Center, all four of them. Besides them, a whole bunch of unknown people packed the place, who were enticed by God-knows-what, but definitely not by a gay Kupala Night. Providing the main event for the evening were, of course, Ivan Petrovych and Petia Bychko. As they had mentioned, they had put together a program especially for the celebration entitled "The Fires of Cairo," which, according to Slavik's—who had been at the dress rehearsal—indisputable affirmation, would blow everybody away. The Bychkos appeared on stage wearing pharaoh costumes, which they had rented from the amusement park. The music sounded. The stage lights went ablaze. Petia Bychko bent down backward, forming a bridge with his body. Ivan Petrovych flexed, grunted, and also made a bridge. The audience applauded. Hrysha Lykhui, who was already drunk upon arrival, even jumped to his feet but lost his balance and knocked over a waiter. The security guards attempted to lift him up and lead him out, but Hrysha resisted. He knocked one of the security guards on his ass and was able to free himself of the other. Sanych noticed the fight and tried to break it up. The middlemen, who had already managed to take their neckties off, saw that Hrysha was being roughed up and, forgetting the recent past, set out to help him.

Meanwhile, Hrysha tossed the second security guard onto the stage, and the latter cut himself on a truss that the lights were hanging on. The truss collapsed and fell onto Ivan Petrovych, who was still bent over in the form of a bridge. Bychko Jr. saw none of this because he too was bent over in a bridge. The public leapt to pull Ivan Petrovych from under the truss but Hrysha was in their way, fighting both the security guards and the middlemen, not ready to give in to either of them. At that moment, Bychko Jr. finally turned his head and saw his dad lying under a mound of metal beams. He stretched toward him but his father commandingly lifted his hand, as if to say, Go back, onto the stage, you are an artist, so get to it—enchant the audience! And Petia understood him, he understood his father's final command. And he once again formed a bridge. And the audience also understood everything and restrained Hrysha Lykhui and took him to the bathroom to splash him with cold water. "Go ahead Petia, go ahead my son," Ivan Petrovych whispered from under the truss and then a blast sounded—Hrysha Lykhui was offended at everybody and, not having any strength left to resist, pulled a hand grenade from his jacket pocket and threw it over into the last toilet stall. The toilet exploded like a crushed walnut, smoke drifted out of the stall, the audience fled for the exits. Sanych tried to gather the beat-up security guards, Hoha stood by the stage and didn't understand what all the noise and smoke was about. "Heorhii Davydovych! Heorhii Davydovych!" Slavik ran up to him, out of breath. "It's mayhem, Heorhii Davydovych." "What happened?" Hoha asked, confused. "The cashier!" Slavik yelled out. "The cashier, that bastard, he took off! With all of the proceeds!" "Where did he go?" Hoha didn't understand. "He's not far from here!" Slavik continued yelling. "That's it. He must have gone off to blow the money on slot machines! Let's go, we can still catch him!" And Slavik ran for the exit. Hoha, not really wanting to, followed him. Sanych left behind the bruised security guards and joined them. Already waiting for them outside was the hunchback: "Hurry up!" he yelled, "Get in the car!" Besides Slavik, Hoha, Sanych, two workers from the Pioneer Youth Cultural Center, and Petia Bychko, a deafened

Hrysha Lykhui, reeking of smoke, also, somehow, piled into the car; the latter was yelling louder than anyone else, as if it was his money that had been stolen. The hunchback floored it, Slavik was showing the way but he kept being interrupted by Hrysha, whose jacket, missing one sleeve, was still smoking. The hunchback was angry but kept flying, the workers from the Pioneer Youth Cultural Center were shrieking with every turn, until, finally, the hunchback lost control of the steering wheel, and the taxi, having crossed over the oncoming lane, slammed into a newspaper stand. Newspapers flew all around, like startled geese. It was 4:00 AM, all was quiet and calm. A truck drove by, hosing down the street with water. The doors of the taxi creaked opened and the passengers began crawling out. The first to crawl out was Hrysha Lykhui, wearing a jacket missing one sleeve; he saw a stack of newspapers, grabbed one paper, and walked down the street. Behind him, with snakelike dexterity, crawled out Petia Bychko, wearing the pharaoh costume. Behind Petia, San Sanych stumbled out, pulling out the two workers from the Pioneer Youth Cultural Center. Pushing the two workers out of the car was Slavik. Then they pulled out Hoha. Hoha had lost consciousness, probably from anguish more than anything else. The hunchback was able to get out on his own; it seemed that his back became even more hunched. Actually, one of the workers from the Pioneer Youth Cultural Center, Anzhela, had probably got the worst of it—Hrysha Lykhui had knocked out one of her teeth along the way. San Sanych walked off to the side and pulled out his phone, which had been turned off since yesterday. He tried to turn it on. He looked at the time. Four fifteen. He checked his inbox for new messages. There were no new messages.

Within a month's time, Hoha renovated the place again, paid off his debt, and filled the Sub with arcade games. The hunchback was now working as his new cashier. Slavik, together with Raisa Solomonovna, set off for the Far East. Sanych left the business. Hoha had asked him to stick around, stating that they would soon make some money off of the arcade games, and begged him not to abandon him alone with the hunchback. But Sanych said that everything was okay, that he didn't need a cut of the proceeds and that he simply wanted to leave. They parted as friends.

But that's not all.

One time, at the beginning of August, Sanych ran into Vika on the street. "Hey," he said, "you've got some new piercings?" "Yes, I didn't even wait for the scars to heal," Vika answered. "Why haven't you called?" Sanych asked. "I'm flying to Turkey," said Vika, not answering him. "I'm gonna try to convince my girlfriend to come back. It sucks without her, you know?" "Well, what about me?" asked Sanych, but Vika just caressed his cheek and, without a word, set off for the subway.

A couple of days later, Sanych received a message from Doctor and Busia. "Dear Sanych," they said, "we're inviting you to our place to celebrate our beloved Doctor's birthday." Sanych reached into his stash, took the remaining cash he had in there, bought a plastic amphora at the gift store, and set off for the birthday party. Doctor and Busia lived in the suburbs, in an old single-family home, together with Doctor's mother. They greeted him joyfully, they all sat down at the table and started drinking some dry red wine. "What's new with the Sub?" Doctor asked. "The Sub is no more," Sanych replied, "it sank." "That's a shame," Doctor said, "that was a nice place." "So what are you going to do now?" "I'm going into politics," Sanych said. "Elections are coming up." Unexpectedly, the phone rang. Doctor picked up the phone and got into a long argument with someone, after which he curtly excused himself and disappeared, slamming the door behind him. "What happened?" Sanych inquired. "Oh, that would be mom," Busia laughed, "that old hag. She's always getting on Doc's case, she wants him to ditch me, she sneaks off to the neighbor's house and calls from there. But Doctor doesn't give in. Good for him!" Busia slid closer to Sanych. "Listen, Busia," Sanych said, after having thought a bit, "I wanted to ask you something. So, you and Doctor are gays, right?" "Well . . . ," Busia began saying diffidently. "So, fine, you're gays," Sanych interrupted him. "And you live together, correct? Well, and of course you love one another, if I understand everything correctly. But explain one thing to me—are you physically satisfied with one another?" "Physically?" Busia didn't understand. "Well yeah, physically, you know, when you're together, is it good?" "And why do you ask?" Busia was lost. "No, I'm sorry, of course," Sanych answered, "if this is an intimate topic, you don't have to answer." "No, no, it's fine," Busia was even more lost. "You understand, Sanych, what I want to say is that, in essence, it's not so important, I have in mind the, uh, physical side, you understand? What's most important is something else." "What then?" Sanych asked him. "What's most important is that I need him, you get it? And he needs me, at least it seems so. We spend all our days together, we read together, we go to the movies together, we jog together in the mornings—did you know that we jog?" "No, I didn't," Sanych said. "We jog," Busia confirmed. "But physically, I honestly don't really like it, well, you understand, when we're together. But I never told him this, I didn't want to upset him." "The reason I'm asking," Sanych explained, "is that I've got this acquaintance, she's very cool, except that she drinks a lot. And once we spent a night together, can you believe it?" "Well," Busia said unobtrusively. "So, I'm in the same situation—it was great being with her, even without the sex, you understand? Even when she was drunk, and she would be drunk all the time. And all of the sudden she gets up and takes off for Turkey, can you believe it? And I just don't get it—where's the justice, why can't I, a normal, healthy guy, just be with her, why does she take off for Turkey and I can't even stop her?" "Yeah," Busia replied, deep in thought. "Alright," Sanych looked at him. "I thought that at least with you guys, with gays, everything works out okay. But you gays have to deal with the same bullshit." "Yep," Busia agreed, "the same deal." "Well then, I'm off," Sanych said. "Say hi to Doc." "Wait up," Busia stopped him. "Just hold on for a second." And he ran off to the kitchen. "Here, take this," he said and handed Sanych a bundle of something. "What is this?" Sanych asked. "A turnover." "A turnover?" "Yes, an apple turnover. Doctor baked it, especially for me. It's just that there are things that always make me cry. This turnover, for example. I know that that he baked it especially for me. You asked about sex, well, I'll tell you. How can I leave him after this? You know, I had an acquaintance who explained to me the difference between sex and love." "What is it?" Sanych asked. "Well, generally speaking, sex is when you're fucking and afterward you want them to get out of there as soon as possible. And love, correspondingly, is when you're fucking and after the fucking you want them to stay for as long as possible. Here, take this," he extended the bundle to Sanych. "So what," said Sanych, after thinking for a bit, "so this is justice?" "No, no, it's not justice. It's just a pastry."

And he set off toward the bus stop. Along the way, a dog began to tag along with him. And that's how they walked, up front was Sanych with the turnover, behind him, the dog. The warm August twilight unfolded around them. Sanych got to the stop, sat down on a bench, and began to wait. The dog sat across from him. Sanych stared at it for a while. "Alrighty," he said, "you mutt, today is your lucky day. In honor of International Gay and Lesbian Day, you're getting a turnover!" The dog was licking himself with approval. Sanych pulled out the bundle and broke the turnover in two. Each of them got about half.

STANISLAV ASEYEV

THE BELL

translated from the Russian by Nina Murray and Zenia Tompkins

AFTER RETURNING FROM THE FRONT, HE realized he was losing his talent. His talent as a writer, to which he had attached so
many hopes, was slipping away. Writing, like boxing, required constant
training, and he was completely out of shape after being held captive.
His young eyes stared at blank sheets of paper, and he couldn't get down
a single line—despite having seen enough pain and grief to fill a novel.

That wasn't his only problem though. For the entire time that he
was held a prisoner of war, he had felt as though a giant bell was hanging over him—tons of vibrating metal. He looked at the world through
a thin slice of light that, on sunny days, slipped under the rim of the
giant iron object above him. Shadows flitted around him, and he was
surrounded by the reverberating ringing of the bell.

Being freed had broken down the bars on his windows, but the bell
hadn't gone anywhere: instead of being the size of his narrow cell, it had
now grown to the size of the entire country. Now it was the quiet around
him that stunned him. After the explosions and the tanks, and the bang-
ing of a rifle butt against an iron door, ordinary city noise sounded as
flat as the sound of a graveyard to him. Every day he expected to hear
a bang against a mass of metal and sometimes ducked while walking
down the street where he had grown up, much to the amusement of

the neighborhood children. Work could distract him, but not for long. His mind was completely possessed by the mystery of the ringing that rippled out, like a circle on the water, through the souls of hundreds of people like him. At night, when he kissed the warm lips of the woman he had been dreaming about for so long, he didn't dare do anything more so as not to betray himself. If she looked into his eyes, she might think he no longer loved her or was thinking about another woman, but that wouldn't be the truth. He loved her, even more, more strongly than before, but the bell meant that he was alone in a way he could not share with her. His eyes that had once sparkled so brightly were fogged over, and the thing he most feared hearing was that he was being understood.

One day in the store where he worked stocking shelves, the manager found him frozen with a can of corn in his hand: he just stood there and stared into the space before him. God only knows how long he had been like that—he certainly couldn't tell you himself—before the manager called out to him. "Hey there," he said, gently taking the can from his hand and speaking in a voice one uses with a volatile, disturbed person who could easily take offense. "You might be a hero and all, but you're no good at shelving corn today. Why don't you go home."

Losing his job didn't bother him; he was about to quit anyway. As he wandered the city aimlessly, he walked into a suburban neighborhood of family homes. The small cottages, their green tidy lawns, and the night sky full of glittering stars put him in a daze. This was the instrument he had forgotten how to play, and only distant noises reminded him of the music he had once heard and could no longer comprehend.

Where are the walls that hold me inside and the bars that section off the sky? Where is the monstrous concrete smokestack rising behind the gray fence? It rises triumphant, as if there were nothing else left of this world except the wind, the cold walls, and the smokestack itself. Is the smoke that comes out of it not a belch of hell, and are these landscapes not those of the underworld? Where is your might, you heavy dull lights in rusted frames? How many men have you watched put a noose around their necks in your low light? Who can tell how a drop of despair becomes a wave—and carries away, through the coal fire, the souls of those who couldn't find it in them to wait for freedom? How bitter must it be to perish, staring at this smokestack through the bars on the window? But you, thick walls, and you, rusty bars, do not know the secret that is higher than this smokestack: freedom comes when everything else is taken away. The freedom of death—the one beyond your power. It laughs at you in the silence of this night, louder and harder as the lights grow dimmer. The right to die is not given by God: it pours into us with the smoke out of this very smokestack.

Such were his thoughts while he stood, unaware of time, for more than an hour near a small church, whose stone steeple gently pierced the night.

All at once, he came back to his senses, leaped over a low fence, and stopped under a tree whose branches brushed the roof of the church's vestibule. He clambered up the branches and from there slipped onto the roof of the church, feeling strange all the while, as if he'd found what he'd been looking for for so long. A few more agile moves and he had reached the belfry and was looking down at the city drowning in hundreds of bright lights. Suddenly, only for an instant, he thought he was looking not at the tidy cottages, but at their ruins, with thin plumes of white smoke rising here and there. In the same instant he felt the urge to leap, headfirst, but some force made him look up, and he saw what he had come there to see. Above him was the bell, no bigger than three feet in diameter, with a rope hanging down, as if from a void. The bell looked nothing like the giant thing that had been tormenting him for months, and still his body trembled all over, once. He grabbed the rope and began to ring the bell wildly. He ripped at it with all his strength, with everything his tortured mind was capable of, and for the first time in many years, a smile touched his face. Oh, it was happiness: he was happy as soon as he felt that the ringing of loneliness had vanished. He thought of the woman from whom he had fled so foolishly earlier that day and knew that they were together, the two of them: he was no longer alone.

Doors opened in the homes below him, and people came out onto the street that had been dozing so peacefully. Some pointed at him, others just grumbled under their breath.

He dropped the rope and squeezed his eyes shut, but not before he saw the flashing lights of a police car speeding toward him on this, his first night of peace.

TANJA MALJARTSCHUK

FROGS IN THE SEA

translated from the German by Zenia Tompkins

IF PETRO HAD HAD CHILDREN, THEY likely would have asked him how he had come upon his occupation. Children like asking things like that. They idealize work, so long as they don't have to go to work themselves. I'd like to be a police officer, they say dreamily, or a ballerina, or a doctor, or an astronaut. No one says, I'd like to be a garbage man. No school teacher ends her lesson with an encouraging, "Study hard, children, so that you can become good Christmas tree sellers." Petro had been both a Christmas tree seller and a garbage collector. Neither job was to his liking. Selling trees is a last resort, especially if they've been smuggled in from the Carpathians. Being a trash collector would have been fine—it's less smelly than people think—but they demanded Petro's passport after the first day of work. As soon as he heard that word, he took off right away. For seventeen years he had lived in Austria with no passport. He had been told that you get along better with the police without papers: then you can pass yourself off as a refugee. Otherwise, Petro, they'll stick you in jail if they catch you, he was told. The prisons in this country are full of us, Petro, full of us, he was told.

He had ripped his Ukrainian passport into little pieces and, on a lovely, sunny Sunday afternoon, thrown them into the Danube. As he did so, Petro thought with a smile that a piece of him would return back home with the Danube waves. Before swallowing the first page of the passport for security reasons, Petro even spat in the water, as if wanting to seal the magic ritual with his saliva. Then all he had left was a first name and a memory. The first name he needed for the multitude of days he no longer counted, and the memory for the multitude of nights he lay awake.

Petro dissipated among the foreigners, and no one searched for him, not even the police. No one wanted to know what had happened to him. The old streetcar with the three steps up was replaced by a modern one; twice, there were devastating floods. Years pass quickly when you don't value your own life. Petro did a little of this and a little of that, until at some point the opportunity arose to be a park sweeper in Frog Park, which was attached to a small castle of the same name, on the northern edge of the city. The owner of the castle never asked for Petro's papers and paid him every week in cash—sometimes more, other times less, depending on his mood. Sometimes he would say, You're a good park sweeper, Petro, which would please Petro very much. He was thin and spindly: a broom suited him perfectly.

In the summer there were more park visitors and consequently more work, too, while in the winter it was just the crows hovering over the wide avenues. He would sit on a bench then and breathe the coal exhaust that spread through the park, as many of the castle rooms were still heated with coal. The smell was too much for Petro. The tiny village he was from in Ukraine had smelled just like that. Of frost and coal. Sometimes of walnuts, too, sometimes of horse manure.

"How lovely," sighed the old lady who took a walk in the park almost every day despite the cold.

Petro thumped his chest with a fist and replied, "There's a dragon stuck deep inside me."

"A dragon?" The old lady raised her almost invisible eyebrows.

"He hasn't stirred in a long time," said Petro. "He lets me believe he is finally dead. But sooner or later something happens, something insignificant—like a whiff of these fumes—and the dragon slowly raises his twelve heads and starts wreaking havoc in my soul, causing absolute destruction."

"How lovely," the old lady said once more and continued on her way. She lived in a magnificent old building with several apartments immediately opposite the park entrance. The house that Petro was born in, right in the middle of the tiny village, had always smelled of food, even though as a child he had never had a full belly. Colonies of ants crawled through the cracks in the wooden floor painted dark red. Many of them with wings. They were particularly clumsy, large, and ugly, and they couldn't fly. Petro's father would spray the ants with kerosene and say that people, too, sometimes grew unnecessary wings, but that only those who had strong legs and could run away as quickly as possible would survive. And that's exactly what his father did: one day he was simply gone.

In order to squelch the inner flame, Petro bought a two-liter bottle of white wine for two and a half euros in the evening and slowly drank the night through, while his roommates—five stalwart men from the town of Bolekhiv—slept as cool as cucumbers after a lightning-speed vodka blitz. All five worked construction and needed to be in top form before sunrise. Unlike Petro, they hadn't destroyed their passports: they each had a number of them. Every time their tourist visa from some Schengen country was about to expire, the men would drive back to Bolekhiv in minibuses and get a new visa, in another passport, at the local travel agency. Some of them had wives and children in Bolekhiv, but Petro had no family. And he refused to leave Austria, even when the driver of one such minibus swore he could drive him across any and every border, unnoticed in the trunk.

Petro was lugging a bag full of black leaves from the previous year when the old lady joined him once again. "Have you ever even seen frogs here in Frog Park?" It was March and ice-cold. "No, never, Mrs. Grill," Petro confessed regretfully, although Mrs. Grill wasn't particularly saddened by this.

"Do you know why?" Her voice sounded conspiratorial. Petro let the bag fall on the freshly swept ground.

"Why is that, Mrs. Grill?"

"Because they all live with me in my house! Cute little animals!"

Mrs. Grill was very, very old, possibly over ninety. That's why Petro marveled that she managed her way to the park almost daily and without any assistance at all. The white-blue skin of her round face didn't sag; it was wrapped tightly around her jaw, forehead, and cheekbones, as if wanting to keep the old lady from slipping out of her body.

Mrs. Grill winked at Petro and padded slowly toward the gate. "You should visit me," she called back. "Then I'll show you my frogs."

After that she never came back.

Mrs. Grill did not even return when the first liverleaves and crocuses in the park sprouted from the earth. She had never before missed this resurrection of nature. Concerned, one day after work Petro went to the building where Mrs. Grill lived. Among the many doorbell nameplates next to the front door, he found Mrs. Grill's. Had the landlord been too lazy to replace the sign when she died? Petro pressed the doorbell and waited a long time. A Turkish woman came out of the building and eyed him distrustfully. She was pushing a checkered shopping cart in front of her.

"Who are you here for?" asked the woman.

"Grill," stuttered Petro and almost regretted having come there. "Mrs. Grill. We are . . . she is . . . I am . . ."

"Are you from Home Help Services?" The neighbor took a step back and let him into the building. "Please, tell your boss that it can't go on like this. Mrs. Grill is completely mad and a danger to the whole building!"

Petro quickly ran up the stairs, noting with envy that the Turkish woman spoke much better German than he did.

On the third floor, he came to a stop. Mrs. Grill was already waiting in the doorway with a friendly smile. Gaunt, stooped, in a stained white blouse and much-too-wide house pants, she looked like a distraught ghost. Her thin lips were painted flaming red.

"Come in," she said cheerily.

"How are you doing, Mrs. Grill?"

Petro entered the apartment, which was big and musty, yet tidy. The furnishings were old-fashioned, and patterned rugs covered the floor. Umbrellas with shafts, ribs, and tips made of wood, likely as old as Mrs. Grill herself, jutted out of the umbrella stand. Petro took off his shoes.

"You've missed the blooming of the liverleaves in Frog Park," he said.

"I wasn't in the mood," replied Mrs. Grill. "I brought you here because I'd like to tell you something, otherwise I wouldn't have disturbed you. We haven't seen each other in forever, Hans."

She walked slowly down the long corridor and bid Petro to follow her. As she did so, she warned, "Careful, don't squash the frogs! They're shy, but they find their way under people's feet sometimes."

Petro murmured that he would be careful.

Mrs. Grill led the way into the bedroom and sat down on the bed.

"Take a seat," she said. "You see, I haven't touched your side."

The other side of the double bed, together with its blanket and two pillows, was carefully covered with a purple-colored lace coverlet. The mound resembled a grave.

Her painted red lips gleamed in the twilight. The daylight faded with each passing moment and wiped the age away, diminishing Mrs. Grill's dementia, her much-too-wide gray house pants, her white blouse with the tomato stains. Now, she was a woman outside of time, one caressing Petro's hand and barely audibly, almost silently, whispering in his ear, "Perhaps we could start over, Hans?"

Petro's posture stiffened. He had said the same thing himself once, whereupon his old neighbor, the beautiful Natalka—alright, she hadn't really been beautiful—merely giggled and shook her sumptuous breasts. A scrawny taciturn boy and a round overconfident girl, who liked nothing more than to dance in front of other boys in the village House of Culture night and day. They weren't a good match. Or were they? One day Natalka would let herself be kissed, take her bra off herself, and the next she would spurn him and say, "God, you're boring." When she danced on Saturdays in the House of Culture, the trembling of the wooden floor drowned out the music. Natalka could have been a heptathlete, she had such force. Alongside her Petro felt secure; alongside her he was no one.

"Hans?"

Mrs. Grill rubbed her lips with the sleeve of her blouse. Ah, the stains weren't from tomatoes after all. "Do you know" she said, "I don't go to the park anymore. There's too little nature for me there. I have a biotope at home." She made a sweeping gesture of the hand. "I particularly like the moss and lichens. Look at how nicely they're overgrowing the photos, the mirror, and the walls. The dragonflies whir, the frogs croak . . . It's so soothing."

Mrs. Grill clapped her hands. Petro stood up quickly and began looking around the apartment. The old lady followed him everywhere. The refrigerator was empty save for several sticks of butter and a few opened, now moldy yogurts. In the freezer there was yet more butter.

"What do you eat, Mrs. Grill?"

She shrugged her pointy shoulders.

"Do you have relatives?"

Here Mrs. Grill cried in annoyance, "Don't you remember my niece? That nice girl turned into a wicked, fat witch, I tell you . . ."

A piece of paper hung in the hallway with a telephone number and a note that said, "Call in case of emergency! Susie." Petro rifled through all the drawers and found a battered green coin purse with fifty euros. He took the money, reflected briefly, and put a ten-euro bill back. Mrs. Grill watched his movements but said nothing. As he ran down the stairs a bit later, she stood in the doorway, smiling.

Petro asked himself whether his mother had also seen things in her old age. Had the black ants continued to crawl out of the cracks in the floor? Shortly before her escape, the sixteen-year-old figure skater Oksana Baiul had won a gold medal at the Olympics in Lillehammer. She had immigrated to the US immediately, and everyone condemned her aloud, though secretly they all would have gladly traded places with her. Making your way abroad meant being exceptionally clever and having great luck. Petro had found an opportunity to go to Slovakia to pick strawberries. Through the dirty window of a white minibus, he saw his fellow countrymen as they set fire to the remnant sheaves of corn on their plots of land, each as big as a wigwam. Gigantic columns of smoke rose up into the sky, and the faces of the farmers were crimson with heat. Right beyond the border, the driver's plans changed. Petro was already beginning to suspect that no one picked strawberries in March, but that didn't matter to him. He only thought, "Am I still boring, you whore? "

Seventeen years later Petro was once again drinking wine till early morning while his roommates, the five stalwart men, slept peacefully.

One of them needed to go to Bolekhiv soon because his visa was expiring shortly.

"Kolia," Petro said to him at breakfast, "do me a favor. Bolekhiv isn't too far from the house where I was born. Could you go there? Nobody lives there anymore. Just swing by, maybe take a few pictures with your phone."

Kolia promised he would.

"Hans?" Mrs. Grill smiled invitingly, her thin lips painted red. "Watch out for the frogs."

Petro went into the kitchen and filled the refrigerator with milk, cheese, and sausage. He left bread and a liter of apple juice on the table. Then he cooked a soup with lots of red beets and cabbage. His mother always used to cook this soup for him: he never liked it. Mrs. Grill ate diligently and chattered.

"Do you know what I'd like to know?"

"No, what, Mrs. Grill?"

Petro was washing the dishes; the forks and spoons were black from time. His mother had always cleaned the dishes with baking soda and the glasses with nettles. She avoided strong chemicals. What would she have said had he explained to her that people here no longer knew about natural products? Here people couldn't even recognize a potato nibbled by mole crickets. Petro's mother always carved out the holey spots with a sharp knife.

"I would be interested to know," Mrs. Grill went on thoughtfully, "whether frogs can live in the sea, too."

Petro contemplated briefly and replied that the sea was probably too big for frogs. "Good point," said Mrs. Grill, and immediately forgot everything again. The following week she asked Petro the same thing, and then once more as they hunted for eggs together on Easter Sunday.

Even though Petro hadn't hidden any (this tradition was foreign to him; in his village people used to eat lots of sausage and do ring dances round the church)—even though Petro had therefore not hidden any, Mrs. Grill nevertheless found one in the living room. Who knows how many years it had spent under the sofa?

Mrs. Grill walked around barefoot in the apartment. He heard how the nails of her curved toes scraped the floor. Petro placed her feet in a plastic basin of hot water, added a few drops of shower gel, and waited till the nails had softened. That's what his mother had done, too. She used to claim that her toenails grew exceptionally quickly.

"I must confess, Hans," said Mrs. Grill, "when you cheated on me with another woman and left, I was broken. I've never forgiven you. But there's one thing you don't know, Hans. I, too, had an affair!" Her eyes beamed briefly in gloating triumph. "With my coworker, Mr. Tratschek."

The young, attractive Mrs. Grill eyed Petro from the photos on the walls. He would have never cheated on her with another. He washed her blouses, yet the red stains wouldn't come out. He stuck one white blouse with a particularly large number of stains in his backpack, his palms burning from its tender touch. "Tomorrow I'll buy a new blouse, Mrs. Grill," promised Petro.

Just then his phone beeped . . . It was from Kolia. "I'm standing in front of your house, Petro, and everything's alright, except that one of the side walls has collapsed. There's a big hole there now. Everything's been stolen except for the icons. You won't be able to sell the house anymore."

Petro sat down on the storage bench next to the umbrella stand. His backpack fell to the ground. The inner dragon flung open its twelve mouths and spewed with all its might: an infernal flame shot out of its throat. The phone beeped again. Kolia was writing, "Natalka, the neighbor, is a very nice woman, by the way. She arranged your mother's funeral. She's furious with you." Petro wept softly, without tears; he didn't want to frighten Mrs. Grill. But she moved closer and pressed Petro's head against her upper body. Her chapped hand stroked his head, dragonflies whirred, frogs croaked.

Suddenly they heard a key in the lock. The front door opened abruptly.

"Disgusting!"

Two women barged into the apartment—the Turkish lady and a stranger with two attack dogs on leashes. Both women jumped at Petro and began to hit him on his back. The dogs barked. Petro didn't resist. He saw that the women had a policeman in their wake.

"Who are you?" the police officer asked sternly and tried to calm the women down.

"He's a pervert!" shouted the younger one. "What he's done to my aunt . . . Oh God, it's unthinkable! She's eighty-seven years old!"

She dumped out Petro's backpack and spotted the stained blouse. "Just look at what he's hidden in his bag! Pervert!"

Petro closed his eyes. He knew what was coming next. The policeman will ask for his passport, and Petro will reply that he ate it. He was just a shadow in the wrong place, a gust of wind that swirled the candy bar wrappers in Frog Park. The one who is no one must finally go home, Officer.

Mrs. Grill rushed to the open window.

"The sea is encroaching," she whispered, terrified. "It'll be here soon. I need to shut all the windows or else my frogs will die. Frogs don't live in the sea."

"Do you have your ID on you?" asked the police officer.

"Mrs. Grill," said Petro, "please, leave the window open."

YURI ANDRUKHOVYCH

SAMIILO, OR THE BEAUTIFUL BRIGAND

translated from the Ukrainian by Vitaly Chernetsky

SAMIILO (SAMUEL) NEMYRYCH, THIS INAPPROPRIATELY forgotten and prematurely extinguished shoot of the tree of our national banditry, attracts attention first and foremost for stylistic reasons. The style of his crimes is based on absolute freedom. Even the most frightening of the murders and robberies he committed can be boldly described as executed with outstanding aesthetic sensibility and imparting an impression of free, inspired creativity.

The life of this Podilian petty nobleman, largely wasted in the 1610s in Lviv, has to this very day been largely ignored by our historiographers, despite their occasional executions. Indeed, what we encounter in Władysław Łoziński's *Prawem i lewem*—or, to render it in Ukrainian, *By Sword and Epistle*—is written tendentiously: the author finds Nemyrych unpleasant merely for not being Catholic and Polish. Besides, he hailed from the same Nemyrych clan as Yurko Nemyrych, the future colonel of the Cossack Army, pitiless hero of the 1648–49 campaign, poet, philosopher, and heretic. (In general, the Nemyryches often fairly willingly went over to Arianism—a trait characteristic not only of them but also of such age-old Ukrainian families as the Potockis, the Wiśniowieckis, and the Tatomyrs).

As for the poem allegedly written about Samiilo Nemyrych in his voice and published in the book *Exotic Birds and Plants* by Yuri Andrukhovych, one should note that the author did not burden himself with any significant effort to plumb the depths of ages past and draw a historical type that would be somehow multidimensional and edifying. The core of this poem is, in effect, the so-called "potato pancake incident"—abnormally emphasized, torn from its biographical context, and hypertrophied; while it did take place in the biography of our hero, it was, one should note, entirely accidental and uncharacteristic.

We now believe it necessary to relate the full truth about this outstanding personality, so little known to modern-day descendants of that heroic time, and thereby liquidate yet another blank spot in the ocean of national history and the struggle for liberation.

Samiilo Nemyrych settled in Lviv beyond the Cracow gates in 1610. The precise date of his birth remains unknown, but we are certain that by this time he was slightly over twenty years old. Brilliant in fencing and horseback riding, impeccably dressed, he takes to buying expensive fabrics from Venetian and Genoese merchants, and he's fond of sherry, Malvasia, good music, and Madeira. His house soon becomes a haven for eccentric exiles from all corners of the Old World—foremost among them, well-known men of ill repute, perverts, circus clowns, serial killers, philosophers, occultists, celebrated alchemists, sodomites, Protestants, fire worshippers, Lilliputians, and robbers. Leisure time is spent in banquets, blasphemous singing, and religious disputes. Almost every day Nemyrych, accompanied by his cohort, journeys through the noblest of the city's taverns, where with great gusto and enthusiasm he makes merry: he shoots musket balls at the bottles and hourglasses, nails visitors' beards to counters, breaks their arms and legs, shakes gold and silver coins out of their weighty pockets, shows them his bare behind, smashes windows and mirrors, drowns the police magistrate

Szczepiurski in a vat of freshly brewed coffee and the judge Gołąbek in the toilet, punches out the eyes of the most insolent, breaks their ribs, pisses in their beer, forces them to eat their own excrement, while loudly singing, dancing, and otherwise amusing himself.

A contemporary reader might fail to understand—or, perhaps, even condemn—such expressions of Nemyrych's vital force and healthy spiritual energy; therefore, it is necessary to say a few words here about the customs of that era.

Murder or violence in general, according to the Constitution of 1577 then in force, was not considered something unusual or illegal. Judges in that era treated the crimes they examined in a philosophical fashion rather than from a legal standpoint, and added a significant degree of humor, irony, and Christian mercy toward the violators. Terms of imprisonment were surprisingly short and often conditional. Thus, for the murder by a nobleman of a fellow nobleman (and, at the time, the nobility constituted a good three-fourths of the Polish-Lithuanian Commonwealth's population), one had to spend a year and three weeks in the castle tower and pay two thousand gold pieces to the treasury. The same murder, but with the murderer caught *in ricenti* (that is, red-handed), was given a doubled punishment: two years and six weeks in the tower and the monetary payment of four thousand gold pieces. (For some reason, being caught red-handed was considered an aggravating circumstance—as if to say, don't get caught, you fool, but be smart about your killing, so that no one sees.)

Moreover, no trial of a murder could take place if the family of the victim could not drag his dead body to the courthouse (this was a special legal procedure known as "presentation of the corpse"). Therefore, the main goal for any gentleman who thought of murdering someone was to hide, reliably and in a timely manner, the body of the one done in: to dispatch it with a stone to the bottom of the Poltva, burn it in an oven, bury it deep in the darkest corner of a forest, chop it into small pieces, etc. By the way, in the case of Judge Gołąbek, whom Nemyrych, as it was mentioned above, drowned in excrement, the body of the judge was never found and therefore the case was closed, owing to the absence of a *corpus delicti*, that is, of the judge's corpse.

Murdering came easy, torturing was carefree—in secret and *in ricenti*, in front of society—for even if a trial did take place eventually and a verdict was issued, the convict did not necessarily have to go obediently to the tower; most often he went home or out with his friends to drink wine. The fact is that although there was a strict division between the judicial and executive branches of power, the executive could not, in the end, execute anything, for it was catastrophically short of executors—more precisely, policemen—while each defendant arrived in the company of buddies, relatives, and servants, armed to the teeth with sabers, swords, chains, cues, brass knuckles, halberds, and scimitars; hence only someone insanely zealous for justice or someone with clear suicidal tendencies would try to take the defendant to jail by force. Such an attempt undoubtedly would have yielded rather sad consequences for the justice system and its defenders.

Thus, in July 1612, some good friends ran into Nemyrych in Makolondra's tavern in Zamarstyniv. He was in a good mood, with a glass of sherry in one hand and a corpulent wench in nothing but Turkish pantaloons by his side, and to their question as to what he was doing there he responded, "Ha-ha, I am doing my time in the tower, gentlemen! I killed old Isakovych and got my three weeks and a year. And do it I must, gentlemen, and that can't be helped."

(Isakovych, a baptized Karaite, traded in counterfeit Lviv rugs, which he would pass off as Persian, since you truly could not tell them apart in any way from Persian ones. One day Nemyrych, together with his closest desperado buddies—Yatsko the Wart, Genyk Schulerman, and the Portuguese Moor Joelinho—caught Isakovych's son Zachariah at the Four Tits bordello, where the young Karaite was squandering his daddy's fortune. They forcibly pried him away from the bordello employee Susanna Waligóra and dragged him to the Vynnyky forest, where they deposited him, bound and gagged, in a cave, leaving behind the half-blind Lilliputian Ptuszek as a lookout. In the meantime, they telephoned old Isakovych, demanding five thousand Austrian gold sequins from him, threatening otherwise to chop young Zach into eleven pieces and later mail the old guy his (his son's, that is) head, stomach, and genitals. Old Isakovych, having grabbed his prized coffret with sequins, hurriedly set off in the direction of Devil's Rock, where the meeting with Nemyrych and his team was to take place. In the meantime, young Isakovych managed to free himself from the ropes (he had seen this trick performed many times by wandering magicians and thus executed it with ease), stunned—that is, killed—the sleeping Lilliputian with a stone, and set out on foot, crossing the forest and the Halych-side suburbs, back to the Four Tits bordello, since he felt he had not yet partied to his heart's content. Angered by his escape, Nemyrych & Co. riddled old Isakovych with bullets, spending all of eight magazines on him. To top it all off, in the coffret they found not gold sequins but silver thalers, worth much less on the hard currency market of the day, which the old man had in the dark, no doubt, mistaken for sequins. The ending of this story is already familiar to the reader: the city courthouse and Nemyrych's banquet with friends at Makolondra's tavern in Zamarstyniv.)

Between the killing of old Isakovych and the robbing of a Wallachian diplomatic mission headed by the boyar Gheorghiţa, which in the fall of 1615 was en route to the encampment of the king of Sweden, carrying valuable papers pertaining to the Transylvanian succession, Samiilo Nemyrych dedicated himself to science and the arts. In 1614 he published in Dresden a treatise in verse titled *De Papavere Curatione et Natura Cannabis* (*On the Medicinal Use of Poppies and the Nature of Hemp*), which was highly praised by his contemporaries but, sadly, irrevocably lost. He played musical instruments a lot, traveled around the environs of Lviv on a proto-bicycle he had invented, hunted game on occasion, and wrote polemical epistles denouncing the Uniate bishop Ipatii Potii, unaware that the latter had left the realm of the living more than a year earlier.

The robbing of the Wallachian envoys turned out to be the most notorious of Nemyrych's transgressions, excepting, of course, the story of the lady with the potato pancakes mentioned by Łoziński—the story that led to Nemyrych's arrest and imprisonment in the tower. In our days of unrestrained political correctness and the triumph of the internet hashtag #MeToo, even a cursory mention of that episode is far too risky. Therefore let us move away from it and back to safer ones.

Having sprung a trap in the notoriously thick Black Forest, which in those days began near Halych and Kalush in the east and, with a few gaps, stretched all the way to Munich in the west, Nemyrych & Co. lay in wait for the Wallachian mission and, having met them with a wall of tear gas, managed to leave the boyar, the other envoys, and their guards lying facedown in the muddy autumnal road, paralyzed either by the tear gas or by fear. Having filled their sacks with Wallachian ducats, topazes, and amethysts, as well as the secret papers sealed in an ebony box inlaid with ivory and mother-of-pearl, having ripped the hats and furs off the envoys, Nemyrych and his friends disappeared into the depths of the Black Forest. Joelinho the Portuguese Moor also grabbed a nine-year-old muleteer to whom he had taken a great fancy, but the latter soon died from abuse. Nemyrych adroitly returned the diplomatic papers to the Transylvanian court, demanding twenty thousand Swiss francs for doing so; but Prince Rákóczy did not express much enthusiasm for such an arrangement, so they had to settle for eight and a half thousand.

By then the king and the Diet of the Commonwealth had already thrice declared Nemyrych *infamis* (that is, deprived of political rights and the status of a nobleman) and twice declared him an outlaw (that is, deprived of all rights and protection by the state and society). This meant that anyone at any moment could rub him out without facing any responsibility in the eyes of the law and even earning His Majesty's gratitude. However, those eager for such gratitude were, for some reason, hard to find, and Nemyrych wandered insolently about Market Square in a gold-embroidered *kontusz* in the company of the valiant cutthroats Schulerman and Joelinho and the former theology student Innocent Sylvester Kotsky, dismissed from college for masturbation and freethinking. (Yatsko the Wart was by then already at the Zaporozhian Sich, where he would soon become hetman by deposing Sahaidachny. Eventually, however, he would lose his head near Khotyn, having brought the famed Zaporozhian Cossack army to the edge of collapse.)

The last in the series of banishments received by Nemyrych was announced in connection with the so-called "case of the menagerie," a story reeking with colorful exoticism. In 1616, around May or June, Pohulianka Park witnessed the arrival of a traveling bestiary owned by a certain Michelagnolo Romano (this was an alias used by the well-known counterfeiter and poison-maker Gustav Suppe, originally from Thuringia, to hide from the Inquisition). It included fourteen cages with various kinds of Indian beasts, namely, lions, panthers, lemurs, rhinoceroses, unicorns, giraffes, antelopes, hippopotamuses, baboons, zebras, echidnas, vampires, incubuses, etc. Daily and especially on Sundays, the most refined specimens of Lviv society gathered in Pohulianka Park, where for a fairly high fee they could look at all this exotic fauna, which, truth be told, also stank a great deal.

One Sunday, Nemyrych and his friends, descending like a whirlwind on the bestiary, opened all the cages and set free all the unfed animals. Joelinho the Portuguese Moor unfortunately perished during this operation: the old lecher and zoophile was trampled to death by a female rhinoceros that he had very imprudently tried to seduce, having just let it out. The frightened residents of "Leopolis, the most faithful among the Crown's cities," ran for their lives in all directions, while the released animals, having torn a few of them to shreds and satisfied their hunger, streamed down Lenin Street (today's Lychakivska) toward the town center and soon occupied the abandoned city, amusing themselves in flower beds, fountains, and monastery gardens and snacking on the occasional passerby. The menagerie's owner, Michelagnolo a.k.a. Gustav Suppe, was beside himself with grief, and so Nemyrych asked for a thousand Sicilian ducats to put all the animals back in their cages. Suppe gladly agreed and placed an advance of three hundred ducats on top of a barrel (the conversation took place at the Headless Fish Brew Pub). The following day, the beasts were indeed all returned to their cages. Using curare poison from Brazil, which they had purchased earlier in van der Vanden's pharmacy at Hetman's Ramparts, Nemyrych and his band sedated all the monsters with well-aimed arrows and brought them, still sleeping, to Pohulianka Park. This was one version, but there was another one, according to which the animals obediently returned to their cages, yielding peacefully and quietly to the tune Nemyrych played on an end-blown flute. Whatever the case, Suppe did pay the remaining ducats to Nemyrych and the same day left Lviv in a hurry, together with his entire caravan. The ducats turned out to be counterfeit, each and every one, and so, on the night of June 22, Nemyrych and his boys caught up with the swindler on the Great Silkworm Road, where they chopped everyone to pieces and transferred the animals together with their cages to the Vagabundo Circus: Nemyrych and its director were linked by some dubious schemes.

The aforementioned pharmacist, van der Vanden, was likewise quite closely connected to Nemyrych, since he prepared for the latter various narcotic potions and pills. Being the main supplier of opium to the court of the Turkish padishah and of cocaine to the caliph of Baghdad, the clever Dutchman was a connoisseur of forbidden substances of every kind. Following his advice, Nemyrych started shooting up and remained a junkie for several long years, chasing away all his pals and girlfriends and spending his time in melancholy solitude. He did not rise from his bed for days, lost a lot of weight, and seemed to waste away, but never missed a vein when injecting. He watched endless mysterious, colorful visions and kept rereading the latest work of the famous Saxon theologian Abraham von Aschenbach, *The Divine Egg, or the Instrument of Sinful Tortures*, which he had preordered from the Sorbonne. His notes in the margins of this quarto evidence his profound mastery of the subject and possible intention of composing a polemical response.

But the true reason for his generally melancholy—indeed, depressed—state was his love for thirteen-year-old Amalka, daughter of the city executioner, Stefan Neboraka. Nemyrych saw her for the first time from behind bars when he was doing time in the tower for— let us mention it for the third and final time—the notorious "potato pancake incident." The girl took daily walks to her daddy's workplace, which was located close to the tower: she brought him hot lunches in pots wrapped in woolen kerchiefs. Once, while on her way, she squatted to pee in the bushes next to the tower. This was when Nemyrych noticed her and immediately fell in love more completely than he had ever fallen in love with anyone before. The walls of his cell were soon covered with Amalka's name; additionally, he used a chip of a brick to draw countless hearts pierced with arrows, female lips, other body parts, etc.

The tragedy of this affair lay in the fact that young Miss Amalia scorned his love. On leaving prison, Nemyrych confessed his love to her in writing, offering to take her hand in marriage. He added to the letter his acrostic sonnet, "Amalia Neboraka." Alas, the girl replied in a rather cutting way that she would never think of marrying such a delinquent and debauchee; moreover, she was from an esteemed, respectable family whose dignity would suffer from such a shameful union; and, besides, she had long been in love with her fiancé, Piotrus, the butcher's son, whom she loved for his curly hair, cheerful disposition, and incomparable skill at turning animal guts into blood-and-buckwheat sausage. The following evening, Samiilo Nemyrych met Piotrus the butcher's son in Kulparkiv and disemboweled him, but this was of no help: to the end of her days—and she lived to be ninety-three—Amalia was in mourning, remaining faithful to her fiancé and keeping her virginity intact.

Gradually coming to the conclusion that all efforts and attempts at changing something for the better in this absurd world were futile, Samiilo Nemyrych turned passive and withdrawn. It seemed that he had finally understood several simple but depressing things. Back when he punished the rich and took possession of their wealth, he only redistributed it, but this did not save the needy from need and the hungry from hunger. Women offered themselves to him willingly and often, but not because they appreciated his mind or his heart, but because he could satisfy them. His contemporaries generally did not understand his scholarly and artistic efforts, and more often than not his writings were burned, on the orders of the Inquisition or the tsar of Muscovy. His brilliantly executed, artistic crimes produced in response only denunciations, a failure to understand, yet another suspension of rights or banishment, yet another court verdict and jail term, but never became a subject of the dignified aesthetic interpretation and thoroughgoing moral analysis for which poor Samiilo so desperately longed. He had to drink to the bottom that bitter cup of tragedy that all great men share: incongruity with the time into which they were thrown by Providence.

But the bitterness of Nemyrych's cup is of a double nature: one not only of time but also of place. Samiilo Nemyrych had the misfortune of being a Ukrainian and living in a Ukraine devoid of its own statehood, jurisprudence, its own history, and, finally, of its own criminal world. In America, he could have become a president; in Rome, a pope or, at least, a cardinal; in England, he could have been Robin Hood; in Germany, Bismarck or even Goebbels. But in Ukraine he could only be a bandit and a pogromist. There was indeed a ring of truth to the Polish saying from that era: "Sow Jesuits in Ruthenia, and you will still reap thieves!"

Samiilo Nemyrych was tonsured as a monk on October 18, 1619, and under the name of Brother Theodosius he quietly spent the rest of his years in a cell at the Pochaiv Lavra. After his death in January 1632, from an unknown nocturnal illness, documented minute-by-minute by a hidden camera, with the intention of a future upload to YouTube, his body did not decay, and on the fifth day, retaining its resilience and warmth, it began to smell of hollyhocks. He was not, however, canonized, despite the expressiveness of this unambiguous anomaly. Allegedly the reason was that his birth certificate was nowhere to be found. Gradually people stopped believing in the very fact of his existence.

Acknowledgments

The stories listed below have appeared previously in the following publications:

Artem Chapeye, "The Ukraine," trans. Zenia Tompkins, *The New Yorker*, April 4, 2022.

Olena Stiazhkina, "From *In God's Language*," trans. Uilleam Blacker, *Apofenie* 10 (January 21, 2021), https://www.apofenie.com/fiction/2021/1/21/an-excerpt-from-the-novel-in-gods-hands.

Kateryna Babkina, "Richard the Chickenheart," trans. Hanna Leliv, *Washington Square Review* 41 (spring 2018), https://www.washingtonsquarereview.com/kateryna-babkina.

Vasyl Makhno, "Brooklyn, Forty-Second Street," trans. Zenia Tompkins, *Apofenie* 7 (June 17, 2019), https://www.apofenie.com/fiction/2019/6/12/brooklyn-forty-second-street.

Sophia Andrukhovych, "An Out-of-Tune Piano, an Accordion," trans. Vitaly Chernetsky, in *The White Chalk of Days*, ed. Mark Andryczyk (Boston: Academic Studies Press, 2017).

Sashko Ushkalov, "Panda," trans. Iryna Shuvalova, *Words Without Borders*, August 2014, https://www.wordswithoutborders.org/article/panda.

Tanja Maljartschuk, "Me and My Sacred Cow," trans. Oksana Maksymchuk and Max Rosochinsky, in *Best European Fiction 2013*, ed. Aleksander Hemon and John Banville (Champaign, IL: Dalkey Archive Press, 2012).

Oksana Zabuzhko, "Girls," trans. Askold Melnyczuk, *Words Without Borders*, April 2005, https://www.wordswithoutborders.org/article/girls-oksana.

Oleg Sentsov, "Grandma," trans. Uilleam Blacker, in *Life Went on Anyway: Stories* (Dallas, TX: Deep Vellum, 2019).

Natalka Sniadanko, "When to Start, What Not to Pay Attention to, or How to Fall in Love with George Michael," trans. Jennifer Croft, *Brooklyn Rail*, August 2010, https://intranslation.brooklynrail.org/ukrainian/the-passion-collection-or-the-adventures-and-misadventures-of-a-young-ukrainian-lady/.

Serhiy Zhadan, "The Owner of the Best Gay Bar," trans. Mark Andryczyk, in *The White Chalk of Days*, ed. Mark Andryczyk (Boston: Academic Studies Press, 2017).

Yuri Andrukhovych, "Samiilo, or the Beautiful Brigand," trans. Vitaly Chernetsky, *Ukrainian Literature* 5 (2018).

Authors

Sophia Andrukhovych is an author, translator, and essayist. She has written six books of prose, most recently *Amadoca Lacus*. Her 2014 novel *Felix Austria* was awarded that year's BBC Book of the Year Award (Ukraine). In 2015, she was awarded the Joseph Conrad Korzeniowski Literary Prize by the Polish Institute in Kyiv. Together with Mariana Prokhasko, she coauthored the children's book *The Chicken Constellation* in 2016. Sofia translates from Polish and English and has translated, among others, works by Kazuo Ishiguro, C. S. Lewis, and Tony Judt. *Felix Austria* has been translated into several languages, including German, Hungarian, Polish, and Czech. In French, it was nominated for the Jean Monnet Literary Prize in 2018, and the English translation, forthcoming in 2022, was the first Ukrainian work to receive a PEN/Heim Translation Award from PEN America.

Her story "An Out-of-Tune Piano, an Accordion" was written for the Opowiadania International Short Story Festival in Wrocław, Poland.

Yuri Andrukhovych is a poet, novelist, essayist, and translator from Ivano-Frankivsk. In 1985, together with Viktor Neborak and Oleksandr Irvanets, Yuri founded the literary performance group Bu-Ba-Bu, which stands for "burlesque, farce, and buffoonery." He has authored six poetry collections, eight collections of short stories and essays, and seven novels. His works have been widely translated and include English editions of the novels *The Moscoviad* and *Twelve Circles* (Spuyten Duyvil, 2008 and 2015), *Perverzion* (Northwestern University Press, 2005), and *Recreations* (CIUS Press, 1998); the poetry collection *Songs for a Dead Rooster* (Lost Horse Press, 2018); and the essay collection *My Final Territory* (University of Toronto Press, 2018).

"Samiilo, or the Beautiful Brigand" is from Yuri's novel-in-stories *Darlings of Justice*.

Stanislav Aseyev is a writer and journalist from Donbas, Ukraine, who for two years following Russia's invasion of Eastern Ukraine authored unbiased reports about the on-the-ground reality in occupied Donbas for media outlets in Ukraine under the pen name Stanislav Vasin. In June 2017, Aseyev disappeared, having been unlawfully imprisoned by militants from the so-called Donetsk People's Republic (DPR). Sentenced to fifteen years on terrorism charges, Aseyev spent thirty-two months in unsanctioned Donetsk prisons, where he was brutally and routinely tortured. *The Torture Camp on Paradise Street*, a memoir of his imprisonment and an exposé of the DPR's underground prison system, was published in English in 2021 as a limited print run in Ukraine and will be available in the US in 2022. *In Isolation: Dispatches from Occupied Donbas*, a collection of Aseyev's reportage from war-torn Donetsk, was recently published by the Harvard Ukrainian Research Institute. Aseyev is also the author of a novel, a collection of poetry, and a play. He is the recipient of the 2020 Free Media Award, the 2020 National Freedom of Expression Award, and the 2021 Taras Shevchenko National Prize for his journalistic writings.

"The Bell" is from Stanislav's memoir *The Torture Camp on Paradise*

Street and was written while the author was illegally incarcerated at the Isolation torture camp in Donetsk.

Kateryna Babkina's published books include five poetry collections, two story collections, a novel, a novel-in-stories, a play, a screenplay, and four children's books. Kateryna is a regular contributor to a variety of Ukrainian and international publications, including *Esquire Ukraine, Focus, Business, Le Monde, Harper's Bazaar,* and *Insider,* among others. Her work has been published in German and English, and a number of her stories have been made into short films featured at festivals in Ukraine, Serbia, and the US. In 2016, a short film by Kateryna was screened as a Young Director's selection at the Cannes Film Festival.

"Richard the Chickenheart" is from Kateryna's collection *Happy Naked People.*

Artem Chapeye is the author of four novels and four books of creative nonfiction and is a four-time finalist for the BBC Book of the Year Award in Ukraine. He is an avid traveler who has spent approximately two years living, working, and traveling in the US and Central America—an experience that has greatly informed his writing. His work has been translated into seven languages and has appeared in the *Best European Fiction 2016* anthology and in publications such as *The New Yorker* and *Refugees Worldwide.* Artem is a past recipient of the Central European Initiative Fellowship for Writers in Residence (Slovenia) and the Paul Celan Fellowship for Translators (Austria), as well as a finalist for the Kurt Schork Award in International Journalism.

His story "The Ukraine" is from his collection of the same name, forthcoming from Seven Stories Press in 2023.

Kateryna Kalytko is a poet, prose writer, and translator who has authored two collections of short stories and nine poetry collections. Her poetry collections have won myriad awards in Ukraine, and her second story collection, *The Land of the Lost, or Frightening Little Tales*, was awarded the 2017 BBC Book of the Year Award (Ukraine). Kateryna's writing has been published in English, Polish, German, Hebrew, Russian, Armenian, Italian, and Serbian translations. She is also the founder of the Intermezzo Short Story Festival, the only festival in Ukraine exclusively dedicated to the genre of the short story. As a translator, Kateryna works from Bosnian, Croatian, and Serbian.

"Vera and Flora" is from Kateryna's collection *The Land of the Lost, or Frightening Little Tales*.

Oksana Lutsyshyna is a writer, translator, and poet who lives in the United States. She has authored three novels, a collection of short stories, and five books of poetry, the most recent of which, *Persephone Blues*, was published in English by Arrowsmith Press in 2019. Oksana's latest novel, *Ivan and Phoebe*, was awarded the 2020 Lviv UNESCO City of Literature Prize and the 2021 Taras Shevchenko National Award in Fiction, both in Ukraine. The novel is forthcoming in English from Deep Vellum. Oksana holds a PhD in comparative literature and is currently a lecturer at the University of Texas at Austin, where she teaches courses in Ukrainian language and Eastern European literature in translation.

Vasyl Makhno is the author of twelve collections of poetry, two essay collections, a short story collection, and a novel. His first book of fiction, the short story collection *The House in Baiting Hollow*, earned him the 2015 BBC Book of the Year Award (Ukraine), and his first novel, *The Eternal Calendar*, was awarded Encounter: The Ukrainian-Jewish Literary Prize in 2020. His multiple other literary awards and prizes include the Morave International Poetry Prize (Serbia), the Order of Merit (Ukraine), and the Kovaliv Fund Award (US). Vasyl's work has been translated into twenty-four languages. In English, Vasyl's poetry and essays have been published widely in journals such as *AGNI*, *Krytyka*, *Solstice*, and *Hawaii Review*, as well as in anthologies published by Black Lawrence Press and Academic Studies Press. An insatiable traveler, Vasyl has been living in New York City since 2000 and holds a PhD in literature from the National Academy of Sciences of Ukraine.

"Brooklyn, Forty-Second Street" is from Vasyl's collection *The House in Baiting Hollow*.

Tanja Maljartschuk is the author of five collections of short stories, two novels, a middle-grade novel, and a poetry collection. Her work has been translated into over ten languages and is widely available in German. She is a winner of the Joseph Conrad Korzeniowski Literary Prize (Poland and Ukraine), the Kristal Vilencia Award (Slovenia), and the Ingeborg Bachmann Prize (Austria). In 2016 Tanja won the BBC Book of the Year Award (Ukraine) for her novel *Forgottenness*, after previously being a two-time finalist for this award for the novel *A Biography of a Chance Miracle*, published in English by Cadmus Press in 2018, and the collection *Downwards from Above*. Her work has been supported by grants and fellowships from various German, Austrian, and Polish arts foundations, as well as the Federal Chancellery of Austria. Though Tanja continues to write primarily in Ukrainian, she has also been writing creative nonfiction in German since 2014.

"Me and My Sacred Cow" is from Tanja's collection *Downwards from Above: A Book of Frights*. "Frogs in the Sea," the only fiction that Tanja has written to date in German, won her the 2018 Ingeborg Bachmann Prize in Austria.

Taras Prokhasko is a novelist, essayist, journalist, and translator who has authored over fifteen books. A representative of the so-called "Stanislaviv phenomenon," a group of Ukrainian writers who defined themselves in relation to their hometown of present-day Ivano-Frankivsk in the early 2000s, Taras was awarded the 1998 Smoloskyp Prize in Ukraine for his debut novella, *Anna's Other Days*. He is also a winner of the Joseph Conrad Korzeniowski Literary Prize (Poland and Ukraine, 2007), the Yuri Shevelov Prize (Ukraine, 2013), and the BBC Book of the Year Award (Ukraine, 2019) in the nonfiction category. He has coauthored several children's books with his wife, Mariana Prokhasko, one of which, *Who Will Make the Snow?*, won the 2013 BBC Book of the Year in the children's category.

"Essai de déconstruction (An Attempt at Deconstruction)" is from Taras's novella *Anna's Other Days*, scheduled for publication in English in 2022.

Oleg Sentsov is a filmmaker and writer from Crimea, best known for his 2011 film *Gamer*. Oleg was arrested in May 2014 in Crimea on suspicion of "plotting terrorist acts," after participating in the EuroMaidan demonstrations that led to the overthrow of the former Ukrainian president and helping deliver supplies to trapped Ukrainian troops during Russia's occupation of Crimea. He was sentenced to twenty years in prison, causing an international outcry by human rights groups, who condemned his imprisonment as a fabrication by the Russian government in an attempt to silence dissent, and called for investigations into reports of torture and witness coercion. In 2017 he was given the PEN/Barbey Freedom to Write Award. Oleg's work includes several scripts, plays, and essays, as well as two short films, *A Perfect Day for Bananafish* and *The Horn of the Bull*. In May 2018, he went on a 144-day hunger strike to protest the incarceration of Ukrainian political prisoners in Russia. His published books include two story collections, a science fiction novel, and a prison memoir titled *A Chronicle of a Hunger Strike*, forthcoming from Deep Vellum.

"Grandma" is from Oleg's collection *Life Went on Anyway: Stories*, published by Deep Vellum in 2019.

Natalka Sniadanko is a writer, translator, and journalist who has authored nine novels and a short story collection. Her work has been translated into eleven languages, including book translations into German, Polish, Hungarian, Czech, and Russian. She is a winner of the Joseph Conrad Korzeniowski Literary Prize (Poland and Ukraine), as well as a past finalist for the Angelus Central European Literature Award (Poland), the BBC Book of the Year Award (Ukraine), and the Lviv UNESCO City of Literature Award (Ukraine)—an award in honor of the city in which she has spent most of her life. Natalka's writing has been supported by fellowships and grants from various culture and arts foundations in Poland, Germany, Austria, and Hungary. She has worked extensively as a journalist and is the translator of over a dozen books from Polish and German. Natalka's essays and stories have appeared in publications such as *The New York Times*, *The Guardian*, *The New Republic*, *Brooklyn Rail*, and *Two Lines*.

"When to Start, What Not to PayAttention to, or How to Fall in Love with George Michael" is from Natalka's novel *The Passion Collection, or The Adventures and Misadventures of a Young Ukrainian Lady*.

Olena Stiazhkina is a writer and professor who holds a PhD in historical sciences and, until the Russian invasion in 2014, taught at Donetsk National University. After fleeing the occupation, she founded a nonprofit organization, Deoccupation. Return. Education., and has since transitioned from writing in Russian to writing in Ukrainian. Olena is the author of eleven books of literary prose, as well as an array of academic books and essay collections. Her *Zero Point Ukraine: Four Essays on World War II* was published in English in 2021 by ibidem Press. Her most recent novel, *Cecil the Lion's Death Made Sense*, is scheduled for publication in English in 2023.

This collection features an excerpt from Olena's novel *In God's Language*.

Sashko (Oleksandr) Ushkalov is the author of poetry, drama, and prose, as well as a translator and literary scholar. He has authored five books, notably the novel *BZhD* and the story collection *Zhest: Sho(r)t Stories*. His fiction has been described as some of the most "compelling, comic, and absurd" in its depictions of life in twenty-first-century Ukraine. Sashko has also coauthored two children's books with his father, the renowned Ukrainian literary scholar Leonid Ushkalov. He translates contemporary German poetry and prose into Ukrainian.

"Panda" is from Sashko's collection *Zhest: Sho(r)t Stories*.

Oksana Zabuzhko is one of Ukraine's most prominent writers and leading intellectuals. The author of over twenty books of poetry, fiction, essays, and criticism, her works have been translated into over twenty languages. Three of Oksana's books have been published in English by Amazon Crossing: the collection *Your Ad Could Go Here: Stories* (2020) and the novels *Fieldwork in Ukrainian Sex* (2011) and *The Museum of Abandoned Secrets* (2012). Oksana is the recipient of numerous domestic and international literary awards, including the Angelus Central European Literary Prize (Poland, 2013), the Shevchenko National Prize (Ukraine, 2019), the BBC Book of the Year Award (Ukraine, 2020), and the Women in Arts Award (Ukraine, 2020). She has previously taught at Harvard University, Penn State University, and the University of Pittsburgh.

Serhiy Zhadan is a poet, novelist, translator, essayist, musician, and radio host. A native of Eastern Ukraine, he has authored twelve books of poetry and seven novels. Serhiy's various national and international awards include the Angelus Central European Literary Prize (Poland, 2015), the Jan Michalski Prize for Literature (Switzerland, 2014), and the BBC Book of the Year Award (Ukraine, 2006, 2010, and 2014). Among the most widely translated works by contemporary Ukrainian writers, Serhiy's books are available in over twenty languages. Four of his novels are available in English: *Depeche Mode* (Glagoslav Publications, 2013), *Voroshilovgrad* (Deep Vellum, 2016), *Mesopotamia* (Yale University Press, 2018), and *Orphanage* (Yale University Press, 2021). Two of Serhiy's poetry collections are also available in English: *What We Live For, What We Die For* (Yale University Press, 2019) and *A New Orthography* (Lost Horse Press, 2020), which was named a finalist for the 2021 PEN America Award for Poetry in Translation. In 2017, the author founded the Serhiy Zhadan Charitable Foundation to help people living on the frontlines of the war zone in Donbas.

Translators

Mark Andryczyk administers the Ukrainian Studies Program at the Harriman Institute, Columbia University and teaches Ukrainian literature in its Slavic Department. He has a PhD in Ukrainian Literature from the University of Toronto (2005). He is the author of *The Intellectual as Hero in 1990s Ukrainian Fiction* (2012). In 2008–2016 he organized the Contemporary Ukrainian Literature Series. Andryczyk is editor, compiler, and a translator of *The White Chalk of Days, the Contemporary Ukrainian Literature Series Anthology* (2017). Other published translation include Yuri Andrukhovych's *My Final Territory: Selected Essays* (2018) and Volodymyr Rafeyenko's *Mondegreen: Songs about Death and Love* (2022).

Uilleam Blacker is associate professor of comparative East European culture at the School of Slavonic and East European Studies, University College London. He is the author of *Memory, the City and the Legacy of World War II in East Central Europe: The Ghosts of Others* (2019) and coauthor of *Remembering Katyn* (2012). He is also coeditor of *Memory and Theory in Eastern Europe* (2013). He has translated the work of numerous contemporary Ukrainian writers, including Oleg Sentsov's short story collection *Life Went on Anyway* (2019).

Vitaly Chernetsky is a professor of Slavic languages and literatures at the University of Kansas. A native of Odesa, Ukraine, he received his PhD from the University of Pennsylvania and has been translating poetry and prose into English since the mid-1990s. His translations into English include Yuri Andrukhovych's novels *The Moscoviad* (2008) and *Twelve Circles* (2015) and a volume of his selected poems, *Songs for a Dead Rooster* (2018, with Ostap Kin); a book by the Ukrainian artist Alevtina Kakhidze, *Zhdanovka* (2006); and two children's books by Romana Romanyshyn and Andriy Lesiv, *Sound* (2020) and *Sight* (2021).

Jennifer Croft won a 2022 Guggenheim Fellowship for her novel *Amadou*, the 2020 William Saroyan International Prize for Writing for her illustrated memoir *Homesick*, and the 2018 Man Booker International Prize for her translation from Polish of Nobel laureate Olga Tokarczuk's *Flights*. She is also the author of *Serpientes y escaleras* and *Notes on Postcards*, as well as the translator of Federico Falco's *A Perfect Cemetery*, Romina Paula's *August*, Pedro Mairal's *The Woman from Uruguay*, Tokarczuk's *The Books of Jacob*, Sylvia Molloy's *Dislocations*, and Sebastián Martínez Daniell's *Two Sherpas*. She holds an MFA from the University of Iowa and a PhD from Northwestern University.

After graduating from Cambridge University's Slavonic Studies Department in 2018, **Daisy Gibbons** moved to Ukraine and took up translation of Ukrainian literature. She has translated various nonfiction books for Ukraine-based Osnovy Publishing and has translated Tamara Duda's Shevchenko Award-winning novel *Daughter*. Her cotranslation of Vakhtang Kipiani's *WWII, Uncontrived and Unredacted: Testimonies from Ukraine* was the recipient of a Ukrainian Book Institute translation grant and was published in 2021. She is currently translating novels by

Artem Chapeye and Oleg Sentsov and hopes to one day delve into (re-) translating Ukraine's feminist classics.

A former Peace Corps volunteer, **Ali Kinsella** lived in Ukraine for nearly five years. She has been translating from Ukrainian since 2012, and her work has appeared in *Solstice, Kenyon Review, Apofenie,* and *Guernica.* Her translations have been supported with grants from the Ukrainian Book Institute and the Peterson Literary Fund. *Eccentric Days of Hope and Sorrow: Selected Poems by Natalka Bilotserkivets,* a collection she cotranslated with Dzvinia Orlowsky (Lost Horse Press, 2021), is a finalist for the 2022 Griffin Poetry Prize. She lives in Chicago, where she also sometimes works as a baker.

Hanna Leliv is a freelance literary translator based in Lviv, Ukraine. In 2017–2018, she was a Fulbright fellow at the University of Iowa's MFA in Literary Translation. Her translations of contemporary Ukrainian literature into English have appeared in *Asymptote, BOMB, Washington Square Review, The Adirondack Review, The Puritan, Apofenie,* and elsewhere. She teaches a literary translation workshop at Ukrainian Catholic University in Lviv.

Oksana Maksymchuk and **Max Rosochinsky** are scholars, poets, and literary translators. They coedited *Words for War,* an award-winning anthology of contemporary Ukrainian poetry. More recently, Oksana and Max cotranslated *Apricots of Donbas,* a collection of selected poems by Lyuba Yakimchuk, and *The Voices of Babyn Yar,* a book of poems by Marianna Kiyanovska. They hold PhDs from Northwestern University and were fellows at the Institute for Advanced Study at the Central European University. Their work has been supported by the Fulbright Scholar Program, Fritz Thyssen Foundation, Peterson Literary Fund,

National Endowment for the Humanities, and National Endowment for the Arts.

Askold Melnyczuk's book of stories, *The Man Who Would Not Bow*, was published in 2021. He's the author of four award-winning novels. He coedited *From Three Worlds: New Writing from Ukraine* and is the founding editor of both *AGNI* and Arrowsmith Press.

Nina Murray is a Ukrainian American poet and translator. Her translation of Lesia Ukrainka's *Cassandra* won the 2021 Ukrainian Institute London's Ukrainian Literature in Translation Prize. Oksana Lutsyshyna's award-winning novel *Ivan and Phoebe* is forthcoming in Murray's translation from Deep Vellum.

Iryna Shuvalova is a poet, translator, and scholar. She holds an MA in comparative literature from Dartmouth College and a PhD in Slavonic studies from the University of Cambridge. She has authored five award-winning poetry collections, including *Pray to the Empty Wells* (2019) available in English, and coedited the first anthology of queer writing in Ukraine. Her latest collection, *stoneorchardwoods* (*kaminsadlis*, 2020), was named poetry book of the year in Ukraine by Litakcent and won the Special Prize of the Lviv UNESCO City of Literature Award. A member of PEN Ukraine, she lives and works between Kyiv, Ukraine, and Nanjing, China.

Zenia Tompkins's translations have been supported by grants from the Ukrainian Book Institute, the House of Europe, and the Peterson Literary Fund, among others, and include Tanja Maljartschuk's *A Biography of a Chance Miracle*, Olesya Yaremchuk's *Our Others: Stories of Ukrainian Diversity*, Vakhtang Kipiani's *WWII, Uncontrived and*

Unredacted: Testimonies from Ukraine, and Oleksandr Shatokin's *The Happiest Lion Cub.* She is currently translating books by Stanislav Aseyev, Oleksandr Mykhed, and Maljartschuk (forthcoming late 2022 and early 2023). She has served as the lead English translator for The Old Lion Publishing House, Ukraine's premier literary press, since 2019.

Ross Ufberg is a writer, translator, and cofounder of New Vessel Press. His writing has appeared in a variety of publications, including *The New Yorker, The Wall Street Journal,* and *Vice,* and he has published several translations from Polish and Russian, including *Beautiful Twentysomethings* by Polish author Marek Hlasko.

Thank you all
for your support.
We do this for you,
and could not do
it without you.

DEEP
VELLUM

PARTNERS

FIRST EDITION MEMBERSHIP
Anonymous (9)
Donna Wilhelm

TRANSLATOR'S CIRCLE
Ben & Sharon Fountain
Meriwether Evans

PRINTER'S PRESS MEMBERSHIP
Allred Capital Management
Robert Appel
Charles Dee Mitchell
Cullen Schaar
David Tomlinson & Kathryn Berry
Jeff Leuschel
Judy Pollock
Loretta Siciliano
Lori Feathers
Mary Ann Thompson-Frenk & Joshua Frenk
Matthew Rittmayer
Nick Storch
Pixel and Texel
Social Venture Partners Dallas
Stephen Bullock

AUTHOR'S LEAGUE
Christie Tull
Farley Houston
Jacob Seifring
Lissa Dunlay
Stephen Bullock
Steven Kornajcik
Thomas DiPiero

PUBLISHER'S LEAGUE
Adam Rekerdres
Christie Tull
Justin Childress
Kay Cattarulla
KMGMT
Olga Kislova

EDITOR'S LEAGUE
Amrit Dhir
Brandon Kennedy
Dallas Sonnier
Garth Hallberg
Greg McConeghy
Linda Nell Evans
Mary Moore Grimaldi
Mike Kaminsky
Patricia Storace
Ryan Todd
Steven Harding
Suejean Kim

Symphonic Source
Wendy Belcher

READER'S LEAGUE
Caitlin Baker
Caroline Casey
Carolyn Mulligan
Chilton Thomson
Cody Cosmic & Jeremy Hays
Jeff Waxman
Joseph Milazzo
Kayla Finstein
Kelly Britson
Kelly & Corby Baxter
Marian Schwartz & Reid Minot
Marlo D. Cruz Pagan
Maryam Baig
Peggy Carr
Susan Ernst

ADDITIONAL DONORS
Alan Shockley
Amanda & Bjorn Beer
Andrew Yorke
Anonymous (10)
Anthony Messenger
Ashley Milne Shadoin
Bob & Katherine Penn
Brandon Childress
Charley Mitcherson
Charley Rejsek
Cheryl Thompson
Chloe Pak
Cone Johnson
CS Maynard
Daniel J. Hale
Daniela Hurezanu
Dori Boone-Costantino
Ed Nawotka
Elizabeth Gillette
Erin Kubatzky
Ester & Matt Harrison
Grace Kenney
Hillary Richards
JJ Italiano
Jeremy Hughes
John Darnielle
Julie Janicke Muhsmann
Kelly Falconer
Laura Thomson
Lea Courington
Leigh Ann Pike
Lowell Frye
Maaza Mengiste

pixel ||| texel

EMBREY FAMILY
FOUNDATION

ADDITIONAL DONORS, CONT'D

Mark Haber
Mary Cline
Maynard Thomson
Michael Reklis
Mike Soto
Mokhtar Ramadan
Nikki & Dennis Gibson
Patrick Kukucka
Patrick Kutcher
Rev. Elizabeth & Neil Moseley
Richard Meyer

Scott & Katy Nimmons
Sherry Perry
Sydneyann Binion
Stephen Harding
Stephen Williamson
Susan Carp
Susan Ernst
Theater Jones
Tim Perttula
Tony Thomson

SUBSCRIBERS

Margaret Terwey
Ben Fountain
Gina Rios
Elena Rush
Courtney Sheedy
Caroline West
Brian Bell
Charles Dee Mitchell
Cullen Schaar
Harvey Hix
Jeff Lierly
Elizabeth Simpson

Nicole Yurcaba
Jennifer Owen
Melanie Nicholls
Alan Glazer
Michael Doss
Matt Bucher
Katarzyna Bartoszynska
Michael Binkley
Erin Kubatzky
Martin Piñol
Michael Lighty
Joseph Rebella

Jarratt Willis
Heustis Whiteside
Samuel Herrera
Heidi McElrath
Jeffrey Parker
Carolyn Surbaugh
Stephen Fuller
Kari Mah
Matt Ammon
Elif Ağanoğlu

AVAILABLE NOW FROM DEEP VELLUM